BOOKS BY PAUL GALLICO

FURTHER CONFESSIONS
OF A STORY WRITER

FURTHER CONFESSIONS OF A STORY WRITER

Stories Old and New

by
PAUL GALLICO

1961

Garden City, New York
DOUBLEDAY & COMPANY, INC.

ORCHESTRATION FOR TWELFTH NIGHT first published in Esquire
Magazine December, 1956

Contents

Introduction

SOME years ago I was flattered to receive an invitation to address the members of the Eton Literary Society upon some subject connected with writing which might be considered of interest to this young generation. The flattery contained in this, as far as I was concerned, was that I was the first American writer, and perhaps the only one, to be requested to give such an address.

It was, however, not my first connection with this famous school, for each year on St. Andrew's Day I am also invited to journey thither as a member of a fencing team to fence *épée* against the Etonian swordsmen. Thus I had learned to know Etonians and what they were like.

They were, it seemed to me, like any other boys who were quite likely to be bored stiff, even if they were members of the Literary Society, through being compelled to sit still for an hour while some adult caracoled about on his literary hobby horse. I thought my young hosts might be grateful for a little unexpected entertainment.

Therefore at a preliminary get-together at dinner before the lecture when I was asked by a most gorgeous young man (who was clad in the school uniform of white tie and tails to which was added a colored waistcoat of stunning magnificence, denoting that he was a member, I gathered, of "POP," a most exclusive and exalted society) what the title of my address was and I suggested "Belles Lettres versus the Punch in the Nose, or How to Begin a Literary Career From the Horizontal Position," I could feel the shock waves extend all the way back through the centuries.

The young man took the attitude that I was pleased to be facetious and he tried hard not to show too obvious disapproval. I said I was never more serious and thereafter refused to elucidate any further. The gorgeous young man and his acolytes were baffled and bewildered, but game. But I could see mental reservations forming about asking any more Americans.

The evening was notable in the annals of the Literary Society from the fact that to the great joy of its members the lecture avoided the subject of literature and was devoted to pugilism and the brief moment when my career and that of Jack Dempsey, the former heavyweight champion of the world, touched in a training ring at Saratoga Springs, New York. This was in the year 1922, when Dempsey was training to defend his title against the giant Argentine, the late Luis Angel Firpo.

It did not take long to affirm the validity of the title I had suggested, for I told them the story of an unknown sports writer who was sent to cover the training camp of the champion and who conceived the idea of entering the ring to spar with the latter in order to be able to write more convincingly what it was like to have the fist of the world champion connect with one's chin in battle.

The young sports writer found out and had plenty of time to reflect while sojourning on the canvas, where he had been deposited by a Dempsey left hook, listening to the referee toll off a count that could have proceeded to one hundred and fifty for all I was concerned.

The point was that this brash stunt tickled the fancy of J. M. Patterson, publisher of the *Daily News,* for whom I was working, and led him not only to promote me to the sports editorship of his newspaper but to let me take on the writing of a sports column.

Perhaps it was something of an American exaggeration to hold that my career as a writer was based upon this stunt and this knock-out, but the sports column, a thousand words in length, appeared thereafter for thirteen years, seven days a week. It was uncensored and uninhibited; it had to be in the hands of the composing room no later than six o'clock in the evening and the ideas transmitted to the cartoonist who illustrated it even earlier. It forced me to write every day, rain or shine, whether

I felt like it or not, sick or well, happy or unhappy. It gave me that discipline without which no writer can ever hope to succeed. It formed working habits and thinking habits, since a new idea had to be presented each day or an old theme treated in a novel manner so that it seemed like a new idea. But, above all, it made me write, write, write. Roughly over that period, not counting other sports stories and coverages of sports events, I turned out some five million one hundred and ten thousand words. I must reiterate: if one wants to be a writer, there is no substitute for writing. Talking about it or just thinking beautiful thoughts isn't enough. Writing, like everything else, is a muscle, and the more you use it, the more flexible and useful it becomes.

I had wanted to be a writer for as long as I can remember. My infantile years were filled with fantasies and imaginings and castles sent soaring into the sky. I wrote my first short story at the age of ten, one evening in a hotel in Brussels back in 1907 when the World's Fair was held there and we visited there, my parents and I, on their annual summer holiday.

They left me alone in the hotel one night, to my distress, while they went out to do the town. There was pen and ink and hotel stationery available. The creative urge was overpowering. I had had this idea for a story for some time, ever since I had passed a construction site on Madison Avenue in the Sixties near where we lived, where a new building was going up.

I am going to insist upon telling you the plot because I was unable to get it published at the time and this has rankled.

Briefly, a little boy wanders past the site and notices a pile of colored pebbles on the sidewalk, and a large "Eyetalian"—all construction workers in New York in those days seemed to be Eyetalians—is engaged in shoveling these stones into a wheelbarrow.

The small boy is fascinated with these pebbles and, wishing to acquire some, for purposes never quite made clear in the story, begins to fill his pockets with them. The large Eyetalian, either apparently outraged by this bald-faced larceny or simply failing sympathy with the needs of small boys, flies into a temper and cries, "Hey you, beat it! Wotsammara you? Garrada here! Put-a dem stones-a back. Beat it."

Terrified, the little boy puts the stones back and beats it. The Eyetalian finishes his stint of shoveling the stones into the wheelbarrow and thereafter is summoned to other duties atop the steel skeleton of the building thirteen stories above the ground.

There sudden disaster overtakes him! A misstep, a slip! He falls, yet manages to seize a girder with his hands and there he is dangling in mid-air thirteen stories above certain death.

Fellow workers shout to him to hang on until they can reach him. Help is almost at hand as they converge upon him. The Eyetalian holds on for dear life, but, alas, feels himself tiring, his strength rapidly waning, his grip beginning to weaken. Closer and closer comes the rescue party. Tireder and tireder grows the "Wop," as they were called in those days. Will he be able to last? Can they reach him in time?

Looking back over the years, I am pleased to note that even at a tender age I had some feeling for the element of suspense. Had this been a serial, here would have been the place to have written, "Continued next week." However, this was to be a complete short story with all the unities preserved.

Now for the twist! Willing hands are almost upon him, reaching forth to cheat the angel of death, when the desperate clutch of the Eyetalian's fingers is loosed and as he plunges with a shriek to his death this awful retributive thought passes through his mind (I was too young and inexperienced then to know that, of course, what would have flashed through his mind at that point was his past life).

"Oh" thinks he, "would that I had not been so cruel to that little boy who wished to fill his pockets with pebbles earlier this afternoon. Had I permitted him to do so, there would have been one less shovelful of stones for me to shovel and I would have now had just that one little bit more energy and strength I needed to hang on until help arrived."

Too late, too late! As the Eyetalian plunges past the twelfth, eleventh, and tenth floors, more Eyetalians working there hear him murmur regretfully as he passes, "Just a li'l shovel of stones-a, just a li'l sh-shovel full-a stones-a!" And after that only the well-known dull and sickening thud.

The title of this story was "Just a Shovel of Stones" and I was charmed with it. These were the days before psychiatry, psycho-analysis, and the cult of the head shrinkers, and it has been suggested since that at the bottom of this juvenile Grand Guignol lay the fact that I hated my Italian-born father and wished to kill him and that I turned him into the big Eyetalian construction worker and neatly dropped him from the top of a building.

I doubt this. I may have been irritated with my old man that evening for parking me in the hotel while he and my mother went forth to revel, but not to the point of vicarious assassination. Consciously I adored my father, though I was sometimes terrified of him. I am now too old a fox to bet either on or against the subconscious, but I had been carrying this short story around with me for many months in my mind monkeying with it and polishing it up before I set it down on paper, a process nowise changed in later life professionally. I have carried stories around inside me for over a year before they came right, to the point where they warranted setting down on paper.

I can tell you better why I am publishing it now and why a version of it also appeared in an earlier edition of these stories when my father was still alive. Eight or nine years later when I was a young man and bombarding the magazines with short-story attempts, which, like homing pigeons, returned inevitably to the doorstep a day or so later with a printed rejection slip, I used to have Mozart thrown into my face.

I am still amazed that Mozart remains my favorite composer and that I can never get enough of listening to his music, for in my youth he was held up to me as an example. Mozart, at the age of twelve, according to my father, himself a pianist and a composer, had already composed several symphonies, an opera or so, innumerable quartets, and, what is more, had had them performed, while here I was a lolloping big looby all of eighteen to nineteen years and already a failure. I could not even get a short story accepted and printed.

From which you will gather that I was no infant prodigy and that I was likewise born into a European household transplanted into America where the young were expected to produce.

I published this originally so I could say to Dad, "Who was this Mozart of twelve? An old man! Get me at ten Pop, here it is in a book." Father roared with laughter; by that time he was reconciled to the fact that his son was irremedially a late starter. I reprint it herewith dedicated to his memory.

My father, Paolo Gallico, was an Italian of Spanish extraction, a concert pianist, composer, and teacher, born in Mantua in Lombardy. My mother was Austrian. In 1895 they emigrated to New York, from whence my father went on a number of concert tours throughout the United States. I was born in New York City in July 1897, just in time to avoid the twentieth century. In one generation I became more American than the sons and daughters of the American Revolution. I was educated in the free public schools of New York—Public School 6 at Madison Avenue and Eighty-fifth Street, Public School 70 at Seventy-fifth Street and Third Avenue, and the De Witt Clinton High School at Tenth Avenue and Fifty-ninth Street.

In 1916 I entered Columbia University and graduated in 1921 with a Bachelor of Science degree, having lost a year and a half due to World War I. On my twenty-first birthday in 1918 I enlisted in the U. S. Naval Reserve Force, where, due to defective eyesight, I was placed in the loathsome category of yeoman.

Once in the service, however, I managed by means of high-school football experience to effect a transfer into a combat branch and emerged after Armistice Day with the more respectable rating of gunner's mate. Discharged from the Navy, I spent half a year working for a small newspaper syndicate and then returned to Columbia to take my degree.

The science degree is a part of the story, for I had intended to be a doctor.

This is no contradiction to what I said earlier: that for as long as I could remember I wished to be a writer. I still wished to be a writer, or rather a story-teller, but I was not at all certain that (a) I could be a good one and (b) earn a living with it. For some reason never quite clear to me, writing was hooked up in my youthful mind with insecurity. Perhaps in some subtle fashion I was aware that writing was a kind of luxury profession, just as was music and piano teaching. I think there was a financial panic once during my childhood and I must have heard my parents refer to the fact that when money got tight the first thing that happened was that people stopped junior's piano lessons. But these same people never stopped calling for the doctor, no matter how tight money might be. At that age I didn't realize that they just didn't pay him.

I shudder to think of the number of lives saved by my abandoning medicine. But when I was a boy around New York I did have a certain flair for it; I was the kid who had the first-aid kit, and when one of the gang hurt himself or acquired a cut or a bruise, I know how to wash it out with hydrogen peroxide, daub it with iodine, and apply a fairly competent bandage.

I cannot remember any time from my earliest days when I was not aware that I would have to earn a living and that I must prepare myself for that day. We were not poor people, but neither were we well off, and I think from an understanding of this and of the precariousness of a professional life stemmed a curious kind of cowardice which led me at the age of fourteen or fifteen to rearrange my ambitions and organize my life along the following lines. "Medicine," I said to myself, "is a secure and certain profession. People will always need a doctor. Therefore I will become one and always have the means of earning a living and I will write on the side. Then it will make no difference if I fail to sell what I write." Accordingly, when at the age of nineteen I entered Columbia University as a freshman, I registered for the premedical course, which called for two years of ordinary college study with the emphasis on chemistry and biology—in other words, the sciences—after which I would go into the College of Physicians and Surgeons, the medical school known as P. and S. Two close boyhood friends of mine were embarked upon the same course. During those two years I wrote stories constantly and with no more success. Mozart, it was pointed out to me at this age, was a European celebrity. I couldn't sell a story to a 10¢ pulp magazine.

At the end of my sophomore year, as the time drew near to enter medical school, I took stock of myself and my ambitions, the plans I had made, and arrived at the conclusion that they were infantile and that I was just plain yellow. I knew in my own heart that more than anything else I wanted to be a writer and that the whole idea of embracing medicine and becoming a doctor was cowardly and an evasion.

I can still look back and remember having one of those moments of clarity which sometimes illuminate the dark pathway. And in that moment I realized that I would be a fool to dissipate my energies and that success in anything called for the utmost concentration in that field. If I genuinely and honestly loved writing as I felt I did, then I ought to concentrate upon becoming a writer and let nothing else divert me or stand in my way.

This was a decision that not only had to be arrived at by myself but also implemented by me. Without taking my parents into my confidence, I withdrew my application to enter medical school, threw over the premedical course, though I was committed to majoring in science, added as many subjects in writing and literature as I could and put medicine out of my life. The bridges were irretrievably burned.

During all my four years at the university I lived at home but maintained my independence by working my way through, paying my tuition and keep by means of a variety of jobs—tutor, translator, longshoreman, usher at the Metropolitan Opera, librarian, gymnasium attendant, laborer in a spark-plug factory, college correspondent for a downtown newspaper or whatever odd jobs the employment agency at the university could dredge up for me. I also took part in university activities, won my numerals and letters rowing on the freshman and varsity crews and functioned as captain in my senior year.

And what about writing at this period and the immediate results of the great decision? Looking back, the best I can say is that I never gave up trying, and success was meager. I did proceed from the horrid impersonality of the rejection slip to the personally type-written note from the editor, a few brief lines to the effect that while the story submitted had not quite made the grade, they would like to see more of my work at some future date. And I can tell you this come-on was enough to have me walking on air for weeks. I had almost made it. Perhaps the next one would hit.

When I was twenty-one I sold my first story to a pulp magazine. I think it was *Blue Book*. I haven't the faintest recollection of what it was about, but I got $90 for it, which is probably more than Mozart got for his first opera.

During my interim job as office boy for the Otis F. Wood syndi-cate between emerging from the Navy and returning to college, I learned something about the syndicate business: chiefly that if one had a salable literary property, one could dispose of it a number of times to various newspapers in different cities of the United States. During my last two years at Columbia I devised short fiction sketches—what would be called "short shorts" today—modeled after the late American story classicist O. Henry, who was fashionable then and whose style and formulas were the basis of study in every short-story class in those days. O. Henry was the master of the unexpected twist at the end—a twist that incidentally was care-fully and unobtrusively planted in the narrative at the beginning of the story. Even today anyone wanting to write short stories would do well to read O. Henry.

These stories I syndicated and sold myself, submitting them to Sunday papers in Boston, Philadelphia, Detroit, Chicago, etc. I regret to say New York remained unimpressed and absent from my list of customers. These newspapers paid me space rates for these stories. Sometimes I got as high as $20 apiece for them.

During my years at the university I went through the mill of short-story writing classes. I studied with John Erskine, Helen Hull, Dr. Blanche Colton Williams, Walter Pitkin, Donald Lemon Clark, and Thomas Uzzell. Some of these classes were given in the university extension school and others were private evening classes conducted by these teachers and into which I paid my way. I am compelled to report that I was an undistinguished pupil who sold none of the efforts or exercises written for those classes. There were others who did and received checks from *Harper's* or the *Atlantic Monthly,* or even the big slicks. I was consumed with jealousy.

I attended classes, wrote stories, had them reviewed and criticized, learned the jargon to which the art had been reduced by the pedagogues, and sold nary a line. But I have a dreadful recollection that not only did I not sell, but I became so saturated with the rules and regulations of story craft, the mechanics and mathematics of construction, that I actually taught the stuff to small groups outside the university to eke out my college living. Why my students went for it and ever paid me money, or what good they got out of it, I shall never know.

When beginning writers ask me whether they should take a short-story course, I tell them yes, because I feel it cannot do them any harm and it might do them some good. If nothing else, it sets them to writing regularly.

Eighty-five per cent of the students of every writing or story course are made of frustrated and utterly talentless and feckless folk who are lured by the gold in them thar hills and the apparent ease with which successful writers appear to be able to tap the vein. They may be encountered in the extension courses year after year, hopefully but unsuccessfully pursuing the chimera. The simple truth is that they are neither writers nor story-tellers and never will be, if they go to school for a hundred years.

But where a man or a woman has a natural talent for expressing himself with the written word, originality, and a good ear for reproducing the speech of others, these classroom sessions unquestionably, to my mind, can help him. They frequently provide short cuts and save him time. If he must struggle and suffer and learn what to do and how to do it by himself, at least he can acquire there a foundation in what NOT to do.

I never heard of a writer coming to any harm in such a class, and in 1948 when I was asked by Columbia whether I would teach an advanced short-story class in the extension school, I accepted on condition that I be allowed to choose my students on the basis of some submitted work. I didn't want to waste time on the hopeless ones.

I worked for a year with a bright, talented group and oddly enough experienced here the thrill of success which had eluded me when I was a student. Several members of my class sold stories to magazines either during or immediately after the course. I am sure they would have sold them anyway, but the pleasure of having assisted at their incubation to development was inescapable. I gave up teaching because I couldn't bear to be tied down to the academic year.

After graduating from Columbia in 1921, I married, and took the first job that was offered to me by my friends in the university employment office. This was as a review secretary for the National Board of Motion Picture Review, which was the voluntary censorship to which the motion-picture producers agreed in the face of the threat of state or federal censorship. Half a year later I became motion-picture critic for the New York *Daily News*, the fledgling tabloid founded by Joseph Medill Patterson, of the Chicago *Tribune*, and there I lasted exactly four months and twenty-nine days. On the thirtieth day I was removed from the chair by Captain Patterson because my reviews were too smart-alecky. I was not fired from the *News*; this was not the custom of the publisher. He merely, in a fit of exasperation, told his managing editor, Phil Payne, to get "that man" out of the movie department. Payne hid me in the sports department as an anonymous and un-by-lined sports reporter, odd-jobs and rewrite man.

And here we return to the subject of my discourse at Eton: namely, how to begin a literary career from the prone or horizontal position.

Assigned to write some "color" from the Dempsey training camp at Uncle Tom Luther's at Saratoga, myself a heavyweight still in good condition after four years as a galley slave but with no experience of boxing, I asked Dempsey if he would let me into the ring with him in order that I might find out firsthand what it was like.

As I have indicated, the results were drastic, since I was unknown and for all Dempsey and his camp knew might be a ringer sent to injure him or make him look bad. But at any rate, after one minute and twenty-seven seconds I was flat on my back with a cut lip and a prize headache. But I also had a story. In an old-fashioned narrative one might say that in this manner my fortune was made. Certainly it was the beginning. There were other elements, but the fact was that the left hook Dempsey whistled to my unprotected chin changed the frown on the face of Captain Patterson to a smile.

I wrote no more fiction for nearly eight years but applied myself to my job as sports editor and columnist of the *Daily News* and the necessity of earning a living for my family and myself. But while fiction was temporarily shelved, I was at least writing sports. I was writing, writing, writing, day in and day out, Sundays included.

Every writer has a different story of his beginnings and of how he obtained the needed practice and training for his craft, including those geniuses who need no training but do it right the first time, but for me sports writing was a wonderful incubator. Reporting the American sports scene was story-telling, a rich and inexhaustible lode of dramatic material. Daily I was in contact with those necessary elements of drama—good against evil, suspense, frustration, climax, and success. Every contest had its villain as well as its hero. We wrote partisan sports in New York. Our teams, our boys, were white knights, the visitors black. I lived and worked in an era of great personalities in sports—Dempsey, Babe Ruth, Helen Wills, Tilden, Ty Cobb, Johnny Weismuller, Man o' War, Paavo Normi, etc.—all of them highly colorful and dramatic men and women—a quality that often was reflected in their contests. Reporting sports was a constant exercise in presenting dramatic material in a dramatic fashion.

I became involved at the same time in sports promotion and was led into curious bypaths, which, oddly enough, were grist to the mill of the would-be writer, for they taught me showmanship, though I was aware of none of these things during those years.

Shocked by the wretched and sordid manner in which amateur boxing was conducted in New York in those days, I persuaded Captain Patterson to let me stage an amateur tournament, and invented the Golden Gloves and thereafter, in addition to my work as editor, reporter, and columnist, promoted such sports extravaganzas as roller- and ice-skating races, water circuses, golf-driving contests, and a thoroughly mad canoe race around Manhattan Island.

It was a fast, gay, wonderful, and completely thoughtless life. Winter sports merged into summer sports; the seasons and the years flowed by. To increase my understanding of the men and women about whom I wrote and to make myself a better writer, I tried everything: a speedboat ride with Gar Wood, a spin around the Indianapolis track with Cliff Berger, attempts to catch the fireball of Lefty Grove and the football passes of Benny Friedman, faced the tennis drives of Helen Wills and Vincent Richards, and played golf with Bobby Jones. I learned to fly, won a pilot's licence, logged five hundred hours, and took to covering some sports events from the air.

Nobody censored my copy or told me what to write or what not to write, or what to do or where to go or what to cover as long as I remained within the laws of libel. My column became known as the *News* increased in circulation and stature, and myself a minor celebrity recognized by taxi drivers as one of the "young men of Manhattan" along with Damon Runyon, Bill Corum, Dan Parker, Joe Williams, etc. Our seats at the working-press benches in Madison Square Garden had our names emblazoned in bronze plaques.

Here was success from an unexpected quarter—financial, social, etc.; the would-be fiction writer became submerged but never forgotten. I still looked forward to the day when I would "make" the *Saturday Evening Post*. It took me twenty-five years to achieve this ambition—that is to say from 1907 when I was ten, the age at which I wrote my first story, to 1933 when I was thirty-six years old.

I began gradually to break into the better magazines with sports articles. This was the easy way, for I had all of the material at the tips of my fingers and the writing muscle was limbered. It was just a matter of acquiring the more leisurely slant of the monthly publication as against the immediacy of the daily journal. And here I had another stroke of luck. I wrote and sold several articles to *Vanity Fair,* which in those days in class and sophistication occupied the position the *New Yorker* does now. Its editor was the late Frank Crowninshield, and the late Don Freeman was managing editor. The associate editor was Clare Boothe Brokaw, afterwards Congresswoman and then Ambassadress Clare Boothe Luce. I was invited to join their staff as an associate editor.

The publisher, the late Conde Nast, gave us all a free hand and the magazine was a wonderful and crackling proving ground for young writers. It printed anything I wrote, and the editors egged me on to try all kinds of things including short pieces of fiction. In addition to my own by-line I had five assorted pen names under which I wrote. Sometimes I had as many as three pieces in one issue under different names. The schooling and the encouragement I received were priceless.

In 1931 I acquired an agent, Harold Ober, with whom I had been associated until last year, when he died: I felt that I had lost a second father.

Oddly enough, it was not sports or a sports story that sparked my demolishing the barrier between the big time and myself and enabled me to break into the *Saturday Evening Post* after so many years of endeavor and desk drawers filled with rejection slips, but the city side. A news story broke one Christmas; a night editor performed a near miracle of getting it into the paper and thereby excited my imagination and capacity for hero-worship. The story of this story and its subsequent landing me in the *Saturday Evening Post* is told in the preamble to "McKabe," the first short story in this book. Its sale and publication resulted in giving me the one thing I had lacked up to that moment, and without which, I maintain, no writer can function. That lack was self-confidence. From then on, all my "writing on the side" was concentrated upon fiction and my stories began to appear regularly in the *Saturday Evening Post* and later in other magazines as well.

This is not intended as a blueprint for anyone who wishes to become a professional writer; I am just telling you what happened to me.

In 1936 I took the decisive step of changing my entire way of life. I resigned my job as one of the then highest-paid sports writers in the country, setting off a perfect holocaust of bridges, and went abroad to try in the future to earn my living as a free-lance writer of fiction, make or break. I was thirty-nine and running scared.

What was I scared of? Of failing and having to go back to sports writing! Previously I had become aware that I was in danger of letting the wrong kind of success go to my head and becoming that prize bore, the veteran sports writer, of having years creep up on me with my boyhood and life-long ambition unfulfilled, of being a success in the eyes of the world and a failure to myself.

Once while I was sitting at the ringside in Madison Square Garden preparing to send a round-by-round account of the main event to my office, a colleague arrived late, climbed into his seat while the principals were being introduced, and, standing up, took his own sweet time about parking his typewriter, removing his overcoat, and looking over the house. An irritated customer sitting in one of the ringside seats whose view was being blocked shouted, "Siddown! You're nothing but a sports writer!"

I think—in fact I am certain—that my decision to go for broke dated from one evening that took place some time in 1934. It was two years before I was able to implement the decision, but it had been made and I knew that I would go through with it. In 1936 one of my short stories sold to the movies for $5000. It was a stake that would enable me to live for a while and write stories. If they sold, well and good. If they didn't . . .

I resigned from the *Daily News*, went to England, and rented a cottage in the little fishing village of Salcombe on the South Devonshire coast, 214 miles from London, and remained there a few months before going on to the Continent.

Ever since then I have earned my living as a writer. I never forgot my cottage in Devon or the charm of the little village town.

Eventually I bought it, and now use it as a holiday retreat and base for one of my hobbies, salt-water fishing. The annual bass run off Salcombe in November is something to gladden the heart of any fisherman, and I rarely miss it.

Twice thereafter there was a kind of halfway turning back, not because I had failed to sell my stories, but rather because I felt that through fourteen years of watching and writing about athletes I had become one-sided. I was still sufficiently naïve as to believe that I had to experience things properly to write about them. I had not yet wholly learned to trust my imagination and even more my instincts. In the winter I went back to the *News* as a reporter on the city side to learn the business or to come in contact with that thing known as "life." The following winter I signed with INS as a feature writer to do special stories.

I soon found out that this nonsense was costing me money, since my assignments interfered with my writing and since, furthermore, working as a news reporter was not teaching me any more about things and people than I already knew. I was simply wasting my time. Thereafter I did no more reporting except for a brief period during the war when I took a job as a war correspondent.

In connection with the above I might say that life for a writer, at least for this one, is a constant series of alarums and excursions, of self-pamperings and self-delusions. There is always some distant place, a thatched cottage in England, a hacienda in Mexico, where, if you could only be, you would turn out the lyric prose and deeply significant stories that you find you cannot do wherever you happen to find yourself.

This, of course, is sheer nonsense, but it is a harmless kind of nonsense. It keeps one hoping and helps one to get around. I managed to achieve the house in England and the villa in Mexico and many other places, and they were never the answer. One of the few stories that ever gave me any satisfaction was written in snatches on railroad trains and hotel rooms while I was batting around the country as a reporter. I have written in furnished rooms, on boats, in the city, in the country, and in airplanes. If I have something that I want to write, I know that I can do it anywhere and under any conditions. But I will not relinquish the cherished illusion of the need for far places. I don't even mind knowing it is a fake. It is delightful window dressing. What one actually needs to write is an idea, a typewriter, a roof over one's head, and three square meals a day, because writing is physical as well as mental work and therefore hungry-making. All one really gets out of the delusion that ideas will burn and words flow three or four thousand miles away from the place where one is at the moment is a pleasant and diverting way of living and the broadening that comes with travel.

One is always seeking the touchstone that will dissolve one's deficiencies as a person and a craftsman. And one is always bumping up against the fact that there is none except hard work, concentration, and continued application.

From 1938 on I have been a free-lance professional writer, turning out short stories, serials, novels, film scripts, articles, and essays. My market at first was limited to American magazines—the *Saturday Evening Post, Cosmopolitan, Good Housekeeping, American Magazine*, and the defunct *Collier's* and *Liberty*. I have also written for *Reader's Digest, Esquire*, the *New Yorker*, and many others, and in later years my stories have appeared in publications abroad and in translation.

Some of my books have become best sellers, others have appeared and vanished without so much as causing a ripple, and others still, to my greatest satisfaction, have maintained a quiet and steady circulation over a long period of years. I have had a few minor triumphs, some failures, and down through the years an extraordinary amount of luck. If you were to ask me what so far in my thirty years' career as a professional writer has given me the most satisfaction, I would tell you that it is the fact that in the Times Book Shop in Wigmore Street in London, as well as in Foyle's, Hatchard's, and one or two other bookshops, at Christmas I have my own individual table where all of my books are displayed from *Snow Goose*, which was published more than fifteen years ago, to perhaps include this current volume.

All these evidences of popularity—a comfortable way of life, a house in the south of France, etc.—are accounted in this world as solid success with every indication of security. I am still dissatisfied with things that I write and I am still insecure.

Since these are listed as confessions, I will confess to you that from the time I resigned from the *News* a quarter of a century ago up to and including this very moment I have never had a single moment of security. Mark this down as one of the occupational hazards of free-lance writing for a living. Or if this is too gloomy a view, ascribe it to my own personal neuroticism and perhaps infantilism, for even today when I have completed a manuscript and sent it to agent or publisher I await the verdict with the same anguish, fear, and doubts that I did when I was a boy and dispatched a manuscript to a magazine with the usual stamped addressed envelope enclosed for return.

The euphoria connected with an acceptance lasts for a week or ten days, after which the reaction sets in. Can I keep it up? Will I be able to do it again? What will the next one I write be like?

I should be more upset at these palpable evidences of neuroticism if every writer, male and female, with whom I have exchanged shop talk had not confessed to some similar instances of disillusionment and insecurity which expressed themselves in one form or another. And we were all agreed that nothing was quite so shattering as a rejection or a sour notice or criticism from an editor, and the further along we went in our professions, the more damaging were the results of such a rejection. The first thought that arises to harass every writer when a piece is bounced, for whatever reason, is "I'm through. I'm all washed up. This is the end. I can never write again. I've lost the touch." One feels as helpless, dejected, and amateurish as the veriest tyro or beginner, as though one had to start learning all over again.

Of course it is sheer nonsense, of course one writes again because one must, and if the subsequent piece is accepted with hosannas, or merely accepted and paid for, all one's oozed confidence comes flooding back again and one rides atop the world—until the next fall.

I have always maintained that every successful writer is primarily a good editor, a premise that usually drives editors into tantrums when I tell it to them. But when the writer sits down to his typewriter to tell a story that he will offer for sale, he has already fulfilled most of the functions of editor. He has chosen his subject for timeliness, reader interest, the style of the magazine at which it is aimed, the known likes and dislikes of the editor of that particular literary vaudeville show, and the current state of mind of the public. He trims his material and sews his seam in a manner designed to be pleasing to all concerned. I maintain that's editing. The editor in the end merely confirms or denies one's judgment.

The hazards remain large, even after you have what the layman likes to call a "name," and very often the greater the name, the stricter the standards set by the editor. The writer invests an idea, research, time, energy, and hard labor in the preparation of a story. At the end of three weeks or a month he has some fifteen to twenty pages of typescript. If the editor nods "yes," it is worth from $1,000 to $5,000 depending on who the writer is and how big the demand for him. And if he says "no thanks," the income-tax people will let the writer deduct the market value of twenty sheets of used foolscap and depreciation on his typewriter, and the manuscript can then be used to light a fire. You can't afford to be wrong.

Short stories and novelettes that get into magazines in the class of mass circulation of the *Saturday Evening Post, Good Housekeeping,* or *Cosmopolitan* are counted as successful because, if nothing else, they have had to meet certain standards that, if not highly literary, are at least a guarantee that they can be published in a highly competitive field to divert ordinary people. They have passed editorial tests and hence are original, amusing, instructive, entertaining, and readable. Working as a professional writer with a reasonable understanding of my medium, I have long been aware that there are often more interesting and exciting things about a story than meets the eye, and among these is the story of the story, for there always is one connected with every effort.

Not that I hold with the frequently perpetrated theatrical cliché that the writer per se is a romantic and fascinating fellow. His delineation on the stage, hacking away at a portable in the middle of an expensive indoor set somewhere on Long Island, pausing for thinks, ruffling his fingers through his hair, making *moues* and lighting endless cigarettes, always makes me a little ill. Nothing is quite so static and unromantic as a chap sitting at a typewriter. And, paradoxically, nothing is to me quite as exciting and fabulous as the preparation of a story or the realization of the hundreds of kaleidoscopic flashes of the human mind, both conscious and sub-conscious, not to mention bits and pieces of the liver and lights of the writer that go into it.

For there is no creative product that so exposes the past life, the background, the adjustment or lack of adjustment to life, the fears and foibles, the failings and the strivings of the human being behind it as does writing. Music is an emotional abstract, and painting and sculpture in themselves provide few clues to the personality of the artist. But everything a man ever thought or did, or was or hoped to be, will eventually find its way into his copy.

Why does a man write a story? For many reasons—an urge, a bite, a gripe, the need of a buck, the need to get something off his chest, the desire to support his family, the hope of expressing something beautiful he feels inside him, the wish to entertain, to be admired, to be famous, to overcome a frustration, to experience vicariously an unfulfilled wish, or just for the pleasure of taking an idea and sending it flashing through the air, like a juggler with many silver balls, or the dark satisfaction of pinioning that same idea or thought or human experience and dissecting it to its roots.

"To write beautifully of beautiful things" is enough for any man's ambition, but the ingredients that go into this writing are myriad and fascinating. No matter what the subject, the store-house of the mind is opened and a million relics of a full life are there from which to select and choose. There are human experiences, memories, dreams from both night and day, fantasies, people real and imagined, places one has seen with the naked eye and places one has hungered for in the spirit, scents, snatches of long-forgotten conversations, old and troublesome emotions one had thought packed away, the memory of a caress, dislikes, hatreds, love and fear, serenity and passion, all waiting to help you in the telling of your tale. Many of these are unrecognized, but sometimes one is able to see through a finished story and know how old and how characteristic are some of the things contained therein.

Even superficially the events gathered behind a story are interesting, the why and wherefores of the background, the actual experience that touched off the idea, and the means used by the writer to add substance and drama to a happening, an episode, a fantasy, or an idea. The writer appears in many guises throughout his stories, and each of them has a meaning and a reason, some valid relation to his character or person or the kind of human being he is.

This book is intended to be neither a biography nor a self-analysis, but rather a glimpse into the workroom of a professional storyteller, somewhat like wandering through an artist's studio where you will find displayed some of the ingredients he uses in his work scattered about—his paints, palettes, canvases, and lay figures, old work and new, good ones and bad.

Such a visit, it seems to me, might be interesting merely from the point of view of curiosity; it might also be helpful to the beginning writer and perhaps even furnish here and there a hint or a clue as to how to go about confecting salable fiction. Yet I am offering it only as entertainment. If any of it should prove to be instructive, so much the better.

Over a period of twenty-five years I have written some one hundred and thirty published short stories, novelettes, serials, and books. Of these short stories I have selected twenty, ten of which were written before or during the war, and ten between 1945 and today. To each of these I have written a preamble or introduction that, to the best of my recollection, is the story behind the story, the background of the idea, the reason for writing it, the design, the method, the things that animated me or, for that matter, whatever came into my head about it as I looked back. Whether these writings are true or false is debatable. When I write about motivation or emotions connected with the telling of a story that happened years ago I am trying to write, not as I feel and think today, but as I hope I remember I then felt and thought. I am most certainly no longer the person I was when I began to write, nor do I write in the same style or upon the same subjects. Some of the things I write about, my stories, may be exaggeration and some even delusion, but everywhere I think I have managed to imbed some kernel of truth.

Half of these preambles were written years ago when a version of this volume first appeared in 1946. I have now edited them and brought them up to date in the light of being older and, I hope, that much more experienced and knowledgeable.

There is a question I am always asked and it is not confined to the layman. It is: "How do you work?" The content of this question varies from the vacuous probing of the ninny who wants to know whether I have to wait for inspiration and write on both sides of the paper to my colleagues who are as interested in my working hours and methods as I am in theirs.

Briefly, then, I work from half past nine in the morning until twelve thirty or one, break three hours for lunch and rest, and return at three-thirty for a two- or three-hour session in the afternoon.

Up to two years ago, when an illness suddenly robbed me of the use of my fingers, I did all of my work myself at the typewriter, punching out first and second drafts and then sending the corrected and interlined material to my agents for copying. And, incidentally, the illness that affected the nerves of my hands was occupational. Forty years of bending over a hot typewriter had caused changes in the vertebral column at the neck, pinching the nerves. Faced with a loss of output and recovering in the hospital from an operation to ease the condition, I engaged a secretary and in a few months had taught myself to dictate.

The use of my hands was restored, but I am now accustomed to dictating, like it, and find that it has increased my output and I can work longer hours. It is also better for my dialogue. Say a silly line to your secretary and even as you are saying it you know it won't do. She may have been trained never to turn a hair no matter what idiocies you might utter; nevertheless, you know that *she* knows the line is a dud and you kill it before it has a chance to go any further.

When I was typewriting my own material physically and was working to develop the plot or an idea of a short story, I used to talk to myself on the typewriter, rambling on, setting down thoughts and ideas, praising or cursing them, calling myself names, etc. This had the effect of unblocking myself. Original and valid ideas then would float up from the subconscious and present themselves, and I have solved many a difficult story in this fashion. Today I can achieve the same effect by rambling on to my secretary, dictating my thoughts upon the subject. Pages and pages of these notes are then discarded, but they have accomplished their purpose of letting through the story I really want to tell.

Short stories are initiated from ideas, the tickle of an absurdity— "Wouldn't it be funny if . . ."—an item in the newspaper, a story told by a friend, an emotion or a character one encounters. The difficulty then is to translate this beginning germ or incident into a full-fledged dramatic plot preserving the unities.

This is the hardest work of all, for it requires thinking. I begin by writing a trial synopsis and plot outline, adding, discarding, changing, messing about until a clear line for the beginning, middle, and climax begins to emerge, after which a final synopsis is written.

Next, this final synopsis is broken up into scenes and so many pages allotted to each scene and transition of the story. The average-length short story is limited to between five and seven thousand words. Five thousand words is about seventeen typewritten pages. This does not give one much room to turn around in and calls for all the tricks of economy, brevity, and suggestion, which is the nature of the art of short-story writing.

When I am satisfied that I can tell my story within the allotted space, I spend two or three days writing character sketches, setting down all and everything I know about each of the characters in the story. Like the iceberg, seven eighths of this material remains submerged and doesn't show, but the characters have now taken on life for me and I am able to think and speak and act as they might.

The above is the work part; then comes the fun part, the writing. If the story has been properly constructed, this can be a joy and a delight. It is at this time that one makes little discoveries and adds those small touches that are often the contribution a director makes to a moving picture, and that help to bring story and character to life. After I have written the first draft, I let it cool for two or three days or a week, by which time I can detect the soft spots and weaknesses. The second writing usually eliminates these. I write double space and on one side of the paper, margin of twenty, two hundred and fifty words to a page. This makes for quick and easy reading by the editor.

Final corrections are made with pen and the story forwarded to my agent, who has it copied and bound and sent to the publisher for whom he thinks it is best fit. I sit at home chewing my fingernails, waiting to hear if all this effort and planning is to be a success or a failure.

Herewith, then, some examples:

McKabe

"McKabe" is the first fiction story I sold to the *Saturday Evening Post*. It is made up of a kind of hero-worship I entertained for the working newspaperman, the killing of a notorious gangster, and the urge to imitate a short story by Rudyard Kipling, "The Devil and the Deep Sea."

The background for this story and the two others included in this section is New York's first tabloid, the *Daily News,* and all the characters are drawn from the editors, reporters, and photographers who worked there. The era is the lush period between the two wars.

The *Daily News* of that time was quite different from the mammoth of today. It was young, virile, vigorous, roughneck and rowdy, tough, and sensational, a consistent battler for the little guy, witty and humorous in its approach to life and the coverage of great stories. It was fighting tooth and nail for circulation and conducting the fight first from a ratty old building on Park Place opposite the Woolworth Building and later from its own neat skyscraper home on East Forty-second Street, which it still occupies.

I think that newspapers, like people, like everything in nature on earth, are young, grow up, change, age, and pass. I am glad that I lived with and was a part of the *Daily News* during its ebullient youth. It was the greatest shop in town in which to work and turned out some of the best newspapermen and women of the era.

Behind these people, animating them, supporting them, egging them on, was the young Captain Joseph Medill Patterson, publisher of the paper, just home from the wars, with a record of socialism and liberalism behind him in Chicago, a man filled with the gusto of living, who had then a sense of sparkling mischief without malice, whose understanding of the mass mind of the American public was infallible, and who never lacked the courage to admit when he was wrong. Working for him meant fun and excitement as well as good pay, and most of the men

Saturday Evening Post, August 12, 1933.

on the other sheets would have given a right arm to become a part of the *News* organization.

The newspaper as well as the people who worked for it used to fascinate me, and long before I thought of it as background for a series of fictional stories I used to duck away from the sports desk and roam through the other departments, watching, asking questions, getting the foremen or heads of departments to explain their work to me, trying to familiarize myself with the daily miracle that took place before my eyes, the smooth amalgamation of highly differentiated parts of a human and material machine leading to the inevitable climax of going to press on time.

I wandered through the darkrooms of the photographer's laboratory, where they could whip you out a print in less than five minutes after the cameraman had come bustling in from the scene of the accident or crime, the photo-engraving department, where pictures were turned into metal cuts to be laid next the type, into the library, where the intricate files were kept, files on the lives and misdeeds of hundreds of thousands of people, down to the composing room, where the chaffering batteries of Linotype set the type for the paper and the headlines were autotyped. I spent time in the inferno of the stereotype room, where the plates from the presses were cast, and from time to time when the battery of presses looking like the innards of an ocean liner or a battleship would begin to turn over slowly, commence to roll, and then, picking up speed, rise to an earth-shaking crescendo of noise and fury, I would be standing up on the iron balcony, hanging on the vibrating steel rail, drinking in the sights and the sounds and the smells as the pink papers with their black headlines poured forth from the hopper and were stacked for the delivery room.

One of my favorite people on the *News* was Gene McHugh, night editor, a bushy-haired, hollow-eyed genius with ulcers, tough, wise, decent, full of city-savvy and news instinct.

The morning of the day before Christmas in 1932 Gene was on the lobster shift, running the paper between the hours of midnight and eight A.M. His job was to supervise the final edition, which was put to bed at four o'clock in the morning, and prepare the schedules for the day men.

Shortly after six o'clock in the morning Gene received a telephone call from our Albany correspondent to the effect that Legs Diamond, notorious bootlegger and gangster, had been mowed down in a hail of machine-gun bullets in an Albany lodginghouse. It was a clean and sensational scoop, but might just as well have been delivered in Choctaw for all the good it could do either McHugh or the *News*. Because our run was off for the morning, the linotypers, stereotypers, and pressmen dispersed, and the printing plant shut down, to all practical purposes.

This was the problem that faced McHugh. The earliest he could hope to get this temporarily clean beat into the paper was the next day's pink edition, which went to press at six o'clock in the evening. By that time the afternoon papers would have killed the story.

But McHugh was a newspaperman from his toes to his flying thatch, and the fact that he couldn't get his news onto the street in his edition galled him more than his ulcers. He knew it was impossible. And yet a stubborn and invincible spirit surged within him. He went to work.

There were several of Rudyard Kipling's short stories that were special favorites of mine, and one of these was that epic of man against machinery, "The Devil and the Deep Sea," which appears in the volume called *The Day's Work*, in the authorized edition. If you don't remember it, it will pay you to look it up. It is the story of a little British steamer caught pearl-poaching in the East Indies and brought to bay with a five-inch shell through her engine room. It deals with her chief engineer, Mr. Wardrop, who attempts the impossible—namely, to bring order out of the horrible tangle of steel, copper, and iron junk and repair the damage sufficiently to escape.

The analogy between this story and the story of McHugh, Wardrop's problem, and McHugh's problem, struck me at once. Here was a chance to try to emulate a writer who was a hero to me and attempt to write a story like that.

Emulate should not be confused with *plagiarize*. The theme of man against the elements is as old as literature, and that of man against machinery at least as old as machinery. McHugh sang in my heart as Mr. Wardrop must have made Kipling's blood course faster. To put it mildly, the two stories and their treatments are entirely different. Rudyard Kipling remains undisputed champion, but I was able to achieve at least one lifelong ambition, and that was to make the *Saturday Evening Post*.

It took three months to work up the courage to try it. The burning urge to celebrate one hero, McHugh, and break a lance with another, Rudyard Kipling, overcame fears and inertia. I went to see my agent, Harold Ober, who had handled articles for me, and told him the idea. He arranged an appointment the following week with Mr. Tom Costain, the *Post* editor, who made a weekly shopping trip to the New York literary market. After listening to the yarn and my ideas for fictionizing it, Costain said, "Write it." This is all the commitment the *Post* will ever make. It never orders and it never guarantees to buy.

I pity all who have never known the thrill of "making" the *Post* for the first time. Like the moment of the first solo flight in an airplane, it can happen only once, it can never be experienced again, and there is no feeling to which it can be compared. The Messrs. E. McHugh and R. Kipling are hereby thanked.

As a final footnote to this history of a new start in life, the *Post* paid me $500 for the story. Following its publication, I was sued for libel by a printer whose real name I had inadvertently used, though in connection with another character, a bit of sheer aberration on my part, but indicating how closely I was working with real characters. I won the libel suit, but my lawyer's bill for the successful defense was $900, which left me with a $400 deficit on the deal and the determination to be careful in bestowing names on fictional characters in the future.

THE city room was nothing but a feeble pulse in the somnolent body of the paper when, a few minutes after six thirty in the morning, the day before Christmas, the number-three telephone of the city desk of the *Morning Blade* jangled. The paper had gone to bed hours before, when, at four A.M., the last edition had come thundering off the block-long battery of presses. The emergency crews had been released and sent home.

Gene McKabe, lobster-shift editor, looked up from the overnight assignment sheet on which he was working, preparatory to turning it over to the day relief, when and if it should decide to show up. McKabe was a thin, grayish, old-looking man at thirty-eight, who suffered from stomach ulcers and inferiority. Irritably he flipped the receiver off the hook and prepared to take a story from some tipster that two milk wagons had collided on a slippery street, or that a drunk had fallen down a flight of steps and was lying in the gutter. This was the usual run of news that came to McKabe in the early hours, stories in which he played no great part beyond weighing their importance in reporting them to the day shift for coverage. Well, someone had to take the trick from midnight to morn.

McKabe mumbled, "Desk—McKabe," into the mouthpiece, with his mind half on his assignment sheet and half on the dull pain that gnawed at his middle at that time of the morning. The *Blade* operator said, "A Mr. Giller is calling you from Albany, New York, and wishes you to pay for the call."

"Oke!" grunted McKabe, and wondered what could be getting their Albany correspondent, a not too alert individual at best, out of bed at that hour of the morning.

"Will you accept the charges?" repeated the operator.

"Yes, yes, yes," said McKabe. "Put him on." He checked off an assignment for one of the day photographers to make some pictures along the Bowery and instinctively glanced around the deserted local room while he waited. A Negro janitor was hauling off huge wire baskets laden with paper and trash. Two charwomen were on their knees in the aisles between the battery of rewrite desks. The art department was empty. The big horseshoe-shaped copy desk was untenanted. Monk, the lobster-shift office boy, the only other person in the vast room besides himself, had pushed two of the reporters' desks together and was lying atop them with his coat rolled up under his head, his shirt open at the neck, his mouth a gummy cavern, snoozing and snoring in an unlovely manner. The long-distance operator said something in a distant, far-off bleat, and the *Blade* operator replied in her singsong, "We are ready with Mr. McKabe. He is on the li-yen." McKabe heard Giller's voice, at first indistinct and then clear and plain as the operators closed their keys. It was shaking and surcharged with excitement. He said:

"Hello! Hello! Desk? Who is this?"

"Hello, Giller—McKabe. What's biting you?"

"Who is it? . . . Mac? Listen, Mac. They got Feet Schindler up here half an hour ago. Blew his head off."

"What?" said McKabe, and glued the receiver more firmly to his ear. "Lemme have that again." Instinctively his eyes leaped to the clock over the desk. Six thirty-seven. The *Times* and the *Tribune* had shut down at five, the *American* and the *Mirror* a half-hour later. But the afternoon papers—

"Listen! Wait," said Giller, his voice sounding odd with the pressure of excitement. "Hello, Mac? They got Mimi, his girl, too, and Little Hymie and Joe Colonno. It's a slaughter."

"Sweet Peter!" said McKabe. "Wait a minute." He called over to the sleeping office boy, "Monk! Hey, Monk!" Then he threw a telephone book at him, which struck him in the chest. Monk sat up, bleary-eyed and indignant. McKabe bawled at him, "Get on extension 457 and help me check this story."

Monk ambled over to the desk, working his mouth, and picked up pencil, paper, and the receiver from the extension of McKabe's phone on the other side of the desk.

"Shoot!" said McKabe, his own pencil poised.

"Listen," said Giller. "I'm coming home about an hour ago from a little party at my wife's sister's. I'm a little stiff, see?"

"You're not stiff now, are you?" asked McKabe, suddenly suspicious.

"Listen," replied Giller's voice, and its deadly earnestness convinced McKabe. "After what I just seen, nobody could be stiff. So the wife is inside and I'm just putting the car away when the World War busts loose on the other side of town. It's way on the other side, but it's so clear and quiet I can hear it. Machine guns. It takes me a half-hour to find it."

To himself Monk carefully repeated the address Giller gave, and marked it on his sheet.

"The state troopers were there already. They were all dead."

"Who was dead—the troopers?"

"No, no! Feet and his doll and all of them. They made a clean getaway."

"I thought you said they were dead."

"No, no, no! The mob that done it made the getaway. They drove up in a car, walked up two flights, and machine-gunned 'em. Feet and Mimi and Little Hymie and Joe Colonno must 'a' come up from Kinderhook and took a room in this joint. It's just a rooming house. I guess they were all celebrating Feet's acquittal. They caught 'em cold. There was a lot of busted gin and whisky bottles around that got shot to pieces."

"How many in the mob?"

"I dunno. They made a clean getaway in a car—"

Monk edited this statement automatically and wrote, "Clean getaway in a high-powered car."

"—but from the slugs that's in the bodies and the walls, there must 'a' been at least four of 'em pumping sub-machine guns, and maybe a coupla lookouts. The walls was all shot to pieces, and the lights. Feet and the girl were sitting on the bed when they got it. Joe and Hymie were at the table, drinking. The floor is all blood and plaster out of the wall and ceiling and pieces of glass. They didn't take a chance on Feet getting away this time. Got all that? Is that something? None of the other guys are out here yet. We got an hour's start. Is that something?"

"Yeah," said McKabe. His eyes went to the clock again. It now showed a quarter to seven. "That's something, all right. But what the hell good does it do us? We're locked up. The run's off. The crews have all gone home. We're dead. Get it? Feet's been knocked off for the afternoon papers. That's your luck and mine. The devil himself couldn't get out a paper at this hour. I'll rout O'Rary out and fly him up to get some pix. Stay on it. Call me back in an hour."

There was a pregnant silence from the other end of the telephone.

McKabe hung up the receiver and chewed at his pencil, his eye on the clock again. His face went suddenly ash-colored and he swore. Excitement always made his stomach bad. Monk hung up the receiver to his extension and blinked across the desk at McKabe, who sat looking old and shrunken. The copy time-clock stamp went "click" as another minute popped itself into eternity. Six forty-seven—the day before Christmas. Merry Christmas, Feet. Blown to hell. Feet, Feet, Feet. The name marched through McKabe's skull and trailed behind it black ribbons of headlines.

The enormousness of the story suddenly struck home. Feet Schindler, the headline pet, big-time racketeer, killer, booze and dope runner. Feet, the much-shot-at, who had survived five murderous attacks and who carried enough slugs in his skinny body to founder him, whose latest escape from death had been a seven-day sensation, and whose acquittal the afternoon before of a charge of hijacking and abduction was still smashed over the face of the extra-final edition of the *Blade* which lay face-up on McKabe's desk. It read, "FEET ACQUITTED."

It was wrong. It ought to be shrieking, "FEET MURDERED, FEET SLAUGHTERED, FEET BUTCHERED." The date, "December 24, 1932," on the logotype made "FEET ACQUITTED" stale and a lie. It was six forty-eight the morning of December 24, and Feet, the king cobra of the muscle and roscoe men, was lying in a welter of plaster and broken glass and his own blood in a cheap rooming house in Albany. Yesterday he was acquitted. Today he was dead. Fresher news! Hotter news! His moll was dead with him; Mimi, the pretty redhaired *Follies* girl, and Little Hymie and Joe Colonno lying in the same room. Six-star, extra-final edition. The latest news. December 24, 1932. FEET ACQUITTED. Acquitted nothing! He was either roasting in hell or standing before the last bar of justice confirming his killings. Feet! Feet! Feet!

McKabe looked up at the clock again. The corpse of the paper was three minutes colder. Six fifty. "Call the pressroom," said McKabe. "See if you can raise anybody."

Monk looked at a card stuck under the glass top of the city desk, stuck his pencil butt into the dial face, and spun it around to 346. As he did so, McKabe was dialing 342, the composing room, 3—4—2. Wait. . . . Click. . . . Ring . . . ring . . . ring . . . ring

The phone in the empty office of the composing-room foreman rang again and again. Outside, the vast floor loaded with steel and lead, with the orderly rows of linotype machines set up at one end and the make-up stones with the half-broken forms of the paper resting thereon, was dark, empty, deserted. The purplish-blue overhead mercury lamps were out. One electric droplight that hung over one of the type saws cast deep shadows that reached to the linotypes and darkened the silver-lead pots in which was nothing but cold metal. A single red standing light gleamed over one of the machines and lit up a few of the rows of the keyboards. It had been turned on by the operator to indicate that the machine was out of order.

Three hours earlier, hot type had been dropping from the clacking, chaffering, spinning machines, as line after line of silver lead was set by the flying fingers of rows of operators. The telephone began to ring in the empty room. This was a "swing" morning because of the impending holiday. The day shift wouldn't be on until eight. The telephone stopped ringing.

It rang in the pressroom in the empty office of the pressroom foreman, who an hour ago had ordered the presses stripped, seen them washed down and oiled, and gone away. Outside, the great presses that stretched for a full city block lay dark, gleaming, and silent. They looked like the turbines of a gigantic battle cruiser. When they ran at full blast, they made a noise like sheet iron falling down a mountainside. The floor and the steel gallery that ran around them, and the entire building, trembled. Men, oily and grimy, walked the catwalks between and around them. The papers poured from them like chaff from a hopper. Governors spun, rocking beams rocked, levers and pistons moved back and forth in their complicated counterpoint. The paper whirled white through the cylinders and came out gray-black with news and pictures.

Now they lay, quiescent, sinister mountains of machinery. The overhead lights gleamed from the polished brass and steel and from the oil on the steel floors to which they were anchored. There was in the vast and seemingly endless pressroom no motion, no sound but the regular ring-stop-ring of a telephone.

McKabe called a Garden City number and routed O'Rary, the flying photographer, out of bed, told him what had happened, and ordered him to Albany to make pictures, and then telephoned to a reporter to meet O'Rary at Roosevelt Field and fly up with him to Albany and get on the story. The excitement bell in the A.P. and U.P. ticker room went "Ding . . . ding . . . ding. . . . Ding-ding-ding-ding-ding." Monk pricked up his ears and McKabe motioned him with his head in the direction of the room. When he came back, he had a narrow slip of white paper in his fingers— an A.P. flash.

It read:

6.52 A.M. FLASH. FEET SCHINDLER REPORTED SLAIN IN ALBANY. EDITORS: FOR YOUR INFORMATION. MORE LATER ON VERIFICATION.

McKabe swore helplessly. Now it was out. Feet Schindler reported slain. More on verification! Reported nothing. He was an hour, two hours ahead of them all. He had the story. He had it in his mind's eye. His physical eye looked at the time again. It was five minutes to seven. He saw again the picture that Giller had drawn for him of that dreadful room in Albany. He could get it down on paper—short, pithy, exciting sentences. But it couldn't be cast into type. It couldn't be got onto the presses. He had a moment of complete madness when he contemplated making twenty carbon copies of the story and getting it out on the street— getting something out on the street. Everybody would want to know. Everybody ought to know. Extra! Extra! Feet Schindler slain. Here's the story by Gene McKabe, on a piece of copy paper. Read it and pass it along to your neighbor.

The same Associated Press flash that lay before him was in the offices of the *Times,* and the *Tribune,* the *American,* the *Standard, News-Beacon, Chronicle,* and *Enquirer.* All the lobster-trick editors on the morning sheets were fingering the same slip of paper and cursing their inability to get the news on the street. Lobster-trick editors! Forgotten newspapermen like himself who worked the shift from midnight to dawn. Not the most brilliant editors in the world, but good, sound newsmen who knew what to do in case of fire, flood, or quake. Well, none of them could perform miracles and bring a corpse to life. With a good deal of scrambling, the day forces could get a morning paper out by seven o'clock that night, twelve hours later.

Not so the afternoon papers, due on the streets at ten thirty in the morning. With a sickening sensation McKabe visioned the excitement and the activity in the offices of the *News-Beacon*, the liveliest of the afternoon sheets—editors on telephones to Albany; reporters piling into plane and car and heading north to run down the tip; rewrite men fingering through the clips on the dead Schindler, preparing a biographical sketch of his career; copy pouring into the composing rooms. Time, time, time—fleeting seconds and minutes. They would try to move their press time up, rout out their Albany man, locate the death house, interview the state troopers. Artists would be drawing diagrams and artists' conceptions of the slaying. The vast news-reporting resources of the Associated and United Press were hot on the trail by this time. It wouldn't be long before the bell in the ticker room would ring again, and the first details of the sensational slaughter would be clacked out on the automatic printers. And in the meantime the radio might kill the story.

McKabe jumped to his feet. "Watch those phones," he said to Monk. "I'll be back." He ran over to the elevator and caught it as the porter dragged a load of waste paper aboard.

"Pressroom," he said.

The operator looked at McKabe curiously. "Gallery?"

"Floor," said McKabe. His heart was banging against his chest. His stomach was sore. In his throat was a curious, nervous, excited feeling. He swallowed several times.

The elevator door slid back and McKabe half ran through the door as though to catch the miracle he hoped he would find before it vanished—rolling presses, pressmen, fly-boys—life and activity. But the batteries lay there glistening, quiet, and oppressive. There was no one on the floor. The catwalks of steel were empty. The massiveness of this cold, silent machinery laid hold of McKabe's heart and made him feel the way he felt when he contemplated high mountains—alone, insignificant, helpless. Mountains made men want to scale them. These cold, hard, motionless ranges of steel made a stubborn anger well up in McKabe's heart and throat and brought tears of rage to his eyes.

He stood, a pygmy, on the steel floor, a little, thin man with bushy hair, now half iron-gray, eyes sunk into hollows, unshaven, sloppy-looking, his tie pulled down from his shirt, his vest flapping unbuttoned, pockets bulging with pencils, shaking his fist at the dead presses and then pounding his forehead with the heel of his hand. Men had made these machines, but they wouldn't run without men. He, McKabe, willed them desperately to run, and not a gear, not a cog, not a lever could move. He began to curse them. His voice came clattering back to him from the high vault two stories above. His eye caught the ever present clock—seven three. Then his ears caught a scraping noise halfway down the room. If it were only one pressman—one of anyone who knew what handles to pull, what buttons to push to make those giants roll again—somehow McKabe knew he might do the rest. He ran down that catwalk between the two rows of presses like a sprinter, his feet rapping sharply on the floor.

It was a porter, plunking trash into his wire basket and dragging it along the floor.

"Hey!" shouted McKabe. "You!"

The porter, a Swede, looked at him curiously. "Vat?" he said.

"Ah, hell," said McKabe. "Nobody here?"

"Nah," replied the Swede. "Dey close up, hour ago."

"You don't understand anything about"—nodding his head at the presses—"these?" McKabe hoped vaguely that the man might be an apprentice or an ex-pressman filling in to keep working.

"Haw, haw!" laughed the Swede. "I keep away from dem. Vat you looking for—pressmen?"

"My God, yes," said McKabe. "Do you know where any are? Maybe there's a couple still washing up."

The Swede shook his head. "Proply you find a coople across the street."

McKabe grabbed the porter's arm. "Across the street? The speak?"

"If dey get drunk enough, dey stay there sometimes."

"Wait a minute," said McKabe. "What day is this?" He knew, but he couldn't bring it into his mind.

"Huh?" said the Swede, and looked at him. Then he fished into his wire basket and pulled out a paper. The black headline on it hit McKabe like a physical blow. It read, "FEET ACQUITTED." The Swede looked at the date line—"December 24, 1932"—and said, "You haff a coople drinks already? Tomorrow iss Christmas."

December 24. The day before Christmas—the day the cashier paid the Christmas bonus. Some of the crew might hang around and wait—hang around in the neighboring speakeasies.

"O.K., O.K., O.K.! Thanks!" said McKabe. He was already running down to the end of the room. He ran to the elevator, pressed the button, and then, without waiting, pushed through the door to the iron stairs that led to the street.

A twinge of pain caught him and stopped him, weak and gasping. It passed. Two steps at a time, he ran down two flights to the bottom and out into the street.

McKabe crossed the street to the speakeasy and never felt the cold or the slight morning drizzle. He burst through the ground-glass door so precipitately that the bartender stopped wiping glasses and rather casually dropped his right hand down below the bar, but restored it when he saw who it was, and said, "Hello, Mac. Merry Christmas. Don't come in quite so fast, old boy."

Durkin, the sub-foreman of the pressroom, Farley, an old-time pressman, and a man whom McKabe did not know were sitting around one of the wooden tables drinking Scotch highballs and eating cheese sandwiches. They were all drunk. McKabe paused, looking as though he had seen the Angel Gabriel, mopped his brow, and said, "Sweet Peter, I'm glad to see you fellows."

The three looked at McKabe owlishly and a little resentfully, until Durkin recognized him and said, "Oh, h'lo, Mac, ol' Mac, ol' Mac. Merry Christmas. Will ya have a li'l' drink?"

McKabe shook his head, made the usual gesture toward his stomach, said, "I can't drink likker. It murders me. Listen, are all you pressmen?"

Durkin shook his head. "Billers here"—nodding toward the stranger—"is a sub-make-up. He jus' come on from Milwaukee. Wife's cousin. . . . Billers, shake han's with Mizzer McKabe."

"Can you set type?" said McKabe eagerly, without acknowledging the introduction.

Billers nodded his head solemnly that he could, but said, "I ain't in a long time. I'm a make-up."

"Listen, you birds," said McKabe, his voice choking with excitement. "I want you to come on back with me and help me get a paper out. Feet Schindler—"

Durkin interrupted indignantly. "What the heck are you talking about? 'S shut down. Closed up. Can't get no paper out. Siddown and have a drink."

"No, no! Listen, fellers," said McKabe earnestly, his sunken eyes wide and pleading, and dropped into the vacant chair at the table. "Listen, there's a whale of a story. We got it. They knocked off Feet Schindler and his doll and everybody. Listen, we could beat the afternoon papers out—"

"Ah, forget it, Mac, and have a drink," said Durkin. "You can't get a paper out."

"The hell I can't," said McKabe, blazing suddenly and banging the table so that a slab of cheese jumped the dish. "If you two can plate up a press, Billers can set the story."

Durkin wiped his mouth with the back of his hand. "And who's gonna cast the new plates? Ya gonna have a new One and Three, ain'tcha? Ya can't get a edition out with a rubber stamp. Have a drink and forget about it."

"Stereotypers!" said McKabe. "Aren't there any stereotypers in here?"

Farley peered intently around the empty room and said, "No."

McKabe screwed his eyes shut and ran his fingers through his hair. Suddenly he pointed a bony finger at Durkin. "What's that joint where the stereotypers usually hang out?"

"It's just over on Second Avenue, but there won't be anybody there now. Most of the boys went up to Ed's house to play pinochle. Ferget it, Mac."

McKabe was up out of the chair. "Listen, will you fellers stay here a minute till I get back?"

Durkin said, "You're damn right we'll stay here. We're gonna stay here till tomorrow morning. We're—"

McKabe was already heading for the door. He heard Billers say, "Who is that screwball?" as he went through the door. He started for Second Avenue and the speakeasy frequented by some of the stereotypers and compositors.

The place was deserted except for the sleepy-eyed bartender, who was hanging up his apron. He didn't bother to turn around when he heard McKabe's footsteps, but merely said:

"Closing up."

"No, no. I don't want a drink," said McKabe. "Are any of the stereotypers here?"

"Naw. They been and gone. If you'd come a minute sooner, Otto was here. You know Otto? He just left."

"Which way did he go?" McKabe knew fat Otto Schommers, who worked in the foundry, making the mats from which the plates were cast. The bartender shrugged his shoulders. McKabe ran out into the street. It was deserted. Helpless, he ran a few steps first north, then south, stopped and swore bitterly. Then, two blocks away on Thirty-ninth Street, he saw a squat, solitary figure standing on the corner beneath the elevated. A trolley car was coming up the avenue, northbound. McKabe broke into a run for the figure, shouting, "Otto! Hey, Otto! Otto Schommers! Hey, Otto! Otto, wait." He didn't even know if it was Otto. Or if he had seen or heard him. The trolley clattered closer. McKabe gave one more yell. "Otto! Hey, Otto!" The car blotted him from sight. McKabe ran on. The trolley moved away. The squat figure was still there. It was Otto.

"Otto!" McKabe reached him and caught him by the arm. "Otto! Where you going?"

Otto paused. "Home. Where you think? You make me miss my car."

"Listen," said McKabe between gasps. "Will ya come back and cast a couple of plates? Hell of a story. Wanna get a paper out. Gotta. Will ya, Otto?"

Otto gazed at McKabe placidly. "Sure," he said. "It's O. K. with me. I'll cast 'em. If I ain't too drunk. Anything you say."

McKabe looked at Otto's fat and pudgy face. "Otto, I could kiss you. We'll pick up Durkin, Farley, and Billers on the way." He put his arm around fat Otto's shoulder and they turned back down the street.

It was seven twenty-four when McKabe shepherded his group through the plant door. The block-long double battery of giant presses no longer filled McKabe with quite the same awe. He no longer stood so terribly alone before them. Two of these men with him could master them.

Durkin took his handkerchief from his lips and said, "Now, just what is it you want us to do, ol' boy, ol' boy?"

"Plate up," said McKabe. "Get the plates back on again. I'll write the story. Billers can set it and make it up. We'll send down a new page one and three. Otto says he can make the mats and cast them alone. You get those plates on the cylinders; I'll do the rest."

"Plate up with what?" asked Durkin with sarcasm. "I told you the paper was dead. The plates have been destroyed. Come on back and forget about it. The plates have been melted up already. We don't keep 'em. You can't do a miracle, even if it is Christmas, Mac. I could 'a' told you that."

McKabe said, "Oh, God," and clung to the handrail of number-ten press. Farley began picking his teeth. Billers did likewise. Otto looked fat and placid.

"All right! All right! That won't stop me. We'll cast 'em all over again." McKabe shouted it and then turned to Otto. "Whaddya say, Otto? Cast the whole damn thing over again except one and three."

Otto shrugged his shoulders. "It's O. K. with me. Anything you say. I'll cast a million of 'em. It don't mean nothing in my life. I get time and a half. I hope the mats is all right."

McKabe clutched his head. "The mats. Holy jumping— Otto, you look. I can't." Otto waddled placidly off in the direction of the stereotype foundry. McKabe pounded his skull with the heel of his hand again. His stomach was afire. "If those—" he broke into profanity again—"mats aren't there—"

"You'll have the mats remade out of forms that is broke up," sneered Durkin. "You're off your nut."

McKabe didn't hear him, or if he did, he gave no sign.

They stood around, silent and gloomy, until Otto came waddling back down the iron walk. His features were as expressionless and placid as ever. It was impossible to tell whether he had good news or bad. All four stared at him.

"Well?" It was McKabe who spoke.

"Yeah, the mats is there." Otto scratched his head. "You want I should begin casting? It takes some time."

McKabe looked up at the pressroom clock. It was seven thirty-one. "How long?"

"I dunno. Maybe a hour. I gotta work alone."

"Can't Durkin and Farley help you?"

"We're pressmen, not stereotypers," said Durkin. "You get us the plates; we'll slap 'em on. It'll take Otto a couple hours to cast up all them plates for a seventy-two-page paper. The afternoon papers will be on the street. The *News-Beacon* goes in at half past ten. Why don't you forget about it? What the hell is this hot story, anyway, that can't wait until tomorrow?"

"Come on," said McKabe. He steadied himself on Otto's shoulder and the five went off to the foundry.

Otto divested himself of his coat, vest, tie, and shirt and worked naked from the waist up. He threw a switch and the foundry became bathed in blue mercury light. Durkin and Billers and Farley looked bilious, and Otto like a fat imp from inferno. He looked at the temperature of the molten metal in the casting machine, pressed on a button, and the huge pile of pipes, cylinders, caldrons, beams, and dials came to life and hissed and groaned and clanked, shuddering. Otto cast a blank test plate to try out the machine and the metal, picked it off the revolving casting cylinder with hands clad in asbestos gloves, and shoved it back into the melting pot again. He worked with a sure, deliberate leisureliness that soothed rather than aggravated McKabe. The dead giant was stirring—the first faint flutter. McKabe watched Otto. From a pile in one corner of the foundry Otto took a brown mat, shaped like a half-cylinder, dimpled and corrugated with type impressions, baked stiff and hard like a biscuit. Otto ran his fingers deftly over the inside surface. "Page two," he said, and slipped it into the casting cylinder, made an adjustment, locked it into place, and pressed a yellow button. The machine hissed and roared. Metal parts moved against one another noisily.

The cylinder made a half-turn, and to its outside clung the curved metal plate with the negative type faces on the outside. Otto plucked it off, steaming hot, and carried it to the shaver and pulled the lever. Steel knives pared little curls of silver from the inside. The plate slid on down over the cooler. Jets of oil and water shot up into the inside.

"Come on, you punks, and grab it," said Otto. "What you want me to do—put it on the presses for you? I'm a stereotyper, not a pressman."

Durkin laughed. "Stick it on the conveyor," he said. "We'll catch it outside." He and Farley turned and walked out. Otto set the plate on the moving rollers that led to the pressroom, and the thing moved solemnly out through a hole in the steel wall into the pressroom. A tremendous excitement took hold of McKabe. The moving plate seemed to release him from a stupor into which pain and discouragement seemed to have sent him. Time, seven forty-three. "At-a-boy, Otto!" he shouted. "I'll get the story out as quick as I can! . . . Come on, Billers!"

They went upstairs in the freight elevator, stopped at the sixth floor, the composing room, where McKabe unloaded Billers. He had an uneasy feeling that all might not be well there, but after his victory in the pressroom, he lacked the courage momentarily to investigate personally.

"Go on," he said to Billers. "Get familiar with the place. I'll rush the copy down in short takes. The thirty-six-point machines are over in that far corner. The seventy-two and ninety-six is hand-set." It was seven forty-four by the composing-room clock.

"O. K.," said Billers: "take your time. I can't start until eight anyway."

The elevator door started to close. "What?" screamed McKabe.

"You heard me," said Billers. "Union rules. Keep your shirt on."

The elevator door shut. McKabe cursed Billers so that the elevator man turned and stared at him and then had to remind him that they were at the seventh floor. McKabe staggered out of the elevator and over to the city desk. It seemed to him that he had been gone for hours. He expected to see it piled high with A.P. and U.P. copy, but it wasn't. The press associations were evidently having trouble on the story. Monk was asleep at the desk, his head buried in his arms. McKabe shook him until he awoke, blinking stupidly.

"Come on. Get on the job. Hustle out to the library and get me all cuts on Feet Schindler—the big ones."

Monk dragged his leaden feet. McKabe yelled, "I said hustle!" and threw another telephone book at him. Monk ducked and kept on going at no faster speed. McKabe inserted a sheet of paper in the swinging typewriter at the city desk and from sheer force of habit typed in the upper left-hand corner, "Schindler slaying, McKabe REW Giller"; wrote, "By Eugene McKabe" in the center of the page, and then exed it out. He was an editor and had no authority for a by-line. He then wrote:

Silent night, Holy night. . . . The world sleeps.
Only the Holy Christ child keeps lonely vigil.
The carillons of St. Anthony's on the hill in Albany, New York,
rang out the old hymn in the cold, clear dawn before Christmas and
then were drowned out by the roar of four sub-machine guns
exploding simultaneously in the dingy top-floor room of a cheap
boardinghouse at—

McKabe checked his notes to make sure of the address.

The slugs that poured from the flaming cannons obliterated Feet
Schindler, the king cobra of the racket men, tore his girl, Mimi

Fredericks, to shreds, and blew the life out of two of his henchmen,
Little Hymie and Joe Colonno, in the greatest underworld slaughter
since the St. Valentine's massacre in Chicago.

McKabe stopped and read it over and liked it. It was a good lead.
He knew that if old Bill Waters, chief of the copy desk, were in the
slot, he would probably cut out the stuff about the Christmas hymn
and the carillons. But he wasn't. McKabe was rewrite, copy desk, and
editor in one. His head drooped and he braced himself on the typewriter, and then realized that the telephone on the city desk was
ringing again. It shocked McKabe to consciousness again. He got
the receiver off the hook and to his ear, and was surprised to hear
his own voice saying somewhere inside his head, "Desk—McKabe."

The voice at the other end said, "Hello. Hello. That you,
McKabe? This is Billers, down in the composing room. Listen, you
can't set no type here. The machines is all cold."

"What? What the hell are you talking about?"

"I said, this is Billers, in the composing room. The lead in the
pots is all cold. You can't set no type here."

McKabe shouted into the telephone, "I'll be down!" and hung up.
Wrath cleared his head. Not set type? Not get that paper out? He
would go down and beat Billers to a mush. He got up and made
for the stairs. He saw Monk issuing from the library and called to
him, "Bring 'em all down to the composing room, and bring that
copy out of my typewriter." He half fell down the flight of steps
and burst into the composing room, a disheveled madman, frightened the wits out of Billers, who was sitting on a make-up stone
reading the paper and smoking a home-rolled cigarette.

"Now, what the hell is this?" gasped McKabe.

Billers nodded his head toward the silent rows of linotype
machines. "Them lead pots is cold. You can't set no type."

"Well, heat 'em up!" snarled McKabe.

Billers spat into a type rack. "Take you two hours," he said.

"The hell it will! Stoke 'em up. Force 'em!"

"Can't. Gotta bring it up gradual. Else the lead won't set. Them
machines is cold. Here, come over here and take a look."

He and McKabe went over to the first of the linotype machines. Billers rubbed some oil and grease from the face of a small dial on the side. The needle registered two hundred and ten degrees.

"How much should it be?"

"Between six hundred and six fifty. Take you two hours. You gotta bring them up gradual or you can't set no type. Might take a chance in a hour and a half. Don't figure it no use trying."

McKabe looked helplessly up and down the rows of dead machines with their white keyboards grinning like mocking ivory teeth. A few hours ago they were hot. Men were sitting at them and sending the brass letter casts tinkling into the casting racks, molding the bars of type, line after line. A few hours ago—

McKabe grasped at the thought. "Wait a minute," he said. "Maybe they weren't all shut off at the same time. Maybe some or one worked later than others. We could bring that up. Come on."

Billers came reluctantly, saying, "They're cold, I tell you." They went down the first line, scanning the temperature dials. One of them was up to two hundred and seventy. The second row of machines was stone-cold. McKabe was moving ahead of Billers. He had learned to read the dials. At the fourth machine in the last row he let out a whoop.

"Hey, Billers, four hundred and fifty degrees."

"It'll take you an hour."

"Make it in a half."

"Takin' a chance she won't flow."

"I'll take it. Boost her. Pour it to her."

Billers looked at the machine. "That's fourteen-point Vogue. That's an advertising type. You can't use that." He saw the look in McKabe's eye and hurriedly pressed a switch. There was a low hum from the machine. Billers looked at an indicator, adjusted something, and shrugged his shoulders. "It's O. K. with me. Only we don't do things like that in Milwaukee. I'll set it in thirty-six-point Old English, if you say."

"You're damn right you will. . . . What are we going to do about inside heads?"

"Nothin'," said Billers. "Them machines is all damn near froze. You got hand type, ain't you?"

"Yeah, seventy-two and ninety-six. We'll smack the word 'slaughtered' across page one. Maybe we've got some one hundred and twenty-point. Come on, let's take a look and see what's in the pup."

They went over to the corner of the room where the Sunday predate edition lay on the make-up stones, locked in the forms. McKabe's practiced eye skimmed over the reverse-type: Broker in Lovecult Trap. Kiss Slayer to be Executed This Week. Governor Ill at Albany. Wife Sues Rich Mate. Charges Blonde in Hide-out. Tale of Kentucky Vengeance. City Slums Breed Gangsters. Babe Ruth Not Murderous Hitter of Yore. The Sunday-feature headlines ranged from 36-point Bodoni to 48-point Chelt and Century. McKabe whipped out a pencil and began to scribble on the back of an envelope. Finally he handed it to Billers. It read, "Trap Gangster at Albany Hide-out—Executed in Murderous Vengeance."

"Here," he said, "fix that up. She'll go in two lines of three-column."

Billers looked at it stupidly. "The machine is cold—" he began.

"Dig it out of the pup and saw it up!" howled McKabe. "It's all in there. What the hell kind of printers do they have these days? Here, pick out that 'Broker in love-cult trap,' and saw off the 'trap.' Get it?"

Billers mumbled something about Milwaukee, unlocked the form, lifted the line out, and took it over to the saw. McKabe teetered back to the make-up desk, where Monk waited with the cuts.

"Gimme," he said. He spread the metal likenesses of the dead gangster out before him on the desk. There was a big three-column cut of Feet's head with a cigarette drooping from the weak mouth. He wished it were five columns. There was another three-column full-length of Feet and his girl Mimi. Three and three were six—one column too many. Across the bottom of page one of the edition was a five-column cut showing Feet and Mimi and Little

Hymie and Joe Colonno in the courtroom at Kinderhook. It was too deep, however. From the other end of the room came the ring and whine of the metal saw as Billers cut through the headlines: "Wee-e-e-e-ow! Wee-e-e-e-e-ow!" McKabe held the cuts stupidly in his hand for a moment while a spasm of pain swept over him. "Wee-e-e-e-ow!" McKabe came to life again, fighting the pain down, ripped open the desk drawer, and took out a large white sheet the size of the front page, crisscrossed with red lines into squares and marked, "Dummy—Page 1." He laid the three cuts on the sheet and with a pencil and rule marked off the overshoot on each. He cut Feet out of the deep three-column, leaving Mimi in two-column size, with a few pieces of Feet on the border, and laughed at the idea of Feet being dismembered again. He cut the legs off all of them on the five-column courtroom scene. Then he hobbled down to Billers.

"I can't find 'murderous'," said Billers.

"On page fifty-six, Sports," snapped McKabe. "Never mind that a second. Crop these cuts for me where I got 'em marked. Saw 'em off. Step on it."

"R-r-r-r-ring! Wee-e-e-e-ow!" McKabe caught "Schindler Separated from His Sweetheart" as the saw bit through, and fired the piece into a near-by hellbox. Billers cropped the other one.

"That's page one," said McKabe grimly.

"Ain't you gonna have nothing tells who they are—whataya call 'em—captions? Or anything?" asked Billers.

"Hell with the captions," said McKabe. "Everybody knows who they are. When I smack that line 'slaughtered' across the top of the page, they'll get it. Get these lines sawed up."

McKabe returned to the desk. He dared not exult. It was too soon. If the lead didn't heat up, if something went wrong with the casting or the presses—two men, and both drunk, to plate up— But in his ears already rang the cry of the newsboys: "Extra! Extra! Special Extra!" A sudden panic laid hold of him. What newsboys? Where would he get them? What good was a newspaper on the pressroom floor? He grabbed the telephone on the make-up desk.

"Hello, honey—McKabe. Listen, get me Jim Dixey, the circulation manager, at his home. Hurry it." He heard her dial the call. A man's voice answered the telephone sleepily.

"Hello, Jim. This is McKabe. Are you awake? Get me now. Hell of a story. Feet Schindler and his mob knocked off in Albany. I'm gonna get a paper out and—"

"Wait a minute—wait a minute. Who is this?"

"McKabe. I—"

"What's the matter? You drunk, McKabe? What time is it? You can't get a paper out now. Why the hell didn't you call me earlier?"

"Listen, you dumb Irish——" raged McKabe. "Did you hear me tell you I was going to get a paper out? You and every other dumb so-and-so have been telling me I can't for the last hour. I'm getting it out, I tell you—getting it out!" His voice rose hysterically.

There was a silence from the other end of the wire. Then, "At-a-boy, Mac. How soon you going to be running?"

McKabe looked up at the clock. It was twenty-one minutes past eight. "Half an hour with any luck, three quarters, maybe sooner. The afternoon papers can't move up more than forty minutes."

"You gimme the papers. I'll get 'em around."

McKabe was suddenly suspicious. "You ain't humoring me, are you? I tell you I ain't drunk, I'm—"

"Listen," said Dixey. "If you're drunk or kidding me, when I get there I'll beat your head off. Go ahead, get her rolling."

Get her rolling. Rolling, rolling, rolling—those dumb, immovable, lethargic giants below. "Billers! Billers!" bawled McKabe. "Come on down here! We got to get her rolling!"

Billers came strolling until McKabe bawled, "Move!" at him. Then he shuffled. They went over to the linotype machine. The lead in the pot was a liquid, glistening silver. The dial read six hundred and ten degrees. Billers sat down at the keyboard, shrugged his shoulders, and said, "I don't think she'll be any good. It come up too fast." Then he ran his fingers over the keys lightly. The type casts tinkled musically into the rack. McKabe leaned over to the casing to read the line "Now is the time for all good men to come to the ai—" Billers stepped on the pedal; the machine hissed and clacked, chuttered, and then delivered the silvery bar of type. McKabe pounced on it. It was so hot it burned the ends of his fingers, but he held it. Billers scrutinized it. The type face was a little pockmarked, but legible.

"Let's go!" shouted McKabe.

"O. K.," said Billers. "You got the copy?"

"Sweet Peter!" said McKabe. "The copy! Here, I'll dictate it."

"Dictate it? You mean, tell me as you go along? I never done that in Milwaukee."

"You'll do it here. Set it in two columns. You ready? I'll go slow." He remembered every word of his lead. "Silent night, Holy night—" What he hadn't been able to write upstairs through fear and exhaustion, he now told to the printer at the machine. They were a mad pair—this McKabe, gaunter and grayer than ever, his eyes nearly disappearing in the shady caverns of the sockets, his hair disheveled, his lips pulled away from tobacco-stained teeth, seated on a stool, doubled over, telling in short, bitten-off sentences the story of the shambles in Albany, and Billers, the nondescript printer, a big, scraggly man with a large, expressionless face running pudgy fingers delicately over the hair-trigger keys, unemotional and uninterested.

Then followed a period that to McKabe was the blackest—the make-up. Billers had resolved himself into a slow-motion picture. He refused to be hurried. He was that most dreaded of make-up men—an old maid at the stone. He puttered, he fussed, he straightened, he measured, he went on long expeditions down to the end of the composing room for rules and dashes. Often when on the make-up trick, McKabe would dream a nightmare in which the edition was an hour late and he stood in front of an empty page while printers wandered about and did nothing to fill it. All make-up editors are subject to the same dream, which wakes them in a chilly sweat, reaching for their watches to see if it is really past edition time.

Billers was the dream come true. McKabe pleaded, argued, bullied, screamed, raged, begged. Billers moved unhurried. Against his lethargic movements the hands of the clock spun around the

dial: seventeen minutes to nine . . . sixteen minutes to nine . . .
fifteen minutes to nine . . . fourteen; thirteen. What if by some
miracle an afternoon paper had managed to get on the street with
his story?

"What you want to do with this divorce story? We need more
room," Billers would ask.

"Yank it out. Get it out of there. Come on, Billers, for God's sake,
hurry a little."

"You can't throw it out without you break up page four. It jumps
to page four."

"I know it does! The hell with it!"

"You gonna let the jump ride without what goes ahead?"

"Yes. . . . Yes. . . . Yes!" Once Billers had slid his make-up
rule into his pocket and said, "I don't got to let you talk to me like
that. I don't work here anyway. I quit."

McKabe practically went down on his knees to him. The composing room was new to Billers and he had to look for everything
he needed. The inside drop heads that McKabe had taken from
the pup had to be resawed to fit. Five minutes were wasted looking
for the 120-point type for page 1. Once the half-crazed McKabe
picked up a paragraph of type and jammed it in the page, and
Billers quit again, and meant it.

"You touched type," he said flatly. "I quit. That's against the
union."

McKabe chased him, a heavy leather type-leveling mallet in his
hand. Frightened, Billers came back. At five minutes after nine the
two pages were finally locked up, page 3 a solid mass of black
display type with crazy, odd-sized headlines, no two words in the
same type; page 1, sawed-off captionless cuts beneath the one
startling word. Otto poked his round, sweating face through the
composing-room door.

McKabe greeted him eagerly. "O. K., Otto. Just locked 'em up.
All set, down below?"

Otto shook his head. "I didn't dare tell you," he said, "but Durkin
and Farley said what was the use and was gonna go home, unless

I come right up and told you. Page twenty is lost. We can't find the mat."

McKabe only nodded his head. "O. K., Otto. Shove these two pages through. Get going!"

"But whatta you going to do about page twenty? The mat's gone."

McKabe laughed loudly. "Go in without it. It's only the editorial page. Do you think you're gonna stop me now?"

"But you gotta have a plate, Mac."

"All right, cast a blank one. Cast page eighteen twice. Cast the calendar. Cast anything."

"It's gonna look funny."

"Hah!" exploded McKabe. "If you want to see something funny, wait till you see these two pages. But it's a paper, damn you, Otto! Shove it through!"

McKabe and Billers went over to the steam table and watched Otto lay the composition mat over the form, cover it with a blanket, and send it humming through the steel rollers, which exerted two tons of pressure and stamped the impressions of the reverse type into a positive on the mat. Otto started to dump the mats down the chute to the foundry, but McKabe stopped him.

"Don't do that! Something might happen to them. We'll carry them down."

Otto shrugged his shoulders. They rang for the elevator. While they waited for it, McKabe was sick. Billers held him up and said, "Why don't ya take it easy now and lie down?"

"Stop it, will ya?" said McKabe when he could talk again. "She ain't rollin' yet."

It was seven minutes after nine by the foundry clock. Under the blue mercury lights McKabe looked like a corpse. He held on to a steel table while Otto methodically sent the two precious mats through the mat-former, which shaped them into half cylinders, oiled them, and then dried them on the gas-heated scorcher, which turned them out looking like well-done waffles. He put them through the automatic plater. The hot lead hissed into the cylinders.

The machine chaffered. Six minutes to a plate. Nineteen minutes after nine. McKabe clung motionless to his support, his deep-sunk eyes following every move Otto made. How much had those after-noon rags been able to move up their edition time?

"You got any choice what page you want to duplicate?" Otto asked. He had to ask twice before McKabe heard him. He shook his head. Otto selected one at random.

"Page eighteen. Moider mystery," he said. "They can read it twice." He slipped it into the automatic molder and then stuck his head down by the door through which the plates traveled and bawled, "Starter coming!" McKabe pricked up his ears at that, but was too far gone to exult. The pain from his stomach had exhausted the last of his strength. Otto looked at him as he whipped the plate from the cylinder and sent it through the shaver and cooler. He gave it a final inspection and set it on the rollers. It sailed out of the foundry. McKabe followed it with his eyes.

"You don't feel good, do you?" said Otto.

"I'm all right. What can go wrong now?"

"Plenty," said Otto, "but maybe your luck will hold out. Want a hand in?"

He went to McKabe and slipped his arm around his shoulder and they hobbled onto the pressroom floor. It was nine thirty-one. Farley was in the bowels of the number-four press, plating up. Durkin stood at the row of red, yellow, and blue buttons.

"You're plenty lucky," Durkin said. "Number four had paper on her rollers. Me and Farley never could have got the rolls on alone. . . . What's the matter with you?"

"He don't feel very good," Otto explained.

"This is a hell of a looking page," commented Farley from inside the press. "What do you want to print a thing like that for?"

The dull remarks in the quiet pressroom brought some strength back to McKabe. "Roll her!" he shouted. "Get her rollin'! What the hell are you waiting for? You got your paper! Roll her!"

Durkin shrugged his shoulders and pushed a red button. The white light bulbs alongside the press turned to red. A bell rang long and loudly, and as it stopped, the sound changed to a low, sweet hum, which grew higher and higher in pitch. The wheels began to turn slowly and smoothly. Countless rocker arms, pistons, tappets, and levers went through their appointed motions. The sheets of paper, wide, flat, and white, stretched over the rollers and spindles, began to travel to their common meeting place, dead white until they reached the turning cylinders, passed over them, and came away gray with print.

McKabe could see the individual pages as they traveled past his eyes. Then the hum grew louder and the press started to clatter as it speeded up. The printed paper turned to gray ribbons that hurled themselves from all directions into the vortex of the machine. The noise became a battery of machine guns, and then, as the press rolled into high, turned into deep, rolling thunder that flooded McKabe and went to his core like a symphony. He still stood swaying in the center of the now quivering room. He couldn't even see the astonishing rows or aisles of neatly folded papers that began to climb irresistibly from the mouth of the press, even rows with every fiftieth one turned crooked to mark the count. He didn't see the black headline—SLAUGHTERED—or the weak face of the dead Schindler, or Otto and Durkin and Farley and Billers, each with a paper, looking through it and shaking their heads.

He felt and heard rather only the sweet, shaking rumbling of the rolling press, and seemed to hear, too, the orchestration in it, the clattering of the trucks bearing the extra edition to the newsstands, the cries of the newsboys: "Hyah! Special extra!" The rumble of the subways, the chaffering of the sub-machine guns that, a few hours ago, had blasted the life out of four people, the scream of the stricken girl, the motors of the vanishing murder cars. All of these he heard in the counterpoint of the whizzing, whirling, spinning, pounding machinery. Papers! Extra! Murder! Exclusive! Paper? Yes, sir. Special extra. Two cents. Only the *Blade*'s got it. . . . Silent night! Holy night! Feet Schindler and his girl and two bodyguards butchered. . . . Noel. Noel. . . . Only in the *Blade!* . . . Give it to 'em! Bang-bang-bang-bang! Extra! Extra!

Dixey, the circulation manager, came into the pressroom, rubbing his hands.

"O. K., kid. We've done it," he said to McKabe. "The country edition of the *Standard* is up, but it hasn't got a line. The *News-Beacon* won't be up for half an hour. It's a screwy-looking paper, but it's news."

McKabe began to laugh softly and to himself at first, and then, gaining like the press, louder and louder. He dropped to his knees and swayed there, still laughing. "Ha, ha, ha, ha! Ha-a, ha-ha-ha-ha!" His long, bony finger was pointed again, but this time at number four, the giant of steel and copper and iron and brass, the glorious rolling press that was thundering out his story, twenty thousand an hour.

"Ya big bum, ya!" he bawled. "Ya big bum! I made you roll!"

Expense Account

The grass, as you may have heard, is always greener on the other side of the fence, and during the many years that I was sports editor of the *News* I used to admire, envy, and romanticize the reporters and photographers who toiled in the city room just down the corridor from the sports department. The men and women of the city-side staff were endlessly fascinating and exciting people to me. Everything, in fact, about newspaper work was gaudy and thrilling with the exception perhaps of my own field, which work I took as a matter of course.

And as you might expect, the sports department was looked upon hungrily and with great longing by all the men on the local side. To *them* sports with its association with prize fighters, baseball players, horse owners, and male and female champions of every kind, its free tickets, the thrilling events, its luxurious Pullman travel, and, above all, its freedom of expression, was looked upon as the one exciting and romantic spot on the paper. They were always trying to transfer into it.

Just as they would hover over our baseball and boxing wires or drift in to inquire about the real inside story of some prize fight or football game, so I used to spend the slack hours, when nothing was coming in over the wires, hanging around the city desk and listening to peppery Harry Nichols, the assistant city editor, answering the telephone as his minions called in from the jobs they were on or handing out assignment. I would sit there eavesdropping and reveling when the leg men returned from the scene of the crime and spilled their adventures and stories, the unprintable as well as the printable parts.

We were a picture newspaper and the studio darkroom was a thrilling place too, tiny red-lit cubicles to which each photographer retired with his bag after coming in off the street, and one might stand breathless at his elbow with him and watch the drama he had imprisoned upon his plate slowly emerge in light and shadow from his developing emulsion.

The city editor struck me as a kind of unfettered impresario, drawing upon a variegated stock company of men and women and in a way casting them to fit the raw dramas enacted throughout the city day and night: murders, fires, robberies, kidnapings, scandals, hoaxes, and whatnot. He had, for instance, a reporter by the name of Max Lief whose peculiar specialty was the unmasking of bogus princes, of which we appeared to have a spate in that era. He had a pallid, exquisite blonde, Imogene Stanley, who, besides being the best picture thief in the business, had the beauty and social graces to attract the Prince of Wales to dance with her at the time of his famous visit to the United States. Edna Ferguson, the Jenny Jones of "Expense Account," used to be a parachute jumper at county fairs and didn't know what fear was. They were all willing to risk their lives. Julie Harpman nearly got herself killed investigating the Hall-Mills murder. Norma Abrams, a human she-bloodhound from the Northwest, had a narrow escape while on the Weyerhausar kidnaping. Grace Robinson, who turned overnight from writing society to reporting murder, had the presence that got her in anywhere. Florabelle Muir and Julia McCarthy were two first-class operators.

On the male side there was a similar cast, men of gall and courage who were as efficient detectives as any in the police department, such as Red Dolan, Eddie Doherty, and Gil Parker, who incidentally looked like Perry Brown. There was Marty Sommers, Art Mefford, Jack Miley, and a host of others, clever men who could pretend to be something they were not, who'd use every trick of the trade to come back with the story. We even had one mad Englishman, a younger son, Davidd Bath, who often with his British accent succeeded where Americans failed.

Forth from the studio issued the lens hounds, Captain Eddie Jackson, Jack Tresillian, Marty McEvilly, and fat and nerveless Al Willard of the night side. They were all fearless when it came to getting a picture or taking awful risks to get something onto a negative. You will meet Al Willard as Al Vogel, the literal-minded photographer in these stories, and many of the others, either as individuals or composites.

Sometimes they got into trouble, sometimes they got hurt. It was all in the day's work. From the comparative safety of the sports department, I loved and admired and envied them all, and this story is a kind of celebration of them, a gallant and wacky crew, and of the brave, risky, and often foolish things they did to get their stories.

Everyone who has ever worked on a newspaper knows of the constant feud carried on between the business and the editorial offices. The auditors squeeze and pinch pennies and complain about the extravagances of the city side, the reporters spend money like drunken sailors, and between the two somehow the paper gets out and the owners make money. But it is a constant battle, and our shop was no exception.

We had an editorial auditor on the *News*, a chap named Mike Feerick, called "Iron Mike" by the reporters, whose thankless job it was to edit the expense accounts of the lads and lassies upon their return from an out-of-town assignment. He was a nice guy and I always got along splendidly with him in spite of his questioning and disallowing some of the gaudier items appearing on my swindle sheets, but in the city room the feud between Iron Mike and the leg men was serious and of long-standing duration. It was simple to understand. The latter were untrammeled spirits, literary geniuses, alfresco detectives, combat troops who worked on the line of fire. Mike was a man of money, columns of figures, and balance sheets, with an uncanny memory for the fact that you could take the Illinois Central to get to the suburbs of Chicago, or the elevated, and didn't need to spend six bucks for cab fare.

Out of the feud, and not from either the individuality or personality of Mike Feerick, grew the idea for the character of Icebox Dodd, the penny-pinching editorial auditor of the *Daily Blade*. Him I cast into the obvious stereotype of the miser in order to highlight the nobility and selfless sacrifice of the men and women I spent so many years hero-worshiping. It's an old trick, and it always works. One of the things you learn very quickly in this business is not to despise old tricks, particularly if you can manage to freshen them up. And in the battle between the two departments, in spite of my personal liking for Iron Mike, my sympathies lay with the editorial side. It still does. The moneybags and magazine budget boys sitting upstairs just don't understand the needs and temperament of us poets; otherwise they wouldn't holler so about raising us a paltry thousand or so.

Well, to get back to "Expense Account," there WAS an airship blew up off Barnegat, and some of our people got themselves messed up trying to cover the tragedy. A few of the things that happened, or could have happened, you will find in this story.

Iron Mike Feerick was a good sport about "Expense Account" and the ribbing he took from the gang after it was published, but the only thing he ever said to me a few months later was, "Gee, you sure made me out a fine guy! . . ."

My conscience hurt me a little, so I made him a promise rather lightly given. I said, "Never mind, Mike. Tell you what I'll do: I'll make you the hero of the next one. Will that be all right?"

We shook hands on it. I might add that I kept my promise in a later story.

P ENRYN DODD, editorial auditor, better known as Icebox Dodd to the reporters on the floor below, frowned over the sheets on his desk before him, splintered the end of his pencil with his teeth, shook his head testily, and even pounded the top of his desk with a small bony fist, so that three stenographers and two junior auditors looked up from their typewriters and balance sheets. When he was sure they were still looking at him, Dodd, his mouth pursed, drew a vicious ring around an item of an expense account he was examining.

He was a small, oldish man, with sparse, reddish hair, as dry and brittle as a dead leaf. He had the sharp pointed nose and narrow eyes of one who can pursue a missing dollar through five years and ten ledgers and never lose the scent. He made dry clucking noises with his mouth and set aside the expense account of Perry Brown, reporter for the *Blade*, headed, "Assignment: *Columbia* crack-up, March 6," and running through a miscellaneous set of items, ending with his signature, to which Perry had appended, "So help me," and the bold countersigned initial C over the word "Approved," which was the O.K. of Wyatt Court, who was the *Blade's* city editor.

A junior auditor nudged a clerk next to him and whispered, "I'll bet that's Perry Brown's."

Dodd slammed the desk again—this time in real anger—pushed the next sheet he had been examining aside petulantly, and reached for his telephone. He dialed 333 and said, "I want to speak to Mr. Court. . . . Hello, Court! Dodd, auditing. You free a minute? . . . Be right down." He hung up the receiver, caught up the expense accounts on his desk, dug into a desk drawer for another handful of papers, and moved for the door, his head carried in front of him, his lips tight.

The junior auditor nudged the clerk again and said, "Four alarms. Must be two bits involved."

Dodd picked his way through the local room on the floor below, with an expression of distaste upon his thin face, as though something did not smell good. Without looking up from his typewriter, a reporter picking away at his machine turned up his coat collar as Dodd went by, and shivered quietly. The Brooklyn man said, "Oh, oh! This is going to cost somebody dough."

Dodd stopped at the city editor's desk. Wyatt Court was scanning the overnight assignment sheet and didn't look up. Dodd cleared his throat like dry wheat rustled by the wind.

Court looked up. "Well?"

"Ah—these expense accounts on the *Columbia* crash. Mr. Brown, Miss Jones, Osgood."

"Well, what about 'em?"

"Ah—you O.K.'d them."

"Certainly I O.K.'d them. Can't you read?"

"Yes," said Dodd sharply, "but you no doubt overlooked several items. It is not the policy of the company to purchase Scotch whisky for its employees or eighteen-dollar hats for the female members of the staff. I question these items I have ringed here."

Court killed a cigarette butt and glanced at the accounts. Between two items—"Share of boat hire, offshore, Atlantic City . . . $75," and "Cab, North Atlantic City—Atlantic City . . . $3.80," Perry Brown had typed, "One quart Scotch (and was it lousy) . . . $6.50."

Jenny Jones's account was a single sheet. It was headed, "Flight over *Columbia* crack-up, March 6," and contained only one item. It was: "One special hat—please . . . $18.00."

"I do not recall," continued Mr. Dodd, "that our coverage of the *Columbia* disaster was such a conspicuous success that it might warrant payment of these items as a bonus. I also question whether we are responsible for this bill for dental bridgework to the amount of"—he studied the bill on Court's desk—"a hundred and nineteen dollars for Photographer Osgood. We—ah—have a dental department for employees. Mr. Haley, in the business department, said to me last week, 'Here is another bill for a new Liskow camera for Photographer Joe Osgood. It is the third in a month. He is costing us more than he is worth.' Mr. Haley feels that if a newspaper photographer has—ah—not sufficient tact and address to protect his equipment—ah—" Mr. Dodd faltered. Court was looking up at him with a strange and unfathomable look on his cold, bland face, and his eyes had unpleasant lights in them. But he dropped his head and examined the expense accounts again. He lit a fresh cigarette and said:

"Ah—you are quite right, Mr. Dodd. As you say, our coverage on the *Columbia* disaster was—ah—not a conspicuous success."

The cabdriver leaned far out of his hack and inspected the gray, rickety, two-story house at the end of the road by Beckett's Cove and then said, "This is it."

Perry Brown climbed out of the car and lent a hand to Al Vogel, the fat photographer, with his gear. It was cold, damp, and raw. Although it was a quarter to five in the morning, there was no sign of any dawn in the east. A single lamppost cast its shadow on the sandy road and illuminated the unpainted door and the blindless windows.

Vogel turned up the collar of his overcoat, rubbed his hands together, and said, "Nice place, ain't it?"

Perry Brown said curtly, "Charming," and then knocked on the door. "You'd better wait," he told the cabdriver: "this may be a washout," and the driver said, "Oky-doke." There was no sign of life from the house. He knocked again. A shrill, woman's voice suddenly answered, "Yeah, yeah. Who is it? What do you want?"

"The voice of romance," said Perry Brown to Vogel, who was blowing into his hands, and then aloud, "Is Captain Borrow there?"

The voice, angry, harsh, and unpleasant, called out, "Who wants him? What is it?"

"We want to hire his boat!" Perry Brown shouted. "Newspapermen! Want to hire his boat! Is he there?"

There was a moment of silence and then the voice, still more strident: "He don't want to hire no boat! He ain't got any boat! Go away! Go away! Don't bother us!"

"She says he ain't got a boat," said Vogel.

"Wait a minute," Perry said, and then raised his voice again. "Listen!" he shouted. "There's been a terrible accident! The airship blew up! Do you hear me?"

There was another moment, and then a light gleamed in the second story. The woman's voice said, "What happened? What's that?"

"The *Columbia* blew up and fell into the ocean," Perry shouted back, "at eleven o'clock last night! The big airship!"

There were sounds of footsteps. The door opened. It framed a short, stocky man, hair matted and face thickened with sleep. He was clean-shaven, but his face was deeply lined and hard. His feet were bare and he wore a gray flannel shirt, open at the throat and hastily stuffed into dark trousers. In one hand he held a large-calibered automatic pistol. He said, "Well?"

"Listen," said Perry Brown, talking rapidly, with an eye on the gun. "I'm Perry Brown, of the *Blade,* the picture paper in New York. The *Columbia,* the big Navy airship, blew up last night off Barnegat and fell into the ocean. I guess most of 'em are dead. We want to go offshore and try and find her."

The man remained motionless, but jerked his head toward Vogel. "Who's he?"

"That's Vogel, our photographer. We want to make pictures."

"What's that gear?"

"Cameras. You're Captain Borrow, aren't you?"

The man nodded, then asked, "Who sent you?"

"Joe Passaleoni."

"You know him?"

Perry nodded.

"Talk some more," said the captain.

"Sure," said Perry. "We got the flash in the office at a quarter past eleven. She was hit by lightning off Barnegat. A tanker saw her go down. We caught the midnight out. When I hit Atlantic

City I went over to the Candle Club. I always go there when I'm in town. Joe said you had a boat and to say that it was okay."

The captain reflected a moment, and then flipped his gun, caught it by the butt, and stowed it in his trouser pocket. "How much?" he asked.

The woman's voice yelled, "Who is it, Bill? What do they want?"

The captain, without turning his head, called back, "Shut up!"

Perry Brown sighed with relief. "Fifty bucks," he said.

"Nothing doing. Hundred and fifty."

"Listen," said Perry Brown, "I've got eighty-five bucks. That's all I've got." The captain shook his head. "Wait a minute." Perry spoke to Vogel. "Al, you got any dough?" The photographer patted his pocket and said, "I got eight bucks."

"Nothing doing." The captain glanced up at the black sky, which in the east had a faint grayness. "It's going to be dirty out there. If I risk the boat, I get paid. Hundred and fifty." There was the noise of an approaching car, and two headlights turned down the lane from the asphalt road. The captain reached down into his pocket and fished out the automatic pistol. The car stopped. It was another cab. A single individual got out. He was tall and spare and had a thin, bony face and the complexion that goes with pinkish hair. He stepped into the circle of light made by the headlamps of the two cabs, blinked for a moment, and then said, "Hi, Perry," in a cheerful sort of way. He showed no surprise at seeing Perry Brown, or Vogel, or the captain, or the captain's pistol, except to remark innocently, "Why the cannon?"

Perry Brown said, "Not exactly calling hours. Hey, you got any dough on you?"

The stranger said, "Uh-huh. About ninety-five bucks."

"O.K.," said Perry Brown. "You're in. The captain wants a yard and a half to go offshore. I haven't got it. Neither have you. Kick in seventy-five and we go."

"Right," said the stranger, and dug down into his pocket. He came up with a roll of bills and began to count off tens.

The captain spoke to Perry Brown. "Who is he?"

"Ed Smallens, of the *Gazette-Star*. He's O.K. Between us we can make up the hundred and fifty. Let's go."

The captain looked puzzled. He said, "Ain't he from a different paper than you?"

"Sure," Perry replied. "What's the difference? It can't be helped. He's a good kid, and smart, or he wouldn't be here. Anyway, he hasn't got a photographer, so that balances. Nobody gets to go alone, so we go together. When can we start?"

Vogel paid off the cabdriver and picked up his cameras. The captain led the way inside and lighted an oil lamp. He said, "That all the clothes you fellas have? It's still winter out there, and wet." All three men wore overcoats. Vogel's was thinner than the other two. Perry Brown shrugged his shoulders. The captain said, "I got a couple sweaters and some oilskins. They won't do much good to keep you warm, but you're welcome to them. Wait here. I'll put some clothes on." He went upstairs, and they heard his voice mingling with the woman's in muffled conversation. When he returned, he was thick with clothing. He wore rubber boots and oilskins. He picked up the lamp and said, "Down this way," and led them through a door that opened upon some wooden steps that led down into the cellar below.

It was no cellar, but a boathouse, opening out into Beckett's Cove. In it lay a forty-foot craft, stout, heavy-set, open like a dory, except for a small pilothouse screened on three sides and having room for one person. Aft were two large rectangular engine hatches. The captain nodded for them to get in. Perry helped Vogel store his cameras in the shelter of the pilothouse. The captain pulled on an overhead rope, and two doors to the cover slid back.

The *Gazette-Star* reporter nudged Perry Brown and whispered, "If there aren't a couple of four-hundred-horse-power bootlegger's-special Libertys under those hatches, I'm a copyreader."

The captain threw a couple of sweaters and an armful of oilskins into the bottom of the boat and said, "Sit aft." The three men disposed themselves in the stern of the boat. The captain cast off and then entered the pilot shelter. First one and then the other engine exploded like a battery of three-inch fieldpieces, and in the confined boathouse the racket was frightful. Smallens winked at Perry and at Vogel. The engines throttled down, and there came a coughing and burbling from under the stern. They moved out into the quiet water of the cove and headed east toward the inlet. All the world was a dark gray now, and there was a stinging wind from the northeast.

Spot Reilly, pilot for the *Daily Blade,* set the hand brake of the *Blade*'s little four-place cabin Airwing and jammed the foot brakes with both feet, revving up the engine. He checked the oil pressure, temperature, and tachometer. Fred Courvis, the flying photographer, was in the administration office getting weather when the one-lung cab snorted through the field gate and discharged Jenny Jones in a new spring hat and with the inevitable bag of oranges under her arm. It was six o'clock in the morning, and the field, except for Spot and the mechanics from the *Blade* hangar, was deserted. Reilly pulled back the throttle, letting the motor idle quietly, and called out the window, "Hi, Jen! Got an orange?"

Jenny favored him with a sweet and winning smile and, reaching down into the bag, produced one. "Uh-huh! Got 'em in an all-night place on the way out. Good."

Courvis came out of the administration office, frowning, and said, "H'lo, Jen," and accepted an orange. Reilly asked about the weather.

"Plenty of it, and all bad," said Courvis. "Visibility eight hundred at Atlantic City, and six hundred at Asbury. Low moving in from the northeast. There'll be another report at eight o'clock."

"M'm'm," said Jenny, and licked a finger. "Mr. Court wants us to go right away. He woke me up out of bed. All the boys are in New London, so he sent me."

"Court should fly this jalopy through that stuff," Reilly said bitterly.

"He would," said Jenny, "only he can't. Fly, I mean," she amended. "Are we going soon?"

"Ugh!" Reilly grunted, which might have meant anything. Then he asked, "How long since you've flown a ship?"

"Three years," said Jenny, and looked up at him brightly. She was a tall, thin girl with long, ash-blond hair that she did in a thick rope and bunched at the back of her head, whence it was always threatening to tumble. She had extraordinary sweetness in her face and a naïve air that masked more pure gall and nerve than was possessed by any other reporter on the staff, man or woman.

"Get in," said Reilly. "Sit in the front seat, next to me, and don't touch things. Keep your dogs off the rudder pedals.

Jenny climbed in, sat in the right front seat, and fastened the safety belt. "Don't be a sil," she said. "You know I hate planes. They're dangerous. I wouldn't have come, only Mr. Court asked me as a special favor. He knows I don't like them."

Courvis stowed his cameras on the wide rear seat and climbed in beside them, shutting the door. Reilly shouted, "Map!"

"Right!" Courvis produced a map out of his inside pocket and unfolded it. It was a replica of the Jersey coast. There was an X some eighteen miles due east of Barnegat Inlet. "Location sent out by the Government. That's where the tanker saw her go in."

"They saved three," Jenny said. "The rest, Mr. Court thinks, are dead."

"There's a thirty-five-mile wind," Spot Reilly said. "By this time, what's left of her may be down past Atlantic City and forty miles out. We'll drag the drift when we get down there," and added viciously, "If there's any ceiling left when we get there." He shouted down out of the window, "Stand clear!"

The wind was northeast then, so he merely swung the ship around a quarter turn and opened the throttle. The Airwing was off the ground before they reached the end of the concrete apron.

"Blowing like hell," Reilly shouted. "If this blows one of those fogs in, it's going to be just lovely." They climbed to the end of the field and then banked to the left. The canopy of gray above them hung at a thousand feet. Reilly flew southeast at eight hundred. There were street lights below and the green-and-white Department of Commerce beacon whipped on their tail and flashed across the windows.

Courvis shouted, "What are you supposed to do, Jen?" All their conversation was shouted and bellowed, to reach above the roar of the Thunderbolt motor.

"Color story."

"About what?"

"About anything we see."

Spot grunted. "Always the optimist, darling."

"Today is my day off," Jen said. The lights of the boardwalk at Coney Island shone below them and they were low enough to see the long curved lines of white hammering upon the beach. "I was saying to Luella Dixon yesterday afternoon—" She stopped suddenly and, without warning, screamed at the top of her lungs. Both men jumped and the Airwing fell off to the left. Reilly twisted the wheel, and the aileron brought her back level. Jenny screamed again, and then wailed, "Oh, dear! My hat!" She clapped her hand to her head. Courvis fell back on the seat and mopped his brow. Reilly turned on the girl angrily. "What about it, you nitwit?"

Jenny's face was pale, and stricken with anguish. "I've got it on."

"Well, where would expect to have it?"

"H-home," said Jenny. "I didn't mean—I had it on my pillow beside me. Oh, dear! When Court telephoned, I got all excited and grabbed up anything. He said to hurry. I—I paid eighteen dollars for it. I never paid eighteen dollars for a hat before. I got bewitched."

She lifted it tenderly off her head. The lights from the instrument panel reflected from her hair. The hat was of shiny dark-blue straw and was tilted forward. At the back was a small garland of artificial mignonettes, blue and white. Gathered at the top of the brim and protruding slightly was a short, stiff veil.

"It's a good-lookin' lid," said Courvis. "So what?"

Jenny was still wailing, her face grief-stricken. "I spent all my money on it. I saw it in a window. It was eighteen dollars. I thought I put on my old felt. This one isn't meant for airplane riding. Oh, dear, if something should happen to it, I'd never forgive—"

"If something should happen to it, sister," Reilly shouted, "it will also happen to us!"

Jenny wriggled around in her seat and said, "Fred, be a lamb and put it somewhere where it will be safe. Isn't there a shelf somewhere?"

Courvis took the hat and set it on top of his big camera.

"No, no, in back. Isn't there a place—"

Courvis muttered something unintelligible and stowed the hat in the luggage compartment. It was growing faintly lighter. Reilly had crossed the lower bay and was skirting the Staten Island shore. Jenny saw a light go on behind a window curtain in a house below. She said in Reilly's ear, "Those were pretty curtains. Fly a little lower. I want to see if the price tag is on them."

The pilot said savagely, "Look aloft."

There were ragged gray wisps, torn from the ceiling, curling over the top wing, and ahead there was suddenly a gray bulge that hung downward. Reilly pressed the nose down and they passed beneath it.

"She's closing in!" he shouted.

"Oh, dear," said Jenny. "Freddy, give me my hat."

"Listen, sister, for—"

"Give it to me."

Courvis fished behind in the compartment and handed it over. Jenny pressed it to her cheek for a moment and then put it on again and tried to catch a glimpse of it in the rear-vision mirror.

"We ought to turn back!" Courvis shouted at Reilly.

"Mr. Court wouldn't like it," Jenny said.

Reilly said, "Nuts!"

"Would you like an orange?" Jenny asked.

"No!" said Reilly. Rain was being swept off the slanting windshield, but stuck to the side windows in large drops. The compass showed that they were headed due south. They kept on.

The boat rose, and rose again, its bow pointing sheerly into the fog and driving rain. It dropped first straight and then veered sharply sideways as a wave crashed it. Gray frothy water poured like lava over one side. The captain spun the wheel to the right, caught it in time to send it headlong into another gray sweeping wall, and shouted aloud over the wind, "Bail!"

Perry Brown began scooping at the water that sluiced around his feet. Vogel remained where he had been for the last hour, and in the same position, in the stern of the boat, one arm clinging to the gunwale, the other tightly wrapped around his camera. His fleshy face was blue-white, his lips purple. Smallens, the *Gazette-Star* man, raised himself to his knees in the bottom of the boat, where he had fallen. There was a dark bruise on the side of his face.

"Bail!" the captain shouted again.

Smallens said, "My arm's hurt. I can't move it."

"Bail!" said the captain. "Use the other one!"

Perry Brown stopped bailing and shouted, "Wait a minute! He'll go overboard!" He lurched over, splashing, and threw his arms around Smallens. The reporter's eyes closed. Perry felt all his weight suddenly. The boat crashed again and threw them both into the stern, Perry beneath.

In a cracked voice, Vogel cried, "Perry! Hey, Perry!"

Perry yelled, "I'm O.K." He wriggled out from under Smallens and stared at the reporter's right arm. The hand was twisted, palm outwards, and pointed away from his body. "His arm is broken. He's out!" he called to the captain. "He's out cold!"

The captain stared straight ahead, but with one hand unfastened a length of line and threw it backwards from him. "Lash him," he directed. "Get him between the engine hatches."

Perry Brown looked to Vogel, but the photographer was apparently too paralyzed with terror to move. His eyes were bulging, and he croaked something. Perry waited for a downward lurch of the boat and heaved Smallens' body sideways between the two hatches, the broken arm uppermost, and lashed him. His left shoulder was under water.

The captain shouted again, "Bail!"

The rain changed suddenly to sleet that stung harder than the bullets of spray shot from the torn wave tops. The sky was touching the sea, the sea lashed at the sky. The wind tore patches out of the sky, and smoky fog filled the gaps again. The boat shuddered horribly to every beat of the engines. The sea all about them was alive with noises, hissings and seethings and sometimes dry crackling when the wind drove the sleet into the surface of the water close by. The wind ripped another gray patch out ahead. The water was dark and swollen, and straining and heaving itself as though unbelievable forces from within were fighting for freedom. Perry Brown suddenly noticed something darker.

"Hey!" he shouted. "Hey! Look! Captain Borrow!"

The floating figure was dressed in dark blue. It was face down, the head under water. A motion of the water rolled it, and Perry caught a flash of gold at a sleeve. Behind him floated a small piece of wreckage with a twisted bit of metal sticking up like a mast.

Perry clutched the side of the boat with both hands, yelling again, "Hey, captain! Get him! It's one of the officers. Oh, God, get him!"

The captain glanced to the side. He said, "He's dead. We've got our own skins to think about." He drove the boat straight ahead.

"Al! Al!" Perry was screaming at the photographer. "Grab a shot! Grab it! It's one of the crew!"

The photographer made a futile struggling little movement, like something small trying to break out of a cocoon. Tears welled into his eyes. He found his voice and swore, and then said, "I'm stuck, Perry. I'm frozen fast. My hand is frozen. Perry, I'm stuck. Can you git at the camera, Perry? I'll tell you how to work it."

The dark figure swept astern. Perry had another glimpse of the gold band at the cuff. The mist closed in again, a solid curtain of rain.

Perry was at Vogel's outstretched right arm beating and tearing at it. He shouted to the captain, "How far?"

"Thirty-five miles offshore."

"Make it?"

The captain shrugged. Vogel's arm came loose. A patch of skin was torn from his wrist.

"It don't hurt none," Vogel said.

"It's gonna, fella," said Perry, and pounded it. The boat yawed and fell away. A gray wall, white-capped, sucked past them, and part of it reached in and sheared off one side of the tiny pilothouse. The captain was swept back on top of Vogel. Perry managed to turn and fall on him, his bulk pinning him down. The boat veered and spun.

"Chees!" Vogel yelled. "My cameras!"

The captain fought his way clear, hoteyed.

"Burn your cameras!" he said. "The next picture you'll make will be in hell!"

It was suddenly clear to Perry that they would very likely not get back, and it came almost with a sense of relief. He was soaked, frozen and aching, and dog-tired. He had forgotten that there was a world to return to, that there was any world but this one of gray, battering, lashing torment.

"How long?" he asked.

The captain hauled himself back to the shattered pilothouse. "If the motors stop, right away." He paused, and then continued angrily, "I brought a hundred and fifty cases through worse than this. But we're too far offshore. The wheel's smashed."

Smallens opened his eyes.

Perry yelled over, "O.K., kid? How long you been back?"

"Coupla minutes. I have been passing the time thinking of places I would rather be than here. There is a bar on Fifty-second Street that has big soft, red leather chairs." He stopped. "Is the arm gone?"

"It's bent a little," said Perry. "Stay with 'em, kid."

The captain fought his way back again and thrust a tiller bar through a hole in the rudder post. Vogel was in the way, and he yelled, "Get out!"

"I can't," said Vogel. "I'm froze fast."

"Give way all you can," the captain said, and braced. The boat fought its way out of the deep trough and crashed a wave again. "My old lady will be sore as hell," the captain said. "The insurance wasn't paid up. She can jaw."

"I'd like to be sitting at a show," Vogel said, "close up. I never been any farther front than the thirteenth row."

"I'd like to be looking at Rusty," Perry said, "across a dinner table at the Crillon."

"If any of you can pray," the captain said angrily, "you'd be better off."

They fell silent; a wave pounded and spun them. The captain, cursing, strained against the tiller, and Vogel cried out in pain.

"Lord," said Perry quietly, "we are frightened. Help us not to be."

Vogel said, "Amen." The captain bowed his head for a moment. Smallens laughed sharply and then said, "Sam, meet the best bartender in the United States. Two of your specials, Joe."

The captain looked up angrily, but Perry said, "He's off his nut." Fog replaced the rain. It blanketed everything but the nearest waves. It was a white fog. The captain lifted his head, sniffing. "Hah! There'll be no more wind with this."

"Is there a chance?" Perry was too tired to care.

"If she don't sink. Thank God I put real money into them motors! Bail!"

Perry bailed. The physical exertion numbed his mind. Nothing had happened since he had stopped bailing. He hadn't stopped bailing. He had always been bailing. He was at a task in inferno, to bail for a thousand centuries. Had the thousand centuries passed so quickly? He heard a familiar voice say, "Ease off. You can quit. We'll be inside in a minute." His last conscious move was to throw the dipper over the side. The blackness was peaceful.

He came back out of darkness and heard someone say, "He'll lose his arm. . . . Lucky. . . ." Perry had no thought but for Vogel, and yelled, "No. No. Leave him alone. Don't do that to him."

They were in the parlor of the captain's house. There was a large, heavy-set woman bending over a figure on a low couch, slapping and chafing a limb. The captain and another man, obviously a doctor, were grouped around someone who was stretched out on the table. The captain was holding up a lamp.

"Vogel!" yelled Brown. "Al, are you O.K.? . . . Leave his arm alone." He got up waveringly from the chair in which he had been slumped.

The doctor, a dark, elderly man, turned and looked at Brown. "Which is Vogel?" he asked. Perry Brown stared at the figure on the table. It was Smallens, still unconscious. "That's Ed Smallens," he said. "Will he be all right?"

The doctor shook his head. "His arm will have to go. The other man is all right. I can save his hand."

"We had to use an ax to chop your man loose from the stern seat when we came in," the captain said.

Perry Brown went over to Vogel. The captain's wife was still working on his hand and arm. His eyes were open. Perry said, "O.K., kid?"

"O.K. I could 'a' got that shot, only my hand was stuck."

Perry turned back to the table. "What time is it? Did they find the *Columbia?*"

The captain said, "Half past ten. The fog is still in."

The doctor shook his head again. "Not a sign. There's been hell to pay. A Navy blimp went down in the ocean a hundred yards off Seaside, trying to get back in the storm, after searching. Three were drowned and two are in the hospital. A terrible disaster."

Perry Brown turned back to Vogel, who was sitting up, his face screwed up in pain. "Bad, kid?"

"Needles and knives."

"Uh-huh. That's good. You're lucky. Anything I can do?"

"Gee," said Vogel, and stopped to catch his breath. "A drink would help."

"It would. A lot," said Perry Brown. "Is there a drink in the house?"

"Didn't bring anything with me," the doctor said. "Should have."

"I've got a bottle of Scotch," the captain said.

"Break it out."

"Cost you six fifty."

"For Scotch? You're a dirty pirate. Scotch is four bucks a bottle."

"Six fifty," repeated the captain imperturbably. "It's pre-repeal. Some I brought ashore off a boat. It's the last. I was savin' it if my old woman took sick."

Perry Brown felt in his pocket and noticed for the first time that he was wearing strange dry clothes. The captain motioned with his head to a sideboard. "Your money's there. We're not thieves."

Perry Brown went over and counted out six wet dollars and a

fifty-cent piece and gave them to the captain. The thick-set woman went out and returned with a bottle and opened it. They all drank except the unconscious man, who twitched uneasily once and then became quiet again.

Photographer Jack Osgood was in photographer's heaven. It had been pure hunch that had taken him to Seaside, when he had been assigned to Asbury, and the same blind hunch that led him to the top of the lookout tower of the Coast Guard station. He was cold and wet, but he kept his lens covered, and when the cigar-shaped Navy blimp came fighting her way out of the storm, beating desperately for land, he was ready. He photographed her bucking a sixty-mile wind, unable to move forward, slipping backward, less than three hundred yards offshore. He photographed the Coast Guard crew and natives on the beach, waiting to grasp the ground rope trailing in the water. She caught a moment's slack and beat to within a hundred yards. He photographed her when she buckled in the middle and hung for a moment like a wet dishrag, and he caught her again as she plunged three hundred feet into the fuming sea and black specks fell from her like ants shaken loose from a stick. Three men died and he snapped the tiny dots of their heads on the gray sea before they vanished. He performed miracles of speed changing plateholders and made shots of the lumpy, distended wreckage hurled ashore by the combers, and of the Coast Guard men launching their boat into the impossible surf, and another of the boat, its prow raised almost vertically skyward by the sea, the men braced against their oars. He worked madly and happily, whistling into the gale, whipping out plateholders, jamming home new ones, focusing, snapping. He was down on the shore, photographing, when the big lifeboat hurled itself ashore with the survivors. And his cup of happiness ran well over when, with the last shot made, a cab drew up to the Coast Guard station and discharged a small, sallow man carrying a camera and plate case. It was Krauer, of the *Evening Star-Leader*. The *Star-Leader* and its methods were not particularly beloved by the craft. Krauer he particularly disliked.

The *Star-Leader* man showed unpleasant teeth as he recognized Osgood.

"Get anything?" he asked.

"A sackful."

"How about a split?"

"Go to hell," said Osgood cheerfully, and brazenly climbed into the cab and said, "Airport. Get going."

The airport was a small field with one dilapidated hangar with a wind sock atop. A mechanic was lying under the fuselage of a cabin ship in one corner. A man was at a workbench, filing something in a vise. Osgood burst in, yelling, "Hey, got anything that will fly?"

The man nodded to a small, open, two-place job near the closed hangar door.

"She will. But not in this. Nor will anything else."

"How much to go to Newark airport?"

"Thirty bucks. When the weather's good."

"How much today?"

"Hundred."

"O.K. Let's go."

The man went around a corner into an office, examined an instrument, and came back.

"If the wind drops ten miles, I'll take a chance."

Most of the hour they waited, Osgood spent outside the hangar, cursing the gale and the rain. He did not know that it had decreased until he heard the hangar doors rolling back and saw the two men pushing the little ship out. She started immediately and the pilot warmed her up. The mechanic gave Osgood a pair of goggles and a helmet. The man said, "Get in." Osgood piled into the front seat, after first stowing his plate case and camera. A car squealed to a stop and a man ran out of it. It was Krauer. "I want to hire a ship!" he yelled.

The pilot throttled the motor down and yelled back, "Haven't got another!"

"Hundred and fifty to go along," said Krauer.

Osgood twisted around in the cockpit and said, "Hundred and

fifty to go alone." The pilot sized up the two men. He was young and had a flier's eyes. "Hundred's the price," he said. "She's yours." He called down to Krauer, "Sorry. Chartered. No can do." To Osgood he said, "There's going to be fog. Can you stand hedge-hopping? I know every foot of the ground."

Osgood grinned and said, "Yup!"

The pilot swung the ship around. Krauer had a sickish smile on his face. "I hope you make it, pal," he called.

"Yes you do," said Osgood. The motor roared and the little ship took off quickly and banked sharply. Osgood looked down. The last he saw of Krauer, the *Star-Leader* photographer was penciling some-thing on the back of an envelope.

The altimeter of the *Blade's* Airwing registered eighteen hundred feet. Spot Reilly had the earphones of the small receiving set clamped around his head, and his face wore a worried look. His brow was perspiring, and he mopped it every so often. Jenny Jones was peeling an orange and dropping the curling strips of rind back into the bag. She had hung her hat tenderly, by the elastic band designed to go beneath the hair at the back of the head, over the hook on the side of the cabin to which the earphones normally were attached. Courvis, in the rear seat, was shifting from side to side, looking for a hole or the faintest sign of shredding in the yellow-white fog through which they flew. The motor hummed sweetly, the enshrouding dampness an aid to carburation. Reilly tuned a small dial on the receiving set and concentrated. His frown deep-ened and beads appeared on his upper lip where his waxed mus-tache left it bare, as well as on his brow.

"Nice program?" asked the photographer sympathetically.

"Lovely. She's closed down all along the coast. No flights in or out of Newark. What a sucker I was to go out!"

Jenny gave him her sweet, bright smile and asked, "Will we be there soon?" and stuffed a triangle of orange into her mouth.

The pilot glanced at her savagely and yelled, "We're there now! How do you like it?"

Jenny said, quite innocently, after looking out and down from her window, "I can't see anything." Reilly bit his lower lip and ignored the remark. Jenny continued. "Don't you think we ought to fly lower, where we can see something?"

"The Department says the stuff is right down to the ground, and filling up basements," Reilly said.

"They aren't always right," Jenny said seriously. "They once told me the weather into Tulsa was fine, and when I got there, it wasn't."

"Do you want to take a chance?" Reilly addressed Courvis rather than Jenny.

Courvis shrugged his shoulders. "If there's a surface wind, we may get a look."

Reilly whipped off his earphones and bawled at Jenny, "Get that lid off there, will you?"

"Oh, dear!" Jenny wailed. "Wait a minute!" She wiped the orange off her finger tips and lifted the hat down tenderly and held it in her lap. Reilly throttled the engine back sufficiently to lose flying speed, but not entirely, and began to inch down in a wide, delicate circle, his eyes leaping now to the altimeter, now to the window and the impenetrable fog without. It was easier to talk, now that the engine was quieted, but no one did. Courvis examined his Ullmann camera with the fast lens and inspected the shutter and film-changing mechanism.

It was no lighter at a thousand feet. They circled slowly. Once Reilly muttered, "I wish this damn thing had more wing." He was flying with one hand on the wheel, the other on the throttle. The altimeter showed two hundred feet. Reilly called out, "From here on it's guesswork! Hold your hats!"

"I am," Jenny said simply. She hunched as far forward in the seat as her belt would permit and cradled the hat with her arms and body. The ship continued to sink. "There's no bottom to it," Courvis said, his face pressed to the glass.

"Hey!" yelled Reilly suddenly, and half his cry was drowned in the roar of the engine as he jammed the throttle bar home. The ship nosed up at a forty-five-degree angle. For the fraction of an instant they caught a glimpse of a gray, wallowing sea and white-crested peaks that moved with incredible speed. Then they were back in the fog again. Reilly waited until the altimeter was at five hundred before he reduced the angle of the climb. He was white. "That's your look," he said. Courvis, too, was shaken, but he managed to grin and touch Jenny on the shoulder.

"You've got your hat on backwards, Jen!" he shouted.

Jenny turned around and looked at him, blinking, and said, "I was scared to death," and tried an unconvincing smile. "I don't remember putting it on." She adjusted it again in the rear-vision mirror.

"How far offshore?" the photographer asked the pilot.

"About twenty-five miles. I can't tell how strong the drift is."

"Let's get back."

"You're telling me!" He nodded his head toward the compass. The black ball had slewed around from southeast to due west, the white W showing exactly at the center line. At two thousand they stopped climbing and flew along in silence. The pilot looked at his watch. It was a quarter past seven. Twenty minutes later he glanced at it again and said, "We're on shore." Then he took the earphones down again and adjusted them, but put them back again immediately, with a frown, saying, "The next weather won't be until eight."

At eight o'clock Reilly took the weather report, and hung up the earphones without saying a word. Nobody asked him what it was. With the engine throttled down to its lowest possible cruising speed, they flew blindly, wide, groping circles. At half past eight Courvis inquired, "How much gas?"

The pilot checked his tanks, and merely said, "Plenty."

Jenny leaned with him when he checked. She said, "You really haven't, you know. I can tell."

Courvis repeated, "How much?"

Reilly said, "Half an hour, maybe."

"Chutes?" Jenny inquired.

"Two. You and Fred bail out if you have to. I'll get her down somehow."

Jenny looked at him wide-eyed and smiled sweetly, but earnestly. "Oh, I couldn't, really," she said, shaking her head. "I promised Mother I'd never make another jump. I broke my leg, you know."

"Don't be an ass," Courvis said to Reilly.

The chutes were not mentioned again. At five minutes to nine the engine popped, faltered, and picked up again. Reilly, who was heading west, circled the plane around. "The wind probably shifted due east when it brought the fog!" he shouted.

"I'd better get ready, hadn't I?" Jenny said. She readjusted her hat in the mirror and then opened her handbag and took out lipstick and powder compact. She touched up her mouth with two firm strokes and patted her nose, and then examined herself with great pleasure in her hand mirror. "I'm glad I bought it," she said definitely.

Courvis was unscrewing the lenses from his two cameras—the Ullmann and the big Bertha. From a side pocket he took some half-greasy waste and wadding and wrapped them carefully. The large one he stuffed into his overcoat pocket, the smaller one inside his suit coat. The engine popped twice and stopped. The ship nosed down. There was then three thousand feet on the altimeter. "This is it!" Reilly said, shouting first and then dropping to normal as his voice rang too loud through the cabin. "Bail, Jen: you've got time."

"Hush," said Jenny. "Fly your ship." A thousand feet vanished into the fog.

"Roll your windows down," Reilly called, and began to wind his. "Less glass." Jenny turned her handle. The cold wet fog piled in, thick enough to feel.

"Keep your seat belts fastened, but keep your left hand on the catch," Reilly warned. "When we hit, throw your right arm up in front of your face. We'll find out how lucky we are in a minute." He reached over and flicked off the switch, and said, "Switch off."

All three sat with their eyes glued on the altimeter. At two hundred feet Reilly saw Jenny stiffen and called out, "Relax. You won't break so easy. Let yourself go." His next was a shout, as the smoky fog suddenly thinned. "Hey-hey! Trees! I'm going to squash into 'em. If they're heavy enough, we'll be okay." They were low over a wooded patch. It was just below them. Gray-green skimmed beneath them for a moment as Reilly leveled the ship off. There was no place else to go. He began to ease the nose back. "Easy does it. The tail will hit first." Higher and higher rose the nose of the ship.

There was a slight shock and a tearing sound that suddenly became a terrible, ripping crash, a cracking of boughs and a swishing of twigs against canvas, then a smashing thud. They were pitched violently forward, then upward, as though they had gone over a short rise on a roller coaster again, then forward again. The forward thrust that snapped her head down almost to her knees saved Jenny's life, because the piece of broken bough with a point as sharp as an assagai that stabbed up through the cabin floor was pointed for the back of her head. Reilly saw it and helped her avoid it on the rebound. Then they came to rest and were rocking gently back and forth.

Reilly flipped the catch on his belt and leaned over and opened Jenny's too. "Come on!" he yelled. "Get going! Fast! There's no telling how long she'll hang here! We've got to cash in quick! . . . Freddy, go first and find the quickest way down! Move!" The ship tilted upwards at a slight angle and still rocked. The photographer opened the door gently and fastened it back. Both wings were crumpled—how badly he could not tell. A parent bough to the limb that had speared through the bottom of the ship led to a sizable trunk and came up close to the door. "This will do it. This one right here."

"Get going!" Reilly yelled. "And fast! I'll be next and hand Jen down! If she slips, we've both got a chance to break her fall! Will it hold?"

Courvis called up, "O.K.! O.K.!" Reilly stretched out, wrapped an arm and a leg around the bough, and reached back to the door, calling: "Fast, fast, Jen, and don't be squeamish. You're gonna tear your clothes, but you'll live to tell about this one." The girl was still in the cabin. "But you gotta be fast, Jen!" Reilly yelled. "Please! If this load slips, we're cooked! Kick off your shoes and throw 'em down to the ground!"

He heard Jenny say, "O.K., skipper. Coming." He dropped a

little lower and reached up and held Jenny's foot while she clamped onto the bough. They slid to the trunk.

"The one on the left—the big one!" Courvis called up. "You can reach it if you hang! The rest is a cinch! Follow me!"

They hung and caught the next branch with their feet, then slipped, slid, and scrambled lower. The branches increased as they neared the bottom. The photographer was on the ground, reaching up and saying: "Jump."

"And run when you hit the ground, until I tell you to stop!" Reilly added, jumped, reached up and caught Jenny as she hung and dropped. The three of them set off on a dead run for what looked like the edge of a clearing.

Reilly stopped and panted, "Got it. O.K." He glanced quickly at Jenny, who was unhurt except for a long scratch on one arm. She was gazing at him still with her bright smile. She said, "Spot, you're a pilot."

The photographer was patting his breast and his right side pocket. He grinned. "Saved my lenses," he said.

Jennie's hands flew to her head. It was bare and the thick coil of ash hair was sliding loosely down her neck. Her lips parted.

"Look," said Reilly. He pointed upwards. Some ten or fifteen yards away they saw the cream-colored ship pinioned at the top of the still swaying trees. Both wings had been ripped loose from the cabin and were folded sharply back, but still held. A streak of white showed where a huge limb was cracking. A gust of wind shook the tops of the trees again, and they heard again the terrible ripping sound. A wing tore completely loose and fell to one side. A branch broke, and another, and the tail of the ship began to slide toward the ground. The speed increased. The damp heavy air was full of the snapping and crackling of the branches and the harsh ripping of canvas. Jenny screamed once, a dreadful scream, just before the tail hit the ground, and with a final shocking smash the heavy engine crashed its way down through the cockpit and cabin, burst like a shell from the ruptured fuselage and rolled to rest a few feet away.

Reilly mopped his brow and looked at the photographer, whose teeth were bared and whose face was very white. Then both men noticed that Jenny was on her knees between them, her face in her hands, sobbing.

The pilot dropped to one knee beside her with an arm around her shoulder.

"Hi, Jenny," the pilot said. "Nix. Come on. You're out of it. You're alive. It's all over. Come on, cookie: nix on the hysterics. They told me that you were different."

The girl uncovered her face. "I'm not hysterical! I'm not, I'm not! Oh, dear, oh dear!" Her body swayed as she cried, and the knot of hair gave way and fell about her shoulders.

"Well, then, what is it, sister? Are you hurt?"

Jenny shook her head. She took her hands again from her tear-marked face and caught her breath for a moment, her features grief-stricken. Then she wailed, "My hat! My beautiful hat! My beautiful, beautiful hat!"

"Oh, my Lord!" said the photographer. "Where is it?"

Jenny's anguished wail rose again. "I—I left it! I was afraid I would spoil it climbing down! I thought it would be safer in the ship!" She looked up helplessly at the two men. "I—I never had a hat like that—"

Photographer Osgood waited without and a little to the side of the Oilco Hanger at Newark for the cab for which he had telephoned. The young pilot had left him there, because he said the air lines did not like private planes taxiing up to their ports. The cab station was just across the field, and as he watched, he saw one detach itself from the cluster behind the main building, back out, turn, and head for the main road. It was about a half mile away. He grinned and lit a cigarette and sat down on his plate case.

A limousine drew up in front of the Oilco Hangar. Five men got out and walked over to where he sat. He recognized one of them as Young Suez, a former prizefighter and now a circulation slugger for the *Star-Leader*. Photographer Osgood flicked the cigarette away and got up with his plate case under his arm, his fingers feeling for the strap buckle. He was cursing himself. Why hadn't he telephoned the *Blade* to have him met at the airport? He swore again. He remembered Krauer penciling something on the back of an envelope or a piece of paper as he had taken off. The cab was a hundred yards down the road.

"Hello, Jack," said Young Suez. The other men stood around him with their hands in the pockets of their overcoats.

"Hello, Suez."

"Understand you got some pretty hot stuff."

"Nope," said Photographer Osgood, knowing it was useless to lie, but hoping to gain time. "Light was bad. Most of the plates are fogged."

"Now listen, Jack," said Young Suez. "We think we ought to have a split. Why don't you be regular?"

"I didn't get anything. I tell you the light was bad."

"Now, Jack," said Young Suez, "we know different."

"Oh, hell!" said one of the men. "Quit wasting time. He's asking for it."

They closed in, but Photographer Osgood had the catch to the plate case open. He smashed a half-dozen by crashing them in a bunch to the concrete apron in front of the hangar. The rest he spilled to the ground by turning the plate case upside down and was stepping on them when they reached him. Young Suez struck him in the mouth with a piece of lead, and he felt his teeth smash and was sickened. But he managed to pick up his heavy camera and hit Young Suez over the head with it, and the slugger fell to the ground. The other four piled on him. There was no sound but heavy breathing, scuffling of feet, and blows. One of the men kicked Photographer Osgood in the stomach, and he went down. Another beat him over the head, and a third kicked him again and again as he lay unconscious. The fourth examined the shattered plates and said, "You dopes. They're all busted. Come on."

Two of them dumped Young Suez into the rear of the limousine and climbed in after him. They all climbed into their car, turned it around, and drove off. The cab passed them on the way out. The cabdriver pulled up to the hangar, goggle-eyed. Then he began to blow his horn and yell, "Hey! Hey! You guys in there! Hey! There's a guy been slugged!"

Men came running out from the hangar and around to the side.

"No," repeated Wyatt Court, "not what you might call a conspicuous success." He sighed a little wearily and closed the thin line of his mouth, and then, curiously, his eyes, too, for a moment, so that Dodd could not see them. He was thinking of the young men and women who went where he sent them without a question and did what he asked them to do to the best of their ability, and came wandering back to lay their adventures on his desk. He could still hear Perry Brown saying to him, the day after he returned from Atlantic City, "Listen, boss: say something nice to Vogel. He's heartbroken because he didn't get that shot. He thinks he muffed it and you're sore. Honest, they chopped him loose from that boat. He couldn't move."

He was remembering Jenny Jones at his desk, an old felt hat over her ash hair, her mouth tremulous, and then breaking into her bright smile, and the smile vanishing again as she said, "Do you think it would be all right, Mr. Court? You see, it's more than I ever spent. I know I shouldn't have done it, but I just couldn't resist it. They didn't find anything of it."

And he was remembering how Osgood had looked.

"Well?" said Mr. Dodd.

Court opened his eyes with a little start and said, "Well what?"

Mr. Dodd tapped the sheaf of expense accounts. "These."

Court turned his head slowly and looked at the cold, dry man. He looked at him through quite narrowed lids and with the shadow of a smile on his own thin mouth.

Then he said softly, "Go upstairs, Mr. Dodd, where you belong, and stay there. I have no scruples about hitting an old man."

The autditor started. He saw that the city editor's right hand was clenched. He swelled with anger. Court pushed back his chair gently. The auditor began to back away, white with rage. Court was still smiling faintly.

When the man was a few yards away, the city editor suddenly picked up the expense accounts and held them toward him. "Take these with you, Mr. Dodd," he said, "and be careful how you handle them. There's blood on them."

Flood

Some stories haunt one before, during, and even after they are written. "Flood" was such a one. I remember that I was traveling a great deal at the time I was writing it and I carried it around the country with me doing bits of it here and there, on trains, airplanes, and in ugly hotel rooms. I always seemed to be under its influence during the time and never quite able to escape from the atmosphere I was creating, or perhaps the atmosphere it was creating for itself.

I think now, looking back, that writing must often be an opener of doors to the long-buried past within. One hits upon a character or a situation and while concerning oneself therewith provides a release to the subconscious. Old, long-forgotten, or even wholly unsuspected ghosts and specters emerge to invade the typescript. I sometimes think it works in the same manner as the genuine mystic or seer with his crystal ball, or silly lay-out of packs of cards. The glass sphere or the Jack of Spades engages them optically and physically and this perhaps makes it possible for them to tune in.

I recall that I was at a curious stage of my new career as a free-lance writer, and perhaps this story was, among other things, a kind of subconscious negation to the positive and foolish things I was doing consciously.

The nature of the foolishness was this: Having concluded a successful year as a free-lance writer abroad, I returned to the United States late in October and asked the *News,* the newspaper that I had quit as one of the highest-paid sports writers in the country, to give me a job at the minimum guild salary of $70 a week as an ordinary city-side news reporter and leg man. Captain Patterson, the publisher, who must have thought I was quite mad, consented and I was assigned to work under the late Harvey Duell, the city editor. Having written successful fiction about newspaper reporters for some three years, for by this time Perry Brown was an established *Post* character, I was now

85

deliberately trying to turn the clock back and become one myself to gain experience.

I was telling myself that if I was to continue to write about newspaper people I ought to know even more about them. I believed that fourteen years in the sports department had left me one-sided and out of balance toward that something pronounced "laif" and that, of course, was the sheerest nonsense.

And so I went bucketing about the country covering strikes and murders, labor leaders, crackpots, and politicians, and all the time "Flood" was gnawing at my vitals and crying to be written, and it had nothing whatsoever to do with what I was seeing or covering or writing about those days, but only with emotions and fantasies that were going on within me. None of the things in "Flood" ever happened beyond the natural catastrophe after which the story is named, nor had I ever seen or covered one of those periodically disastrous Mississippi floods.

Yet fatuously I was proud of myself that I was a real reporter at last, earning my $70 a week. And this pride closed my ears to the inner person saying, "Don't be a fool, Gallico, you're wasting your time careering about looking for adventures. Calm down and listen to what comes from inside you." I couldn't hear, and when Patterson raised my salary to $100 after I had scored a small beat, I was as pleased and excited as the day I landed my first short story in the *Post*. And I went bucketing on with even greater energy to try to absorb more "life" and more "copy" and in the meantime stealing moments on train rides or in hotel rooms late at night to work on this "Flood" story and its people, who would give me no rest, until in the end apparently "Flood" got itself written in spite of me.

I suppose there is no way to learn but the hard way. In the spring of 1937 I went back to Europe to make use of this wonderful living material I had acquired as a reporter and wrote a novel around the great sit-down strike I had covered in Flint, Michigan. The results were quite ghastly, as I myself had very little to say about the strike, its causes, its effects, and the people involved in it, and thought that it was sufficient to put a set of characters similar to ones I had met through their paces in a background with which I had familiarized myself. It is true that the novel was published as a one-shotter by *Cosmopolitan*, but buried it in the back of the magazine where it quietly died, the fate it deserved.

Realism and the personal-experience gambit had taken an awful

licking, but did I learn? Not yet. Back I came to New York in the fall
and took another job as a reporter, this time with International News
Service. I never used a line of the "material" I gained in this further
experience, but again while I was chasing around the country I pulled
"The Roman Kid" out of the back of my skull and wrote it.

Gradually the idiocy of what I was doing began to dawn on me. First
of all, to help me along there was the economics. The so-called material
was not useful and the salary insufficient. More and more editors were
inclined to use my fiction talents for feature stories. As I was then beginning to enter the higher brackets as a *Post* writer and the newspapers
were getting my work at a fifth of the price the magazines would pay
me, the unsoundness of the scheme finally managed to penetrate. But
slowly the point was also making itself clear that I was wasting my time
and that this kind of forcing was utter nonsense and wholly juvenile
for one who had ambitions to become a writer. Writers write. Writers
write from experience, naturally, but everything—living, breathing,
walking the streets, doing one's job, encountering people—all this is
experience; all the past one has accumulated is experience. Imagination
and fantasy does the rest. Some of the greatest writers have never
stirred from their doorsteps.

These ideas should not be confused with the necessity for traveling
to do legitimate research to gain accuracy and proper background for
telling a story. But it is ridiculous to place the cart before the horse.
First one ought to have something to say—an idea, an emotion, a fantasy that needs to be expressed. Thereafter it is time enough to go about
searching for the knowledge or experience to enable one to say it well.

All kinds of things of which I was not aware at the time I was writing "Flood" seem to have come welling to the surface in the story.
Loneliness and yearnings and dark and unsuspected things out of my
childhood and adolescence, transmuted into the feelings and emotions
of two characters.

This story might also serve as a complete refutation of the canard,
one of the favorites of both the amateur and would-be writer as well as
the high-brow critics, that a "slick" or popular magazine such as the
Saturday Evening Post will not publish a story unless it has a plot,
which plot follows a formula, and unless it has a happy ending. I warn
you: "Flood" has no plot in the usual sense; it has no happy ending; in
fact, now that I come to think of it, it has no ending at all. If anything,
it is a story of a casual adultery, two frightened people drifting together

into a curious kind of love and union through loneliness and terror—not the kind of story you would expect to find in a "family" magazine, yet there it was, and here it is.

Nobody ever found out what happened to Perry Brown on the flood assignment down through Ohio, Kentucky, and Tennessee. He came back to the *Blade* office at half past eleven one night to get his mail and had very little to say.

He had been gone fifteen days and had filed exactly four stories. There had been one good one from Cincinnati on the fire that had devastated the business section, and two from Louisville before all the wires went down. And one night a radio amateur located in Winesville, Kentucky, had made an abortive effort to transmit a story to the *Blade* short-wave receiver, purporting to come from one Perry Brown, but there was bad static and interference, and the amateur suddenly went off the air and could not be located again.

There had been a hiatus of some seven or eight days when they did not hear from him at all and were a little worried about him, but then came an appeal from Memphis from Perry for funds, although there was no story. And shortly after that he came home.

Reyburn, managing editor of the *Blade*, was curious and asked Perry Brown, in a friendly enough fashion, what he had been up to, and to give an account of himself. Perry looked up from the envelopes he was examining. He was pale and looked older. He was a big man, and bulky, but he was thinner, and his clothes fitted him less than they ever did; seemed to hang on him instead. He replied by asking Reyburn a question. "Where's Rusty?"

"She's still in New Milford on the Agathy trial," Reyburn replied. "She was worried until we heard from you from Memphis. What happened to you? You look as though you had been put through a wringer."

"Nothing," said Perry curtly, and began to stack his envelopes.

Reyburn grinned at him. "Didn't like our flood, eh?" he said.

Perry Brown swore bitterly, and Reyburn suddenly saw that something lay behind his eyes. Perry then said, "I wish to God you had never sent me out on that story," stuffed his mail into his overcoat pocket, and went out of the office. And that was the last thing anybody ever heard him say about the assignment. A week or so later he seemed quite normal, except that when Rusty McGowan was in the room with him, he never took his eyes from her.

After they had covered the flood and the subsequent fire in Cincinnati, Perry Brown and Al Vogel, the fat photographer, went to Louisville, where they became separated. Vogel was having his troubles getting his pictures back out of the flood area, and Perry was having his own problems piecing together a coherent story out of the chaos of rising water, fear, and rumor. The city officials and the Army engineers were working against growing terror and panic, and the press was not welcome.

There was a curious quality to this horrible rising of the Ohio River that defied Perry. He had covered floods before and had seen those dreadful misshapen islands in muddy water, made by slanting roof tops of houses showing just above the surface, but about this one there was a cold, frightful relentlessness that he could not get onto paper. From the moment he arrived he never moved without fear in his heart. The ceaseless downpour of rain from heavy gray skies helped this. Unless the rain stopped, the end of the world was at hand. Water beneath, water above, Perry felt the stratum in which he still lived and breathed, and witnessed death and life, narrowing, closing in.

Everything that was done seemed helpless and futile because of the rain and the rising river. He watched whole families, miserable, frightened, shivering, panic-faced, moved to higher ground, and knew that if the rain did not stop, soon there would be no more higher ground, that earth water and sky water would meet and the world in between would cease.

Perry had got a break when he encountered a colonel of engineers he had met on another story, and the colonel had remembered him and let him ride south with him, skirting the flood, in an Army car, and so deeper into new flood area than any other newspaperman had been. And it was while floating in a small hired rowboat over the remains of a little town called Winesville that Perry first experienced the vanishing consciousness of any other world beyond that one which was drowned in moving water, death, and desolation.

A unit of newsreel men who somehow, too, had penetrated to Winesville had captured a corpse. It had caught their cameras unprepared on its lonely, bobbing ride, ferryless, across the Styx, and they were hiding it close to and screened by the gunwales of one of their boats until they could retrain their lenses properly. It had been an old Negro dressed in overalls and a cotton shirt. Their camera boat was held fast to what seemed to be a brick wall rising out of the water, but wasn't, because it was the second story of a bank building. There was a window just around the corner with gold lettering on it: A. A. Clakins, D.D.S., Crowns, Bridgework, Office Hours 9 a.m.—3 p.m.

The newsreel men were frightened at first when they saw that Perry knew, and clustered around in their boat until they recognized him. He had seen them before. They were a crew from Imperial Picture News. He lifted his face out of the collar of his slicker, in which it had been buried, and called over, "A little ghouling, boys?"

One of the cameramen, a big chap, with the rain streaming down his face, called back, "How'd you get here? Hey, nix; row off a little. Don't look. If one of those soldier boys got wise to us, he might do a little shooting. They killed a looter about a mile down, an hour ago. We're just gonna float this guy by again for a shot."

"Jeepers," said Perry, "and we're supposed to be hard-boiled."

"What the hell," said the cameraman. "He don't care any more. Row off a little, willya?"

Perry put pressure on his oars, moved the boat across what had been the main street, and with short tugs kept the nose of the skiff in the current. Two of the camera crew in another skiff began to row slowly up the street. One of them was leaning over the side of the boat, holding on to something in the water. They just kept on rowing, and pretty soon the man who had been leaning over the side was sitting up straight, and a dark object came floating down with the stream, turning over and over with a queer, hapless grace.

The large cameraman in the other boat had his right eye jammed against the rubber-cupped finder of his camera and was grinding rhythmic circles, panning his lens just a little ahead of the floating body.

It was then that Perry Brown suddenly was astonished to find himself seriously wondering where ever they were going to show the pictures they were making. Who would look at them? The earth was laid waste by water. It was impossible to think of dry streets and moving-picture houses, and men and women standing in line waiting to buy tickets, and automobiles passing, and boys on bicycles, and traffic policemen standing at intersections. He looked down the watery avenue of what had once been a town. There was the top of a curved electric sign sticking up above the water, with the letters *BIJO* legible in red and orange-colored electric bulbs. Perry's quick mind supplied the *U* that lay just beneath the yellowish surface of the stream, and his imagination created an unbelievable, forgotten picture of the Bijou Theater on Saturday night, with slick-haired boys, and girls with bright red lips crowding the lobby and being sucked in through the portals as the water was now sucked down the main street.

The dark rotating object passed his boat and kept on going. The movie men, their shot recorded, were letting it go. Two militiamen in a boat, with rifles slung across their backs, shouted up at the newsreel men, "Hey, you guys! Lay offa them kinda pictures!"

The big cameraman waved back. "O.K., O.K., buddy!" and they started to row away, but Perry noticed that one of the other men was grinding away at the camera with a long-focus lens. The militiamen stopped Perry's boat and examined his military pass. It was then three o'clock in the afternoon. The gray rain was falling slantwise because there was a wind that was beginning to freshen into a gale. An old motorboat came chugging past. A man in a black slicker with a red cross on his arm was at the wheel. The boat was low in the water with the weight of its burden of men, women, and children wrapped in sodden blankets. Only the men and the children were looking ahead. There were four women in the boat, and all of them were gazing backwards in the direction from whence they had come.

Perry let his boat drift with the sluggish surge of the flood stream.

He heard some yelling and guided his boat in the direction from which it came, down a waterway that had evidently been a side street off the main thoroughfare. There was a cluster of boats there manned by natives in thigh boots, slickers, and caps. They were evacuating men, women, and children trapped on the upper floors of houses. The first rise of the water must have been extraordinarily rapid in Winesville, from the number of people trapped in houses and driven to the second story and, in some cases, the roof.

The yelling was coming from a man who was hanging out of a window a few houses down. The water level was about five feet below the sill. He was gaunt and unshaven, with sparse gray-black hair, dressed in trousers, collarless shirt, and an open vest.

He had his hands cupped to his mouth and was bawling, "Get a doctor, quick! I gotta get a doctor! D'ya hear down there? Get a doctor! She's gotta have a doctor! Get a doctor over here!"

Nobody paid any attention to him. Perry asked one of the men in the rescue boats where he could find a doctor. The man shrugged. "Dunno! I ain't seen a doctor for nine hours. We could use a dozen of them. They had 'em at the city hall, but that's under now. That guy's been yelling for three hours. Wife's gonna have a baby. We've had a call in for a doctor with the Red Cross soon as they can spare one. They're all busy."

Perry Brown rowed over beneath the window. The man leaned down eagerly.

"For heaven's sakes, hurry, Doc! It's almost here! Make your boat fast to the bottom of the shutter! I'll give you a hand up!"

Perry called up, "I'm not a doctor. They've sent for one from the Red Cross. I'll try to get you one."

The man suddenly lost all control and began to scream curses at the top of his lungs, interspersed with cries for a doctor, as though the very loudness of his voice would bring him what he wanted. He was completely in the grip of panic. From behind him within the room came a woman's cry. Perry wanted to dig his oars into the water and pull hard and keep on pulling until he no longer heard those cries. He found himself thinking suddenly of white-tiled operating rooms and nickeled tables and instruments, and cool surgeons in white, and blessed anesthetic. But that was a dream of ages yet to come. This was the Deluge. So must Leah and Rebecca and Mary have cried their agony in lonely huts when God was angered and His waters covered the earth.

The man reappeared at the window, his face livid. He had a shotgun in his hands. He screamed, "Damn you, Doc! Get in here or I'll blow your head off! I'll blow your head off! D'ya hear?"

The shotgun, at the time, didn't impress Perry. His mind was already made up. He fastened the painter of his boat to the shutter and shipped his oars. He said, "Put that gun away, you fool, and give me a hand."

The man reached down and hoisted Perry up over the sill like a child, and Perry was a big man. A woman lay on a white iron bedstead over in a corner of the room. Her face was white and wet with sweat, and her mouth was twisted, her untidy hair damp and loose. Perry took off his coat. His knees were trembling and he was afraid that he would not be able to walk. When he was a cub, he had many times seen interns arrive, drop off the backs of still moving ambulances, and make curbstone deliveries in streets, taxicabs, or drugstores. His mind, suddenly, with amazing clarity, reviewed for him those things that must be done. He moved over toward the bed, rolling up his sleeves. . . .

Some time later another man came through the window. He had a small black bag with him. He saw Perry and said, "Ah, Doctor, I see you got here ahead of me."

Perry said, "I'm not a doctor. I did what I could. For heaven's sakes, take over. I want to get out of here."

The doctor shrugged his shoulders, looked surprised, and said, "There isn't much more to do except get 'em out of here. The water's still rising. . . . H'm'm'm. That isn't a bad-looking boy."

Perry went out the window and dropped into his boat. He felt sick and shocked. When the world went back to the waters from whence it came, no one took death or life seriously any more. He dug his oars into the water, now choppy with the high wind, and let the rain sting into his face. He paid no heed to the direction in which he was going. He didn't care. He was himself close to panic. He felt his tiny boat bobbing under him, and imagined it was the dead streets beneath, struggling to free themselves from the choking water. Chairs floated alongside in the water, and signs, and barrels and boxes, and soggy lumps of feathers that had been chickens. The incessant rain was heavy and made his oar handles slippery. He grated one of them against a piano that was floating on its back, with its ivory teeth showing, and nearly lost it. A dressmaker's dummy stuck its torso half out of the water, and he passed a water-logged perambulator.

He was conscious that he was suddenly making unusual speed, but not aware why. He thought it was just the desperate power he was putting into the short oars that were always coming out of the wooden rowlocks. It was not until too late that he discovered that he had been rowing directly toward the river. The Army men had warned him against it. With the river gorge under him, he found himself sucked along and helpless amid the forlorn flotsam of the flood. He tried to stem against the current, nearly turned the boat over, and finally spun around in a dizzy circle, caught in a whirlpool. The wind had lashed the surface of the water into wavelets that were dangerous, because they hid the debris and floating objects that might upset him. Between rain clouds and twilight, it was getting dark.

Perry tried pulling across stream, and was succeeding when the current caught him again and whirled him into the top of a tree that showed just above the surface. A branch struck him a glancing blow on the back of the head and knocked him flat on his face in the bottom of the boat, less than half conscious. When he sat up again, his nose was bleeding. The boat was turning around and around with the current. Both oars were gone. It will still raining. It was dark. Only occasional objects rising from the surface of the water were darker than the sky and the horizon, and therefore faintly distinguishable.

There were no sounds but the rain and the wind and the rush of the stream beneath him, and the scraping of his sodden shoes on the bottom of the boat as he shifted his position. He had a tin dipper in the skiff, and he bailed it fairly dry, and then lay down in the bottom of the boat for better security of balance. He felt that he could no longer sit up in the black void through which he was plunging without falling over out of the boat.

He then gave way to the curiously gentle and soothing sensation of being a lost atom, utterly without power to help himself or shape his course. When his boat banged and scraped against solid objects, he found himself wondering vaguely what they were, and once he struck against something that was soft and there followed a great splashing. At that time, and during that passage, he was not afraid, because there was nothing of which to be afraid. Perry had found that fear was very often occasioned by responsibility and having to do something about something. There was nothing he could do in his present situation but wait for morning. He must have slept for a while—how long he did not know, because the luminosity was worn off his watch dial and it was pitch-black when he woke up. The nearest light seemed to be miles away on an elevation, and he caught the flash of a distant airways beacon.

He was not afraid even then; had no premonition of danger or disaster until his boat suddenly bumped, grated, rolled over, and was gone. Even in the fraction of a second's time occupied by the disaster, Perry was somehow prepared for the cold shock of the water, and kept his head above the surface. He began to fight for his life immediately. He lashed out in the darkness with his left arm and smashed his hand against something wooden and solid, hurting it and running splinters into the palm. He moved his legs automatically to keep his head above water, twisted around, and thrust out more gingerly with his right hand. He encountered solid wood again, but ridged. His fingers sought for something to cling to, but the current was sweeping him onwards. Then his grasping right hand and arm suddenly thrust through a void; the ridged wood was no longer there, and the next moment he felt a hard blow on the muscle of his upper arm. Involuntarily he contracted it. The palm of his hand come into contact with a smooth surface.

His arm was around a projection of some kind—what, he could not imagine; but the desperate passage was momentarily stopped.

The current sucked and tore at his legs and body. He held fast. He tried to think. It seemed impossible to marshal thoughts against the vindictive tugging and sucking at his body, the cold heavy grip of the water, sluicing rain, and the blackness of the night. He was a thinking animal, but the attacks upon him were all physical and came out of darkness. He finally said aloud to himself, "I still have my hat on. That's funny." Something floating past batted him violently on the shoulder and nearly dislodged him. And now that he was no longer moving through the water, he was badly frightened. His right shoulder felt numb and he did not know how long his strength would hold. He maneuvered to get his left hand up to reinforce his right in its grasp of the unknown projection. His fingers closed over what seemed to be a narrow strip of wood with an indentation running down the center in which lay what seemed to be cord.

His finger tips suddenly created a picture in his mind, and his free hand, hurt though it was, wandered avidly to verify it. It was true. His right arm had been thrust through the open window of a half-submerged house—probably the second story—curled around the side, and his hand was touching a wall. Cautiously he felt for the sill with his elbow. But it was more than two feet below the surface, and he could not reach it and keep his head clear. Was there room overhead? He felt for it, but apparently the entire window was out. He thrust against the powerful current with all his strength, pulling with his right arm, pushing with his left, kicking desperately with his legs against the heavy drag of shoes and pants and enveloping slicker. He banged his knee against the sunken sill, but found a purchase on it and got a leg over, and suddenly the pressure on his body was gone. He was in still water up to his waist, but his feet were on solid flooring. He was inside a room of some sort. His legs and whole body began to tremble with fatigue and nervous reaction. He was so cold that his teeth chattered. But he could think again. The immediate danger was over, he knew.

Was there another floor overhead, or was he at the top of the house? Was there any way to reach the roof? Was the water still rising, and how quickly? He felt that the last was not immediately important, because remaining in the icy water much longer would kill him eventually anyway. He knew that somehow he must go higher, where it was dry. It was at that time that he first heard the scraping sound from overhead, or thought he did.

Perry waited and listened. He heard rain falling on a roof, and the rushing and gurgling of the flood outside, and his own splashings as he moved closer to the window and jammed his legs up against the space below the sill to steady himself. He tried desperately to stop the chatter of his teeth. He thought that it might have been the branch of a floating tree scraping against the side of the house. Then he heard it again. It did come from overhead and inside the house. If there were human beings above, they might help him.

He called out into the darkness, "Hey! Hey! Is there anybody up there? Can you hear me?"

His voice sounded dead to him. He felt that it had hardly carried beyond the confines of the window frame, that the darkness was stifling it.

He heard no reply, and called louder, so that his throat hurt him and his voice cracked like that of a boy. "Is there anybody up there? Hey! Is there anybody there? Can you hear me up there?"

He heard the scraping sound again and then, directly over his head, the noise of a window being raised. Then a woman answered him. She said, "Who is it? Who's there?"

The voice was low and rapid, as though the woman's heart were in her throat, as though she were frightened, yet eager. It was throaty and half-whispered. She called again, "Is anybody there?"

Perry Brown stuck his head out of the window, holding on with both hands to the lintel. The rain drove into his face. He could see nothing.

"I am!" he shouted. "Can I get up there? Where are you? I lost my boat! I caught the window as I was being swept by! Is anybody up there with you?"

The woman replied, "I'm alone! Where are you from?" Her voice was heavy and languid, with the speech of the district.

Perry called back, "I'm a reporter! Newspaper! I got caught in the current! My boat rolled over! Is it dry up there? Can I get up?"

"You can try! I'm in an attic room! Reach up!"

Perry, feeling his way carefully, climbed to the underwater sill, his back to the flood. The water pulled at his legs again. He held on to the side of the window with his right hand and felt above him with his aching left. He touched a woman's hand and arm, newly wet with rain. Then, out of the water-laden darkness, something curious fell athwart his face, startling him. But it was soft and had a strange, damp fragrance. In the blackness his perceptions sharpened. He realized that it was a woman's hair. The arm was firm and round, the hand rough. He pictured the color of the hair. Because of the darkness that surrounded him he saw it as glossy black. He took in his the hand that he had found in the darkness, and it gave him a queer strength and comfort.

He said, "Howdy. My name's Perry Brown."

The woman said nothing, but he thought he heard her sob, or cry out softly. Her fingers in his were suddenly limp. Perry said, "Buck up, sister. There's two of us now." He released her hand and reached above. He felt the sill of a small window. It was not far above his head. He wondered whether he could make it, with the water below sucking and dragging at his legs, and hampered by the weight of his wet clothing. Then he found an iron bracket sticking out from the side of the window, tested it, and found it firm. If he could make it on the first pull-up, he might scramble through before his strength failed.

He said, "Better duck back inside. I'm going to try to make it. I'll either make it on the first try or not at all. When I say 'Three,' that's it."

He relinquished his grip on the side of the window with his right hand, seized the iron bracket, and grasped the edge of the sill above as firmly as he could with his injured left. There was not the least glimmer of light to aid him. He had to rely solely upon the picture he had formed in his mind by his sense of touch as to what lay above. He was not afraid, although he had a perfect mental image of what would happen should he miss—felt himself gasping and struggling in the water, turning over and over, beaten and ground and crushed by the vicious flotsam in the current, or swirled under water.

He said, "This is it, sister—one, two, three," and with all his strength kicked off and pulled upwards. He felt the upper sill at his chest and threw his head forward into the opening of the window, at the same time striving to get a bend in his arms to brace himself through.

But the drag of the water had been too much and robbed his spring of a needed few inches. He hung there, gasping and fighting, kicking, his arms aching and cramped, and he knew that in another moment there would come a weakness that would be the end. There was fire shooting before his eyes, and his chest was aflame. In terror, he cried out, "I can't make it!"

Then hands grasped at his collar and shoulders and tugged. In the moment's respite he battled for breath, gave a last kick, and found he was braced on his numbed arms. The tugging continued. The upper half of his body lay across the sill, inside the room. He waited for a moment and then dragged his legs over after it, and collapsed on the floor and lay there, trembling and sobbing for breath.

After a while he recovered a little and said, "Thanks, sister. Where are you?"

He sat up and felt the woman brush up against him, and found her hand and clung to it. She was trembling. He asked, "What's the matter?"

Her voice came out of the darkness close to him, low and desperate. "I'm hungry. Have you any food?"

"Jeepers," said Perry, and clapped a hand to his coat pocket. He always made it a point to carry chocolate bars with him. They kept him going when he was unable to get regular meals or any meals at all on an assignment. He still had two, wet, soggy, but intact. "I've got some chocolate. How long since you've eaten?"

"Two days, I think. I don't remember."

Perry broke off a piece of a bar and peeled the wrapper from it. He put it into her hand and said, "Go easy, sister. Eat it slowly. You've got to. I'll give you more a little later, but you've got to start easy."

He heard her eating it in the darkness. When she had finished, he asked, "Better?"

She said, "Oh, yes. Yes. Give me more."

"No. Later. You've got to go easy. It'll hurt you if you eat too much now."

"When can I have more?"

"Soon. Soon, sister. Be patient. Who are you? How did you get stuck here?"

There was a moment or two of silence. Finally the woman answered, "I wouldn't leave. The others left when the water started rising. I hid. I couldn't leave."

The heat of Perry's exertions had worn off. He was cold, and a chill shook him. He thought for a moment and then said, "Sister, I've got to take my clothes off. They're wet. I'm freezing."

The woman's voice answered him, "Yes, you must take them off. I have a blanket you can take."

Kneeling, Perry stripped off the wet, heavy garments. He heard the woman closing the window. He rubbed himself as best he could, trying to get dry and warm. He heard the woman say:

"Where are you?"

"Here," said Perry, shivering and stretching out his hand. He felt a rough blanket and took hold of it. He wrapped it around himself. The woman took his hand and led him. She said, "There's a mattress over here in a corner. You can lie down there."

His feet touched the mattress. He knelt first, feeling its length and direction, and then lay full length upon it, huddled in the blanket. The rain was like the distant roar of surf on the roofing overhead. Another chill rattled Perry's frame. He shook from head to foot, and his teeth began to chatter again. He pulled the blanket around his neck and tried to stop it, but could not. The cold came from deep within him, from his mind as well as his shocked body, and from the pictures he was making in the darkness of the things he had seen that day. Now his heart was frozen with fear as his body was with chill.

He heard the woman speak softly from close by. She said, "You're cold."

Perry said: "Y-y-y-y-y-es. I'm s-s-s-sorry. I can't s-s-stop it."

Then her voice came out of the impenetrable darkness again, deeply and quietly. "I'll warm you."

He felt the blanket tugged gently, and relaxed his grip. He was shaking terribly, and his bruises were throbbing. The woman quickly lay down alongside him, pulled the blanket over them. She was wearing a dress of some material that had the texture of cotton, open at the neck. Perry felt her warmth through it. Her arm was under his head. His shaking continued. Once she said to him, "Sh-h-h," as though speaking to a child. His shaking stopped for a moment and he secured a respite before it began again. The woman held him closer. Perry's head rested in the hollow of her neck and shoulder. The fits of shaking were fewer now. They came at longer intervals. The fear was easing from his heart too. A strand of her hair touched his face. Her arms were strong and warm and brought him deep comfort; helped to banish the dreadful pictures from his mind as the cold was slowly leaving his body.

He had strange powerful thoughts as he lay there, warmed and soothed. Who was his unseen companion in the darkness? A woman. Or woman disembodied, the essence of womanhood? He had not seen her. He did not even know her name. She had spread wings over him. She warmed, sheltered, and comforted him, shielded his body and was tender to its hurts. As a boy, in reading, the phrase *"Mater Omnium"* had stuck in his mind. His own mother had died when he was very young. But he had remembered her, and as a child, in his daydreams he would picture himself to her bosom, wrapped within the folds of her robe, warm and safe and in refuge. Was this, then, she? Was he, Perry, a child again and dreaming, as he sometimes did, of the reality of his dream? *"Mater Omnium, Omnium Mater"*—the words chased themselves through his head. Mother of all, mother of the world, mother of man. Through the darkness came only the strong womanhood of this person he could

not see. He was warm now and drowsy, hovering between consciousness and sleep. Journey's end—the end of the world—one man
and one woman left alive. He said, in a half-whisper, "Thank
you!"

"Sh-h-h," said the woman once more. Perry fell asleep. When
he woke up, the room was full of gray murky light and it was gray
out of doors and still raining. The woman was kneeling by the
window with her back to him, looking out. He saw that she had
blue-black hair that hung down to her waist.

Perry said, "Good morning," and she started, and then turned
around. Her face shocked him. She was not beautiful. Her features
were so heavy-boned as to be almost coarse. She was young—could
not have been more than twenty-six or seven. Her eyebrows were
black and strongly marked, and there were hairs between them.
Her cheekbones were high, and more prominent because she was
thin. The nose was long and straight, the mouth large, full-blooded.
The jaw line that ran from ear to chin was slanting, bony, hard.
Beneath her cotton dress swelled large breasts, and she was tall
and wide-hipped. He was shocked, because he was a romanticist.
He knew that he had expected standard beauty. Her eyes, too,
were quite dark, her skin pale and roughened.

She said, "You all right?"

Perry sat up and wrapped the blanket around him. "Thanks to
you. I guess you saved my life last night. A couple of times."
They were in a small bare attic chamber. The roof came to a low
inverted V, directly overhead. In it were two trunks, a battered
chair with but half a back to it, and the mattress upon which he
lay. A cooking pot with a lid on it stood on the floor. Perry asked,
"Who are you? What's your name?"

"Mary Rud. Rudscienski. They call us Rud for short."

"Polish?"

"Not me. My husband. I come from around here." She said it
with a kind of pride.

"Where is your husband?" Perry wished then that he had not
asked, but the girl shrugged her shoulders.

"He got out, I guess—with the kid. He made a sort of raft."

"And left you here?"

She shrugged her bony shoulders again. "I don't know. He called. I wouldn't come. This is my home. I just couldn't leave it. See, it was my home. I hid. I looked out the window after. The raft was spinning around. It was half sinking. I guess he couldn't hang on any more to the house. Maybe the current took him away. Maybe they're all gone."

Perry realized that in a matter-of-fact way she was saying that her husband and child might be dead. He felt again that she was a primitive, but in a different way from the experience he had had the night before. The capacity to suffer deeply called, to some extent, for breeding and imagination. This girl must have been bred close, close to the soil, to be so strangely immune to disaster. She had made her choice, and it had been to remain. He had come upon that trait before in the flood. The men got out quickly enough, but the women, many of them, had to be removed forcibly from their homes to save them. Their homes. It was all they had that was stable and unchangeable and that repaid them love for love. The girl's inarticulateness moved him to a queer compassion for her.

He said more softly, "And then what happened to you—after?"

Mary Rud stirred and shifted her position, so that she sat on the floor with her back to the window, her hands in her lap, and her head tilted a little to the side at an angle that suddenly struck Perry as inconceivably tender and childlike. It softened the harsh jaw line, and the blue-black hair fell to the floor past her shoulder.

"I had to come up here. The water came faster than I thought it would. I moved some food to the second floor, but it was all washed away. I got a pot of water up here. It's almost all gone now. I had a half a loaf of bread, but that's gone. Have you any more chocolate?"

Perry broke off a piece of a bar and gave it to her. She bit into it quickly with good white teeth, stopped suddenly, and held it out to him, saying, "You?"

Perry shook his head. "I had a big meal yesterday afternoon. Go ahead. You need it."

But she stopped eating and sat there looking at him with her large dark eyes. Finally she asked, "Where are you from?"

Perry told her at length. When he told her about New York, her eyes grew larger. She could not understand why folks in New York should be interested in what happened to people on the Ohio River, but she wanted to hear stories about the city—fabulous ones. She had never even been to Louisville. She had been born and raised on a farm. For a while she had worked as a waitress in a café in Winesville. As she told of this, Perry, whose mind always made pictures when he was listening to anyone, saw her, short-skirted, full-breasted, in white apron or overall, with her black hair coiled in a knot at the back of her head and a pencil stuck into it, carrying a tray full of dishes, her hips swinging as she walked, and men at tables turning their heads to watch her passage. There she had met Jan Rudscienski, the farmer she had married. She was then nineteen. She said that he was good enough to her. She seemed to dismiss him with that. Perry, city-born and bred, was amazed at her casualness. It was his first experience with the placidity and resignation of those whose constant struggle is with the soil and the forces of nature.

The blanket wrapped around him, Perry went to the window and looked out. To the left, and under water, he saw the slanting top of the roof of a small porch. It was this that had upset his boat the night before. It was still raining. There was water as far as he could see, but no houses. There were the branches of many bare trees rising from the flood about the house, and these had entangled debris of every description—barrels, troughs, gates floated off their hinges, crates and boxes and hencoops. The water was a dirty yellow in color. Perry raised the window. There was no sound but the falling rain and another like the sighing of wind through a leafy grove, which was water rushing through the light twigs of the trees, and another, which was a deeper gurgling as the stream bent its way around solid objects.

Perry asked, "What's around on the other side?"

"Water," replied the girl. "The nearest house is three miles."

He looked down at the window below, from which he had climbed during the night. It was gone. The top of the frame was barely showing level with the surface of the water. "Hey," he said, "it's gone up since last night. It's still rising."

The girl was not surprised. Of course it was going up. She had been watching it rise for days. She had come to accept it as natural. It would continue to be higher and higher.

Perry examined his clothes. They were damp, but he decided to put them on, hoping the heat of his body would dry them. He turned his back and climbed into them laboriously and, curiously, without self-consciousness. They chilled him at first, but he moved about briskly and managed to warm them a little. He looked into the waterpot. It was a third full. He had a bar and a half of chocolate left. He went over and knelt at the window beside the girl and said, "Look, kid, we're in a nasty spot."

He was kneeling with his hands in his lap, she sitting with hers folded, and so they looked at each other. She said nothing, but there was sympathy and a wonderful warmth in her eyes, and a little twisted smile played at the corner of her mouth and disappeared. If he was worried and afraid, she was sorry and wanted him not to be. She was inarticulate, but not with her eyes and body.

Perry thought that she had leaned ever so tiny a fraction closer to him. He could not help himself then. His hands still in his lap, he leaned forward gently and kissed her lips.

That night they huddled again in the darkness and became as one, naturally and without question. But their union was compounded more of pity and loneliness than of passion. When they awakened late in the morning of the second day, the yellow waters outside were still rising.

There was no telling how high the water would go. When it came pouring into their attic room, it would drive them to the roof. If it continued to rise, it would sweep them away. The rain never stopped. Perry managed to fill the waterpot with rain water, but they faced starvation. The remaining bar of chocolate was reduced by half. Perry rationed it, managing to give her the large share of the small amount they dared eat. She had been without food longer than he and already was growing weak.

Mostly she lay on the mattress, while he told her stories of New York. She would lie very quietly and listen to him, and sometimes ask him questions. She knew a smattering about moving-picture stars from movie magazines and occasional visits to the Bijou in Winesville. Her knowledge was limited and bounded by her life. She talked seldom, except to ask him for more stories, but she spoke with simplicity and directness always. And her growing weakness lent her a beautiful dignity.

Perry was amazed to find how beautiful she had become. Each of her strongly marked features had grown dear and tender to him. He was continually discovering beauty where he had seen none before. It was the same face that he had first seen when she turned around in the gray light of the flood morning, but now he found something clean and moving in the slanting line of her jaw-bone. He loved the heavily drawn eyebrows and the long straight line of her nose that dropped straight from her brow. It reminded him of heads of Minerva he had seen. Her hair was his delight. And her hands, to him, had lost all their roughness, when sometimes she held his head between them.

He never thought of the world he had left, but only of the small one he inhabited now, and the woman who was a part of it and of him. They had so little, and what each had they shared completely. Even as she grew weaker, her fund of tenderness and womanly compassion seemed never to end. Her mouth grew softer and more childlike as it drooped with hunger. Sometimes her dark eyes were glassy.

They never spoke to each other of love. That, too, seemed to be a part of the lost dead world. Perry felt, somehow, in their isolation, that the word was reduced to an absurdity. Once, his mind took him back to a night club in New York—small tables, men and women jammed knee to knee, mingled smell of perfumes, food, and bodies, the crashing of dishes and the jamming of a band, and a woman with yellow hair and a red mouth, wearing a black satin sheath dress, standing in the spotlight caterwauling about love:

Life's just a game and we play it,
But I've got to keep hearing you say it,
Tell me it's love; tell me it's love.

She sang it with her arms outstretched in a pleading gesture. Men and women at the tables looked at one another, their lips moist and eyes sparkling. Love, love, love. They had to hear the word a thousand times over, read it in print, see it in pictures, to believe it.

The girl had interrupted his thoughts with a half-whispered "Is there any more chocolate?"

Perry held her then tightly in his arms, shaken with tenderness and compassion. Also he gave her the last of the chocolate bar—a scrap hardly more than an inch, because he hoped it would lessen in her the awful pangs he felt tearing at his own vitals. She ate it and sighed and clung to him.

Just before nightfall Perry thought that they were going to die, that even the small remaining corner of an expiring world was due to become blotted out. The yellow torrent of water was a scant six inches below the level of the window sill. Some time during the night or early morning it would spill into the window and invade their room, cold, stinking, lethal. Flight to the roof was now out of the question. The girl was too weak to help herself. Perry knew that his own strength was insufficient. Morning would find them standing waist-deep in icy water. The next night would find them dead.

Perry didn't tell Mary what he had seen. And that night which was to be their last, he found their positions reversed. Now it was he who still had strength and compassion and human warmth to give.

As long as there was the faintest of gray light, and long after it was gone, Perry strained his eyes to see her face, to catch the last line of the beauty of her features.

The window was open. There was no use in trying to stem the monster when it came for them. He heard the rush and gurgle of the water outside, and once the excited chattering of a bird. In the far distance he heard another rushing sound, higher in pitch than the rain and the torrent. As he listened, it was accompanied by the drawn-out throaty wail of a locomotive, and it made him draw the girl only closer to him. He refused to believe it. And yet, for a moment, he found himself thinking of Rusty, and the *Blade* office, the city room of his powerful, vital newspaper, with the typewriters clacking and the telephones ringing, and the editors and reporters busy at their desks, and outside the throb and roar of the city.

But of those realities he thought as he had thought of the night club—as things of a thousand years ago, memories bred in him rather than remembered; as once when he had walked the Roman walls of a border city in England, he had felt suddenly that he had been there before, that time and space were nonexistent, and that there, where he stood on the ancient stone and mortar, gazing down into the tangled underbrush at the wall's base, he had stood once before, with the hair on his neck creeping as it was creeping then, awaiting an enemy.

Rusty he had loved in the past and would love again. She was dear to him for what she had been so many centuries ago. In the darkness with this woman in his arms he was again close to the ages that came out of darkness and returned to it. This brief passage, then, was over, and he was not unhappy, because he was not alone. He knew that not at any time did man face any terror more fearful than to be alone, and was grateful. The girl was asleep when he kissed her good-by. Soon he fell asleep too. When he awoke, the sun was shining in through the half-open window. The room was still dry. He got up and looked out. The yellow waters were still below the level of the sill. The sky was cloudless, blue, and brilliant. He heard a scraping sound from around the corner of the house. A rowboat appeared, and then another, a large, flat-bottomed barge. There were men in them. One of them wore a Red Cross brassard on his arm.

"Hey!" called Perry. "Hey!"

They saw him and rowed over to the window.

The man in the small rowboat was a powerful fellow with blond hair and huge hands. His name was Jan Rudscienski and he was the husband of the woman who lay asleep beneath the blanket in the corner of the room. He looked at Perry without suspicion, but asked, "How you get here?"

Perry told him briefly. He grunted and climbed into the room and asked, "Is she hokay?"

"We're—she's starved," Perry said. "We haven't had any food except a little chocolate I had." He seemed to be thinking and talking like the normal human being he had been, except that he was weak with hunger.

Rudscienski leaned out the window and called, "Hey! She's here. Bring some o' that soup."

A Red Cross man came in with a vacuum bottle. He went over to the girl and raised her head. She opened her eyes for a moment. Expressionless, they traveled to Perry, to the man who was her husband, and to the man who held her. She drank a little of the hot broth and closed her eyes again. The Red Cross man gave some to Perry, who drank sparingly.

Mary opened her eyes. "Is Alvis all right?" she asked.

Her husband replied "Yup" and then said to the Red Cross man, "We better get her out o' here."

They lifted her across the sill and into the Red Cross barge. In the sunlight Perry noted how blue-black her hair and brows were, and again saw the firm pillars of her neck. He put on his slicker and climbed into the barge too, and they rowed away from the house, Rudscienski following in his boat. There was no wind, and it was warmer. Perry saw high land that had previously been blotted out by the rain, a mile or so away. He heard the sound of a motorboat. It came over to examine them. In it was his friend, the colonel of engineers, and two or three other officers.

"Hey," said the colonel. "So there you are. We've had an alarm out for you. Are you O.K.?"

Perry nodded his head.

"Want a lift?" asked the colonel. "We're going down as far as Owensboro. You can get transportation out there."

Perry nodded again. He was feeling too sick to talk. He drank another cup of broth while the motorboat came alongside, and then, with the help of one of the officers, climbed in. They cast off immediately and headed south. Perry stood up in the boat, propping himself by the gunwale, and tried to call good-by, but his throat was dry and his head swimming. Mary Rudscienski opened her eyes for a moment and saw him. A half-smile visited her mouth for the shadow of a moment and then vanished. Perry waved, and Jan Rudscienski and the Red Cross men waved back. Then the farmhouse came between them.

"For God's sake," said Perry Brown, "has anybody got a drink?"

"Not officially," said the colonel. "Give him the unofficial bottle, Joe."

One of the officers passed Perry a half-full quart bottle of rye whisky. He drank a good third of it and did not remember very much after that.

Once, when he returned to a consciousness that, for a few seconds, was not fraught with memories of Mary Rudscienski, he found himself in bed in a hotel room. A Negro bellboy was standing at his side, gazing at him with large eyes that showed their cream-whites.

"Where am I now?" Perry asked.

"De Acropolis Hotel, Memphis, suh."

"How'd I get here?"

"'Deed, Ah don' know, suh. Yo jus' came here, Ah guess. Ah been takin' care o' you, suh. Yo clothes is all cleaned and pressed, and I had yo underthings washed. Yassuh, boss!"

"Have I eaten anything?"

"Guess so, boss. You et everything Ah been bringin'. Ah been takin' care o' you, boss!"

"Is there any more whisky?"

"Fetch yo some, boss."

While he waited, Perry's eyes wandered about the room. There was a telephone on the bedside table, and a Gideon Bible. A Whistler print hung on the opposite wall. He got up and went to the window and looked out, and was shocked when he saw no limitless expanse of turbid yellow waters with the naked treetops breaking the surface. The street below was crowded and noisy with traffic, cars and trucks, and hurrying people skipping between them. There was a five-and-ten-cent store directly opposite, and for a while he watched the women thronging in and out the doors. The sanity of the familiar store sign and the display of merchandise behind the plate-glass window was healing.

He remembered times in the last few days when he had awakened so full of a nostalgia for something that was gone beyond recapture that there was no fight left in him. Miserable beyond comprehension, he drank quickly, only for the anodyne of unconsciousness. As a boy, Perry had often for a day been haunted by the escaped beauty of a dream. What had happened to him in the flood-bound house had already taken on the quality of a dream, but it still shook him, physically and mentally, beyond bearing. Perry Brown was a reasoning animal, but it was not either with or against reason he was fighting, but against a terrible sense of loss of something that had been beautiful. At times he was half driven to the insane determination to find Mary Rud again, to try to ease the pain by once more pressing his cheek to hers, to feel the softness and sweetness of her mouth, and to close his eyes in the peace of her arms.

But he knew that that really was not his loss. He recognized that he had been in a world to which he could never again return; that he was shut out from it as though what had taken place had occurred on another planet, hundreds of light-years away. It was then that he would drink again.

The view from the window helped. People, cars, policemen, newsboys, stores, and the wholly concrete and soothing display of bottles and paper flowers and cheap glassware and knickknacks in the five-and-ten opposite—this was, after all, a world he had known and loved and could live in. It was still there. With a sudden rush of tenderness and shame he thought of Rusty, with her copper-colored hair and gray-green eyes, and wide mouth with the half-humorous smile. Somewhere, busy, keen, alive, she would be on the trail of a story. When she saw him again, her face would light up with that look he loved, half amused, half tender, and wholly loyal.

He shook himself and went away from the window. The objects in the room no longer looked strange to him. They no longer hurt him. This was where he belonged. He picked up the receiver of the telephone and replaced it again; then lifted it and sent a telegram to the office to send him a hundred dollars.

The bellboy came back with a bottle of whisky. Perry paid him for it and then gave it to him with a ten-dollar bill, saying, "You keep it, son. I don't want it. Beat it. Tell the porter to get me space on the night train for New York."

Three hours later he put on his clothes, paid his bill, and went home.

Did You See the Coronation?

Some stories are timeless and some so dated as to become period pieces, and such a one is "Did You See the Coronation?" which not only goes back to the Coronation of the late King George VI but likewise to the slang current among the debutantes of New York and Chicago a quarter of a century ago and now replaced by "beat" talk, with which I have not yet had time to catch up.

In the spring of 1936 I was on my way to England on the S.S. *Statendam*. During the course of a progressive bridge game in the ship's lounge I encountered two young ladies who, when we introduced ourselves, announced that they were "Two debutantes—from Chicago!"

The way they said it gave an unmistakable importance both to the profession or state of being of debutantism as well as to the fact that they hailed from Chicago, which they seemed to feel made them even more unique and distinctive. They were eighteen and bound for England to spend some time as paying guests in Devonshire, later to be joined by their mothers on the Continent. One was named Jane and her nickname was "Swing," and the other Adair. In the long series I wrote about them which ran in the *Saturday Evening Post* from 1937 to 1945 I kept the name Swing and changed Adair to Audrey.

One was a quiet, dreamy, bookish child, the other a lively, bouncing, merry, and athletic little cricket. And they spoke a jargon such as never before had assailed my ears, a compendium of debutante slang and young thing's idiom full of such aptness, toughness, and gaiety that I was captivated. I just wanted to listen to them talk so that I too might learn this marvelously expressive language that could convey ideas and shades of meaning from which apparently ordinary English-speaking people were quite hopelessly cut off. It had a considerable vocabulary all its own, and eventually they helped me to compile for my own use a kind of debutante dictionary, which was constantly enlarged and added to as new expressions came up.

But there was more to them than glossology, for in addition to superb manners, good breeding, and sweet natures, there was their outlook on life. Daughters of wealthy and prominent families in Chicago, they had made their debuts, or "come out," simultaneously—up to that moment the crowning event in both their lives, to which they had apparently pointed from the cradle. They were clothed and cloaked in debutantehood. They accepted its majesty like training for the throne, which, once achieved, from then on armored them both against all and any troubles, from minor emotional disturbances to major cataclysms that included fire, flood, and earthquake. Their thinking and feeling, everything they did or that happened to them, were seen or evaluated from the point of view of two who had had the great good fortune to be brought up as debutantes—from Chicago. Nothing was impossible to a girl who had gone through that mill, or could be expected to faze her. All life could be rationalized to fit into some compartment of this training. It gave them an impregnable and wholly charming self-assurance.

We met again in Devon, and later in London during the Coronation, and when Audrey's mother joined them in England, they were my guests in Devon for a week, during which time I pursued my studies of their language assiduously, because by this time I knew I wanted to put them into a story just as they were. And "Did You See the Coronation?" was the result.

The plot of the story is pure fiction. No such thing happened, of course, but with Swing and Audrey on the loose in England, it could have happened. The girls and their speech, however, and their outlook upon life and the infectious and sometimes touchingly gallant youthfulness that animates them are, I think, accurately reported. They were always helpful and considerate and breathless and wriggling with zest for life and always about to perish with excitement, I mean absolutely pass out and quietly die from hysterics over whatever was going on or happening to them.

It wasn't until the story was published and the *Post* asked for more that I realized that here was a pair of fiction characters who could be carried on from story to story and whose unique way of looking at life could be used to satirize almost anything that seemed to need it, both in England and in the United States. The decision to use the device of having one of the girls appear as narrator of the goofy events was made for verisimilitude and credibility and enabled me to tell the tale in the queer private language of the young things of that day. I finished the first story before they left Salcombe and read it to them. They corrected some few minor philological errors and then announced that they just couldn't bear it, it was just too divine, they meant absolutely extra-amusing.

My Swing and Audrey are long since married—I went to Swing's wedding in Chicago—and now have grown children of their own, who I suspect when they read this preamble and this story will turn horrified upon their maternal parent and cry, "Oh, Mother, how *could* you be such a square."

As a point of interest to writers, I should reveal that these are what is known as formula stories: that is to say, the preparation, exposition, and narrative and twist at the finish follow a pattern. Incidents, background, characters, plot, and so forth change, but the pattern remains constant.

For the exposition of this formula I shamelessly pinched the opening gambit used by Mary Roberts Rinehart in her wonderful Tish stories— namely, an almost incoherent and scrambled rehearsal of the initial difficulties, plus a forecast of some of the awful things about to happen. This type of opening serves a double purpose. It is a come-on to hook the interest of the reader, and at the same time it serves as a kind of innocent blind in which to bury four or five "plants," ridiculous or innocuous-sounding statements all of which have a later bearing in the story. You encounter the principles of the "plant" nearly every time you go to the theater to see a play. When, for instance, in the first act a character goes over to a desk, opens a drawer, takes out a pistol, examines it to see if it is loaded, replaces it, and closes the drawer, you can be sure that before the evening is over someone is going to be shot with it. It is a cardinal rule of story writing, and one, as I recall, that is taught in all the courses, that the reader must be put into possession of all the facts. You are not permitted to spring surprises on him in the professional league.

It has always seemed to me that a little such technical knowledge would increase the average reader's enjoyment of a story. A skillful plant enhances rather than interferes with the narrative, and it is fun after finishing a story to check back over it and see whether the author has played fair with you throughout. If he hasn't, you are entitled to complain twice—once to the writer and again to the editor who let it go through. That's what editors are for.

DID you see the Coronation? Wasn't it just too snappy for words? It was so divine when that old love of an Archbishop lowered the crown on top of the King's head. I simply wept. I've never been so touched in my life. Swing said the King looked as though he were trying to duck, but then Swing simply hasn't any reverence for anything. She was perfectly furious, and didn't want to come at all first, because they had made Edward abdicate, but then, after all, what was the use of being in England and not seeing the Coronation, especially when it was so easy?

Wasn't it too ridiculous, all the fuss they made about how hard it was to get seats, and all the crowds and everything? Why, we had no trouble at all. Well, practically none, unless you count Swing's getting the hiccups just as the Queen was being crowned, and, of course, being so close—that is, standing right behind her, almost—it was really awful for a moment, until she suddenly caught a glimpse of that perfectly dismal Captain Fizz, and that frightened her so she stopped. Oh, and then, afterward, when Captain Fizz chased us into the Sultan's carriage, it was a little awkward for a moment. I mean it might have been, but the Sultan turned out to be extra-genial, even if he was a dinge. And Swing made such a hit with him when she worked his fly-swatter for him. He wanted to marry her right away. I just had a picture of Swing breaking in on the family in Chicago, with an airy "Hello, darlings: this is the Ambeok of Negotora, Sultan of Amu Penang. We're going to be married." Can't you just see their faces? Oh, and of course Captain Fizz turning out to be who he was was rather fortunate, because our families never would have understood it if we had gone to jail, although the jails are quite different over here, and they never put anything into the papers, even if it's true.

You see, we never would have been at the Coronation at all if Swing weren't such a fiend at bridge, and, of course, I always hold the cards, and that nasty Major Putrington and his wretched wife trying to take advantage of us just because they knew our families had plenty of chips—I mean it served them right—and so, when we did have the chance to buy two tickets for the Abbey cheap, it seemed as if we ought to do it.

And, of course, when Captain Fizz kept trying to put us out, it really wasn't his fault, because he didn't know who we were then, and although it was Swing's idea to take the sandwiches with us, it was mine to give some to the pathetic old gentleman who looked so tired and hungry, and, of course, when he turned out to be the King's uncle, we were almost as surprised as Captain Fizz was. I mean Captain Fizz knew he was the King's uncle, but not that he knew us, and Swing's reaching down and retrieving the Queen's handkerchief helped, too, because when she dropped it, all those stiff English women just stood around with egg on their faces. And now, because the Queen smiled at her, Swing is giving herself airs just as though she had been presented at court, though we could have been if we had wanted to. Perhaps it would be better if I explained everything.

You see, we are debutantes from Chicago.

Swing and I came out together in Chicago. It was the biggest party of the year. We had three floors at the Palmer House. Never saw so many college boys boozed at one time in all my life. Well, after that it was a plenty hectic season; we just had to keep going, and, of course, Swing and I acquired a couple of stooges, awfully nice boys, and we really were more than a little fond of them—I mean we were serious, even though we were only eighteen— and then—well, I mean our families stepped in. So that's how Swing and I came to be parked in Devonshire together for six months to cool off, at Grammorton House, Fenly Moors, Little Downey.

Well, we had been plenty free with the family chips last winter, so we didn't at all mind being put on an allowance. I guess Swing will come into ten or twelve million when she comes of age, but you would never guess it, to be with her, and though Dad isn't exactly a pauper, he has always made me count my pennies. You see, Swing is really Janet Pierce, and Mr. Pierce—Harriman Pierce—is the owner of the Harriman Pierce five-and-ten-cent stores, only I call her Swing, and I am Audrey Westmar, and if you have to look at our pictures in the rotogravure sections all the time, it isn't our fault; we really only came out to please our families, and if you think it is an easy life being a debutante, you just try it some time.

So there we were, sort of under the thumb of Mrs. Grammorton, down in Devon, and it really wasn't so bad, even if we did have to dress for dinner every night, and some of the other guests there were just too peculiar for words; but, of course, there was just no chance of our going up for the Coronation, because we had promised not to exceed our allowance and we knew everything was just frightfully expensive there and we really did want to see England, and it wasn't so bad being away from our stooges, because one good thing about a stooge that's anywhere half decent is that he'll keep. So we really just gave up the idea of the Coronation— that is, until the bridge game.

You see, we used to play bridge after supper with the other guests at Grammorton House, and, of course, we never play for more than sixpence a hundred, and somehow we always found ourselves at a table with Major Putrington and his wife. The major was old and maggoty and all sort of stringy, with a most dreadful wife. Swing said she always looked as though she were getting ready to answer a telegram that had bad news in it. So one night, about a week before the Coronation, the major asked us if we didn't want to increase the stakes, and we thanked him and said no, that we never played for more than ten cents a hundred back home, which was quite true, because once I played for half a cent a point, and Dad heard about it and nearly had a kitten.

Mrs. Grammorton gave us a sickly-sweet smile—Swing said later that it reminded her of eating pomegranates—and said, "We understand here that in America one always plays for very high stakes."

"Well, we don't," said Swing, "because we can't afford it."

"Aha!" laughed the major, just like that. "Aha, aha! Jolly good. Can't afford it. Aha! I say, that's jolly good. It's been so dashed dull here. Thought you might want to stir things up a bit. Can't afford it. Oh, you Americans! Aha! Jolly good!"

I caught the "I-want-to-talk-to-you-alone" signal from Swing and went up to our room. She came up a moment later and said, "How much money have you got?"

I said, "Eight pounds. But it's got to last me until the end of the month."

"Give it to me," said Swing. "I've got seven. That makes fifteen. We'll just have to stay home if we lose it. Our rent's paid here, so we can eat and sleep."

I said, "Oh, Swing, what are you going to do?"

She said, "Play that pair of maggots. They've found out that our families are chip-heavy and they want to take us for expenses. Jolly good sport, milking two eighteen-year-olds. Let's go. And for heaven's sakes, Audrey, no psychics."

"Oh, Swing, I'm nervous."

"You hold them, I'll play them," said Swing. "Anyway, the Putringtons are still playing out of the book we threw away three years ago. Am I ever glad I was educated as a debutante."

When we came back, Swing said sweetly—she has beautiful manners—"So sorry we kept you waiting. What stakes would you like to play for?"

"Eh? Eh?" said the major. "Oh, I say, that's jolly good. London Club stakes. Pound a hundred suit you?"

I nearly fainted, but Swing said calmly, "That's fine. Shall we cut for deal?"

Swing is a very deceptive bridge player. She looks as if she had no interest in the game at all, or were thinking of something else, or were half asleep. She is a tall, quiet girl with lots of dark hair and a faraway look in her eyes, and when someone bids, it always seems to startle her, but that doesn't fool anybody in our crowd in Chicago any more. But, you see, it completely fooled the Putringtons.

So you see that was how we got the money to go to the Coronation. Mrs. Grammorton always makes everyone stop playing at midnight, because all the lights go out then, and the major had to give us forty-seven pounds, mostly because once Swing woke up out of what seemed to be a sound sleep, not having said anything but "Pass," and doubled their two no-trump bid, caught them with a weak suit, smelled out my strength, and set them 1,400. When Mrs. Grammorton found out the next day what had happened, she was plenty annoyed, and the major and his wife had to leave.

Mrs. Grammorton put her foot down first at our going to the Coronation alone. You see, being English, she doesn't understand that American girls, especially debutantes, are different and can go anywhere by themselves; so we told her we had relatives in London, which was true, except that we weren't going to look them up, because, as Swing said, what was the fun of going to the Coronation if you went with relatives; so she finally relented and said we could go. We called up the Harriman Pierce Stores representative in London and he got us a wonderful room in a lovely old house off Hanover Square. We rode up to London in a third-class carriage and took our lunches with us to save chips, as we figured whatever of Major Putrington's money we didn't spend on the Coronation we would use for shopping.

Of course, nobody could get inside the Abbey without an invitation, and the most we hoped for was to wait until the last minute and then try to buy a cheap seat in a window somewhere to see the procession, and Swing said from some of those windows that had grandstand seats in them we ought to be able to see the plumes in the hats as they went by, if they were tall enough, and why didn't we wait and save our money, and then go to the circus when we got back home.

We tried all over, but the good seats were all $60 apiece and the cheap ones $25 each, and when we thought of the tailored suits we could get in New Bond Street for that, we simply couldn't make up our minds what to do. So when the nice young Englishman we met at lunch at Quaglino's offered to sell us two seats inside the

Abbey for £6 each, which is $60 for both, it sounded plenty good to us. Of course, we didn't actually meet him. I mean he was sitting at the next table and spoke to us after a while. Of course, we don't speak to strange men unless they are obviously college boys and not too tight, but Englishmen are different and all sort of quite harmless.

So, when this man at the next table smiled and said, "You young American ladies are over for the Coronation, I take it," it seemed perfectly all right, so I told him we were, and when he asked whether we had our seats, I explained just how things were to him; he was really very nice, with sort of sandy hair and pale blue eyes and not much chin, but then, all the Englishmen with chins are put right into the Army or the Navy. So then he said, "How would you like to sit right inside Westminster Abbey?" So I said, "That would be plenty good. Can it be done?"

He said he had two tickets and he couldn't go, but inasmuch as we had none, he would be glad to sell them to us for a small sum. He said he would give them to us, except that they belonged to a friend who wanted to get rid of them. Of course we asked to see them, and he explained that he couldn't show them to us there, because in England it was a very great crime to sell tickets to the Abbey, and there were so many people about, but if we would walk a little ways with him, he would show them to us. Swing kicked me and said, "It sounds like a gyp," but I kicked her back and said, "Shut up: he hasn't got our money yet."

So we left Quaglino's with him and walked down Bury Street toward St. James's, and after a while he showed them to us, and even Swing had to admit that she was wrong, because they really were two tickets for Westminster Abbey, and they had the crown on them and everything, and the name of the King, George, with his number after it. They were really extra-official, engraved in gold. So we paid him, and he thanked us and jumped into a taxi and drove away. He really was very nice.

Well, we were simply so excited to think we were really going to be inside the Abbey for the Coronation, until Swing suddenly remembered about clothes, and, of course, we didn't have any court dresses, but, luckily, we had brought our white evening dresses up to London just in case we should meet anyone who would ask us out, and I said we could go to Selfridge's and buy some white elbow gloves and some white feathers to put in our hair, and Swing said that you didn't wear feathers to a Coronation, you wore tiaras; feathers were for presentations; so we had a fight about that, but we finally bought a pair of rhinestone tiaras and a few odds and ends, and then we got all the papers and read the instructions, and found that we would have to get up at half past five in order to be at the Abbey at six thirty in the morning, and Swing said that that was a lot of nonsense, that the ceremony didn't begin until half past ten, and she wasn't going to get there until nine o'clock, which was early enough.

I said that the papers warned that nobody would be allowed through after seven o'clock, but Swing said that with those tickets we had we ought to be able not only to get through but to sit next to Queen Mary, which was funny, because the way it turned out, it was Elizabeth we were next to, and not Mary, and she is a lamb, and just as sweet as she can be, and I wished we could have given her some of our sandwiches, poor dear; she did look so hungry.

Oh, yes, I almost forgot about the sandwiches. You see, it said in the papers that guests in the Abbey would have to go eight or nine hours without eating, and of course Swing just hates to go more than three hours without a bite, and so we made up some sandwiches to take along, and then found we didn't have any place to put them, because we weren't taking any bags or anything, and I said we couldn't walk into Westminster Abbey carrying our lunch, and Swing said she wouldn't mind carrying her lunch and a bottle of beer, if they didn't mind, and then I saw her looking at my dress in a very strange way, and that solved it, you see, because although it was a very simple dress, it had two panniers of white satin at the side, and so we just cut the panniers open and put two sandwiches on either side and basted them up again, and it really didn't hurt the dress at all—in fact, it helped it a little, making it sort of old-fashioned, like a bustle.

I wanted to start early, the morning of the Coronation, but Swing said that was silly, that they just said that to frighten people and that we should be there in plenty of time, and so we didn't get up until eight o'clock and put on our white evening gowns, and, of course, no make-up at all, because it would have looked just too horrible in daylight, and our tiaras really were quite stunning; and so we left the house at a quarter to nine and found one of those funny little taxis cruising around—only this was an antique, and plenty decrepit; Swing said she was sure it had been used for Queen Victoria's Coronation—and we got in and told the driver to take us to Westminster Abbey.

He gave us a very funny look, though I'm sure it wasn't because of the way we were dressed, because people in England wear evening dress at some of the oddest hours, and then he said, "Will I drive you right up to the haltar, miss?"

We said no, just to take us around to the front entrance. Then he climbed down from his seat and came and opened the door and looked at us for a moment, and shook his head and climbed back into the seat. He said we would be lucky if he got to within a mile of the Abbey, and then he started the machine's one lung and we drove off.

We seemed to be driving around for a long while, and all of a sudden we came down a narrow street and up behind a crowd and stopped. We told him not to stop, but to go right on, and when he said, "Yes, miss, will I go hover or hunder the people?" Swing told him not to be a bore, but to blow his horn, because we had tickets, and it startled him so that he did, and a policeman came over and said, "Here, here, what's all this? Going to the Coronation, Bertie? Didn't you read the regulations? Come on, out of it now, quickly."

Swing said, "Tell him we're debutantes," but I let down the window of the cab and showed the policeman our tickets. He looked at them for a long time as though he were completely baffled, and even took off his helmet and scratched his head, and then put his helmet back on again before he said, "Well, now, young misses, I've seen a lot of queer ones in my day, but this beats them all. Did you buy these tickets?"

I told him we had and had paid £6 for them, and wanted to go through because we were late for the Coronation, and would he please fix it so our driver could go ahead?

At that he gave us a most dismal smile and said, "Well, now, young misses, I am very sorry, but I am afraid you have been took in. You cannot go through here with those tickets, and the reason you cannot go though is—"

Well, we never found out what the reason was—at least not then—because at that moment there was a terrific honking in back of us from an enormous limousine that seemed to have pulled up behind us, and a voice shouted, "Here, here, Jenks! What's all this? Clear the way here! This car must get through!"

The voice came from another policeman, only he was older and had a mustache and more stripes than our policeman.

Our policeman saluted and said, "Sorry, sergeant. I was just explaining to these here two young ladies as how they couldn't go through because—"

"Never mind the two young ladies, Jenks! Come, come, show some life! His Grace's car must be let through! Lively now! Get that taxi out of there!"

Well, there was no room to turn around, so the policeman opened up a way through the crowd and waved us on through, saying to the driver, "Hup, go on, Bertie. And see that you turn off inside, or I'll have your license."

So that is how we got through into the Coronation area, except that Bertie—if that was our driver's name—couldn't turn off when he got inside, because we were on a sort of a circle, or circus, as they call them in London, and another big limousine with a crest on the door shot out from the side and got in front of him and the big one in back of us closed in behind, and there we were, in a sort of procession of big cars. I asked Bertie which way we were going, and he said, "To the Abbey, miss. I can't turn off now. I'm caught."

"Well," I said, "that's where we wanted to go in the first place."

"I wonder what's the matter with our tickets," Swing said.

I said, "Nothing. You'll see! The policeman was just being difficult. They all are."

So that's how we got to the Abbey, and it was perfectly simple, and when we got there, our taxi had to wait in line while the people got out; and I must say, I never saw so many beautiful uniforms in all my life. Swing said they all looked like lion-tamers. And finally our taxi drew up to the little side door and we got out, and while Swing paid Bertie, I got out our tickets, and then we went up to the door, and there were two attendants there in sort of medieval costumes, and one perfectly stunning man in the most gorgeous uniform, with gold lace and a lot of medals on his chest and a red band around his hat and a short mustache and the most perfect white gloves; so we showed them our tickets and just prepared to sweep on by, when the two attendants stopped us, and they called to the stunning creature, and he came over and had a look at our tickets, and first he got red in the face and then he began to fizz in the strangest way, just like something boiling over, and he gave Swing and me an awfully black look and finally said:

"I say, look here. You know, you can't do this."

"Can't do what?" said Swing. "We're not doing anything. We're just going to the Coronation."

The man fizzed again, and got quite purple before he said, "No, you're not! What dashed cheek! Americans, I'll wager!"

I said, "Certainly we're Americans. We're debutantes from Chicago. And we have our tickets for the Coronation, and we want to go in. I know we're a little late, but you needn't be so fussy about that. So are a lot of other people."

"Late? Late? I should think you are late. Dashed insolence. Look here. You'll have to go right away. Those tickets are no good at all."

Swing whispered, "Oh, oh. I knew there was something peculiar about that man."

But I wasn't going to go away without an argument, so I said, "Oh, yes, they are. We paid six pounds apiece for them. How dare you say they're no good when they have the crown and everything on them, and the name of the King and the Abbey?"

Well, this time the man really fizzed. He was so mad—you see that's why Swing and I named him Captain Fizz—and then he took the tickets and held them in front of us and said, "Can either of you young ladies, by any chance, read?" So, of course, we told him we could, and then he said, "Well, then, would you oblige me by reading this"—and he pointed with his finger. So I read out, "Coronation of His Majesty George—"

"Yes, go on," said Captain Fizz. "And what comes after that?"

"Why a—a five," I said. "George the Fifth. What's wrong with that?"

"Oh, I say," said the captain, after having fizzed terrifically. "What's wrong with that? Oh, nothing, except that this is the Coronation of George the Sixth. That ticket was good twenty-six years ago, but not today."

"Oh, come," said Swing. "Don't be a boor. What difference does it make? It's almost George the Sixth. And, besides, we paid for them."

"Can't be helped," said the captain, fizzing frightfully. "You must go right away from here, or I shall have to call a policeman. Look here, now; you're holding up all these people. . . . Oh, I say; now you have done it!"

You see, he had turned around to see who was waiting. And of course it was the people who had been in the huge limousine right behind us, and the man was sort of tall and grayish, and really wearing a most wonderful uniform, and as soon as he saw him, poor Captain Fizz turned quite red and straightened up and gave him the most intense salute, and the two attendants at the door who had sort of things like boat hooks in their hands, they got quite rigid and presented their boat hooks, and so, while they were saluting, Swing and I just walked on in, because, after all, it wasn't our fault they had put the number of the wrong George on the ticket, and, as Swing said later, if it had been King Edward, as it should have been, that never could have happened, and anyway we had paid for the tickets, and just because our families have plenty of chips is no reason why we should simply throw money away.

So, you see, that's how we got into the Abbey, and it really was quite easy, and I could never understand why people made such a fuss about how difficult it was, because there we were, inside with the wrong tickets, and I'm sure we could have got in just as easily with no tickets at all.

Swing said we'd better find seats right away, so we started looking for some; but of course the Abbey was simply jammed—I mean I never saw so many people—and of course it was the most glamorous sight, and most of the time we just stood around and stared like a couple of goops at all the robes and the ermine and the jewelry, and every time we would get settled somewhere, someone in a different kind of uniform would come along and make us move out; really, I never felt so hunted in my life. We held on to our tickets, but we wouldn't let anybody see more than a little bit of them, for fear they would notice they were for the wrong Coronation.

And then, of course, we got lost in the Abbey; it's the most tremendous place you ever saw and just full of tombs, and we kept wandering around and hiding behind them whenever we saw anyone with a uniform who looked like an official, and finally we thought we saw an aisle leading down to a place that seemed to have some empty seats, and we thought maybe the people who had the seats wouldn't come, and anyway, if they did, we would be there first, because, you see, it was getting late, so we fairly whipped down the aisle and ran straight into Captain Fizz. I was simply terrified.

Well, you see, we had no way of knowing that the seats we had seen were the ones the King and Queen and the peers and things were going to sit in until they were crowned, or, of course, we never should have gone near the place, and all of a sudden there we were, surrounded by archbishops and things, and poor Captain Fizz was quite purple with rage, and we knew he was about to do something dreadful to us, because, really, I have never seen a man so mad in all my life; so we turned and streaked, only, in the excitement, we ran the wrong way, with Captain Fizz and a lot of men who looked like butlers or footmen after us, and just then the organ began to play and then a lot of people in costume came walking up the aisle where we were.

First there were three sorts of heralds, right out of *Alice in Wonderland,* and then some men in the most beautiful costumes, carrying a lot of jewelry, and, of course, we would have recognized the Queen, even if there hadn't been six sort of butlers holding up her train, and all the little boys up in the gallery simply screaming, *"Vivat Regina Elizabeth!"* at the top of their lungs, and a lot of women walking behind her, and maids of honor in white dresses and tiaras. You see, we had walked right into the Queen's procession, and there was the captain right behind us, fizzing most horribly.

Well, everyone was giving us grim looks, and the captain had turned absolutely violet when Swing, who wasn't a bit upset—she never gets upset, which, I guess, is another good thing about the training of a debutante—said to Captain Fizz, "Calm down now, and tell us what you want us to do, and we'll do it. If you hadn't hunted us so, this wouldn't have happened."

Well, the captain's eyes simply started from his head, and the procession was practically on top of us when he found his voice and whispered, "Fall in. For God's sake, fall in or I'm ruined."

Swing grabbed my hand, and before I knew what was happening, we were walking in the procession with the maids of honor, and it was all done so quickly that nobody really knew what had happened. I whispered to Swing, "Swing, my knees are knocking together so hard I'm sure everybody can hear it," and Swing whispered back, "Shut up and keep going. We'll just do what they do. It looks as though we were going to have a good seat for this Coronation." And later she whispered, "Don't look now, but I think the King is walking right in back of us."

Well, of course, we didn't really have a seat at all, because the ladies-in-waiting and maids of honor don't sit, but stand up around the Queen on either side; but, of course, we didn't mind standing a bit, because, you see, we were right where the Coronation was happening, and Queen Mary was sitting in a sort of a box with a lot of people right behind us, looking really royal. Somehow, when we were all arranged, we were standing almost next to Queen Elizabeth, who seemed to be a swell person, and she wasn't a bit nervous, and I was getting over being frightened, except that I whispered to Swing, "If anyone starts counting maids of honor, we're lost," and Swing said, "No one's going to start counting, but if anyone looks at our feet, we're sunk."

Well, of course, English girls have got the most tremendous feet, poor dears, and the maids of honor, who, we later found out, were all peeresses, seemed to have really extra large ones, so Swing and I hid ours under our dresses as best we could, and then the King came along with his glittering procession and his butlers, and I must say I have never seen butlers dressed so beautifully, and, of course, there were the crown jewels, right out of the Tower, close enough for us to touch.

So, you see, that explains how we got right up close to the Coronation; I mean if we had got any closer we would have been the Coronation, and somehow, just before the ceremony started, Captain Fizz managed to slip behind us and fizz, "I'll see you in quod for this. And if you make any kind of slip, dashed if I won't strangle you both."

Swing whispered, "Don't be silly. Compared to the reception line at a debutante tea in Chicago, this is easy."

Well, I was never so impressed with anything in my life as the way that lamb of a King—I think he is much more attractive than Edward—went through all the things they made him do. I mean they were always taking clothes off him and putting others on him, and praying over him, and giving him things to hold and then taking them away from him again before he could really ever get a look at them; and I suppose if he ever really wants to see the crown jewels, he'll have to go to the Jewel Tower and look at them there, because he would hardly get his hands on anything before some dear old Archbishop would dash up and remove it and give it to someone else, and then all of a sudden they handed him a whole lot of things at once, and I honestly never felt so sorry for anyone in my whole life, because he had a golden ball with a cross on it in one hand, and a scepter in the other, and something else in his lap. Swing said the poor man looked exactly like a college boy at a tea party, trying to balance a plate on his knee, with a teacup in one hand and a sandwich in the other.

Then the Archbishop took a sort of golden duck and unscrewed his neck—or maybe that happened before—I mean there was so much happened—and poured some oil out on a golden spoon, and for a moment I thought he was going to give it to the poor King, who looked as though he was ready to submit to just anything, but instead he just dipped his finger in it and made his mark on the King.

Oh, and I almost forgot the part where the Archbishop introduced the King to everybody in the Abbey on all four sides, and everyone shouted, "Long live the King!" and trumpets sounded and I just had shivers all up and down my spine.

It was while the Archbishop was fussing with the crown before putting it on the King—the poor old thing was so nervous it almost slipped—the crown, I mean—that the Queen dropped her handkerchief. Those English girls just stood there and looked at it, or were watching the Coronation; so Swing, who was nearest, picked it up and gave it to her and made her a little curtsy—one she had learned from a French governess when she was just a child—and the Queen gave her the sweetest smile, although right after it I could see she was looking a little puzzled, poor dear. I mean, after all, she was sure she knew all the maids of honor, and there we were, you see; but in the sort of glittery light in the Abbey, our tiaras looked just as real as the others, and I thought I heard the captain fizzing a little.

Well, then there was a lot more ceremony and praying, and I really thought it would never end, and it was really very touching to see the lords paying homage to the King, and while it was all going on, I noticed a really wonderful-looking man in the most gorgeous uniform, standing right near us, and he had all kinds of glittering stars on his chest and things hung around his neck, and I recognized the gentleman who had been behind us when we entered the Abbey, only he was looking sort of pale and worn and terribly tired, and once I thought he seemed to sway a little, and so I whispered and asked him if he was all right, and he said, "Oh, yes, quite. Quite all right, my dear."

But he wasn't at all, and I had a sudden inspiration and said, "Are you hungry?"

He whispered, "Starved, my child. Been up all night, you know. Forgot to eat. Silly of me."

"Would you care for a sandwich?"

"Would I care for a sandwich? Good Lord, child, you don't mean to tell me you have a sandwich?"

So I kicked Swing a little, and she gave me the pin she had brought along for the purpose, and I picked the threads of one of the panniers in my dress and got it open and sneaked him a cheese sandwich all nicely done up in waxed paper, and he almost swooned when he felt it in his hand, and then he sort of backed around behind a pillar, and when he returned he was looking much better, and he whispered, "God bless you, my child. I don't know who you are, but you are obviously an angel dispatched by Heaven. I say, might I send a friend? Poor Crommartin is worse off than I was. Would you have another?"

I said by all means, and when he wanted to know how we would recognize the friend, Swing said out of the corner of her mouth, "Tell him to say you said he was O.K."

So after a while a tall, thin man, in really the most gorgeous velvet cloak I've ever seen, backed over and said, "One, two, three, four, five from the end. Righto, the little one with the light brown hair. I say, my dear, Buckminster said I was O.K."

So we gave him a sandwich, and he hardly waited to get behind a pillar to eat it, poor dear, he was so hungry; and, of course, he had a friend; so we fed all we could, until our sandwiches were gone, and one of them had to do homage to the King, and he knelt there for the longest time, and everybody thought he was trying to swallow his emotion, but he wasn't, he was trying to swallow the last of our sandwich before he spoke his piece, and I was so nervous for fear he wouldn't get it down, I nearly died.

Well, they finally got around to crowning the Queen, and I was simply petrified I'd do the wrong thing, but we just watched the other maids of honor—I mean the real ones—and did what they did and stood where they stood, and there really wasn't anything for us to do, because there were four peeresses who held a sort of a gold awning over her, though Swing and I were ready to step in and grab it if they dropped it, because they didn't look any too certain, the way they held it, and really the whole thing went off beautifully, except just as that love of an Archbishop of Canterbury put the ring on the Queen's finger and started to say, "Receive this ring, the seal of a sincere faith—" Swing got the hiccups, and the Archbishop turned right around and looked at her, and it frightened Swing, but not enough.

Well, just as the Archbishop went to take the crown off the altar to crown the Queen, there was the most awful silence in the Abbey —I mean you couldn't hear anything except, of course, Swing's hiccup—and I'm sure it was the most awful moment of my life, except one night at a hockey game in Chicago when a Yale boy in our party fell right out of our box onto the ice, and both teams skated right over him, and Captain Fizz had evidently made up his mind to end it all and kill Swing first, because I saw him sidling toward us, around in back, with murder in his eye, and, luckily, Swing saw him, too, and it frightened her so she stopped the hiccups, and the Archbishop crowned the Queen.

So after the Coronation part was over and the procession

re-formed, we thought perhaps we had better not go with them any more, so we just went part of the way to where we had met them in the first place, and then cut down one of the cross aisles, because we had seen a door at the end of it; only we weren't quite fast enough, because Swing's heel got caught in her dress and nearly threw her, and Captain Fizz came after us, and we could see that he was still simply furious, so we just picked up our skirts and ran as fast as we could, with Captain Fizz right in back of us, and we did get through the door and out into the street, but there were soldiers on either side, forming a lane, and police behind them, so we couldn't turn off; and Captain Fizz was fizzing and breathing right on our necks, and there was a carriage drawn up at the door, and we were so absolutely panic-stricken we just ran to it and opened the door and jumped in, just as Captain Fizz said, "Got you!" Only he hadn't.

Because, you see, there was this enormous dinge sitting in the carriage—I mean he was really very handsome—and he was dressed in the most beautiful golden cloak I've ever seen in my life, and he had a gold thing sort of like a pagoda on his head, and gold chains around his neck, and a lot of stars and medals besides, and when Captain Fizz yanked open the door of the carriage, he leaned forward and said in just the softest voice:

"Iss something wrong?"

Well, I've never seen anything in my whole life like the look on poor Captain Fizz's face, he was simply mauve with wrath, but he had to step back and salute, and while he was saluting and saying, "I beg your pardon, Your Highness," the carriage drove off.

So that was how we saw the procession after the Coronation. I mean that is how we were in the procession, because we really were, because we were in the carriage of the Ambeok of Negotora, Sultan of Amu Penang, and, of course, he was a savage, though he spoke the most wonderful English, because he had been educated at Oxford; but he was a perfect dear, and he said he was so glad to see us, because he had thought he was going to have to take that long ride over the Coronation route all by himself, and

wouldn't think of us leaving, and he told us all about himself and
all his wives and his jewels, and it was such a relief really to find
someone who had more chips than our families, and we told him
all about Chicago and being debutantes, and about our parties, and
he was quite fascinated, and said he would like to come to Chicago
sometime and visit us, and Swing said: "Yes, do," and he had a
golden stick with a sort of a fringe and little golden tassels on the
end of it, and it seems it was his royal fly-swatter, and Swing offered
to work it for him, and he was so pleased, not that there were any
flies, but he was used to being where there were and just liked to
have it worked anyway.

The streets were just packed with people, and when we drove
down the Embankment past thousands and thousands of school
children, they all cheered, and the Ambeok taught us how to bow
to the plaudits of the multitude. Really we've never made such a
hit—I mean even our families would have been proud of us if they
could have seen—and we were just hoping that some of our Chicago friends would recognize us—I mean we really had something
there, what with the Ambeok grinning and bowing, and Swing
patting him on the neck every so often with the royal fly-swatter,
and me waving graciously—they simply would have died.

We were a great success on Oxford Street and at the Marble
Arch, and going through Hyde Park I suggested to Swing if she
didn't feel we ought to be thinking about going soon, because we
were headed right back toward Buckingham Palace, where we were
almost sure to run into Captain Fizz, who obviously didn't like us,
and maybe the Sultan could drop us off somewhere and we would
get a taxi home; but Swing was having such fun working the fly-
swatter and improving her technique—she said she was just beginning to develop a backhand—that she simply wouldn't think of it,
so we kept right on, and going through the arch on Constitution
Hill, the Sultan asked Swing to marry him and promised to make
her his number-one wife, and Swing, who is a dreamy sort of girl,
said she would consider it, and then the dear, who was really so
polite, asked me to marry him, too, so that we could go on being
together and teach his women how to be debutantes.

Anyway, we promised to look him up at the Savoy, where he was stopping, and have a glass of sherry with him, and the carriage stopped at Buckingham Palace, and we said good-by and he went inside, and there we were on the sidewalk and no taxi in sight, just as we walked right into the arms of Captain Fizz.

I nearly died. He fizzed furiously for a moment, and then took us each by the arm, saying, "Aha! Dashed well knew I'd find you. Unauthorized presence in the Abbey. Interfering with the Coronation. You won't get away this time."

"We didn't interfere," said Swing. "We helped. Stop pinching."

"Not pinching," said Captain Fizz. "Going to turn you over to a policeman. Dashed cheek. Just like Americans."

"I'm going to trip him," Swing whispered to me. "You run." But before she could do it, another state coach drew up and stopped, and the handsome gray-haired man to whom we had fed the sandwich stepped out. He saw us and came right over and said, "I say, Fitzwarrine, what's all this?"

Swing whispered, "I knew his name would have something with a fizz in it."

The captain didn't salute this time. But he straightened up and said, "Caught them, Your Grace. Unauthorized entry into the Abbey. Joining in the Coronation procession. Interfering with the Coronation. Going to hand them over to the police. Teach these dashed Americans a lesson. Can't come over here and mix in our Coronation. We don't go over there and join in their Inauguration."

The old gentleman addressed as "Your Grace" looked at us for a moment and then said, "They're angels, Fitzwarrine. There's been some mistake. They're angels. They gave me a sandwich when I was starving. Crommartin had one, too, and Trevelyan. . . . You haven't another one, have you?" This last he said to me.

Fitzwarrine fizzed a little and then said, "Sorry, sir. Duty. Unauthorized presence in the Abbey. False ticket. Dangerous characters, probably. No other alternative but to hand them over."

The nice old gentleman looked at us again, and smiled and said, "My dears, who are you?"

I said, "We're debutantes from Chicago."

"I'm Janet Pierce," said Swing, "and this is Audrey Westmar. And you can send us both to jail if you want to, and we'll tell how we were swindled trying to buy a ticket to the Coronation. And I want to notify the London office of Harriman Pierce Stores."

"Eh?" said Fitzwarrine. "Eh? Harriman Pierce? Oh, I say. Not Harriman Pierce's daughter. Oh, I say, how awkward! How very awkward!"

"Very awkward for you!" said the old gentleman, who seemed to be enjoying something, to Fitzwarrine.

"I say," said Fitzwarrine. "Now I'm dashed if I know what to do. Most embarrassing. Duty and all that. Unauthorized presence in Abbey. Ought to hand you over."

"Well," said Swing, who has an uncanny way of knowing when she is going to come out on top, "why don't you?"

"It's all very well to say why don't you," said Fitzwarrine, "but it puts me in a dashed peculiar position. You see, I'm Lord Eilton."

Well, of course, as soon as he said that, I knew we had something, because Swing knows an awful lot about her father's business, and Lord Eilton was the chairman of the board of the English subsidiary of the Harriman Pierce Stores, and, besides, he owned several large factories in Manchester and the Harriman Pierce Stores bought just scads of things from him.

So then the nice old gentleman we had fed in the Abbey turned out to be the Duke of Buckminster, the King's uncle, and a perfect darling, and he finally said, "See here, Fitzwarrine, supposing I post-authorize the presence of these two young ladies in the Abbey. Will that relieve you? Blessed if I ever want to have a Coronation again without them. . . . You're sure you haven't another sandwich anywhere about you, my dear?"

Well, that just fixed everything, and Captain Fizz—I mean Lord Eilton—was plenty relieved, and he really is a love when you get to know him and he hasn't got a Coronation on his mind, because it turned out he was something dreadfully official at this one, and he took us through the lines and got us a car and sent us home, but not before he invited us to be in his box at the Coronation Ball at Albert Hall the next evening and talked a lot about hands across the sea, and I am sure he is going to ask Swing to marry him—everybody does—and if he does, I hope she'll tell him she's engaged to the Ambeok of Negotara, Sultan of Amu Penang, but anyway, I've never met so many sweet people in all my life, and we did see the Coronation for practically nothing and with no trouble at all, and yet a lot of people we met afterward told us they couldn't even get near to see the procession.

The Roman Kid

Back in 1933 the *Daily News* sent me to Rome to negotiate with the Italian Government of Benito Mussolini for a team of Italian amateur boxers to come to the United States and fight our New York Golden Gloves team in an international match at the Yankee Stadium.

The party big shots kept me cooling my heels for weeks while trying to make up their minds whether the Fascist State could afford to let the representatives of the new Italian Empire be mussed up by a gang of degenerate New York democrats. While waiting, I used my spare time to do some research in libraries and museums and at the American Academy to see if I could find out what was actually known about sports in ancient Rome.

During this time I met Professor Prentice Duell, the brilliant Harvard archaeologist, who was likewise living at the Hotel Ambasciatori, and we formed a lasting friendship. When you read "Professor" and "Harvard archaeologist," don't get a picture of an old crock with a long white beard. This was a tough young guy. I admired him a lot and he guided me in my research work.

He took me to Tarquinia to see the frescoes on the walls of the Etruscan tombs, to the Colosseum and the Forum Romano, and one day he suggested we go to the Museo delle Terme in Rome, near the old thermal baths, to look at the recently exhumed statue known as the *Sitting Boxer*.

This proved to be a life-size bronze of an ancient bearded Roman gladiator, a boxer, his hands armed with the lethal iron cesti, the Roman version of the boxing glove, which were laced to his hands with bronze reproductions of the leather thongs that crisscrossed his forearms to the elbow. He was seated and there were wounds to be seen, extraordinarily vivid delineations of the wear and tear that comes to a fighter during the course of a rough evening.

Saturday Evening Post, June 11, 1938.

There was little Prentice could tell me about this work; in fact, very little at all was known about it at the time. He said that it was quite obvious that the sculptor had sketched the fighter in his dressing room after his match and that also possibly the figure might have been one of a group, with several others present, perhaps the patron of the show or the lanista or owner of the stable of gladiators to which the boxer belonged. But nothing was known at the time as to either the subject or the artist. It was not until years later that the signature of the latter was thought to be recognized, concealed in the thongs of the cestus.

Now, to a sports editor and veteran boxing writer who had seen many hundreds of professional and amateur fights and boxing matches, the statue and the condition of the old pugil's face and arms and body spoke volumes. Every muscle, his attitude, his hands, the battered ears, and the marks on his features told their story, a story that anyone who had spent as many hours as I at the ringside and in the dressing-rooms of fighters before and after matches could read.

For days I had been sitting literally at Duell's feet, popeyed at his erudition and knowledge of antiquity, drinking in the wisdom he had excavated from the ages. Now for the first time I was confronted with a situation where I knew a lot of things he didn't know, and the temptation to show off to him a little was too great to resist. With somewhat studied casualness I said:

"Well, now, I can't tell you anything about the period to which it belongs or the artist who made it, but I can tell you a little about the big guy himself, what he was like and how he fought, and maybe even something about the chap who mussed him up."

Then I proceeded to do so with excellent results, for now Prentice's eyes bugged; he was the impressed student and I the erudite professor, for a moment anyway, expounding the deeply scientific lore of scrambling ears. I was tremendously impressed with myself and we had to hurry back to the Ambasciatori and have a drink on the strength of it down in the bar. After a couple of drinks Prentice allowed as how by God he'd put me and my exposition of the *Sitting Boxer* into an archaeological book someday. I said, by God, I'd put him into a book someday too, and we had another old-fashioned. Professor Duell told me the other day that he had got around to keeping his promise. Well, by God, so have I. Bartender, another old-fashioned.

It wasn't until five years later, while I was working as a feature writer for International News Service and wanted passage money to get back to England in the spring, that I thought of using the idea of the *Sitting Boxer* in a short story.

It's queer what things come out when you set out to put an idea into story framework. The hero, Tommy Thompson, the sports writer who works for the *Daily Blade,* is obviously autobiographical. But physically I made him into the late Eddie Neale, a sports writer for the Associated Press, for whom I had a great liking and admiration. He quit the sports-writing game to go to Spain as a war correspondent and was killed by a shell while reporting the Civil War, the first of many famous newspaper writers to die in this fashion. I envied Eddie when he left on his assignment. I was saddened when he was killed.

But for the rest I certainly used myself as a model, and in searching for a means of telling my adventure in the Museo delle Terme, fixed on the boy-meets-girl-must-win-her-from-villain cliché. It bothers me now and it bothered me then, so much so that I tried to take the curse off it by kidding the cliché during the telling of the story. But strangely it seemed to bother no one else.

Why did I do it? Just pure bad editorial judgment, I should say, because no editor asked me to write it that way. I discussed the background of the story with Stuart Rose, *Post* associate editor, in Harold Ober's office, and he was excited about the idea, but made no suggestions as to how I should write it. The boy-girl, young love story was wholly my conception of what the *Saturday Evening Post* wanted. True, the *Post* bought it, but it might also have published it had I cast the idea in a more original frame. This type of self-editing is bad, and comes from being a greedy-guts and wanting to sell. One outgrows that too.

In 1945 "The Roman Kid," to my surprise and pleasure, was included by Anthony Boucher in his anthology *Great American Detective Stories,* where it enjoyed considerable success. It never dawned on me that I had written a deductive detective story.

B on *giorno,*" said Tommy Thompson. *"Ubi est* the—" he paused and then concluded that he had made sufficient concession to what he thought was the Italian language, and finished, "Could a guy take a gander at the Tertullian Fragment?"

The girl at the desk of the Antiquity Room of the Museo Romano flinched a little and then cocked her bright head to one side and repeated slowly, with a reflective pause after each word, "Could —a—guy—take—a—gander—guy—take—gander. Gander is the male of goose." She stopped and looked at Tommy with the corners of her mouth drawn down and a sort of despair in her eyes.

Tommy suddenly realized that she had a face of infinite humor, and that the humor somehow managed to disguise its beauty, or rather made you less conscious of it. Unlike the Italian women to whom he had already grown accustomed during his short sojourn in Rome, she had masses of soft hair, the color of early morning sunlight, large light-blue eyes, and a small nose. But Tommy felt that here was a person with whom one instinctively wanted to laugh. So he laughed.

"Excuse it, please," he said. "Maybe I ought to talk English. My Italian is terrible. I wanted to get a squint at that fragment of manuscript by the first Roman boxing writer. I read a piece about it in the Paris *Herald*. They're supposed just to have dug it up and it's the only existing description of an early boxing match. Some Greek fed a Roman plenty of left hands and stopped him. . . ."

The girl shook her head and said plaintively, "Why did they not teach to me the right kind of English?" Her mouth was thin, wide, mobile, and slightly pathetic. She was tiny and dressed in a long, blue smock. "I have taken very high marks in English, but it is the wrong kind. You are an American. Are you an archaeologist?"

"Who, me? Jiminy, no." Tommy grinned again. He was a pleasant-looking man in his late twenties with a broad, wide-open face and a strange two-inch patch of gray that ran through his dark hair from front to back. "I'm a sports writer. You know—boxing, baseball, and stuff. I do a column on the *Blade* in New York. But I'm a sucker for this ancient history. I'm supposed to be digging up a team of Italian amateur boxers to take back to fight our Golden Glovers, but I've been spending most of my time trying to find out what sports were like in ancient Rome. Very tough. If they had any columnists in those days, they buried 'em deep."

The girl gazed at him, her face alive with intense interest. Finally she said flatly, "Americans are wonderful people. Come. I show you."

She led him down an aisle between massive bronzes and pieces of ancient frescoes to a small alcove where there was a little pedestal holding up a flat glass frame. Under the glass was a small triangle of stained brown manuscript that looked like a piece of old rag. It was six inches across the top and about four down one side. Tommy could discern faintly the black brush characters on it.

"That," said the girl, "iss the Tertullian Fragment."

Tommy stared at it and then said, "Oh oh! I knew there'd be a catch to it. It's in Latin, isn't it?"

The thing Tommy liked about the girl was that she didn't crack. An American girl would have said, "What did you expect it would be in, eight-point Bodoni, with subheads?"

Instead she said gently, "I will translate it for you." She leaned over the case, her eyes shining with interest and concentration, and read slowly in her fine, precise English with the slight accent that Tommy had not yet placed:

Falernus, the Senator, in his accusations, pointed to the scandal of the Emperor [Titus, the girl explained] who saved the life of Sinistrus his defeated boxer because of his love for Aula, the sister of the vanquished gladiator. All Rome, he said, knew that Sinistrus deserved to die because by his defeat at the hands of the Greek, Phistra, a small but nimble boxer, who by the quickness of eye and hand and the agility of his legs remained uninjured during the combat, while inflicting many wounds upon his taller, stronger, opponent, the Emperor's gladiator drew the laughter of the multitude, thus bringing discredit upon the purple. Nevertheless the Emperor, with a glance at the box of the patrician Reglus, where sat the girl Aula, and in the face of the tumult of the mob demanding death for Sinistrus, who lay bleeding from many wounds as well as exhausted by his efforts, signified that his life should be spared. These matters, declared Falernus, were common knowledge. . . .

The girl stopped and looked up. "It ends there," she said.

"Gee," said Tommy. "The little guy just stepped around and popped him. A sort of a Fancy Dan. I'll bet it was a lousy fight.

I never saw one of those that wasn't. Maybe it was a splash. Titus sends his bum into the tank and then coppers on the bets. There was a dame angle in those days too, eh? Gosh, you know, you're wonderful. You translated that at sight."

"Perhaps," said the girl, "you will return the compliment and translate for me too."

"I apologize," said Tommy. "I didn't mean to be rude. Whenever I start to talk fight, I fall into that jargon. They were funny guys, those old reporters. They didn't care a hang about the sports and never wrote about them unless there was some political angle to it —like this guy Tertullus. I guess when your space was limited and there weren't any printing presses, you had to stick to things that were important. Nobody seems to know much about what a show was really like at the Colosseum because nobody ever wrote about them. I guess they just stuck up a copy of the results and the box score somewhere in the Forum and let it go at that."

A tall, stoop-shouldered man came through a door that opened from a small office at the rear of the little alcove, and spoke to the girl in German. He was gray-haired, gray-faced, and weary-looking. He wore a gold pince-nez attached to a black ribbon. The girl answered him and then turned to Tommy. "This is my father, Professor Lisschauer, the curator of the museum. Papachen, this is an American gentleman who is interested in the sports of antiquity."

Tommy shook hands. "Thompson is my name, sir. The *Blade*, New York. Sports writer. Your daughter was kind enough to translate the fragment for me."

The old man had a pronounced accent. He said, "*Ja, ja*. Leni haff just tolt me. You do not read Greek and Latin?"

Tommy shook his head. "I—I'm afraid what little education I have, I got the hard way. I mean I had to go to work when I was a kid."

The old man looked at him puzzled and then glanced sharply at his daughter.

"Then how can you be a student of antiquitation? It iss impossible."

Tommy felt uncomfortable. There was a detachment about the

professor that shut him out completely. He did not want to be shut out. He tried to explain.

"I—I'm trying to get the feel of things. I mean the people of those days and what they were like. Behind all these inscriptions and statuary and stuff there were people—you know, human beings. They couldn't have been such a lot different from us. That fighter, for instance, I saw in one of those wall paintings in Tarquinia, squared off with his thumb stuck out ready for a left lead to the eyeball. You could just see him getting ready to say, 'Excuse me, pal,' and then cross the right while the other guy is still blinking. He must have been the Gentleman Jones of Etruria. Gentleman Jones is a light heavy we have around New York. Polite, smooth, and very sporting in the ring, but he loves to stick that thumb in the other guy's eye. What I mean is maybe those old-time fighters were just like that. . . ."

Professor Lisschauer looked baffled, shook his head, and said, "The reading of the ancients requires years of study." He sighed. "And then sometimes it iss nod enough. You are wasting your time. You will excoose me please."

He turned and shambled away. His daughter watched him go. On her face was pain and concern.

"Gee," said Tommy, "did I say something? I guess I'm just a dumb cluck. I didn't mean—"

The girl shook her head. There was a brightness in her eyes. Tommy saw that they were close to tears. "Papachen iss in some trouble. That is all. He did not wish to be impolite. He thinks only of his work. Ach, if I could only help him. . . ."

"Is it anything serious? I mean is there anything I could—"

Leni smiled. "You are kind. I am afraid you would not understand. His integrity. His years of hard work. And then to lose everything." She stopped. "Forgive me. It iss private trouble. I should not bore you."

She hesitated and then suddenly asked, "Have you seen the famous statue of the *Resting Boxer*? It iss in the Museo delle Terme." She raised her head proudly with a significance that

Tommy did not understand at the time. "It iss a discovery of my papa."

"I haven't," said Tommy. "But I will. Do you suppose you— I mean, would you go along with me some time, to—to—"

"Take—a—gander—at it?" finished Leni.

"The once-over," said Tommy.

"The once-over," repeated Leni.

"A quick peek—"

"A quick peek."

"You're on."

"You're on. Does that mean yes?" Leni asked.

"Yes."

"Yes. You're on."

Their laughter joined and echoed from the quiet caverns of the museum. They took each other's hands on it. Something told Tommy that this was not the time to kiss her. But there was nothing to stop him from wanting to.

They met two days later, on a bright, clear, warm spring Sunday, and went to Alfredo's, where Tommy, entranced, watched Alfredo's showmanship as he manipulated the Fetuccini in the melted butter, and later they ate his famous sole in white-wine sauce and exchanged bits of information about their lives.

The Lisschauers were Viennese. Leni's father, a famous archaeologist, was the curator of the Museo Romano. Leni herself had studied with him for many years.

"Gee," said Tommy. "I knew there was something. My mother came from Vienna. My father was an American. And you can read the past as though it were a book. And yet you're sweet and simple. I've never met anyone like you. Shut up, Thompson, you're ga-ga!"

"Ga-ga?" said Leni.

"Soft in the head," explained Tommy, and then added under his breath, "about you," continuing aloud, "You must learn our beautiful language. I'll teach you if you'll help me with my ancient history."

Leni looked at him curiously with her large eyes. "You are a strange boy, are you not? You write about the sports and you are interested in antiquity. I thought Americans only cared about to make money."

"I love it," confessed Tommy—"making money, I mean; but I don't let it get me down. What do you like to do besides read old Latin manuscripts at sight?"

"Oh," said Leni, thinking seriously and counting on the fingers of one hand, "I like to dance, to play tennis, to ski, to . . ."

"That's done it," interrupted Tommy. "There's a tea dance at my hotel at five. What do you say we go and step?"

Leni nodded her head violently in assent. They toasted each other in Lagrima Christi on that. . . .

They kept meaning to go to the Museo delle Terme all through the afternoon. But there was such a fine blue Roman sky and the smell of flowers in the air—Tommy could not be sure whether it was flowers or Leni, who was dressed in a simple white frock with a little girl's sash at the waist, and a big straw hat—and also they acquired a cabdriver named Pietro Dandolo whose fine brown horse was named Ginevra. Pietro sang snatches of operatic arias as he drove—sang them very quietly to himself. And although it was warm, he still wore his rusty blue coat and shoulder cape and battered silk hat, and he sang his orders to Ginevra instead of speaking them, which was why Tommy and Leni grew to love him. Tommy engaged him for the whole day.

He drove them through the Porta Pinciana and the fragrance of the Borghese gardens to the Plaza de Popolo. From there they crossed the Tiber over the Ponte Margherita and went rolling along the muddy river past the Castel Sant' Angelo, and the Salviati and Corsini palaces. It seemed so natural that all the time Leni's hand should be in Tommy's, and their fingers intertwined.

Tommy told Leni something about himself and the curious life he lived in New York—the constant round of prizefights, baseball games, golf and tennis matches. At fifteen he had had to quit school and start in as an office boy in the sports department of the *Blade*. His father had been a singing teacher who had been ruined by the depression. Tommy's education had been continued by his father to the best of his ability. He had a talent for writing and had become sports editor and columnist and lived in an atmosphere of athletes, competition, and sweat. But in Tommy too, there was a reaching for beauty, and a sensitivity to human beings and what made them tick. The bright girl at his side was stirring a yearning in him, one that he felt unable to express, except in the curious language of his life and his trade. On her part, the girl was fascinated by the strangeness of this American, his vitality and animation, but with her feminine intuition she already felt the hungry, incompleted side of his nature and was drawn to it.

They recrossed the Tiber by the Ponte Palatino and drove back through the wonderful, shining city, past the great Victor Emmanuel monument and the Palazzo Venezio to the Ambassadeurs, where they went down to the little café below and danced Viennese waltzes and Tommy taught Leni American slang and she came to look with a fond joy for the wide grin that spread over his face when he interpreted.

"You're the tops. Get it? It means there was never anybody like you ever before. You're the number-one gal."

Leni repeated after him solemnly, "I—am—the—tops."

"Here's another one. Carrying the torch. When you're crazy about someone—like 'Baby, am I carrying the torch for you!' Get it?"

"I get it," said Leni, copying Tommy's intonation exactly. "Can I carry the torch for you too, or is the torch only for gentlemen?"

The whirling waltzes and the unity that comes from the perfect matching of rhythm and movement finished them. By the time they went to the famous Ulpia restaurant, hard by the Trajan Forum, for dinner, they were in love. They sat close together in the damp cool of the grotto below with the magic upon them, their hands tightly clasped, listening to the little orchestra, the guitars and mandolins and the blind violinist with the wonderful throbbing tone. The old grotto was carved out of the tufa of the buildings of the Forum. Dim lanterns faintly showed the garlands of spring flowers, the hanging basket bottles of Chianti, and the bits of old marbles and pieces of ancient friezes.

Tommy said, "Gee, Leni, I've got a nerve to spring this on you this way, but I can't help it. I'm going for you. I've never gone for a gal this way in my life. Do—do I have to translate that for you too?"

Leni took Tommy's hand and held it to her cheek and shook her head that way, holding it. She said simply and directly, "Oh, strange, American Tommy. I am afraid that I going for you too."

"I want to kiss you," said Tommy, flatly. "Would anybody care?"

Leni looked at him with her eyes dancing like wood sprites. "This is Rome," she said. "The old gods would like it very much."

They kissed each other. They kissed each other again until the sweetness was no longer bearable. "Oh gee," said Tommy, "I heard the gods cheering. . . ."

"I did too," said Leni, "only I think it was Benedetto."

Benedetto, the enormous proprietor, waddled over to the table with a bottle of wine. He said, "Bravo! Bravo! Signor, signorina, permit me, the compliments of the Ulpia."

"Looka," said Tommy, after they had drunk a toast with Benedetto, "let's get this straight now. I love you. I'll never love anybody but you. I want to marry you. But quick. I want to take you back to New York with me. I never want you out of my sight from now on."

Leni took his hand and said, "Oh, Tommy. I think perhaps I want to do so much . . ."

And then the dancing went out of her eyes and she caught her breath sharply and let go of Tommy's hand. He could see that something inside her had gone limp.

"Oh oh—" he said. "Trouble. What is it, Leni? Is there another guy?"

The girl suddenly was frightened and a little panicky. "Oh, Tommy—I should not have let myself go so. It iss so different with us here. It has been understood for so long that I will be the wife of Professor Zanni. He is Papa's associate. I know that Papachen wishes it. And we here are different with our families. Papa is everything. He would not understand you. And just now, when he is in such deep trouble. Oh, Tommy, I shall die. . . ."

Tommy spoke a little grimly. "I get it. When I walk into Madison Square Garden or Twenty-one, I'm a big shot, but in this set-up Mr. Thompson of the New York *Blade* is just John Mugg." He paused, and when he caught Leni looking baffled again, said, "Never mind, sweet, that's one I didn't want you to understand. Look, what is the trouble your dad's in? Tell me about it, Leni."

Leni said, "Oh, Tommy," again, and then replied, "It is about the statue of the *Resting Boxer*. The one—the one we did not see. Papa discovered it near the Fosso delle Tre Fontane. It was his great discovery. It is one of the most perfect bronzes ever found. Papa has written that it is in the style and manner of the sculptor Praexus in the time of the Emperor Titus. Mussolini made Papa a Commendatore because the statue is of the Golden Age of Rome. . . ."

"And so—"

"And so a Professor Guglielmo in Napoli has published a paper on the statue, against Papa. He iss a very important man in archaeology. He has written that the statue is—how do you say?—a—"

Tommy whistled. "I get it. A phony."

"Is false. Is a fraud. Three years ago the Manzini brothers were put into jail because they had made and buried many statues that were—that were phony, as you say. Now they are both dead. Professor Guglielmo has written that the statue my father has discovered is a fraud of the Manzini brothers."

"Well, isn't your dad's word as good as his?"

"Guglielmo is an important man in Italy. He is high in the party. And we are Austrians. And proof? What is there but that which Papa has from his years of study, from his knowledge? . . ."

Tommy chewed on his lower lip. "And unless he can prove he's right, he loses his job. Nice. This guy you're supposed to marry. Where does he figure in this setup?"

Leni frowned. "He is terribly unhappy. He is afraid that Professor Guglielmo may be right."

"Just a pal," said Tommy. "And if your father goes out, he goes in."

"Oh, Tommy," cried Leni, "how did you know?"

"It's got a familiar ring to it, sweet." Tommy sighed. "At this point, enter our hero. And what does he do? He does nothing. On account of he's just a dumb sports writer. It's a fine plot, up to there."

"Plot, Tommy?"

"Mmmm. Boy loves girl. Girl's father does not love boy. In fact, he does not know boy exists. Girl's father is in jam. Buckety, buckety, here comes boy on a white horse, rescues father. Father says, 'Bless you, my children.' Boy gets girl. Only this one has me stopped. Cold. As a hero I'm just a columnist. Let's get out of here, Leni, and go for a drive. I want to cool my head off."

They filled their pockets with sugar for Ginevra, the horse. Pietro Dandolo was sitting on the box singing the *"M'appari"* aria from *Martha* to himself, so they fed Ginevra until he had finished and then got in. Pietro said something in Italian to Leni and started off.

"Where is he going?" asked Tommy. "Not that it matters on a night like this."

"He says because there is so big a moon, he is driving us to the Colosseo."

The indeed so big moon shone through the skeleton of the Colosseum and illuminated the simple white cross erected on the spot where the Christian martyrs died. Leni and Tommy wandered in through the main entrance, their arms about each other's waist, picking their way around the pieces of fallen pillars and slabs of tufa and marble cornices. The great shell of the ancient arena was deserted except for the many huge Colosseum cats who lived there. Sometimes the moonlight picked up their eyes and made them glitter. The shadows seemed alive with their slinking figures, and sometimes their shapes were outlined, sitting on the long, broken columns.

Leni and Tommy sat close together on a drum-shaped slab of broken pillar and soaked in the feel of the place, the ancient quiet, and the beauty of the rising tiers of tumbled stone and the silhouettes of the arches.

Leni began to speak in her soft, expressive voice. "There, in the center, is the box where the Emperor sat. There was a great purple cloth that hung from it. The patricians and the Senators were in the near-by boxes, according to their rank. In that little gallery above sat the courtesans. The plebs, the common people, were up at the top."

"The gallery boys," said Tommy. "I guess a chump had no more chance of getting a ringside seat at this show than a guy named plain Joe Doakes could crash the first five rows at a heavyweight championship fight at the Yankee Stadium."

"On days when the sun was too hot, or there was rain, there was a great canopy erected that covered the whole arena like a roof, a canopy of many colors."

Tommy grunted. "We're civilized. We let our customers sit out in the rain at Palmer Stadium and the Yale Bowl."

"They could let in water and cover the whole floor of the arena enough to stage sea battles, of which the Emperor was very fond. Have you seen the excavations at the other end? In the time of Titus the floor of the arena was many levels below this one. We are sitting on the dust of twenty centuries."

"I looked at them. You know what they reminded me of? The basement of Madison Square Garden, our big indoor arena in New York, at circus time. Runways for the animals, cages, dressing rooms. And nobody really knows very much about the shows they put on here, or what it was like, do they, Leni? There is the Emperor's box. There sat the big shots, there the girls. There was a canopy. Men fought with weapons and with their hands. Christians and slaves and condemned prisoners were torn to pieces by wild animals. And that's all."

Leni sighed. "It iss all so long dead, Tommy. One must be so careful of the records one reads into stones."

Tommy sprang up suddenly from the drum of the pillar and took a few steps into the arena. The floor was white with moonlight, and the gray patch that ran through his hair looked like solid silver. He spread his arms wide with his fists clenched and shook them and cried, "But it isn't dead, Leni. Can't you feel it? All the people. There were people here. Thousands of them. Human beings. The place was alive with them. What's two thousand years?

They must have been just like us. Leni, it drives me crazy. I want to see them. I want to bring this place to life."

He stopped suddenly, shoved his hands deep into his pockets, and began to pace, and the dark shapes of the cats scattered to the deeper shadows. He spoke again. "This couldn't have been so different from what we know—World Series day, or fight night at the Polo Grounds, or the Harvard-Yale game at New Haven. Crowds coming in to see the show, pushing and gabbing. . . . If you'll listen, you can hear the scrape of thousands of sandals on the ramps and that excited hum and chatter of a crowd going to a show. You would hear snatches of conversation. They must have talked in Roman slang as they went to their seats the same way we do— 'Who do you like tonight? What do you hear? I've got a good tip on the third prelim. A new guy down from the north—they say he's a honey, fast and shifty. He's fighting for the Blues. . . . Is it true that Decius, or whatever he was called, is out of shape? They say he didn't train a lick. A wise guy. I heard the main go was in the bag. I got it from the inside. Friend of mine who knows the guy who trains the gladiators. I'm gonna have a couple of bucks riding on Drusus. He's a house fighter. Those guys haven't blown a decision yet. . . .' Pushing and shoving, and sweating, and laughing. . . ."

Leni was standing too, now, her face pale, reflected from the white ball of the nearly full moon that now hung directly over the black shell of the old arena. Her lips were parted with excitement. She did not understand much of what Tommy was saying, but the feeling of it was reaching her. "Oh, Tommy. Please go on."

"Crooks, gamblers, sports, pickpockets, actors, writers, just plain people out for fun, guys with their dolls, and the dolls dressed and made up to kill—I've seen their paint pots in the museums, big-shot gangsters, lawyers—Rome was lousy with lawyers, politicians, the regular fight crowd. "Why, you can work right back from the numbers on the portals, Leni. If they numbered the portals they must have had tickets that corresponded to the numbers."

"Yes—yes, Tommy. They were made of bone, I think."

"Then they must have had ticket-takers and directors and ushers.

It was probably a political job. Maybe they even had programs—"
He grinned suddenly, widely. "Can't you see the program-sellers
standing under those arches and on the ramps, and by the stairways
hollering, 'Get your programs here. You can't tell the gladiators
without a program. Names and numbers of the Christian martyrs.' "

He threw up his head and gazed around the great amphitheater
to the entrance arcades. "And what about grub, and concession-
aires? There never yet was a sports crowd that didn't get hungry
and thirsty. There must have been venders selling things to eat
and drink. What would the Roman equivalent have been of our
hot dogs and peanuts and beer and pop?"

"Meat on a stick, probably," said Leni: "yes, and fruit. . . ."

"They probably hollered just the same as ours. 'Get it red-hot
here!' and wine—"

"The *vinarii*," interrupted Leni, almost breathless, "the wine
merchants. They carried it around in skins . . ."

"Red wine and white. Didn't they used to cart snow down from
the mountains to cool it? 'Ice-cold, ice-cold, ice-cold! Get your ice-
cold *vino* here, ten cents a cup. Who'll have a cup? Sweet or sour,
sir?' Noise, cries, excitement, and maybe the bums up in the two-bit
seats stamping their feet because they wanted the show to begin.
And the guys selling souvenirs. 'Show your colors.' The blue and
the white. Hawkers, with blue ribbons and white ones. 'Show your
colors, folks. What's your favorite?' "

"Oh, and little clay figurines of the gods," breathed Leni, "for
the good luck."

"Sure. And statuettes of the favorite gladiators to carry or tie to
your tunic the way the gals who go up to New Haven for the
Army-Yale game pin a little bulldog or Army mule to their coats."

"And girls selling garlands of flowers to throw into the arena to
the victors," Leni said. "There they stand, with flowers in their
dark hair, and the garlands over their arms. . . ."

Tommy put his arm around Leni's shoulder in glee and pointed
to the vast floor of the arena. "They had to get ready, didn't they?
Set the arena for the show? There are the roustabouts—slaves, I
suppose—marking off the combat areas, looking after the props,

preparing the boxes of sand to cover up the bloodstains. There'd be the officials, and judges and referees and masters of ceremony, dressed up to kill and strutting like an A.A.U. official in his hard hat at a big track meet. Officials are all alike. The crowd is sifting to its seats. People are visiting from box to box, laughing and making bets. Whistling breaks out from the top tiers as a gladiator comes out to try the footing and look at the direction of the sun so that if he wins the toss he can get it to his back. I guess man could whistle from the time he had a mouth.

"And can you get an idea of the dressing rooms below? The taping and bandaging and last-minute advice to the fighters, and the swordsmen limbering up and doing knee flexes and lunges and making passes with their short swords, and the boxers shadow-boxing to warm up, the way every fighter has since guys first put up their dukes, and whistling their breath out of their noses as they punched at the air. And I guess maybe down in the dungeons the Christians were on their knees, quietly praying, and the other doomed stood by and watched them. And sometimes over the noise of the crowd and the cries of the candy butchers and wine-sellers and hawkers you would hear from deep down the impatient roaring of the hungry beasts, the way sometimes when the circus is in the Garden and there is a sudden lull and you hear the lions from down below. . . ."

Leni was crying, "Oh, Tommy, Tommy, you have made this place of the long ago so alive. . . ." Her eyes were shining, and now she too stood with her head thrown back and her arms outstretched toward the slender white cross. "These things were so. They were. Oh, they were."

Suddenly she stopped short and spun around facing the man and cried sharply, "Tommy!" and again, "Tommy!"

Tommy was startled. There was such a strange look on her face. Her eyes were so wide. "Sweet, what is it?"

The girl suddenly placed both hands to her temples and held them and spoke in German. *"Ach, lieber Herrje! Es ist nicht möglich—aber doch—doch—"*

"Honey, what's happened?"

Leni ran to him. "Tommy, you must come with me at once. But at once. It is still early. You *will* come with me. I have had—oh how do you say it? Something inside of me, all through me."

Tommy held her off. "Is it a hunch, honey?"

"Oh, yes, yes, Tommy. Is that the word? Something inside of me has told me something."

"Do you want to tell me about it?"

Leni shook her head. "N-no-. Not yet. But you will come . . ."

She took him by the hand and together they ran out of the arena, frightening the cats again. Pietro was so startled that he stopped in the middle of the Toreador song.

"*Trenta*, Via Palestro, *e presto!*" ordered Leni. They scrambled into the carriage, and a surprised and startled Ginevra rattled them over the cobblestones and onto the smooth asphalt of the Via del Impero, at what, to the best of her recollection, was a gallop.

Leni said, "I do not want to say yet, Tommy. Just hold me, please."

The address was a private house, not far from the Museo Romano. "Our home," Leni said. She still had Tommy by the hand as she rang the front doorbell. A pleasant-faced elderly woman in a black dress and white apron came to the door. Leni said breathlessly in German, "Ach, Liesel. Is Papa still up?"

The woman replied, "He is not at home, Miss Leni. The Conte Alberini came. They both went away together. I believe they were to go to the Museo delle Terme."

Leni wasted no time. She cried, "Come. Oh, if it is not too late. *Presto, Pietro, al Museo delle Terme.* The little door on the Via Gernaia side . . ."

Ginevra, thoroughly outraged, clattered them past the huge gray Station Centrale, whipped them around a corner on two wheels and deposited them before a tiny iron door in a high, thick wall. Leni seized a bell pull and jangled a bell wildly and then pounded with her little fist so that the iron door rattled and clanged.

The door was finally opened by an ancient attendant in a faded blue uniform coat.

"I am Leni Lisschauer, Professor Lisschauer's daughter," Leni said. "Is my papa here?"

The attendant nodded. "*Si, si signorina*. It is a little irregular. We are closed. They are all on the second floor with the Conte Alberini. You may come."

He had an old lantern, and by its dim rays he led them, Leni still clinging to Tommy's hand, through a garden in which were many shadowy statues, to the dark and gloomy museum built on the site of the old thermal baths. It grew lighter as they went up the stairs to the second floor. The room at the far end of the museum was illuminated and they heard voices coming from it.

Leni, still towing Tommy, broke into a little run. They burst into the room. The four men there turned and stared.

One of them was Professor Lisschauer. He looked very old. The second was tall and dignified, with a black beard and a monocle. With him stood a short, fussy, bald-headed little man wearing pince-nez. The fourth was a thin man with a narrow face and long black hair combed back from a high forehead.

But the thing that caught Tommy's eye was not so much the men, but the great bronze on a marble pedestal in the center of the room. It was the figure of a naked man seated, his arms resting on upper legs, his hands encased in the iron-studded, hard-leather cesti worn by the ancient pugilists, with thongs extending halfway up to his elbows and ending in a tight leather cuff.

His head was turned to the right looking up over his right shoulder. He was curly-headed and bearded, heavy-muscled. He had been through a terrific battering. On his right shoulder and right elbow and in the crisscrossed thongs of the right forearm were three deep and gaping cuts. His ears were cauliflowered, ballooned, and cut. His nose had been smashed to one side and cut, his lips puffed, his cheekbone swollen and gashed. His eyes showed the heavy ridges of the professional prize fighter, and traces of old scars as well as new wounds. The cesti, which were thick and about two and a half inches wide, covering the knuckles and letting the fingers protrude, had sharp cutting edges, and the two halves were held together around the hand with narrow strips of iron.

The thin man with the lank black hair made a little movement toward Leni, but her father was the first to recover. He spoke to her in German.

"Leni! What are you doing here? Who is this man? Ah yes, he was at the museum. I remember. But why?" He stopped, turned to the group, and said in Italian, "Forgive me. Count Alberini, I believe you have met my daughter. Professor Guglielmo, my daughter Leni."

Leni introduced Tommy. The bearded, monocled man was Count Alberini, State Director of Museums and Art, the fussy little bald-headed man was Guglielmo. The thin, narrow-faced one with the long hair was Armando Zanni, Lisschauer's assistant. Then she turned to her father. "Papachen—what has happened?"

"It is all over, my child. Count Alberini has accepted the statement and the testimony of Professor Guglielmo. The Manzini brothers were once known to have made a statue of a boxer. Zanni has had no alternative but to agree with him. I have given my resignation. The Count has been very kind. He brought Professor Guglielmo here from Naples to confront me and give me a last chance to prove my case. I could not."

Leni turned to Tommy quickly and translated what her father had said, in pain and in panic. The Count was coughing discreetly and then spoke softly and deprecatingly in English. "Your pardon. But this is indeed a very private matter. This young man—" He looked inquiringly at Leni.

The girl turned. "He is an expert—" She was very close to tears.

Professor Guglielmo removed his pince-nez and cocked his head to one side and asked, "Of antiquity?"

"No," cried Leni, her young voice ringing bravely and defiantly through the room. "No! Of life!" Suddenly she turned to Tommy and wailed, "Oh, Tommy—Tommy! Do something! Make him live. Bring him to life for me the way you did the old people of the Colosseo. Tommy . . ."

Tommy caught her by the shoulders and said, "I get it. Keep your chin up. I get the picture." He faced the group of men. "Do all of you gentlemen understand English?"

They all bowed. Zanni said, "But naturally. It is a part of education."

"Good," said Tommy. "Anything you don't understand Leni will translate for you. She's onto my jargon." He grinned pleasantly at Zanni. "Education sometimes has its limits. Leni, tell all these guys to keep their shirts on. I want five minutes with this old chap. Maybe I can help."

He stepped out of the circle and walked slowly over to the statue while the four men and the girl stood watching him. He spoke to himself very slowly as he stood in front of the great bronze, his hands in his pockets, his head cocked a little to one side—

"The Roman Kid, eh? What a licking you took! . . . Gee, shave off those whiskers, and you could be Paolino sitting on the rubbing table in the dressing room at the Yankee Stadium after Max Schmeling got through with him. What a pasting! . . . That's a lovely pair of tin ears you've got, my friend. You just never bothered to duck, eh? What a job—what a job! . . ."

He commenced to circle the statue slowly, examining it minutely. He fingered the three cuts on the right side, went suddenly to the other side and examined the left arm, whistled, and said, "Oh oh, sidewinder!" He inspected the hands carefully and then hopped up on the pedestal, fingered and examined the cuts on the face, the bruises and abrasions and scars. He jumped down to the floor again, and suddenly fell into a boxing stance, looked at the statue again and changed it, and then walked rapidly around it again. Once he addressed himself to Count Alberini. "These cuts," he said, "are definitely cuts? Not accidents? Ages of being buried, or being tossed around?"

"We do not believe it has been buried for ages," the Count replied with a little smile, "but the cuts and marks were all placed there by the sculptor."

"Thanks," said Tommy. "That's all I wanted to know." He made one more circle around the statue and then backed away from it with a little gesture of salute and said, "Thanks, pal. There's been many a guy since your time who's had his ears pinned back just the way yours were." He turned and faced the group, uttered something out of the corner of his mouth to Leni that sounded like "Buckety, buckety," and then said with a fine, studied, dramatic carelessness that delighted him, "Gentlemen, what would you like to know about this guy?"

It was old Professor Lisschauer who grasped at the straw. He said, "What? Iss there anything you can tell us?" There was deep despair in his voice, which made Tommy suddenly ashamed of his fine pose. He dropped it.

"Plenty," he said grimly. "In the first place, the guy was a southpaw."

"A which?" inquired Professor Guglielmo politely.

"Portsider. He was left-handed. I'll bet most guys hated to fight him. Nobody likes to fight a southpaw."

Count Alberini looked interested. "So?" he said. "How do you determine this?"

"Looka," said Tommy. "You can't miss it." He stepped up to the statue, took a pencil from his pocket, and used it as a pointer. "Here! Deep cut on right shoulder. Another on the arm just below the elbow. Another on the forearm inside the lacings. No cuts on the left shoulder or arm whatsoever. Here's how the orthodox boxer stands—" Tommy fell into the regular stance, left hand, left foot forward. "Here's how this guy stood—" He reversed his position and stood with his right foot forward, right arm extended and curled, left arm bent at his side. "Get it?" he said. "The reason he has those cuts on the right arm is because that is the part of him that was closest to his opponent."

For the first time light came back to Leni's face. The Count solemnly walked over to the statue, inserted his monocle in his eye, inspected the three cuts one after another, assumed the left-handed boxing stance that Tommy had taken, straightened up, slapped his thigh, and said, *"Per Bacco!"*

"Uhuh!" said Tommy. "And anyway, the guy's had a busted left duke—hand, I mean. That artist didn't miss a thing. Here, you can see the swelling where it knit badly. He used the left for the

Sunday punch. That would be the one most likely to go. All right. He wasn't a boxer. He was a slugger. All he wanted to do was to get in close enough to lay in that left—which meant curtains. Get it?"

Guglielmo walked over, adjusted his pince-nez, and said, "You can explain that?"

"Look at the ears on him," said Tommy. "Guys who can box don't get marked up that way. This guy's had a hell of a licking. All those bums who take five to give one wind up with pretzel ears and scarred eyebrows. He's got the musculature of a slugger too, and the legs. Here, look at all these heavy muscles behind the shoulders and down the back, and on the arms. The fast boxer and snap hitter has slender shoulders and tapering muscles. And anyway, the cuts on the arm again tell you that. Look here, professor, let me show you. Square off in front of me."

He got Guglielmo in a boxer-like attitude. The little old man seemed to like it and tried to look fierce and belligerent. Tommy ranged himself opposite him in the left-handed stance, but with his right arm and fist completely extended in front of him, and the left cocked at his breast.

"I can keep you off in this way. But this guy fought with his right arm curled in front of his face like a shield as he shuffled in. That's how he got those cuts where they are."

Guglielmo practiced a little, transformed himself into a slugger, examined the statue, went into a pose again, straightened up, looked at Alberini and said, *"Mirabile! . . . E vero. . . ."*

Leni clapped her hands. "Oh, Tommy, bravo!"

Professor Zanni shrugged his shoulders and said, "In the realm of pure conjecture . . ."

Tommy threw him a look, licked his lips, and spoke again. "Now if you'd like," he said, "I think I can tell you something about the guy who whipped him. The sculptor who did this made his sketches in the dressing room or in the arena, immediately after the fight. Now—"

Zanni suddenly showed even, white teeth. "Just a moment, my

friend. How do you know he lost the fight? Perhaps he was the winner, no?"

"Zanni," said Tommy, "you ought to read a book. It'll broaden you. Do you admit that he was sketched immediately after a fight?"

"If the statue were genuine, I would. The artist has been so careful to include every mark with nothing omitted. But he might still have been the winner."

"Then the sculptor would also have been careful enough to include the victor's chaplet or garland which would have been on this guy's head if he'd won," said Tommy with his most charming smile.

"Bravo!" said Alberini and Guglielmo in unison.

"*Herrlich!*" said Professor Lisschauer. He moved over toward Alberini and Guglielmo. There was a little gleam of hope in his tired eyes.

"Thanks," said Tommy. "All right, then. The little guy who licked him was probably a Greek. He—"

It was Zanni who interrupted again with a laugh. "Hah! No, no, no, my friend. That is now pure fancy. You have the true American imagination."

"You sure root for the home team, don't you, Zanni?" Tommy said.

"I do not understand this expression."

"Leni does," suggested Tommy. "Maybe you've read a book, but not the right one. There's one over in the library of the American Academy I can refer you to. Professor Stoddard gave it to me. It tells how the Greeks never punched for the body. They were purely head punchers. This guy hasn't a mark on his body. But look at his kisser. The Greeks, from all I can find out, were much better boxers than the Romans. And make no mistake. The guy who gave the Roman Kid his pasting was a little sweetheart. He fought on a bicycle, and—"

Even Leni joined in the unison chorus, "A bicycle?" They were all hypnotized.

Tommy grinned. "Excuse me. That's one I haven't taught you yet, Leni. He fought in retreat. He knew he had to stay away from this guy or get killed."

"Why do you say a small man?" asked Guglielmo.

"Figure it out," replied Tommy. "Small men are fast. Big guys are slow. This guy is still alive, isn't he? If his opponent had been a big, fast guy with a punch, he'd be dead instead of sitting there. You could cave in the side of a guy's head with one of those things he has on his hands. But the Greek was fast enough to keep away, and probably smaller. He either didn't have a punch or he was afraid to get close enough to let one go. And the direction of the cuts and bruises on the Kid's face indicate that the Greek hooked, or punched up at him, and therefore was smaller. . . . Look at the condition of the right side of the Kid's face, compared to the left. The Greek probably let him have a few right-hand smashes when he had him woozy. But he was a smart little guy and he knew how to fight a southpaw, which is more than most of our fighters do today. He kept moving, circling to his own left and the Kid's right, away from that deadly left hand, and as he circled and back-pedaled, he kept popping him with left hooks—look at the way his nose is bent, the size of his right ear, and the mess he made out of the right side of his face. Even so, he didn't want to risk getting close enough to finish him. He had the fight won, so why take a chance? He just popped him with that left until the southpaw collapsed from the accumulation of punches, loss of blood, and exhaustion. Afterwards—"

Leni suddenly placed her hand to her face and screamed.

Her cry echoed through the high, empty vaults of the deserted museum.

"Tommy! Tommy! Papa!" she was staring. "The Tertullian Fragment! The description. . . . Tommy! Papa!"

They were all talking and shouting at once, Alberini crying, "*Corpe di Bacco*," Guglielmo saying over and over, "*Si, si, si, si, ma si, si-si . . .*" and Professor Lisschauer, "*Lieber Herr Gott. Aber gewiss . . .*"

"I don't get it," said Tommy.

"The Fragment!" cried Leni. "The description of the boxing match before Titus!"

"Holy smokes!" said Tommy. "I had forgotten it."

"The name—The name!" cried Professor Lisschauer. "Sinistrus, the Left-handed One. It iss. It iss. You haff here before you Sinistrus, Roman boxer of the Emperor Titus, defeated by the little Greek, Phistra, and granted his life because of the love of the Emperor for his sister Aula."

It was not strange that Leni and Tommy should be hugging each other, but it was a little unusual that Lisschauer and Guglielmo should be in each other's arms, and patting each other on the back, until the little man suddenly stepped back and cleared his throat and said, "I must have leave to speak. Count Alberini, Professor Lisschauer, I withdraw. I apologize. I have done a great injustice, though my intent was honest. I was wrong. The Manzini brothers have been dead two years. The Tertullian Fragment was discovered less than six months ago. They could not possibly have known of its contents. I hope that I will be forgiven. For my friend Professor Lisschauer I have the greatest esteem and admiration."

The Count adjusted his monocle and said, "Professor Guglielmo, it is no more than I expected from a man of your attainments and generosity. The resignation of Professor Lisschauer is of course not accepted."

Professor Lisschauer somehow made a magnificent job of not seeing where Leni had just been. He came to Tommy and said, "I wish to thank you from the bottom uff my heart, and to make to you my apologies for my attitude and my ignorance in the museum that morning. We are all too far from the realities of life. You have shamed us all. . . ."

Tommy said, "Gee—don't—it catches me in the throat. . . . I'm —I'm just a dumb guy who happens to have been around fights and fighters all his life. . . ."

There was a pause. "I am so happy," said Professor Lisschauer, "I could to sing and cry. We will go to my house, all, and drink some wine. Mr. Thomsen, Count Alberini, Guglielmo, Zanni." He stopped. "Where has gone Zanni?"

"Zanni," said Tommy succinctly, "has taken a powder."

They all looked blank, but Tommy didn't explain. They moved off down the long aisles of glass cases and marbles and bronzes toward the stairs. When they reached the darker portions and the attendant went ahead of his lantern, Tommy did what was requisite.

"You know," said Leni, when she could speak again, "I—I think perhaps boy is going to get girl. . . ."

The Witch of Woonsapucket

People ask me frequently how I get ideas for stories. Sometimes I am ashamed to tell them because the genesis of the idea is frequently nuttier than the story itself. This happens to be the case with "The Witch of Woonsapucket," which was one of a series of business-golf stories I kept going in the *Saturday Evening Post* over a period of years, all written around the personality and troubles of the advertising manager of a concern manufacturing golf equipment, an invented character.

The origin of this story goes back to the particular kind of screwball I am and the days when I was writing my sports column. I used to cover all the big golf matches, the National Open, the Amateur, the Women's, the P.G.A., and I had many personal friends among the golfers, men of whom I was genuinely fond, such as Tommy Armour, Bobby Cruickshank, Bob Jones, Walter Hagen, Gene Sarazen, and many others.

I was never able to take my sports casually, but always rooted passionately for some individual or some team and suffered agonies when my side looked as though it might lose. I never bet a dime on any sporting event, with the occasional exception of a small wager on a nag, during my entire thirteen-year tenure in sports, but I always had a strong personal rooting interest in some team or contestant.

Well, one day (and this is where the narrative becomes embarrassing) I was following a golf match. If my recollection serves me, it was the Augusta Open Tournament, at Augusta, Georgia, and I was rooting this time for Walter Hagen, who was staging a comeback, to win it.

I liked the Hague, who hadn't won a major tournament in too many years. He used to live well and looked upon the flowing bowl with honest thirst and a friendly eye. He was an uninhibited man, loved by the sports writers for his faults as well as his virtues. I wanted like the

Saturday Evening Post, August 5, 1939.
Golf Is a Friendly Game (New York: Alfred A. Knopf, 1942).

very devil to have Walter win this one, because in addition to the personal element it would have made, a great sports news story.

The morning of the final round, Hagen led the field by several strokes, and it looked as though he might be going to turn the trick. But immediately he began to play, he started to slip. Really, Grantland Rice and I were to blame for his downfall, because the night before we kept stealing drinks away from him, so eager were we both to have him come through, and Granny and I practically kidnaped him away from the night club where he had been staying up until four or five o'clock every previous morning during the tournament, and put him to bed in the hotel at eleven o'clock to get a full night's sleep. The shock apparently proved too much for him.

But the last day provided a dramatic finale, with Hagen playing in the same foursome with the eventual winner of the tourney, neck and neck, and, as I say, strokes were slipping away from him. And so I tried to hex his opponent. And I now present the picture of a grown man walking after a golf foursome muttering gibberish to himself.

Of course I wasn't really hexing, but in my eagerness to see Hagen come through I thought how wonderful it would be if I knew some magic words to say that would cause Walter's opponent to fluff a bunker shot, or roll a short putt eight feet past the hole. And so, when matters became tense and the Hague's nearest opponent was about to make a shot, the success of which would put Walter still deeper in the hole, I made up words of magical gibberish in the sort of despairing, infantile hope that they MIGHT be the ones necessary, the words of power that would summon Beelzebub to joggle the fellow's elbow at the critical moment. These charms I mumbled to myself, well out of earshot of the contestants. This was strictly between me and Old Nick.

Well, here the long arm of coincidence consented to be yanked, and Hagen's opponent actually blew two strokes on easy shots he should have made, which, I must say, alarmed me somewhat as well as delighted me. Hagen picked up two sorely needed strokes and I was in a fair way to hang out my shingle as an operating wizard.

Then nature and form took their normal course. Walter's golf wouldn't stand up against his non-hangover jitters, and, magic or no magic, his opponent pulled himself together and went on handily to win.

Years later, while rummaging through the attic of my mind for an idea for a story in this series, I remembered my moment of complete idiocy at the Augusta tournament, and "The Witch of Woonsapucket" was the result.

Any reader for entertainment or student of fiction writing in possession of these egregious facts can see how this story was put together. Using nothing but the original notion of a guy trying to put a silent hex on a golfing opponent, the train of thought would move naturally from hexing to witches, to witch-burning, and thence to the vicinity of Salem, Mass., where the story is laid.

But I wouldn't want to wish on anyone the four months' wrestle I had trying to solve this story and get myself and my characters out of the jam into which I had led them.

This is a formula story, a somewhat despised creation in literary circles, but I must confess I love the kind. They are fun to think up, fun to plan, and fun to write. They come as a lightening of the load and a blessed relief. They fall into the category of what is scathingly known as potboilers, and many a brimming pot I've boiled with them, but I am not content to rest upon the confession that I made frequent compromise sorties into lower levels of magazine taste in order to keep the larder stocked. There was never any writing down in these stories. I always wrote them to the best of my ability at the particular moment. But often I would get as much pleasure, and sometimes more, out of knocking out a Bill Fowler business-golf story, or a debutante yarn, as many of the other, more serious attempts in which I was trying to convey a burn, or a yearning, or an honest emotion to paper.

For these pieces served two purposes. They amused and rested me and they also entertained the customers. They constituted a welcome change of pace for them and for me.

Sometimes I would receive scolding letters from clients asking, "Why do you waste time on junk like So-and-so? Why don't you write more stories like Whatsis?" naming some story that had appealed to them emotionally. But the formula stories also brought in approving mail, and if somebody wrote, "I read that screwball story of yours out loud to my wife last night, and we both laughed until we were sick," I considered that there could not be much higher praise and my time and efforts had not gone unrewarded.

It is the characteristic of the formula story that the basic pattern of the story remains static. Only the scene and incidents change. While top magazines by no means restrict themselves to formula stories, every magazine has one or two pet formulas based upon trial and reader reaction. They vary. The *Collier's* formula differed from the *Post* type, which in turn is quite different from the ones favored by *Cosmopolitan*.

To me, the word "formula" in story means that certain ingredients, as in a prescription, are always present. Here, for instance, are the ingredients of the golf-business story: The hero and narrator, the young and not too bright advertising manager for a golf-equipment manufacturing firm, at the beginning of each story is given some near-impossible task by his irascible and demanding boss. This task is always complicated by circumstances, the honest stupidity of the hero, or the machinations of his not too ethical rival, the villain, who is the advertising manager for the rival firm. The story then moves out on the golf course among the pros, where trouble continues to pile up for the hero. Just when things look blackest, the hero does something dumbly honest, or despairing, or the villain perpetrates the final deed, in which he outsmarts himself, virtue triumphs, and everything turns out just fine in the best of all possible worlds.

It would be churlish to scorn the *Saturday Evening Post* for never tiring of this one when the truth is that the readers served by the *Post* are the ones who never weary of it. Like children listening to fairytales, the oft-told, well-remembered stories are always the best and the ones they wish to have repeated.

To the writer or story-maker the challenge comes in trying to fit new ideas, new backgrounds, and new characters into this pattern and keeping it ever fresh so that the reader is never aware he is reading a formula story. He just feels comfortable and knows he is enjoying himself. Often this work is like a fascinating picture puzzle in which the pieces stubbornly refuse to fall into place. But when they do and things go right, the story can be written at a breathless gallop and with great pleasure. "The Witch of Woonsapucket" was one of these.

D o you believe in witches, keep away from black cats, worry if you bust a mirror, and stay home in bed on Friday the thirteenth? I am only asking, because personally I am not superstitious myself, though I must confess that I am more than a little partial to a small ivory lucky elephant about the size of a walnut that Freddy McRae brought back for me from a golfing tour he made through India one winter and that I carry in my left pants pocket just in case. And, boy, if I hadn't had it along with me that time the P.G.A. Championship got itself h'anted, I hate to think what would have happened to poor Elmer Brown, who was just a big dumb kid, but sweet and decent, and that swell Mary Summers he was so stuck on.

I mean, when it comes to that stuff about witches riding on broomsticks and Old Ned moving into a guy's golf bag and telling him what stick to use and where to place the ball to turn a tough par-five hole into a drive, a pitch, and a putt, your Uncle William Fowler, Esq., just gives it the broad "haw." But there's something cute about that little elephant and it doesn't take up much space anyway; and to think I almost forgot it when I changed suits before I went up to Woonsapucket for the P.G.A. Championship last year because I was so sore at old A.R. spoiling the party for me.

Being the assistant advertising manager of A. R. Mallow & Co., in charge of promotion, means that I do all the dirty work. And that was just what I was called upon to do when, the day before I was to leave for Massachusetts, I went in to see A.R. in response to his buzzer. Any time I am yanked in to A.R.'s office and he is sitting there with his glasses on the end of his nose and a paper in his hand, I know that there is going to be some trouble for William.

"Ha! Ahmmm! Hrrrrmph! Fowler. I have here a memo compiled for me by Mr. Gudgins of the business department. It is a list of the professionals under contract to us and their—ah—accomplishments. Top-heavy! Carrying some deadwood. Uncertain times, Fowler. Business unsteady. Everyone nervous. Good time to retrench. Must cut down, eh? This fellow Brown—hrrrmph!—Elmer Brown from—ah—Osceola, Iowa. What has he done to earn his pay?"

Well, he had me there, because Elmer hadn't exactly set any fairways on fire since I had signed him up three years before when it had looked as though he might be going to win the Open. But he was such a decent, earnest guy that I thought I'd at least have one crack at saving him, so I said:

"Gee whiz, A.R., he's just a kid. He placed seventh in the Open in '36, and had it won if he hadn't folded on the last three holes, and—"

"Ha! Exactly, Fowler. There is no room on the Mallow & Co. payroll for professionals who fold. This young man has done nothing since then, according to my memo, but place ninth in the Los Angeles Open, and twelfth at the Masters Tournament in Augusta. His contract has expired. I do not wish it renewed. He has brought no credit to A. R. Mallow products. Ha! Hum!" With the last "Ha! Hum!" he pushed his glasses back up on the bridge of his nose, which was always the signal that A.R. meant what he said and there was no use arguing.

Of course they would hold the P.G.A. in a place by the name of Woonsapucket, Mass., five miles from Salem, but to the boys who cover for the papers, a thousand miles from anywhere. As far as our business is concerned, the lines are all pretty well laid out in that tournament, which is just for the pros, and there's no scrambling or chiseling or gambling to be done as there is around an Open, beyond a little polite needling. We always like it when one of our pros wins, and advertise it, but it doesn't count with the public like the Open. So for me it's just an annual week's vacation where I can relax, follow the boys around, and have myself some laughs. But it's a bad way to start a good time to have to give a nice kid the heave-oh. I guess maybe I'm just too tender-hearted.

There wasn't even a hotel at Woonsapucket and there was no room to stay at the Woonsapucket Golf Club, which was eight miles outside of Salem, so they had the boys quartered around in private houses, the citizens chipping in with room and board as a matter of civic pride. I found I was sharing a room in a swell old house with our Freddy McRae, who had as good a chance as anyone to win the tournament. I told him that I was going to have to give Elmer Brown the ax. He shrugged his shoulders and said,

"That's a shame. He's a good kid, even though he is an awful hick. That's all that's the matter with him. He hasn't got that hay out of his hair yet. He's shy and scared. Every time he steps onto a tee with someone who's got a name, he's licked."

I went out to the club Saturday morning, the day before the tournament started. It was a pretty course, long, and winding through woods every inch of the way. I had been wondering whether I would break the news to Elmer before or after the tournament. I suppose it would have been kinder to wait until it was all over and keep that load off his mind, but I thought that maybe if I told him right away it would make him just mad enough to go out there and play some golf. And if he could make any kind of a showing in the tournament, maybe I could risk giving A.R. another argument.

I found him putting on the practice green. Not that he was hard to find, because he had a build like a heavyweight. He was grain-fed, big, husky, with corn-tassel hair and blue eyes and broad mouth. He'd been brought up on a farm out in Iowa.

I didn't waste much time after the handshake and the usual about how his game was going. I came right out with it and said, "Look here, Elmer. I'm sorry to have to be the one to tell you this, but you're on the spot."

He straightened up from a putt he was going to make. Gloom was smeared as thick as butter all over his big, good-natured pan. And he looked scared too. He said, "Oh gee. Do you mean—?"

I started to give him a lot of stuff right out of A.R.'s book—retrenchment, unsettled conditions, nothing personal, economy wave, things ought to be better next year—when he cut in with:

"Aw, gee, Mr. Fowler. I know. You don't have to let me down easy. I know I ain't been winning enough to clean the rust off a mashie. If it hadn't been for you folks I'd a had to go back to the farm long ago. I guess I knew it was coming."

There was a sort of silence in which I felt rotten, and he leaned over and banged a nine-footer into the cup. Then he straightened up and said:

"Mr. Fowler, would it do any good if I won the P.G.A.?"

I looked at him. "It would help, kid. It would give me an argument with A.R. Even if the P.G.A. doesn't count a hell of a lot selling merchandise, A.R. is smart enough to know that the man who wins it is also capable of winning the Open, or one of those other big publicity tournaments like the Masters."

He said, "Gee, Mr. Fowler, I just gotta win, then. I just gotta." It was pipe-lined straight from his heart. And before I could speak the question I had written on my face, he said:

"I got a girl, Mr. Fowler. Gee, she's sweet."

I said "Oh-oh!" The last time one of our pros got himself a girl, it came so close to costing us the Open I didn't even want to think about it. But he hadn't heard me. That far-away look of men in love and fighters who have been popped on the chin came into his eyes, and he was off. "Gee, Mr. Fowler, she's the most wonderful person I ever met."

So I got the whole story from him. He had been assigned to the Wellbye cottage, kept by a spinster, Miss Sarah Wellbye, and the house had been in the family for more than two hundred and fifty years. Miss Wellbye's niece, Mary Summers, was staying there with her for her vacation. Mary was a college girl, a stenographer in Boston, and had black hair and blue eyes and wasn't any bigger than a milking stool, but gee, she was sweet and smart as a buggy whip, and he had fallen in love with her the first day he saw her, a week ago, when he arrived there to practice, and he couldn't understand why, but she liked him too, and they were going to be married when the tournament was over; the thousand dollars' prize money would get them started.

Well, the more he rattled on, the glummer I got. There he was, all full of young love and wanting to get married to a nice girl, and I had just fired him. And I knew just how tough it was for a young pro who wasn't winning anything to keep himself fed, let alone marry.

And as for winning the P.G.A.! I didn't have the heart to tell him. As McRae said, he was a shy, hero-worshiping type who got the meemies every time he played anybody with a name like Mac-Donough, or Crabby Wilson, or Craig, or Steubner. All they had to do was throw a ball onto the tee and he was licked. And the P.G.A. was match play against the toughest, coldest, most hard-boiled, goat-getting crew in the racket. He didn't stand any more chance with them than I would of breaking 80 at Pinehurst with a croquet mallet and a butterfly net.

But I gave him a little pep talk and wished him luck and then beat it off to the locker room to have myself a little snort. It certainly was a swell introduction to a lousy time.

They really give a golfer a workout the way they play that P.G.A. It stretches out over a week. The first two days they play eighteen holes, each of qualifying medal play, starting Sunday. The low sixty-three qualify, along with last year's champion, who qualifies automatically, making sixty-four in all. On Tuesday they play two eighteen-hole matches, which knocks the field down to sixteen by nightfall, and from then on, it's thirty-six holes a day to the end.

Outside of Elmer's troubles there wasn't a thing to worry about. All of our boys, and we had four in the tournament, qualified nicely, and, for that matter, so did Elmer, but that didn't surprise me, because the guy wasn't so bad at medal play. He could cock a ball a mile when he really let out and wasn't under pressure. He was so big and powerful that he never used more than a three-quarter swing. But that didn't mean anything, because by Tuesday night Elmer would have departed for Osceola, Iowa. The poor sucker had managed to get himself into the tough side of the draw. And, brother, that upper bracket read just like the Social Register of golf. It was loaded for bear. At least a dozen of them were champions or former champions. Angus MacDonough, the Fairgreen pro who had won the Open that year, was in the lower half, and had a cinch. Also I met Elmer's girl, Mary Summers.

There's something sweet, right away, about the name Mary, and she lived up to all of it. She had that quiet sincerity that seems to go with dark hair and blue eyes. She wore her hair very smooth and glossy so that you wanted to touch it with your hand, but, for all her tiny figure—she came just about up to Elmer's shoulder—she had a good, strong, firm chin and a mouth that looked as if its owner might mean business sometimes. And was she stuck on big Elmer! She didn't seem to mind that he wasn't the brightest guy on earth. All she cared was that he was sweet and kind, and could break her in two, maybe, if he ever took a full backswing before he hugged her. Why do all those cute tricks go for guys like that when here is your Uncle Fowler around just dying for someone soft and agreeable who will soothe his feverish head when he brings it home at night, hot and throbbing from the daily effort of thinking up ways to make more dubs buy more A. R. Mallow products?

We met on the clubhouse porch after the qualifying round. Elmer was drinking himself a glass of milk and kidding with the guys, because they all liked him, he was so modest and decent and unspoiled; and he called out, "Mr. Fowler, I want you to meet Mary Summers. Mary, this is Mr. Fowler of the A. R. Mallow Company. That's the company that—that—I have been working for. He thinks I have a chance to win."

Mary gave me one of those deep, kind, welcoming smiles as though, by thinking that, I belonged, and shook my hand and said, "This is the first golf match I ever saw, Mr. Fowler, but surely Elmer will win because he plays so beautifully. And of course you know why it is so important to us. Elmer told me that—that you know," and she suddenly gave Elmer's arm a little hug with such a natural, tender gesture that I thought I'd got one of our Tuff-Hide balls stuck in my throat because all the time I was looking right over her shoulder at what amounted to Elmer's walking papers. It was the draw-sheet on the club bulletin board, and Elmer was down to play old Archie Crobb in the first round. Uhuh. You got the name right away. It was just like taking a kid out of the amateur ranks for his first professional prize fight and saying, "Come on in here, son, and meet your opponent. His name is Joe Louis."

Archie was a crochety old Scotchman, but he had been around

for years and had the smoothest swing of the pack. And how he loved to take those youngsters apart in match play!

"Do come and take dinner with us at Wellbye Cottage, Mr. Fowler," Mary was saying.

"Gee, yes," Elmer added. "It's the most interesting house you ever saw. It's full of things, just like a museum, from before the Revolution even. . . ."

But I was hardly listening to them. All I could think of was that poor kid trying to tell his girl that he was out of the tournament, out of a job, and flat broke. I mumbled something about thanks and congratulations and, sure, Elmer would come through, and got away. I even had half a notion of going to Archie and asking him not to pour it into the kid too badly, though a lot of difference it made whether he went out three and two or nine and eight. But Arch was too mean, anyway. He loved to rub their noses in it. So I just went into the locker room down to the crying corner where the guys who had failed to qualify were gathered. I felt at home there, it was so nice and gloomy.

Were you ever around a golf tournament on the day when they play those two eighteen-hole sudden-death matches? Brother, it's a shambles, and you know it. The corpses of the famous dead lie piled eight high in the locker room, the grillroom is made hideous with the groans of the wounded and dying, and those that survive come off the course with a look of madness in their eyes. The word "Upset" falls with a monotonous and sickly thud upon the eardrums. I lost Whitey Brompton, one of our best men, to an unknown pro from Alabama who hit the ball as though he had a twitch, and Reggie Ring, another of our topnotchers, had the tough luck to meet Crabby Wilson, the Sweetwood pro, when Crabby was red-hot. That made two. And I just did pull Freddy McRae through in extra holes in the afternoon. Excitement? Plenty of it, with stars dumped right and left.

Oh yes, and Elmer was still in the tournament when the day was over. He beat Archie Crobb on the nineteenth hole, and in the afternoon took over Nelson Rohm, the crack Midwest pro, one up on the eighteenth. I didn't see it happen; nobody did, for that matter, but the scorer who went with them, because they had no gallery. But from what the scorers told me afterwards, Elmer just had all the luck that can happen to one guy at a time. Crobb had him dormy on the fifteenth. On the sixteenth they were both on in two, but off the pin. Elmer had to make a birdie to have a chance to stay in the show, so he jumped at the putt and rolled four feet past the hole. He sank the one coming back, but it was too late then, because Crobb shoved his putt to within eight inches of the hole for a sure half. The old guy waited for Elmer to knock the ball away and concede the victory. Elmer didn't say anything, so Crobb took his time studying the putt, while the kid stood off to one side with a funny expression on his face, staring at Archie. Crobb putted carefully and surely so that he couldn't miss, and then, by gum, the ball shot off in the funniest way and finished eight inches to one side of the hole. Archie glared as though he couldn't believe it and took a five to Elmer's four. Elmer squared the match on the eighteenth and won it on the nineteenth with a neat birdie.

In the afternoon round, against Nelson Rohm, he was cooked again. They were all square on the eighteenth tee. Elmer topped his drive, took an extra one in the rough, and lay four on the edge of the green. Nelson hit a daisy, his best drive of the day, and had the easiest kind of a niblick pitch to the pin for a sure four or a possible three. The scorer said Elmer must have been thinking of that train ride back to Iowa from the horrified way he stared at Nelson while the Midwest pro measured the distance, niblick in hand and got ready to give him the ax. And then, apparently for no reason at all, Rohm hit his niblick shot right up onto the clubhouse porch, nearly killing an eightball who was carrying a tray of drinks. He had to play it off flagstone from behind a pillar and bounced it into some shrubbery and from there into a bunker. He took a nice juicy seven. Elmer won the hole and the match with a six. Funny, huh?

I went to look up Elmer to congratulate him and give him another pep talk. That girl, and luck, were sure working wonders for him.

I found Mary, but she hadn't seen him since he had come off the course. She was a little troubled because, she said, he had walked right past without looking at her, but I smoothed that out by explaining that when a guy comes off the green after winning a tough match he sometimes doesn't know his own mother.

Do you know where I finally found Elmer, and it was late too, and the locker room practically deserted? In the washroom, staring at himself in the mirror with the wildest, scaredest, funniest expression I ever saw on any human face. Funny, too, that he didn't seem to see me come up behind him, because when I clouted him on the shoulder with a "Good work, kid!" he jumped as though he had seen the Devil and let out a yell. He came down on his feet, but his knees were shaking.

He said, "Ow! I—uh—er—th-th-thanks, Mr. F-F-Fowler," and turned and ran right out of the washroom and out of the building too.

I put it down as a case of unstrung golf nerves after a couple of harrowing matches.

Which just goes to show you how wrong Mr. Fowler can be.

And one after another, my guys got themselves kicked out of the tournament. You remember who met in the finals, don't you? That's right, Elmer Brown and Angus MacDonough. Elmer had walked right through Alex Gliddy, Crabby Wilson, and Chubby Craig, three of the best and toughest golfers in the business. I didn't see the matches because I was busy trying to root our stars through, but they said those three played the worst golf in their lives. Gliddy got an attack of hooking and parked five tee shots in a row out of bounds. Crabby Wilson couldn't putt for sour apples. He three-putted seven greens. And Chubby Craig, the greatest iron player in the game, actually got to shanking. Elmer, on the other hand, apparently couldn't do anything wrong. He holed out from bunkers. His ball took all the right kicks. If he got into trouble with his tee shot, he'd blast the next one so close to the cup he could blow it in. It was the talk of the tournament.

Yes, and there was some other kind of talk going on too, and I couldn't run it down. It was more a feeling that was in the air that you couldn't get hold of. The pros were off Elmer. They were giving him funny looks, and not speaking to him or kidding with him any more. And they used to love him. But the strangest thing I heard late Friday, when the semifinals were finished, was that when Elmer's match with Chubby was over—he beat Chubby 8 and 7—Craig refused to shake hands with him. Instead, they said, he waved one fist in front of Elmer's face in a queer way and snarled some word at him, and then turned and walked off the green. I thought maybe I'd better find Elmer and see what this was all about. But I couldn't locate him anywhere around the clubhouse. It was beginning to bother me, so I went into the locker room and had a couple of snorts. All right, maybe I had four, then. Anyway, when I got into my car parked behind the clubhouse I thought perhaps I wouldn't drive it just yet, but would sit there awhile and try to figure things out. I guess I must have fallen asleep, because when I woke up it was dark. It was nine o'clock by my wrist watch. I was just going to drive myself home when I saw a figure sneaking out the back door of the clubhouse. By its size and a flash of light on yellow hair, I knew it was Elmer. At the same time another figure suddenly came up the path. I knew that one too, dark as it was. She said:

"Elmer, dear, I've been looking for you. What—what is wrong?"

The boy stood there in the dark for a moment. "N-nothing, M-Mary."

There was a long silence. Then Mary began to speak again, in a low, clear, steady voice.

"Elmer, this afternoon after the match was over, I was going through the woods to the car. Two of the golfers were walking just in front of me. I don't know their names, but they were two who played and had been put out. They were talking about you. They were saying that you had cheated."

There was another long silence in which I could hear my heart going "bonk—bonk—bonk. . . ."

"I went up to them, told them who I was. One of them said,

'Ma'm, we're sorry, because it's true. He admitted it. If you don't believe it, why don't you ask him?' and then they both walked away. Elmer—I am asking you now. Is it true?"

Did I listen for Elmer's answer? Yes, brother, you bet I did. It was a long time coming. At last he stammered, "M-M-Mary—gee, Mary—I—I—I can't say anything—I can't—I can't. . . ."

So there it was. It seemed like hours before Mary said in a sort of small, hurt voice, "I—I'm sorry, Elmer. I guess that's all, then. I just can't stand a cheat. If you win that tournament through cheating, why—why, don't ever speak to me again."

And then she turned and ran off down the path, and a moment later I heard a car starting and driving off. Elmer waited until the last sound had died away. Then he let out an awful groan, turned, and went back into the clubhouse. Me, I wasn't more than six steps behind him.

I found him sitting in a corner of the darkened locker room with his head in his hands. I slid alongside him, put my arm around his shoulder, and said, "What's the matter, kid? Why don't you tell me and get it off your chest?"

He gave a couple of shudders and finally said, "Mr. Fowler, I want to go home. I want to default tomorrow and get out of here. You can post my default for me. I want to get out tonight, now, right away."

I tried to jolly him. I said, "Oh, come on, Elmer, you can't do that. You're going great. You've got to stay in there and fight for old Alma Mallow. You're the only one we've got left. You can't leave now. If you do it'll cost you your job, and what's more, you'll never get another job because you'll be branded a quitter."

He shook his head and groaned. "I don't care. I don't want another job. I just want to get out of here." Suddenly he stopped, hesitated, and then blurted out all in a heap, "Mr. Fowler, I've done something awful. I—I'm a witch."

I thought it was still those snorts I'd had earlier. "You're a *what?*"

"A—a witch, Mr. Fowler. I—I cheated. I put a hex on Mr. Crobb, and Mr. Rohm, and Mr. Gliddy too, though I didn't mean to, honestly, Mr. Fowler, and I guess it got Mr. Craig too, though I didn't put it on him, but it won't stop. I gotta get out of here, Mr. Fowler, I just gotta. Can't you see?"

He wasn't kidding. He was on the level. He was so much on the level that there were tears in his eyes.

I said, "Listen, kid, why don't you tell me what the hell this is all about? I don't believe you're a cheat, and I don't believe in witches, and—"

"I didn't mean to do it, Mr. Fowler. I didn't believe in it either, but I was desperate. I had to win. Mr. Crobb had a 'gimme' to win the match, and I was out of the tournament and my job, and I couldn't marry Mary. Otherwise I wouldn't have said the words. Honest I wouldn't, Mr. Fowler."

I saw I had kind of to nurse him along to get anything out of him, so I said, "What words?"

"The words in the book."

"Uhuh. What book?"

"The book I found in Mary's house. I just looked into it. It's old-like. They have a lot of things there from before the Revolution—pictures, and arrowheads and guns, and books, printed in the old kind English, and there was this one book I just looked into, one night."

"What was the book?"

It was tough getting the story out of him because he was really unstrung, but it finally developed that he had found a copy of something called *Of Ye Plague of Wytches in Ye Colonies,* by the Reverend Hallelujah Snite, printed in Boston in 1699, and had read the thing out of curiosity and found some sort of words in it which, according to the Reverend Dr. Snite, the witches of old Salem used to summon Old Nick for a party. It was getting tough to keep from laughing, because I wanted to badly.

"Just what were the words?"

"Do I have to say them?"

"Go ahead. I'm a Psi Kappa Psi myself. . . ."

He gobbled a little and finally came out with some balderdash that sounded like "Abrogath Ahrimanes Abaddon," and then looked around him frightened, as though he expected to see Old Harry snap to attention out of a cloud of sulphur with an "At your service, sir!"

"So what happened?"

"Well, I was in this jam and was practically out of the tournament, and then I suddenly remembered those words. I didn't really believe in it, but I had to do something, Mr. Fowler. Mr. Crobb couldn't miss an eight-inch putt. So I said them."

"Out loud?"

"Oh, gee, no. Just to myself."

"Could old Archie see you?"

"No, sir. I was standing behind him out of his line so he couldn't see me at all. . . ."

"And Archie blew the putt! Wow!" I just couldn't hold it in any longer and had to let go with a dozen guffaws that shook the locker room. "Kid, it's the discovery of the age. You write 'em down for me. Will I give it to that louse J. Sears Hammett of the Fairgreen Company the next time I play him a five-buck Nassau."

But the kid wasn't laughing. He said, "But you don't understand, Mr. Fowler. It's no joke. I didn't believe it at first, so when Mr. Rohm had me on the hook, I said them again and Mr. Rohm put his niblick shot into the clubhouse and took a seven. And when I played Mr. Gliddy I guess I must have said them once more without knowing it, and the Devil made him hook five tee shots in a row, and by then I was so scared I swore I'd never use them again, but it's too late now, I've sold myself to Satan. I didn't say anything when I played Mr. Wilson, but there he was just the same, keeping Mr. Wilson's putts out of the cup, and when I'd pull a six iron out of my bag I'd hear him say, 'Wrong club, sucker, it's a seven; play it high and fade it from right to left. Can't you see that wind in the top of the trees?' I've raised him, Mr. Fowler, and I can't get rid of him. If I'd only done it once, maybe he wouldn't have charged just for a demonstration. But he must want me awful bad, because he's working overtime. I can't make a bad shot. And I've lost my girl on account of him."

I said, "Listen, you big dope, those guys would have blown those shots anyway. Didn't you ever jab at a six-inch putt and see it stay out? Or get an attack of sausage fingers and see your game slip away? All that stuff is a lot of hooey anyway, but if it'll do you good and make you think you can beat those guys, what the hell! And, anyway, they don't know about it, so—"

"That's one of the worst troubles, Mr. Fowler: they do!"

"What? How could they find out—?"

"I—I told them, Mr. Fowler—yesterday before I played Mr. Craig."

"You what? Why, you sap—"

It seems that the kid was scared and worried and uncertain whether he really had made a spell, or whatever it was, because he knew from his farm upbringing that Beelzebub doesn't do that kind of work for nothing, so he had asked old Crobb whether he had felt anything when he made that putt, and of course the old guy had said, "Yes, why?" Huh! Show me a golfer who won't grab for an alibi. The poor dope had told him, and of course Crobb had snarled, "Ay, I feltit something pushit my elbow. I no hae missit a wee putt like that gang on thirrty years." And Rohm then chimed in and said when he mis-hit that niblick shot it was just as though somebody else was swinging the club, and Gliddy recalled that coming down the seventeenth fairway he had actually said, "This damn driver of mine must be bewitched." And Crabby Wilson had said, "Hah! No wonder I couldn't get a putt down all day." And then they had all turned on him and accused him of cheating, hexing them, casting the evil eye, and conduct unbecoming a member of the P.G.A. The match when Chubby Craig shanked all day had finished it.

"They're in the grillroom right now, holding a meeting over it, Mr. Fowler," concluded Elmer. "They're going to have me barred anyway. Let me go back to Osceola, Mr. Fowler. I can't go on. Satan's moved into my golf bag. I just gotta hang it up."

I said, "Listen, kid. You stay here until I get back. I'm going to that meeting. Those sharks aren't going to push one of my guys out of a tournament that way. You do as I say, understand?"

And I went busting into the grillroom. I was just in time too. There was a big crowd of the pros there, and Archie Crobb was saying, "All those favoring to expel Elmer Brown and bar him frae the final say—" when I walked through the door and finished it for him.

"Say what? Are you guys nuts? What's the matter with Brown? Can't you birds take a licking without crying?"

Crabby Wilson said, "We can when it's on the level," and Nelson Rohm shouted, "What are you doing in here, Fowler? This is a closed meeting. You don't belong here."

I said, "Maybe I don't, but I'm not going to let you railroad one of my guys out of this tournament for nothing."

"For nothing!" shouted Crabby Wilson. "He put the whammie on me! Every time I'd go to putt, my eyes would water so I couldn't see the ball."

"He admittit himself he called on the De'il," said Crobb. "The mon's a witch. I haven't misstit a wee putt like thot in thirrr—"

I said, "You're a fool, Crobb. There aren't any male witches."

"Aweel, then, callit him a wizard, it's a' the same."

"I'll say he's a wizard, the way he plastered you three straight holes after you lost your nerve and blew a kick-in."

"What about his telling me he put a spell on me before I hit that shot to the eighteenth? The ball went up into the clubhouse, didn't it?" said Nelson Rohm.

"Yeah," I said. "He told you afterwards. I suppose you never missed a green in your life before. Sure, the kid's a little screwy like all you birds, but—"

Angus MacDonough chimed in here. "A mon has no richt to do wi bogles in a gowf match. I'll no have to do wi him. The De'il's in his bag."

I said, "O.K., boys. You do what you want, but I'm going out and dig up a couple of golf writers and give them the story of how a lot of grown men who got licked by a green kid had to work up an alibi for themselves."

I thought that would do it. It did, too. There were a lot of sensible guys there and they talked it over and finally agreed to do nothing and go ahead with the tournament.

"But you tell that young mon I'll no be bewitched," warned Angus. "The fairst spell I feel, I'll magic him wi a niblick."

I went back into the locker room and got Elmer and said, "Son, you'd better get all that nonsense out of your head. They were holding a meeting to consider the course for next year's tournament. You come on home with me and get a night's sleep and tomorrow you'll pin Angus's ears back for good old Mallow."

He shook his head. "Aw, what's the use, Mr. Fowler? I don't want the job any more. I've lost Mary. She thinks I'm a cheat like the rest of them do."

So I piled into him about quitting and gave him a ten-minute speech that any football coach would have paid me for, winding up with, "You can't let this thing lick you this way. Go on out there and prove that you can whip—"

He interrupted me suddenly. A change seemed to have come over him. He jumped up and said, "I will, Mr. Fowler. By crickey, I will. I can make good. I will. *I know how.*"

I took him home with me. Boy, I was tickled to death. Mallow was going to collect another championship. I wouldn't have been so pleased if I'd known what he really meant. . . .

So the next morning we went out to play the final match against Angus MacDonough, with me carrying Elmer's bag. That's right. I had to caddie for him. Elmer's regular boy, a big African from Mobile by the name of Four Toes, met me down by the caddie pen, and he was on his way out, headed south. He said, "You gotta excuse me, Mistuh Fowler. Ah ain' gonna carry dat bag no mo'. De Debbil's done got in it. Ebbrybody say so. Ebbry time Ah give a club to Mistuh Brown de Debbil he say to him to take another. Ah heerd de voice an' seen de smoke commin' outen de bag. No *suh!* Ah ain' touchin' it no mo." All the other caddies had disappeared. I picked up Elmer's clubs and went to the first tee. Elmer didn't even notice that I was carrying for him. He was like a guy all wrapped up in something. Angus turned his back on him and so did Angus's caddie, who was none other than Dutch Steubner, another Fairgreen pro. That witchcraft story had got all the caddies so scared they wouldn't go anywhere near Elmer. It was a good thing there weren't any of the top-flight golf writers around that tournament or they would have been asking plenty of questions. As it was, some of those smart guys from Boston were nosing around trying to track down some of the rumors they'd heard, and I had to tell plenty of lies. There was nothing unusual in Angus Mac-Donough refusing to look at an opponent, or speak to him, because he had the reputation of being a mean, goat-getting grouch in match play, but I wondered whether the reporters would catch on to the surreptitious signs he and Dutch and all the other golfers who were in the gallery made every time that Elmer would look at them—you know, fist doubled up with thumb and little finger sticking out, and X's and circles in the air.

I was glad when we got started. I wanted to get it over with. There were about a thousand or so in the gallery, and they must have felt there was something in the air, because they were sort of hushed when they moved off after us, following two nice drives that split the fairway. Elmer's some forty yards past Angus'. Angus knocked a four iron onto the green, about fourteen feet from the pin. Elmer pulled a number seven out of the bag. I said, "It's a six, kid. There's an upslope in front of the green. If you don't reach, it'll stop the ball dead."

Do you know what that fool kid did? He put his hands over his ears. Then he said, "Stand behind me, caddie." I got it, all right. He meant, "Get thee behind me, Satan." Then he hit a perfect seven iron. Only, as I said, it was a six-iron shot. The ball hit in front of the green, hesitated, and then rolled back down the slope. And his chip hit the bank and stopped outside of Angus's ball. Elmer had to putt first and rolled to within a foot of the cup for a fairly sure five. It was Angus's turn to putt. He took a long time over it and then hit one that certainly was a dilly. I never saw a worse shot on a green. He must have lunged at it. It wound up seven feet past the hole to one side. Angus stared at it as though he couldn't believe it. Then he turned angrily on Elmer, but before he could say anything, Elmer went over to Angus' ball, knocked it away with a "That's good," and walked off the green. There was a murmur of astonishment from the crowd.

I said, "What the devil did you do that for, you sap? He was a sure thing to miss that putt coming back and you'd have halved the hole. Now you're one down."

"No, I ain't," said Elmer softly, "no, I ain't. I'm one up. On that feller you just mentioned. And I'm going to whip him all the way."

So that's how it was going to be. Yes, and that's how it was, too. When I brought him in to the clubhouse at the end of the first eighteen holes, he was exactly fourteen down. He underclubbed, he overclubbed, he conceded putts, he took penalties. The people in the gallery were sore as pups, grumbling and threatening to demand their money back or complain to the officials, but Angus was tickled to death, and so were the other pros. They acted just as though they had it coming to them. The newspaper boys kept barging up to me, asking, "What's he doing, throwing the match? What's the idea?" and I'd yell, "Oh, leave us alone. Didn't you ever see a guy in a slump before? He'll be all right after lunch." But of course that last was hooey. It was all over. I could have killed Elmer, except that for the first time since it all started he seemed halfway happy and some of the fear was gone from his face. I left him alone in a corner of the grill drinking milk and went out by myself. I was too sick to eat. I passed a group of officials conferring in front of the clubhouse and heard they were going to call a meeting before the tee-off again after lunch. They had to, because everybody was squawking. I went into the woods bordering the sixth fairway to cool off. I didn't even want a drink. I had my hands stuffed down into my pockets and was kicking at things.

So that was how I came to haul that lucky elephant out of my pocket, because after a while I got to feeling it there, sort of hard and funny-shaped. I said, "You're a fine damn mascot, you are! You're supposed to be lucky, eh? You're nothing but a Jonah, and here you go," and with that I took a Bob Feller windup and heaved it as hard and as far as I could into a clump of bushes.

There was a gasp, and somebody said, "Ow!" I ran around to the other side of them to apologize to whoever I had beaned. You guessed it. It was Mary Summers. She was sitting on a log. There were tear stains on her face where she had been crying. The elephant was lying at her feet.

I said, "Gee, Mary, I'm sorry. Where have you been? I've wanted to see you. Elmer—"

She began to cry again. "Oh, Bill, I'm so miserable. I accused Elmer of cheating, and left him without giving him a real chance to explain. I don't care what he's done, I love him. He isn't a cheat. And I saw what he was doing this morning. And instead of helping him, I— Oh, Bill—"

So then I told her the whole story, right from the beginning. And sometimes she laughed, but with tears and tenderness behind it, and sometimes she cried and made little gestures with her arms as though she were taking the absent Elmer into them. I wound up, "The poor kid is off his nut. He thinks he sinned saying those words, and has to atone for it by throwing the match to that old sour-puss Angus and beat the Devil that way, even though it costs him his job and the chance to marry you; and Angus, the old goat, behaves as though he had it coming to him, with the other pros egging him on, because by blaming it all on Elmer it gives them an alibi for their lousy golf. The reporters are hot on the trail of the story, though they haven't got it yet, but if it gets out, the kid'll be ruined. The officials are going to call a meeting in the clubhouse private office before the afternoon. Maybe they'll disqualify him right there. I don't know. It's an awful mess."

The girl took a deep breath and straightened up. Gee, she was a sweet sight with her blue eyes shining. She said, "Bill—Bill— we've got to do something. Right away."

"I know, but what? Maybe it's too late."

She was staring down at my elephant suddenly. She said: "Bill, what is that?"

I said, "That's my elephant. I carry it around in my pocket."

"What for?"

"For luck. But the luck was all bad, so I heaved it."

She picked it up, gazed at it for a moment, and then handed it to me. There was a strange look on her face.

"Put it back in your pocket, Bill. Maybe it will turn out to be the best friend you or I ever had." She glanced at her watch and gave a little gasp. "Oh! There isn't much time. Hurry, Bill! Go to that meeting. Don't let them leave. Do anything to hold them. I'll be there at two o'clock," and she was streaking off through the woods like a young deer.

I went back to the clubhouse, but quick. The afternoon tee-off time was two fifteen. At ten minutes to two the meeting was called by the officials. It was attended by Elmer and myself and Angus and Dutch, and all the pros that Elmer had beaten, and half a dozen others. Old Bill Wattley, the chief referee, didn't waste any time. He was boiling mad. He lit into poor Elmer and said that what he had done that morning was a disgrace to professional golfing, that people had paid good money to see a fair match. He lit into old Angus too, and the other pros, and said that he had heard a lot of silly stories, and there and now meant to get at the truth of the matter before he decided what action he would take.

Nobody wanted to say anything at first because, now that it was going to be dragged out in open meeting, they were a little ashamed, I guess; but finally old Archie Crobb spoke up and said, "Meester Wattley, 'tis ony richt he should gi' back to us what he tookit by foul means. He's admittit he has to do wi' bogles and Beelzebub and the sperrits o' the pit. I no hae missit a wee putt like that in thirrrty—"

Elmer suddenly got up, big, lanky, and miserable, and interrupted. "Aw, gee, Mr. Wattley, let me default and get out of here. I don't care what they say about me. Mr. Crobb is right. I didn't deserve to win. I—"

"Oh yes you did, Elmer," said Mary Summers. She had opened the door and come in very quietly. It was just two o'clock. She had a book under her arm, and she threw it down on the table. It was old and yellow, and from where I sat I could see it was the treatise by the Reverend Hallelujah Snite. Everybody stared at it as though it were a snake, including Elmer.

"Oh yes, you deserve to win, Elmer," Mary repeated, and then looked the whole crowd over coolly and a little as though they were insects. "I know the whole silly story. All you gentlemen who are so righteous, did you ever hear this: 'Let him who is without sin cast the first stone'?"

A fly buzzing on the windowpane sounded just like a dive-bomber, it was that quiet.

"Mr. Crobb," said Mary Summers, "turn out your pockets!"

Nobody moved. "Wha—what did ye say, lass?" said old Crobb.

"I said turn out your pockets, Mr. Crobb. Put whatever you have here on the table. At once."

By jeepers, old Crobb did. He was hypnotized. His hands came up from his pockets full of junk which he laid on the table—some bills, coins, a little roll of tape, pocket knife, half a dozen tees, and a little rabbit's-foot set in silver.

"Now you, Mr. Wilson," her voice rising, "and you . . . and you . . . and you . . . all of you. Out with them."

By jeepers, they were *all* hypnotized. Even I turned mine out before I knew it. And then Mary was at the table, picking out objects from each pile and sweeping them toward the center, the rabbit's-foot, punched coins, cat's-eyes, a piece of heather in a locket, framed four-leaf clovers, miniature horseshoes, little worsted Aucassins and Nicolettes, a curiously shaped stone or two, chunks of carved wood, a little silver devil on a ring, pairs of dice, medals, carved elephants, a piece of jade, and a silver pig.

She pointed to the pile. "What do you call these?" she said.

They all grinned sheepishly, and Archie Crobb said, "Eh, lass, what's wrang wi' a mascot?"

"Wrong? Do you know where the word 'mascot' comes from?"

asked Mary Summers. "In old French the word *'masco'* meant a
sorceress or witch. You're all in it, every one of you. There isn't one
of you who doesn't carry a talisman that you think gives you something on the other fellow, an edge, a spell, a lucky charm, something supernatural. And you dare to pick on Elmer? You ought to
be ashamed of yourselves, all of you. That book there, that you're
all so afraid of—" she flipped it open—"do you know what it is? It
was written by a half-crazy, superstitious ninny about a pack of
harmless, innocent old women who were drowned and stoned and
hanged not more than five miles from here in Salem, to the ever-
lasting shame of that city and a monument to ignorance and stupidity. Do you know what that spell is that terrified all you big
brave men so that you couldn't hit a little golf ball? There it is.
It was used by a lot of poor, ignorant, self-deluded wretches to
curdle milk. And it never curdled anything but your dispositions.
There, read it and see if it is any worse than that collection of
ridiculous junk you carry around with you this year of 1942 to ward
off bogies. Grown men, all of you. Very well. You're all even now.
Put your nasty things back into your pockets and try to act like men
and not a lot of frightened old women. Elmer Brown, you go right
out and play that man golf, out in the woods there where everything is fresh and sweet and clean. And—and—" she hesitated suddenly and her lower lip began to tremble—"and—I don't care
whether you win or lose, I'll marry you because I love you, and
I don't care if we s-s-s-starve. . . . Oh, Elllllllmer—"

And she was in his arms, crying, and all the pros were around
her, patting her on the shoulder and apologizing and trying to make
up to Elmer, and Mary kissed Elmer as though nobody was there,
and Elmer suddenly raised up his arms with his fists clenched and
shouted, "I've won! I've won! I've licked it. And now I'll lick you
too, Angus MacDonough. Come on out on the course and take
it. . . ."

Whew! I'm glad I don't have to describe that last eighteen holes
for you. You read about it. The greatest comeback in the history
of golf, they called it. And that Angus was playing too. You don't

catch him giving anything away. But nobody ever saw golf like that kid played. He'd never really hit a ball before as hard as he could because of his size and strength, which might rob him of control. But now he had the control too. When they set par for that course it wasn't for the kind of golf Elmer shot. He simply made threes out of the fours, and fours out of the fives.

There weren't more than fifty people on the tee when we started, but by the time we reached the ninth, there were two thousand galloping on our heels, and Elmer, who had turned in 30, was only seven down. Even the cooks and waiters came out of the kitchen to see the miracle. As I toted Elmer's bag past the clubhouse from the ninth green to the tenth tee, a Western Union boy handed me a telegram. It was from A. R. Mallow, who must have been listening in to the match on the radio. It said:

TRUST YOU HAVE NOT MADE MISTAKE OF LETTING BROWN GET AWAY FROM US STOP IF HE WINS RAISE SALARY TWELVE HUNDRED A YEAR STOP A.R.

Me make the mistake! Wasn't that just like A.R.?

You read how Elmer squared the match on the seventeenth to the greatest frenzy of cheering I ever heard, and then slipped up on the eighteenth to let Angus halve him. Then Angus got into trouble on the nineteenth and was only on the edge of the green in three, while Elmer was on in two, but with a nasty, curling, downhill ten-foot putt. Angus chipped into the cup from off the edge for his four, and the crowd gave him a great hand. A careful, certain four would keep the match open for Elmer another hole. A three would win it. But the putt was downhill, and if it missed the can, the ball would roll on and cost him the match and the championship if he missed coming back.

Elmer knelt down and studied the line. He studied it from every angle, inspected each blade of grass in the path to the hole. Everybody knew that he was going to go for the cup and the match.

He bent over his putt and waited to steady his nerves. And then I saw old Angus MacDonough do a funny thing. He fished into his pocket and hauled forth a little scrap of paper, studied it, glared at Elmer's back, and his lips moved; then he looked back at the paper again. Somehow, out of the corner of his eye, Elmer must have seen him too, for he straightened up all of a sudden, grinning.

Then he said, "The words, Mr. MacDonough, are: 'Abrogath Ahrimanes Abaddon,' but they don't mean a damn thing if you haven't got the golf to go with them. Watch this."

He leaned over and stroked the ball and I shut my eyes. Then I heard a gentle "Bonk!" as it fell into the cup, and everybody was yelling and screaming and dancing, and Mary Summers was in the center of it all, with her arms around big stupid Elmer's neck. . . .

Boy, did I kiss that little old good-luck elephant of mine. Wouldn't it have been hell if I'd left it at home?

The Adventure of Joe Smith, American

This story was written out of a deep conviction. During the black summer of 1940 the bill for a national conscription law was being debated by Congress. I hoped, for the sake of the country, that it would pass. And I conceived and wrote "Joe Smith" with the idea that it might make people understand something of our predicament so that they would be influenced to demand the passage of the bill.

The above might very well pass for a definition of propaganda, and propaganda is exactly what the story was, but of a different kind in that it was inspired by nothing but my own personal feelings about my country, and the suggestion to do it came from no one but myself. I belonged to no political party, no group, no sect. But I felt something strongly. And I had a medium to express what I believed.

Among the things I felt at that time was that we as a nation and a people were in grave danger, for which we were prepared neither physically nor psychically. I think the experiences of my sports-writing career were crowding in upon me and reminding me of the necessity of training for any man going into a fight, whether for sport or for keeps.

There was a popular cliché, subscribed to by practically everyone, to the effect that every American was a born fighter and that one American could lick any six foreigners, whereas the truth was that one untrained American couldn't lick his own shadow, literally, because one three-minute round of shadow-boxing would see him lying helpless and exhausted on the ground, unable to move.

It takes years of practice and training to enable a young man to reach the point where he can fight or box fifteen rounds of three minutes each, a total of forty-five minutes of combat with a minute of rest after each round. The average street brawl, or night-club brannigan, lasts about fifteen seconds, with no more than a half-dozen punches thrown. The silliest thing is the fear with which bystanders regard such combat

Cosmopolitan, December 1940.

and their eagerness to stop it, when all anyone has to do is wait. If it goes a minute, both parties will fall down from their own exertions.

Compared to war, fighting in the prize ring is a joke. The soldier must be prepared to march, attack, fight, carry loads, freeze, suffocate, go without sleep or food for forty-eight hours at a time with no rest periods, and no bell to call off hostilities. He must know the intricacies of twenty different mechanical weapons, as well as the dirty secrets of hand-to-hand combat. Few of us in 1940 were able to so much as chase a trolley car a block without getting the blind staggers.

These were some of the things I wanted to say to people, to make them realize, feel, and experience vicariously the horror of the helplessness of a man who is physically soft and unskilled in the use of arms when he stacks up against an enemy who has been taught and trained in all the arts of brutality and aggression.

There were other things. Many of us were doing a lot of talking about our passion for democracy, freedom, and liberty without ever thinking what it really meant to us should we lose it. And then there was that singular emotion, the love of country, and the need to think upon it and to know that there might be a time to come when we would have to make the choice of placing it ahead of self. The time did come, and millions of American men did just that. But back in 1940 those same millions did not even know their country was being threatened, or how tragically unprepared we were to resist an attack.

Out of these thoughts and worries and emotions grew the common-denominator character of Joe Smith and the story, which has no "plot" in the accepted sense. The melodramatics of the desperate situation into which Joe Smith found himself plunged were already everyday commonplaces in tortured Europe. Men were already facing the horror of finding themselves left with no weapon but the will to rebel against compulsion.

The story was completed in two weeks from the time of original conception and sent to my agent from San Francisco, where I was living at the time. He submitted it to the *Saturday Evening Post*, which rejected it on the grounds that it was too emotional for them and overwritten. If my memory serves me correctly, one of the editors characterized it as slushy. I was miserable over the rejection because of how I had felt about what went into the piece. Perhaps I had let my emotions carry me away. Sometimes that can be damaging to a

story. But *Cosmopolitan* did not think so, for it bought the story immediately. The telegram I got from Frances Whiting, Fiction Editor, more
than made up for the bad time given me by the *Post*.

The piece never had the chance to do the job I intended it for, because, owing to inventory and mechanical difficulties, considerable
time passed before it was published, which was one reason it was sent
to the *Post* in the first place. I wanted to get it into print quickly. By
the time it appeared in the December issue, national Selective Service
had become law. But the story stood on its feet as a tale, apparently,
because the mail reaction was surprisingly high. "Joe Smith" had further adventures. It was bought by Metro-Goldwyn-Mayer and produced
as a "B" picture with Robert Young as the star and contributed another
surprise when it proved a "sleeper" in spite of some of the queer things
the picture people did to it to convert it to feature length. It received
four stars in review and was named among the ten best pictures of the
year.

THERE was nothing about that ordinary Thursday morning in
the fall of 1940 to augur an adventure to Joe Smith. He had
never had one, beyond meeting Anna at Coney Island and
marrying her within six weeks, which was Romance and not
Adventure. Otherwise nothing had ever happened to him more
exciting than locking fenders in a traffic jam, with Anna and the
kids in the old car.

Not that in Joe Smith's own mind he wasn't eminently fitted to
play a heroic part in any hazard that might fall to his lot. He went
regularly to the movies with Anna, and he was in the habit of reading himself to sleep with magazine stories. He had no difficulty
substituting himself for the heroes who swashbuckled through the
pages of periodicals or stalked as gigantic shadows across the screen.

And, besides, he was an American, and being an American had a
mysterious and protective connotation to Joe Smith. It endowed him
automatically from birth with large and heroic qualities. An American, he knew, could lick any five foreigners. An American was
lightning on the trigger and equipped by nature with extraordinary
strength, daring and ingenuity. Much of this opinion he had

acquired during the course of his schooling, which had extended to the third year at high, before he had had to go to work. But mostly it was something that he simply took for granted, like liberty and free speech and two weeks' vacation with pay.

If you had asked him whether he believed in democracy, he would have said "Sure," and if you had inquired further whether he loved his country, he would have replied "Certainly!"

For these things were part of the unquestionable verities that went to make up the contented life of Joe Smith; verities as unchallenged as his cup of coffee in the morning, the car, the radio, the monthly smoker at the Queensborough Elks, the job, Anna, and the kids.

At thirty-six Joe Smith had arrived. He lived in Astoria, in a two-story house that was exactly like every other house in the block. But to him his house had distinction. He owned it, with the narrow plot on which it stood and the tiny garden in back. His car was no more than three years behind the latest model, and he could get London, Berlin, and Rome on his radio and share vicariously in the exciting tragedies being enacted there, though he understood no language but his own.

Anna, his wife, was still a fine-looking woman who did not nag him any more than he had a right to expect and who took care of him, the house, and the children. Joe Junior and Maybelle were two years apart, and both attended the excellent public school not far from the house.

Twenty years ago Joe Smith had quit school to go to work on a lathe in a small factory. Now he was foreman of the machine and tool shop of the Acme Pipe and Tubing Co., Inc., in South Brooklyn, at a salary of $75 a week, and a bonus at Christmas. Old man Padson, Acme's big boss, would not think of putting in a new tool or machine without first consulting Joe.

In a way, adventure had already mildly impinged on Smith shortly before the morning in question. The country was in the throes of its rearmament program, a state of affairs of which Joe Smith heartily approved, just as he disapproved the ways of the foreign dictators and aggressors.

An engineer in Washington, a Colonel Glendiron, had worked out a simple but brilliant tool adaptation whereby, with a few slight alterations, machines used in the manufacture of certain types of steel tubing could be made to produce rifle barrels in quantity for the new semiautomatic weapon recently adopted by the Army.

The invention was sufficiently important to be closely guarded, especially in its early stage, and the Acme Company, manufacturers of large quantities of steel tubing, was selected for the initial make-over experiments.

Joe Smith's mechanical genius and overlordship of every die and machine in the Acme factory made him an important cog in the scheme. He was, of course, proud of the trust reposed in him and did not even speak of the matter to Anna at home. He memorized the blueprint in three days, and his mind was chiefly occupied with and fascinated by the brilliance and simplicity of the adaptation.

At five minutes past eight Joe Smith put down his newspaper and rose from the breakfast table. His house was full of the comforting kind of noise to which he was accustomed. The radio was already on. The children were gabbling in the midst of breakfast, and from the kitchen came the sound of running water and dishes being washed.

Smith kissed Maybelle and Joe Junior on the tops of their heads, went to the kitchen door, and said, "G'by, hon."

Anna was wearing a clean, blue-checked apron, her hair was tidy, and she smelled of household soap. Hard work had aged her more than it had Joe, but her dark eyes were still beautiful.

She dried her hands quickly on a dishtowel, came over to her husband, and they pecked at each other—the good-by kiss of long habit. "Ya gonna be late again tonight?" Anna asked.

"I guess maybe. We're putting in a lotta new stuff."

She did not demur. The factory was *his* world. And, besides, it meant overtime pay. She said, "I'll keep something hot for you."

Joe Smith went out into the sunshiny autumn morning. At many other houses up and down the block, doors were banging, too, as men and women emerged to go to work. He went to the garage,

backed the car out carefully, pounded the horn button in two farewell honks, and drove off.

His route, carefully calculated for speed and avoidance of traffic,
was a detour skirting Brooklyn proper. It was always the same and
landed him at the factory at ten minutes to nine.

Shortly before eight thirty Joe Smith was driving down Pascal
Street in the vicinity of Cypress Hills Cemetery when a large
limousine, containing two men in addition to the driver, came from
behind him on the left and bore over, crowding him to the curb.
By jamming on his brakes quickly, Smith managed to prevent a
collision.

He leaned out of his window and bawled at what was apparently
a careless driver. "Whatsa matter with ya? Whyntcha look where
ya goin'?"

This was the accepted beginning for all negotiations with drivers
who displeased him. Smith knew his rights of the road and was not
prepared to relinquish one iota of them.

The driver of the car leaned across to the open window and
shouted, "Why you no look where you go? What you try do, run
into me?"

The man spoke with a foreign accent that Smith could not place.
Because he was well within his time limit for the factory, the temptation to put the fellow in his place was too great to be resisted, so
he said, "Oh, yeah? A wise guy, eh?" still in the accepted formula,
almost as if he were repeating lines from a play.

The driver replied coolly, "You get outta that car, I show you who
is a wise guy."

This was not according to script. There should have been more
verbal exchange, after which they would have driven on. But there
was an insolence about the other driver that caused a hard and bitter
bead of anger to form at the core of Joe Smith. He jammed on his
hand brake, snapped open the door of his car, and piled out into
the road. The other driver did the same. The two men remained
in the rear of the car.

Smith doubled up his fists. The driver was taller than he, and
heavier. Smith wasn't frightened, because part of his credo was that

he could fight, though he had not been called upon to put up his fists since his high-school days. He did not weigh more than a hundred and forty-five pounds, and although he was not corpulent, he had taken no exercise in fifteen years other than an occasional round of golf or an evening of bowling. He would clip this guy one on the jaw, get back in his car, and drive off. But he should have noticed that the street was deserted and the nearest house a block away.

He said, "O. K. What are ya gonna show me?"

The driver made no reply. Instead he stepped close with a cat-like, gliding motion and smashed his left fist against the side of Smith's head in a whistling hook.

It caught Smith on the temple, stunning him and spinning him backward, so that he would have fallen except that he crashed into the side of his own car and hung there, his legs trembling, the world spinning dizzily. Passion brought him back for a moment, and, pushing off from the car, he hurled himself at his assailant, his arms flailing wildly.

The driver sidestepped and hit Smith again and again, though these blows he did not feel in the heat of the battle. But he had not landed yet, and his own efforts were exhausting him. He had to sob to breathe, and there was a rasping flame burning in his chest. His arms were heavy with pain of fatigue. Summoning his last reserves, he threw his right hand desperately at the chin of the other man. He missed, his arm going around the man's neck. Smith fell into him, clutching to hold and grapple with him. The driver brought his knee sharply up into Smith's groin.

Convulsed with agony, Joe Smith slid to his knees, retching and gasping. Blows knocked his head from side to side. Somehow, he retained consciousness long enough for one bewildered, gasping protest. "You're hitting a guy when he's down!"

Also, he was aware that the two other men were piling out of the car. He felt a shock that seemed to explode inside his head and bring down upon him a splintering, fire-streaked blackness that enveloped him in oblivion.

Joe Smith was not a stupid man. When consciousness returned, he knew that he was in a bad spot. He realized now that it was not an ordinary street fight in which he had become involved, but probably a snatch. Hard as it was for his aching, reeling head to summon consecutive thought, he even suspected that it might have something to do with the factory. But he did not for a moment doubt his ability to get out of it. For that was a part of his credo, too. His had been a world of clear-cut distinctions: the good, the bad; the hero, the villain; a world where right triumphed and was rewarded, where evil was invariably punished, where help came to the good in the nick of time.

He had been conscious for some minutes before his captors were aware of it. They were not looking when his eyes jerked open for the first time and took in the barren room and the men in it. He had shut them immediately and then stolen glimpses from beneath his lowered eyelids. He had seen the figures of five men, a door, windows with shades drawn, a fireplace with a mantel, chairs, a table. There were no doubts as to his own position. He was seated in a straight-backed chair, his legs wired so that he could not move them. His wrists were joined together behind the chair and wired tightly.

In the make-believe world of Joe Smith, bounded on the north by the comic strips, on the east by the radio, on the south by the adventure magazines, and on the west by the screen, escape was always begun by the loosening of the bonds, carelessly tied.

He tried straining at his wrists and almost fainted from the pain in his arms. There was no strength in them, nor would the strength of ten have helped him. The copper wire, wound around and twisted, held them solidly. When he moved, the wire cut into his flesh. He knew that he didn't have a chance.

A sudden deluge of water struck him full in the face, making him choke, gasp, and open his eyes. The man who had beaten him up in the street stood in front of him holding an empty pitcher. He said, "So you awake, eh?" All the other men in the room were looking at their prisoner. Smith stared back at them.

He had never seen any of them before. He tried to distinguish between them. One had very dark hair and a blue chin, and another was so blond that he seemed to have no lashes or eyebrows. His assailant had a broken nose. The fourth had a short gray beard and gold-rimmed spectacles, while the fifth was a huge bull of a man with a massive head and a cleft chin.

Dark Hair and No Lashes had heavy blue automatic pistols in their hands, from whose barrels protruded some kind of attachment. Smith had seen such things in pictures and knew they were silencers.

The room was illuminated by three electric globes in an overhead chandelier, for although it was daylight outside, the dark shades covered the windows. The men, with the exception of Broken Nose, who was standing, were seated around a table. On the table Smith could see paper, pencils, pens, a bottle of drafting ink, rulers, calipers, and a T-square.

When they saw that he was conscious, the four began talking in a foreign language of which Smith could not understand a word. He gathered, however, that Cleft Chin was the leader of the group. They were all foreigners, including Broken Nose. Two of them, Black Hair and No Lashes, he now recognized as having been in the back of the car.

Cleft Chin slewed around in his chair and said, "You, Smit'! Listen to me careful. We going to untie you. You come over here and sit down. There will be a gun at the back of your neck. You drawing then the plans and specifications for the Glendiron Adapter. If you can't draw, you tell him there." He jerked his head in the direction of Gray Beard. "He is an engineer. You do that, and nothing happens to you. You try any monkey business, and you get it. Understand? And don't make any nonsense, because the engineer understands the business and we catch you, and when we catch you, you are sorry. You going to be reasonable, I think?"

The thing that puzzled Joe Smith was the absence of melodramatics. Except for Dark Hair and No Lashes holding the guns, which were not even pointed at him, they were all sitting like businessmen at a conference table. And Cleft Chin had spoken almost like one of the Acme engineers at the shop explaining something.

But Joe Smith could understand the things implied in the speech.

These men were after the Glendiron Adapter. They knew who he was. They were certain that he could supply them with what they wanted. Phrases whirled through his head: "National Defense Secrets," "Fifth Column."

It was Joe Smith who finally supplied the melodrama. He stared at Cleft Chin and said, "You can go to hell, ya rat!"

Cleft Chin rose without a word. He came over to Joe Smith; in his hand was a thick rubber truncheon, with which he smashed Smith in the mouth.

The shock addled Smith's brains again, split his lip and shattered a tooth. Waves of pain coursed sickeningly through his head; he spit out blood and the piece of tooth. There was a puzzled look, a look almost of childish bewilderment on his face, because he could not understand the brutal ferocity of the man who had struck him. He had forgotten his own sentence spoken so bravely, and he was trying to think why this had been done to him.

Cleft Chin sucked in his breath with a hissing sound, leaned down, and struck with the truncheon again, but this time just above the shins, little flicking taps that turned into excruciating agony.

"Oh! Oh, God! Oh! Don't hit me any more!" cried Joe Smith. The shock of pain had cleared his head again, and he found himself doing two things at once: inwardly raging and scheming—the dirty, cowardly rats; if he could get his hands on one of those guns he'd show them! He'd kill the lot of them. Outwardly, he cried his hurt because he could not hold it in. "Oh, God! Please don't hit me again."

Cleft Chin straightened up. He said, "You do what I say?"

"Yes, yes. I'll do anything."

Cleft Chin spoke to Broken Nose in the strange language, and the man knelt down and loosed Smith's hands and legs. That was the way, thought Joe Smith. Get loose. Make them think he was going to tell them. Grab a gun and kill them all. Beat them; that's how it was done.

His hands were loose, but he could not feel his fingers. Broken Nose yanked him to his feet and held him because he could not stand alone. Dark Hair stood behind him, pressing the muzzle of his silencer into the back of his neck. Broken Nose led him to the table and let him slump into a chair. Gray Beard leaned forward, a blueprint in his hands. Joe Smith worked his fingers feebly to bring some feeling back into them.

What was it he must do? Turn the tables! Whirl like lightning! Snatch the gun! Cover them! Kill them if they moved! The moment would come. One spring, and . . .

The waves of pain pulsed through his head again. His beaten legs were trembling and useless. The numbness had left his mouth, and the raw nerve of the shattered tooth was stabbing him with throbbing spasms.

Whirl, then! Spring! Snatch victory from defeat! Oh, God, with what? What was this monstrous lie of invincibility he had believed? Spring with this limp, broken, tortured thing that was his body? Do what heroes do? In God's name, how? For he had nothing left.

The papers blurred beneath his gaze, and he swayed, but caught himself. He heard the harsh tones of Cleft Chin. "Come on! Begin!"

A curious accident happened, for it was nothing more. The weakness came again, and Joe Smith began to fall face forward on the table.

Dark Hair snatched at him to hold him back, and Broken Nose did too, in a sharp movement that clashed against Dark Hair, so that his arm was jarred and the heavy automatic with the silencer attached clattered onto the table.

Hands and arms thudded on the board in a wild scramble for it. But miraculously it was Joe Smith who got it first. And as his fingers closed around the butt, not only courage came back to him but strength, and he thrust himself violently backward, knocking Dark Hair and Broken Nose aside.

Pure instinct was at work, urging him to put distance between himself and his tormentors, and he ran, staggering on his weakened legs, to the wall on the other side of the room. He would have been shot by No Lashes during this flight except that in the flurry of his getting hold of the gun both Cleft Chin and Broken Nose had come between Smith and No Lashes, and the gunman had not dared to fire.

Joe Smith turned, gasping for breath, his legs trembling violently, his heart pounding. But he held the heavy pistol up before him, though his hand was shaking, and through his puffed and bleeding lips he said thickly, "All right, you rats! Stick 'em up!"

All right, you rats! Stick 'em up! That was what one said when one's hand held the compelling magic of a gat. All resistance must melt before this talisman, and arms must reach for the ceiling. Thus were the tables turned; so was victory snatched from defeat.

Yet this was not what Joe Smith saw. None of the men at the other end of the room had obeyed his command.

"Stick 'em up!" said Joe Smith again, but there was puzzled insistence rather than command in his voice. "Drop that gun and stick 'em up, or I'm gonna give it to you." He pointed the weapon at the men and tried to hold it steady.

Cleft Chin gave a quiet command in the strange language to No Lashes. The blond man raised his gun.

Joe Smith gave a yell of fear. "All right, ya rats, ya asked for it!" He jerked wildly at the trigger to kill them all by the violence of his finger.

It was the first time Joe Smith had ever held a pistol in his hand. In the organization of his simple world, guns were owned by policemen, gangsters, and G-men. When guns barked, the righteous survived and the men of evil crumpled and fell. He had never questioned his own ability to handle a weapon. To shoot well was the gift of every American by right of inheritance. These were facts long recognized. He had never had any reason to doubt them.

His gun went "Pcha! Pcha!" and kicked violently upward. Flakes of plaster and dust fell from the ceiling onto the table. None of the men stirred except No Lashes, who squeezed the trigger so that his gun likewise said "Pcha!" before Joe Smith could shoot again.

Fire seared through Smith's hand, and panic rose in suffocating waves. He realized that he had missed, and with his mind he fired his gun again and again into the bodies of the men as they stormed toward him. But there was no noise except the trampling of their feet, because there was no longer any pistol in his shattered hand. It had been shot out of his grip and lay in a far corner.

Futilely, he tried to strike as the five poured over him, beating, clawing, and kicking at him. He received a heavy blow on the head and for the second time that day lost consciousness.

Joe Smith was revived by the powerful fumes from an ammonia bottle held beneath his nose and was brought sharply to a world of bitter truth and realism.

He was again lashed to the chair, and though his right hand was free, it was wrapped in a rough, thick bandage. He was surprised to note that his shoes had been removed and that his feet were bare. His entire being seemed to be one taut, swollen mass of hurt.

As he revived, the door to the room was opened, and Cleft Chin came in. The other four were already there.

The opened door brought an instinctive reaction from Joe Smith. He yelled, "Help! Help! I'm—"

Dark Hair struck him across the face with a small piece of rubber hose. Joe Smith yelled no more. Dark Hair had his arm raised to strike again, but Cleft Chin stopped him.

The leader then came over to Joe Smith and said, "Don't being foolish. There is nobody here within a mile. You see what happens when you make nonsense? We wanting nothing from you but the information of the adapter. You tell that to our engineer, and we let you go."

Joe Smith caught a glimpse of the dial on the wrist watch worn by Cleft Chin. The hands stood at ten minutes past twelve. Because of the light behind the shades, he knew it was noon. What had happened at the factory? Had they telephoned his home when he had not appeared by ten o'clock? Anna would have told them that he had started for work as usual. Then the search must already be on for him. He would be found and rescued. Yes, there was a chance for rescue, and his mind almost automatically formed the phrase: "in the nick of time."

Surely they would find his abandoned car. And then what? He knew suddenly that there would be no rescue. Joe Smith in those few terrible hours had learned much of the world of brutal realities. No one had seen the fight or the kidnaping. The men who had taken him must have planned with care. It might take days, even weeks to find him. And by that time . . .

"Well?" said Cleft Chin harshly. He had been talking, but Joe Smith had not been listening to him.

"What?" said Smith.

"The information. You giving it to us?"

The information! The Glendiron Adapter that would soon be turning out rifle barrels by the hundreds of thousands. They wanted him to give them the information, tell them how it was done. But that was a secret. That would be treason. What did they take him for, a skunk?

He said, "What if I won't?"

Cleft Chin nodded to No Lashes and said, "Show him!"

No Lashes came from behind the table. He had a nasty grin on his face. He held a large pair of broad-end garage pliers in his hand. He knelt and bent over Joe Smith's naked feet. . . .

"Stop! Stop!" screamed Smith. "For God's sake, stop! I can't stand it! I can't stand it, I tell ya!"

No Lashes stood up. Cleft Chin said, "Now you know. That's nothing. We got worse. You want we show you?"

"No, no," Joe Smith moaned. A curious thing was happening to him. His outer mind that functioned from his ears and his eyes was so dulled and shocked from pain and beating that it seemed to take ages before words spoken to him reached his brain or he could speak in reply. But in the meantime he seemed to be able to think a million thoughts at once in his inner mind—things that he had never thought of in his life before.

So this was what really happened to people who got into trouble. The pretty, heroic, pomaded men who romped through the pictures in polo shirt could fight gangsters and villains singlehanded and come through unharmed. Plain Joe Smith was broken, exhausted, incapable of further resistance, utterly helpless.

Helpless! Why was he helpless? Wasn't he an American? Wasn't that enough? He'd had them with a gun in his hand, and what had happened? He remembered. He had shot at them across the room and missed. Missed them when he had them cold!

Why had he never had a gun before? Why had he not been trained to play the man's game of defending himself and his own? Joe Smith's inner mind argued with himself.

"So," said Cleft Chin, "now you tell us what we want to know?"

The question came from far away and passed across Smith's mind like a slowly moving string of freight cars: "Tell—us—what—we—want—to—know."

Yes, tell them and make an end to this. He wasn't prepared to fight these men from another world. No one had shown him how. These were not men as he had come to know men, but creatures from another planet, devils *who did not play the game.* They had hit him when he was down; tortured him when he was tied and helpless. They would find out the secret anyway, sooner or later. If he told them, they would let him go and not hurt him any more.

What else could he do? He had fought them to the limit of his ability and had failed. Men had to be fit and trained to fight. They had to have hard bodies and tough minds. You didn't get a hard body going to the movies or bowling once a month or driving a car. To hell with the country if that was the way it was! What had it done to protect him or make him fit to protect himself? He'd had enough. He'd had all he could stand.

"No, ya rat," said Joe Smith. "I won't."

He had said no! He had heard himself say no, when he had intended to say yes. Which Joe Smith was it that had uttered still another defiance? Was it the one who sagged lashed to the chair, battered and beaten? Or was it a new and unrealized Joe Smith who lived deep inside the aching skull and who struggled and wrestled there, like something newborn, striving to break out of its cocoon?

And what was it that wanted to break forth? What was there left of him? He did not understand this. He could have brought his pain to an end by yielding. It was what he wanted to do. He was no hero. He was just an ordinary guy, on whom a gang of foreign thugs had put the snatch to force him to reveal the workings of a machine.

And so . . . And so something in him which he did not understand, a mad, perverse stubbornness that rose in him, would not let him give in.

Instead he said thickly, "Ya can go to hell, ya rat. I ain't tellin' ya anything." He felt a swelling sensation of satisfaction within him that was almost anodyne to pain.

In all the naïve and simple externals of his life Joe Smith had not yet encountered or even thought upon the power and the beauty of the thing known as the spirit of man.

Cleft Chin gave a command in his language. No Lashes stepped forward eagerly again and knelt down. And Joe Smith learned what was meant by hell on earth.

He screamed for mercy until they taped his mouth. His nerves, attuned to degrees of pain, learned how to convey even greater agonies to his tortured brain. He gave up. He gave up a thousand times. When they stopped to question him, he nodded at last in assent because at that moment he could not do otherwise.

But when they removed the gag and pushed him roughly to the table, and Gray Beard took up drawing pen and T-square, Joe Smith whispered, "I ain't gonna do it. I ain't gonna do it."

It was at that point that Cleft Chin dropped his cold, businesslike calm and lost his temper. Curiously, the giant refrained from physical violence upon what was left of Joe Smith and instead began to scream at him, shaking his fist in Joe's face.

"You fool! You bedamned fool! Do you want us to kill you? Do you want to die? You bedamned fool! I tell you we kill you slowly so it takes you hours before you die. We won't leave an inch of skin on you. Go on, you bedamned fool, tell us what we want to know. You hear? You want we kill you?"

The last was shouted in a half-hysterical yell. It brought Joe Smith to for a moment so that he was able to look upon the black, half-crazed fury of Cleft Chin's distorted face with eyes that burned with discernment and determination.

"Yeah," he whispered. "That's what I want. Ya gotta kill me."

For Joe Smith was no longer helpless, no longer without a weapon. It had been growing within him, and now that it had been shown to him in its simplicity and invincibility, it was clear at last.

He could die and, dying, keep from them the secret they so desperately wanted, take with him the final victory.

They would kill him, but in killing him they were beaten. With his last conscious thought he would know that. Life! His life! Why had he clung to it so? There was no higher card in the deck. He held it in his hand. He laid it on the board. He could die, and this he chose to do.

He no longer feared the agonies he must endure before the end, for when it came, he would not have spoken and, safe in death, could never speak again. The wires and shackles would no longer bind him. He would have escaped. He would be free.

Free! For the first time in his life Joe Smith was close to understanding the meaning of the word "liberty." He had read it and used it a thousand times; had viewed it symbolized in a statue; had heard it bellowed at him from the radio; had learned in school that it was his birthright, bestowed upon him by those heroes of the past known as "our forefathers."

But now his spirit, facing death, was looking upon the truth that liberty was something irrevocably bound up with human dignity, though he could not have phrased it that way. He would have said, "No one's gonna push me around."

Liberty, he knew now, was the first unassailable fortress and stronghold of man, for in the ultimate grave crisis he could choose to die for it. From this—the freedom of death and the disposition to seek it rather than yield to the brutal slavery of force—nothing in heaven or on earth could deter him.

It were better, he knew in this hour of understanding, to live proudly and to fight for it, but in the end, if there were failure, the victory would lie with the dead, not with the living.

"I ain't gonna tell ya," whispered Joe Smith again. "You can kill me." And he closed his lips and waited.

Raging, Cleft Chin himself went at the torture with every refinement of European ferocity to break the will of Joe Smith, American.

To escape the horrors of the physical agonies imposed upon him, Joe Smith fled wildly to the sanctuary of the mind. It was difficult at first because of what was being done to him, yet the way grew clearer as his thoughts progressed, and sometimes it seemed as if these men were not hurting him at all.

He thought of his children. The kids would be home from school for lunch. He did not see his home disrupted, as it must be by the mystery of his absence, but rather as he had known it on days when minor illnesses kept him at home.

Joe Junior and Maybelle would be sitting on opposite sides of the table, and Maybelle would have a colored ribbon in her straight brown hair. Anna would lean backward from the kitchen so that she could see into the dining room and call, "Eat your vegetables, Joe. Hurry up!" He could hear the scraping of forks on plates, and he clung to the dear sound.

Now that he was never to see them again, he no longer thought of them as he had for so many years, simply as the kids. At the club one said, "I gotta wife and kids," the way one said, "I gotta car." There they were. He had them. It was good living with them, but he had never thought about it. They had simply become a pleasant habit.

His mind, opened under the stress of his approaching end, unlocked impressions and tendernesses he had not known existed.

To him there came, as sharply as though the children were there, the sweet smell of fresh skin and recently ironed flannel as they came to say good night, bathed and in clean pajamas. He had been used to laying down his newspaper and pecking at them in return for their kisses and had never known how they had touched his heart.

He could think now of the sweet pressure of Maybelle's arms around his neck, and in the thinking the trusting tenderness of the two thin arms became sharper and more poignant than the thing these creatures were doing to him to unseal his lips.

He wondered how much he must endure before the end would come, and whether he could endure it. And to this expanding mind there came the knowledge that he must and would, because in his veins there ran the blood of others who had endured before him. Those long mysterious and abstract forefathers became something personal and intimate. Their obstinacy and tenacity and love of liberty were in his blood, and he was the survivor of them all. He was the living representative of an unbroken line that had battled out of the dark, prehistoric forests of Europe, down through count-less ages to a free America, triumphing over every catastrophe of nature and man. Perhaps men of his blood had been tortured and had triumphed before him. There would be no defeat in death. Joe Junior and Maybelle were there.

It was curious that his mind did not take him a step farther to think that perhaps because of his sacrifice, because he had not yielded a secret that would help an enemy, the lives of his children would be the safer. It simply did not occur to him that this was a sacrifice.

His mind turned to Anna, and the moment when he had told her that he loved her. They had met on a summer Sunday at Coney Island. A month later they had gone on one of those dark boat rides through the "Tunnel of Love."

Over the agonies that racked him, he could recall the soft bump-bumping of the boat against the sides of the tunnel and feel and smell the presence of Anna. In the damp heat a perfume that she used filled him with sweetness. She wore a thin white blouse, through which he felt the softness of her arms and shoulders, and her dark hair, cut to her shoulders, was clean and fragrant.

The pitch-black tunnel was full of the sounds of lapping water and the whisperings and sniggerings of other lovers in the boat. Her head had touched his cheek, and her youth and fragrance suddenly were no longer bearable.

He had placed his arms about her awkwardly and whispered, "Anna, Anna baby, I love ya. I can't help it. I love ya."

She had turned her head to kiss him when the boat, rounding a corner, had passed one of the illuminations built into the wall—a representation of hell, red-lighted, with sinners stewing in pots and a red devil standing there making a noise that sounded like "Baaaaaaaaaa!"

They had leaped apart because of the light, and Anna had giggled almost hysterically at the sudden apparition.

But when the boat entered into inky blackness again, she had turned to him swiftly and placed her arms around his neck, so that her breasts beneath the thin blouse had pressed against his shirt, and she had kissed him on the mouth with simple passion and engulfing sweetness. Then she had buried her head in his neck and wept, and there remained until the trip was over.

This had been the big moment of their romance, which had faded all too soon, with the work and the struggle and the coming of the kids. In those later years of success and respectability in the community Joe Smith had taken it for granted that he loved his wife, just as he took it for granted that as a father he loved his children and was in turn loved by them. It had all been a part of the simple, orderly scheme of life.

Joe Smith re-created Anna strongly in his mind now, in the increasing desperation of his search for ease, for his need of her was great. And now that he was come to the end, he knew that he had never loved her as he could love her now. For a moment he visualized not her but her blue-and-white checked apron, empty, smelling of celery and the scent she used. It was this that he held to his cheek and pressed to his lips as the symbol of the woman who somehow, without his knowledge, had grown to be the greater part of him.

Romance and glamour had faded as they had grown into man and wife. Anna's body, which had been so appealingly thin when he had first known her, had thickened with time and children, and her skin had coarsened. But the roughness and the stoutness were now dearer and more yearned for than all her shining youth had been.

Now, about to die, Joe Smith had a glimpse of the glamour and the glory of this wife. The thought of her work-lined cheek against his face, or the little smile he sometimes caught at the corners of her mouth when she was putting away the linen she had laundered and ironed for him, built her into a towering and loving goddess, against whom in this hour of anguish and brutal torture he could lean his battered head and, for a moment, find respite from pain.

Under the relentless hands of the men who knew no means to gain their ends but fear and force, Joe Smith grew weaker, as rage at impending defeat replaced the calculated brutality of their work.

Several times his mind wandered, but he groped on hopefully, seeking the darkness that would end the journey. Old thoughts lost their power to heal him, and he was forced to grasp at new ones like a man climbing the face of a cliff where each new foothold crumbles away beneath him.

He though of his country, which he had not found it possible to betray.

His weaving mind carried him back to public school, the kids all standing with their hands outstretched and the short, choppy chant of their voices in the pledge to the flag.

He could remember the words, and the effort to remember helped him again to bear what was going on.

"I pledge allegiance to the flag of the United States of America, and to the Republic for which it stands, one nation, indivisible, with liberty and justice for all."

This he understood now, too. The expression "I love my country" was no longer just words, but a deep, swelling, passionate feeling, as though he could have kissed the asphalt streets, the billboards, the brownstone house fronts, the rubble-strewn lots he used to pass.

Somehow, the Acme Company, the clanking, humming machine shop, old man Padson and the Glendiron Adapter had become confused. He could remember only that somehow his body had come to symbolize a shield that stood between many, many things that he dearly loved and the forces that sought to destroy them.

Liberty and justice for all! One nation, indivisible! People! The nice kid at the garage who fixed his car; the swell guys at the club; the gang at the factory; fat Bill Swoyer, his neighbor.

My country! My country, 'tis of thee! There was a song ... He was back in assembly again, hearing the kids singing. How did the words go?

He was weak from loss of blood, and the words kept slipping away. He fought for them, one by one.

> *My country, 'tis of thee,*
> *Sweet land of liberty,*
> *Of thee I sing. . . .*

I love thy rocks and rills,
Thy something wooded hills;
My heart with rapture thrills . . .

The tape was violently ripped from his torn mouth, and from the distant pain-filled spaces floated the voice of Cleft Chin.

"God bedamn you, you fool! You got enough? You hear me? You give in? This is your last chance. You telling us what we want to know?"

Joe Smith's lips moved. Cleft Chin bent down to catch his words.

"I love thy rocks and rills," Joe Smith was saying.

The last thing he remembered was the savage face of Cleft Chin thrust close to his before, for the third time that awful day, the mercy of darkness rolled over him and swept him to peace.

Cool rain brought Joe Smith to the consciousness that he was not dead, nor was he any longer in the torture room. It was dark, and he was lying on the ground, and in the distance he could see the glimmer of a street lamp. He did not feel that he was bound except by stabbing pain. He could not move a limb or utter a sound. And yet he was alive and free.

A belated homegoer cutting across a vacant lot in East Brooklyn stumbled over his body, and Joe Smith heard him say, "Oh-oh, a drunk!"

But the man stopped and lighted a match to make certain, and in the flare Smith saw a rugged face go white, heard a gasp and a cry.

The homegoer was level-headed. He ran across the lot to the nearest house that showed a light in the living room, knocked on the door, and begged to use the telephone.

A few minutes later a police car tore around the corner and screeched to a stop, and shortly after, an ambulance also arrived.

The intern pushed through the crowd that had gathered and knelt at Joe Smith's side, while policemen held flashlights. The intern was young, but intelligent, skilled, and full of pity.

Kneeling there in the rain, he did things for Joe Smith that saved his life and the use of his limbs. When he was done, he patted Joe on the shoulder and said, "You're going to be all right, old fellow," and jabbed him mercifully with a morphine needle.

Two policemen placed him on the stretcher and loaded him into the ambulance.

The morphine began to work slowly attacking first the hot, throbbing pain centers, soothing, cooling, numbing them, leaving Joe's mind free. And as the ambulance raced along the rain-blackened streets toward comfort, care, and peace, Joe Smith had for a moment a strange, queer vision of things to come.

He knew that he was not going to die; that he would suffer much, but that his wounds would heal in time. The brutes had either not dared or not troubled to kill him. He understood that he had beaten them; that somehow he had won and, winning, was returning to the world he had thought to leave forever. He would see Anna and the kids again, and all those dear things that had been lost to him.

And in the clear insight of his vision Joe Smith was frightened because the world to which he was returning was not the one that he had left. In this new world the shoddy fabrics of his old beliefs were shot through with gleaming threads of truth and understanding. Nothing in it would ever be the same again, nor would he. He had not thought to pray during the time of battle, but now, in victory, he spoke a prayer that those truths and loves that he had found in the depths of his suffering might remain to him and light his way forever.

The Dowry

From my war diary, written in Rennes, France, August 18, 1944, after a day spent in Brittany with the Maquis, the men of the French Resistance:

". . . Every Maquis encampment was betrayed at some time or other by one of three things—loose talk, gypsies, or a woman. The Nazis paid from 5,000 to 20,000 francs for the betrayal of a patriot and found plenty of takers with dirty souls who would sell out a member of the F.F.I. for money. The Maquis knew well enough who was betraying them, but as long as the Gestapo was in the saddle, there was little they could do about it. But now it is different, and all over Brittany sit the miserable, frightened, filthy women with the stain of greed and treachery on their souls awaiting their trial and the certain poniarding that will follow. As one of the Maquis had inscribed on his Sten gun, 'Victoire et Revanche!'

"There is a horrid story of a woman who married some villager, not a German, and gave a wedding breakfast. This wedding breakfast is a big event in Brittany. She invited a patriot member of the underground to attend and then betrayed him to the Gestapo, who surrounded the house during the wedding feast, took him away, tortured and killed him. That is how the woman got her marriage portion. Note: A good short story here. Think about it!"

I thought about it a lot, because I couldn't forget it, or any part of that day of August 18 when Sonia Tomara, of the *Herald Tribune,* Rozelle Hargrove, of N.E.A., herself a born Bretonnaise, and private Johnny Anderson, of Milwaukee, our jeep driver, and myself drove from Rennes to Saint-Brieuc, Pontrieux, and Paimpol in northern Brittany, part of which was still in the hands of the Germans, to find the leader of the Maquis and visit the secret camp of these guerrilla bush

Cosmopolitan, April 1945.

fighters. The story was written upon my return to the United States and published in *Cosmo* under the title "The Dowry."

We four were the first Americans to enter the little Breton seaside village of Paimpol, a few hours after the patriots had captured the town and taken the German garrison prisoner. Later that day we were taken to the secret camp of the Maquis, and there it was that we heard the story of Yolande from the lips of a young captain of the underground who had known her and who but a short time before had had a bitter share in her final destiny.

The tragedy was still fresh in the minds of all, for they had known her since she was a little girl in and around Paimpol. We saw the house in which she had lived and where she sold out the patriot for thirty pieces of silver, and on the execution ground, a small field next to the camp, we stood on the new-packed earth beneath which she slept. The men of the F.F.I. had not waited long to exact justice. The watchword of the Bretons, always a tough and primitive people, was *"Pas de pitié!"*

I remember the first time I heard the phrase, on the way to Paimpol, when we stopped by the bank of a canal and watched them fish the dead body of a German sergeant out of the water. He had been executed for shocking and nameless brutalities the night before. As the battered corpse was laid on the stone landing at the edge of the canal, children were shouting and laughing and the villagers looked down upon the remains with great interest and enthusiasm.

Evidently someone in the crowd must have said something that contained a modicum of sympathy, a passing word for something that had once been a human being, even though he had not lived like one. There was an old peasant on our side of the water in cap and jacket, with snow-white hair, whose ears it reached. He removed his long pipe from his mouth and shouted across the canal, *"Pas de pitié!"* His old voice rang over the water like the bells of doom. It was the voice of all tortured France speaking. This was the hour of revenge.

Yet there had been some pity for Yolande, and that was why I knew I wanted to write her story, because through it I might be able to project something of the France that I saw at the moment of her liberation.

While the essentials of the story, the events and the background, are true, the details of the story, the relationships of the characters and their intimacies, are fiction. I haven't the faintest idea what the readers of *Cosmopolitan* thought of "The Dowry," because not one of them wrote to tell me.

It was in the summer of 1944 that my long-standing ambition to become a war correspondent was fulfilled when *Cosmopolitan* sent me across as correspondent and European editor on the finest assignment for which any writing man could ask, and for this I will owe a lifelong debt to Miss Frances Whiting, then editor in chief, who made it possible.

For it was more than an assignment. There was a bit of soul-saving involved. Miss Whiting was both editor and friend. And as an editor she knew that I was going to pieces as a writer because, owing to circumstances, I had been unable to get to the war. As a friend she saw that this was profoundly affecting me and might have permanent consequences. I was brooding over missing out on the greatest story of all, and my state of mind was reflected in my work.

As it had twice before, *Cosmo* underwrote my trip overseas. My only instructions were: "Go over and look at the war. When you come back, write about it if and when you feel like it. We won't press you." I went to England and France, into Paris with Dick Tregaskis in a jeep among LeClerc's tanks the day of liberation, smelled powder, got scared, got shot at, and came home with my gloom and megrims dispelled and a sackful of material, which before the war ended yielded three articles, three short stories, and a three-part serial. Two of these short stories, "The Dowry" and "Verna," have been included in this book.

With them go my gratitude and affection for Miss Whiting, who helped me around many a rough corner in my career in the past and who by this final assignment did more for me than any other person or persons in the entire editorial and publishing field. And I do not know which is more grateful, the writer or the man. Both of us salute her.

INLAND from the savage granite coast of northern Brittany the country softens to peaceful rolling farmlands, roads winding through brier rose and hawthorn hedges behind which lie, half concealed, the stone cottages and stout barns of the thrifty Breton peasants, sweet lands bathed in sunshine or veiled by the gray curtains of mizzling rain that drift in from the sea, a country whose

outward appearance belies the fierce, primitive, untamed nature of
its inhabitants.

It is a land of giant spreading oaks, of orchards of apple, pear, and
plum, colored with the red and purple fuchsia and flaming laurel,
scented with the blossoms of mimosa, eucalyptus, and camellia. It is
also a land of high romance and dark superstition, of sorceries, ban-
shees and torrigans, and memories of ancient pagan religions whose
monoliths, the druid menhirs, rise like solitary giants from meadows
of purple heather, and the dolmens, and mystic circles of moss-
greened, granite cromlech stones stand half hidden in fields of
gleaming gorse and tangled brier.

Some twelve miles in from the sea sleeps the old market town of
Tregoulac in the Department of Côtes-du-Nord, a village of tall,
archaic timbered houses that lean forward until they appear almost
to meet across the narrow cobbled streets, houses topped with crazily
peaked towers, gables, dormers, and chimneypots, tossing to the sky
like sails and pennons flying from ships of stone.

Tregoulac is thirteen centuries old, but ancient though it be, it is
yet young compared to the antiquity of the bloodstreams that course
through the veins of the Bretons of the district, descendants of Celt
and Briton and Saxon conqueror, Roman and Gaul.

Modern times and improvements have dimmed the old customs.
Life centers in the market square and the church and cemetery of
St. Guldas at one end, and the starched white coifs and full-blown
black skirts and colored kirtles are seen only on the figures of the
very old women who still bring their curved earthen pitchers to the
fountain of the Virgin set in the mossy churchyard wall, and pause
there to kneel and pray for a moment for the living and the
dead.

The Christian religion, overlaid upon the deep-rooted and still
untamed paganism inherited from their ancestors, plays a tremendous part in the daily life of the people. The Bretons live in close
association with death, their friend, the *"Ankou,"* whose ghostly
horse and cart are heard by the peasants, padding and creaking
down the hedged lanes in the dark of night on his tireless rounds.
They have a Christian version of an old saying of the druids: "The

dead are so many, the living so few," and they have no fear of death. For the Breton to die is simply to emigrate.

The war in the spring of 1943 had neither changed nor much disturbed the town or the inhabitants of Tregoulac and the surrounding farms. The Germans had occupied but by no means conquered the country and its people.

The Nazi garrison in field-gray occasionally tramped the narrow, cobbled streets and sometimes tan and green military cars roared into the market square to discharge groups of grim S.S. men in their black and silver uniforms with the death's-head at their peaked caps. The townsfolk simply ignored them. Perhaps, with their departure, a citizen of Tregoulac would be missing thereafter from his usual haunts, never to return. And nothing would ever be said, or even whispered.

Or a glaring black and white poster printed in French and in Gaelic, the language of the Bretons, would appear on the dark wall of the churchyard or the smooth sides of the Hôtel de Ville, the town hall on the market square:

REWARD! 20,000 FRANCS WILL BE PAID FOR INFORMATION LEAD-
ING TO THE ARREST OF THE TRAITOR AND ENEMY OF THE PEOPLE
KNOWN AS "PANTHÈRE," SUSPECTED LEADER OF THE UNDERGROUND.
                      [SIGNED] COL. HEINZ VON BRAUNHELM,
                      DEUTSCHE KOMMANDATUR.

Then the townspeople would pause in little knots before the proclamation to read, silent and tight-lipped, even their dark eyes veiled and quickly downcast as they walked away. If there were those who knew something of the whereabouts or identity of the mysterious Panthère, the information remained locked in the iron cavity of their hearts. For the Breton is above all fiercely loyal and an implacable enemy.

It was as though the Germans felt and feared the deep, mysterious nature of the people and their unchallengeable connection with the dark and stormy past of this haunted corner of France, for they left them strictly alone except for the occasional desperate man hunts aimed at controlling and destroying the slowly growing underground and resistance movement.

Thus life and business went on as usual in Tregoulac under the German occupation. That spring the town was far more concerned with the progress, or rather lack of progress, of the match between Yolande Plouhet, daughter of Jean and Marie Plouhet, proprietors of the little butter-and-egg shop behind the church on the rue Saint-Eloi, and Louis Guizenec, who owned a small but prosperous farm and apple orchard a kilometer or so from the village.

All Tregoulac knew that dark-eyed Yolande Plouhet was madly in love with Louis Guizenec, had been for more than a year; that he favored her, but that the matter of the dowry stood between him and the consummation of her heart's desire. For the parents of Yolande were far from wealthy, and the handsome, blue-eyed, fair-haired farmer was known to be exceedingly thrifty and beset with ambition. He had his eye on the plot of fertile land adjoining his farm.

It had grown to be a kind of standing jest in and around Tregoulac, and natives who left the vicinity on business trips or to visit relatives would inquire upon their return, "Well, has Farmer Louis given way yet on the matter of the dowry and married Yolande Plouhet?" Or, "What is the news? Has Yolande Plouhet managed to raise the cash yet to wed Louis Guizenec?"

But it was no joke to Yolande, who was dying of love for Louis. She was torn between her ardent desire for him and submission to the custom of the country, which acquiesces in the right of a prospective groom to demand that his bride bring him a sufficient dowry to help him rise in the world and thus secure the happiness of the forthcoming marriage.

Yolande, to all appearances, was a modern girl living in a modern age. Like the other youth of Tregoulac, she had abandoned the starched coif of the district, the colorful peasant garb, and wooden sabots. She wore skirt and blouse imported from Rennes, a city she had visited several times as a child in the company of her godfather, a well-to-do tanner of Tregoulac.

She clacked over the cobblestones in high heels, and was no stranger to the ministrations of the hairdressing parlor and beauty shop at the corner of the market square. She was handsome, with dark, brooding eyes and full Oriental mouth, the lower lip protruding slightly. On Sundays she never failed to attend Mass at the Church of St. Guldas, with her parents, a small, brown figure sitting with head bent in piety, hands folded, eyes lowered, except when guardedly and with infinite caution they strayed to the side to catch a glimpse of the sturdy figure and sand-blond head of Farmer Louis.

But beneath her simple, unobtrusive exterior Yolande was a Breton of the Bretons, a smoldering mixture of passion, desire, mystery, and superstition. She was as primitive as her ancient ancestors, the Celts, the squat, dark Oriental race that had come flooding westward through the Carpathian passes in the age of the birth of Europe.

She lived in a world peopled by creatures of old legends, ghosts and sorcerers and pagan gods. She prayed dutifully to all the accredited saints in the calendar, but stepped softly in the presence of the great druid oak at the crossroads outside Tregoulac, and old memories in her venerated the menhir stone on the northern edge of the town, now topped by the Christian cross, its smooth surface carved in modern times with the symbols of Christ.

When first her dark eyes, shining from their square-cut lids, had rested upon the figure of Farmer Louis, one market day, she knew that she loved him; she had gone to the church and lit a candle to St. Anne and prayed that Louis would be made to look upon her with favor. But that night, too, she had stolen out into the fields in the moonlight, lacing sprigs of mystic vervaine into her hair; she had repaired to the dolmen of *Ma Douez* and had performed those ancient rites which were requisite.

And, indeed, the gods, both new and old, had rewarded her prayers, for Louis returned her affection, if not her love, though not to the degree of becoming either dizzy or careless in the matter of the dowry.

Louis Guizenec was a sturdy peasant, close-mouthed and uncommunicative, a little slow-witted, but a man who knew his worth. His was a Saxon strain, which accounted for his fair hair, blue eyes, and tall frame. He lived for his farm and his acres, and was not averse to a marriage that would increase the number of the latter and the prosperity of the former. On the other hand, he was not the kind of man to throw himself away for a pretty face or a neat ankle. A dowry of twenty thousand francs would enable him to purchase the desirable property adjoining his. If the girl who provided it were comely, so much the better, but if not he was no man to complain either. The important thing was to get ahead in the world.

Like so many of the inhabitants of the district, he had traffic neither with the Germans nor with the resistance movement. He was a man who minded his work and his own business, brought his produce to market and sold it for the best price it would bring. All he asked was to be let alone to till his acres and nurse his orchard, and this the Germans were constrained to do. Life under the occupation had not altered for him except for the understanding he had reached with Yolande.

And as for that, he was a patient man and could afford to wait. For the dowry he demanded was far beyond the means of either Yolande or her parents. But it flattered his vanity that the girl was so much in love with him, and when in a night of courting in the churchyard cemetery of St. Guldas, where the couples of Tregoulac came to plight their troth as their elders had done before them, she had promised him with tears in her eyes—nay, sworn by the sacred bones of her grandfather—that she would secure the sum if he would but give her time, he had agreed. After all, he was no worse off than he had been before, and certainly the dark-eyed girl attracted him strongly.

And so, beneath the calm demure demeanor exhibited as she waited behind the counter of the butter-and-egg shop, Yolande burned with desire for Louis as her husband and suffered and planned how she might come by the money and tortured herself with her love.

She was swept between admiration for Louis' thrift and his keen business sense in holding out for the sum he demanded, and poignant, wishful dreams of a Louis who would take her in his arms and whisper that for love of her he would waive the dowry. Then these sweet fantasies would be replaced by fear and anguish and gave rise in her head to ever wilder schemes to secure the sum.

Ah, the war, the times, and the occupation. Before, a girl might journey to Paris and take employment. There were many ways of making money in Paris. Now she could not even journey to Rennes.

Yolande had paid a painful visit to her godfather, Yves Gourin, the wealthy tanner, on one of his infrequent appearances in Tregoulac, for since the occupation his business had appeared to flourish and he was absent on long trips more and more. At least, Yolande had always considered Yves wealthy, but when she told her story and, trembling, made her plea to the old man for the money, he had shaken his silvery head sadly.

"It is not possible, my daughter. It is a large sum that Louis places upon his—ah—desirability. A more modest man might make a better husband. Such a sum, if it were available, might be better spent in these times."

Yolande was to remember this remark later. But now she was only stricken with a sense of hopelessness and despair. She burst into tears.

"But, Godfather, I love him. What shall I do?"

Her question was a memory of her childhood and better days. When as a little girl she had come to her godfather with some childish trouble, she had been wont to turn up her little round face to him and with quivering lips ask, "But, Godfather, what shall I do?"

Invariably the answer had been a gentle smile and the words "Pray, my daughter, have faith in God and pray!"

And it was thus he answered her now. "Pray, my daughter, and perhaps a way will be found. Do not let your desires blind your faith in the good God. . . ."

Not her tears, but anger now blinded Yolande.

Pray . . . pray . . . always pray. Had she not exhausted the pantheon of deities, pagan as well as Christian, with her nightly supplications? And the aching pain of love for Louis that was ever present in her heart was suddenly replaced by hatred for the gentle old man with the sharp, keen face and white hair down to the shoulders of his embroidered jacket. He had the money. She knew it. He could give it to her if he wanted. It was easier to say "Pray" than to part with the sum that would have bought her eternal happiness.

But no sign of her emotions appeared upon her face beyond the tears that still welled from her eyes, tears of desperation and helpless fury, and even these she dried now and took her leave.

She walked through the narrow winding street from the home of her godfather and passed through the market place on her way back to her father's shop. She paused before the poster affixed to the front of the leaning façade of the Hôtel de Ville and read it again:

REWARD! 20,000 FRANCS WILL BE PAID FOR INFORMATION LEADING TO THE ARREST OF THE TRAITOR AND ENEMY OF THE PEOPLE KNOWN AS "PANTHÈRE," SUSPECTED LEADER OF THE UNDERGROUND.
COL. HEINZ VON BRAUNHELM,
DEUTSCHE KOMMANDATUR

The sun was warm and the air soft, but she seemed to grow cold as though the winter mists had begun to blow in from the sea. Twenty thousand francs! The four eyes of the zeros seemed to stare stonily into her heart and she stared back like one possessed. Twenty thousand francs! The sum of the dowry, if one but knew who and where this Panthère might be. Traitor and enemy of the people, the poster said. If one could but be so fortunate as to have such information within one's grasp! Her mind leaped straight to a vision—her wedding party and Louis at her side—Louis forever at her side. The vision dizzied her and she swayed with its delight. It was still with her, wreathing the corners of her mouth in a smile, as she entered the shop.

It was not until late that night alone in her bed above the little garden that opened out behind their house that the thought came to her that whoever this mysterious Panthère might be who was so badly wanted by the Germans, he was a Breton, and a Frenchman, and to betray him would be the blackest crime of which the human soul was capable.

And then she was ashamed and frightened, and cowered in her

bed and wondered whether God, *le bon Dieu* who dwelt high in the spire of the Church of St. Guldas on the market place, had been watching and had looked into her heart as she had stood before the poster in the square.

Time passed. The poster remained on the walls unheeded. Yolande busied herself with concocting one frantic scheme after another for raising the 20,000 francs. Then one day, by a sheer accident of fate, she came into possession of a terrible piece of information. Panthère, the mysterious and unknown leader of the resistance movement in the Tregoulac district, was none other than Yves Gourin, her godfather. There could be no doubt of it, nor of the redoubled efforts the Germans were making to break his identity and find him. A munitions convoy on the coast road had been ambushed and blown up. Tregoulac itself was again filled with S.S. men, and Gestapo agents were everywhere, spying and interrogating. The inhabitants remained tight-lipped, wary-eyed, and unmoved. The flurry would pass. It always had.

And Yolande, grown quieter, paler, more lovesick than ever, carried the dreadful secret locked away in her breast, whence it rose to torture her night and day.

If only she had not stumbled upon it. Sometimes she tried to convince herself that it was not true, that it was only a bit of local gossip. But then there was corroborating evidence—Yves's unusually long and repeated absences from Tregoulac, ostensibly on business. And then she remembered the remark he had made to her about the money. "Such a sum, if it were available, might be better spent in these times."

She knew now what he was doing with his money. And an echo of the anger that had flamed in her heart the day he had denied her flickered up. Resistance movement indeed! One was no worse off under the Germans than one had been before, and, besides, it was obvious that they had come to stay. Twenty thousand francs for a lost and futile cause. Twenty thousand francs for her happiness. And what if Yves Gourin were to die? He was an old man. . . .

Yolande struggled like a linnet trapped in lime against the evil and treacherous thoughts that crept into her head. Time and again she barred and double-bolted the doors to her mind, sealed them with fervent prayers to the saints to protect her, and still they gained entrance. If only Panthère had been someone unknown to her. If only she had never found out. She evoked memories out of her childhood relationship with Yves, his kindnesses and many little beneficences to her, the presents he had bought for her on the great fete days of the *Pardon,* the dress for her first Communion, and the wonderful trips to Rennes.

She went to church more often to ask to be cleansed of all thoughts of evil. But she did not make confession. And she avoided the mystic pagan monuments in the neighborhood. True, they were only old and innocent stones and monoliths of granite, some of them with cup marks, hollows to be anointed with honey, wax, or oil, but the Church had interdicted such sacrifice and the stones themselves, had banished them into pagan darkness, and in that darkness dwelt memories of cults and practices, love of the body of man that transcended all else, love of love.

And yet, for all the torture through which she was going, Yolande knew that never, never would she eternally damn her soul with such a foul betrayal of one who was not only a patriot and a brave man, but a second father to her.

But that was before the talk began to go around Tregoulac about Louis and Henriette Jerzual, the dumpy, snub-nosed daughter of Herve Jerzual, the prosperous owner of the principal hotel on the market square.

It was the kind of talk that suddenly springs up in a village here and there, casual gossip. It was that Henriette had been making eyes at Louis in the tavern room of the hotel, and her father possessed and was willing to pay the sum of 20,000 francs' dowry in order to secure his not too attractive daughter a good marriage. And the farmer who owned the plot of ground adjoining Louis' farm was anxious to sell and had put a price on it, take it or leave it.

The talk stabbed to the heart of Yolande like a poniard.

It was just gossip. Even Louis denied it fervently to Yolande when she taxed him with it, and swore it was not so. And she would be reassured for the moment, but any instant her reassurance would be demolished like a house of cards by a word or a glance or even something imagined. But one kept on hearing things—Louis and Farmer Bodeur, who owned the plot of ground, were seen in long discussion. Louis was spending more time than necessary in the tap-room of the hotel, where Henriette served the tall pitchers of cider and rich slices of local salmon. . . . Who could blame Louis? After all, a man had to think of his future and could not wait forever. And besides, though she was far from a beauty, Henriette was a hard, willing worker and would make Louis a good wife. Too bad about the little Plouhet. . . .

Yolande, filled with the demons of jealousy and fear, went through agonies that were well-nigh unbearable. Where there was smoke, there must be fire, and the thought of losing Louis to another suffocated her until she thought she would die.

She could not sleep at night and would lie in her bed thinking of Louis, the look of him and the smell of him, the feel of him, the way his blue eyes shone from his brown face, the hard roundness of his thighs, tight in his work breeches, the strong jut of his jaws clutched around a pipe stem, and the odor of fields and leather harness, of horses and of man that enveloped her when he held her in his arms.

And from out the dark pits of hell the demons of jealousy brought forth a picture of Louis and ugly Henriette together in their marriage bed and held it before Yolande until she writhed and screamed in the darkness and shut her eyes and hid, sobbing and crying, under the covers, calling his name and the name of the saints, and names of druid gods and sorcerers, too, long forbidden, but never forgotten.

Now she could no longer banish the dreadful temptation to sacrifice Yves. He was so old. What was death but a translation, an emigration to paradise? What was the passage of one who had lived out his time to the necessity of assuaging the fires that were consuming her? An old man would vanish from the scene as so many had before him, and a young, strong-beloved body would be delivered to her arms, hers for eternity.

And who would ever need to know, or suspect, if one were clever

—if one told Louis one thing and her parents another, if one laid one's plans so carefully that there could be no slip, if one made certain the bird would not be flown when the trap was sprung? . . .

The marriage of Yolande Plouhet and Louis Guizenec took place in the early summer of 1943, and the guests assembled in the gay little garden behind the cottage of Jean and Marie Plouhet, after the ceremony at St. Guldas, for the traditional Breton wedding breakfast.

In her little room, overlooking the garden, where she was changing her clothes after the church ceremony and donning the traditional Breton costume of wide flowing black skirt heavily banded with velvet and embroidery, with beautifully worked over-apron of colored satin, Yolande was swept alternately between delirious joy and waves of fear.

Louis was hers, but she yet skated on the brink of disaster. The 20,000 francs in crisp pink and green banknotes reposed in her wedding chest atop the heaps of snowy linens and clothes that would supply her new household. Louis had seen it there and accepted her promise that he would receive it after the wedding. Her parents she had told that Louis had finally agreed to waive the large sum he had previously demanded and accept the more modest dowry that she herself had amassed.

She dressed herself mechanically, hardly knowing what she did, except that consciously she slowed the process, lingering over each movement, and always her eyes would come to rest upon the heavily carved lid of the oaken chest beneath which the money burned. It was not yet hers to bestow. If she failed, she would have to return it. And sometimes when she paused stock-still and found herself staring at the chest, she was seeing the square harsh face of a man bearing a white sword scar and surmounted by a black military cap to which was affixed a death's-head in silver. She would remember what she had said and what she had promised. Then waves of sickening apprehension would flow over her until her legs trembled so she felt she would sink to the floor.

There came a knock at the door. Yolande's hands flew to her

breast to stifle the wild beating of her heart. It was Annique, her best friend and bridesmaid, who said, "Yolande, are you coming? Everyone is waiting. Your godfather, Yves Gourin, has just arrived, and . . ."

Yolande said slowly, "Yves has come?"

"Oh yes, and *Monsieur le Maire* and all the guests are assembled. . . ."

Yolande took her friend by the shoulders, and turned her around, pushing her toward the door. "Go. I am almost ready. I will be down in a moment."

When she was alone, she staggered, her knees collapsing under her, and fell across the carved chest, weeping tears of relief. She had received a message from him promising to return to Tregoulac in time for her wedding. When she had noted his absence at the ceremony in the chapel of St. Guldas, she had had such a seizure of fear and terror that she had hardly been able to give voice to the responses that joined her through all eternity to Louis Guizenec. But now Yves was really there.

She pulled herself together and swiftly repaired the ravages made by the tears. She fastened the fine coif of lace and linen that had been her mother's and her grandmother's before her, and through it she twined a sprig of orange blossom. When she was quite ready, she went to the window looking out upon the rue Saint-Eloi and stood there for a moment, passing her handkerchief once across her brow as though she were faint. Then she turned and proceeded slowly down the stairs and stood framed in the doorway that opened on the scene of gaiety and festivity in the little garden.

There was much to meet her eyes, the long trencher tables laden with the wedding breakfast, round, dark loaves of bread and pitchers of wine and cider, plates of meat and vegetables, the huge *pot-au-feu*, gleaming pink and silver salmon, dishes of sweets and cakes, the two blind *biniou*-players seated with their ancient bagpipes on a raised platform, the ribbons and wreaths and decorations, the milling guests, the imposing figure of the Mayor in his frock coat of office. She saw none of these.

Her gaze rested only on the person of Yves Gourin, whose tall figure and shining white hair falling to his shoulders caught the eye. He was pulling at a long pipe, smiling, his fine face gleaming with pride.

And then thereafter Yolande's eyes sought out and found and remained upon the figure of her husband, who stood at the far end of the garden surrounded by cronies, a cider cup in his hand. She dwelt upon his every feature, the aquiline bridge of his nose, the fair hair at his neck, the slope of his shoulders, the grim pillars of his legs, doting upon them, devouring them with love and swelling passion.

There was first a shout as the guests greeted the bridge, and then on old, old woman of the village, Mère Locmariac, came forward and, kneeling at the feet of the lovely bride, in the old tradition, offered up a prayer for the dead, the dead of the families and all of those assembled there, whose presence and blessing she invoked.

And Yolande Guizenec listened to the invocation of the dead and feasted her eyes upon her husband.

Mère Locmariac finished her prayer. She rose and kissed the bride on both her smooth cheeks and the first shrill wailing of the *binious* arose from the platform of the blind pipers, in a haunting melody that filled the garden, drowning out the rustle and murmur of the guests at the beauty and the paleness of the bride, and drowning other sounds too, the roar of cars in the street without, and the tramping of heavy-shod feet on the cobblestones.

Now that the ceremony to the dead was over, the tune of the pipes shifted to a gay and lilting dance, the traditional *jabadao,* and the guests rustled and shifted and murmured, looking to see who should be the first to have the honor of dancing with the bride.

Yolande Guizenec went straight to her godfather, Yves Gourin, laid aside her bridal bouquet, and made him a curtsy. Then, to the applause of the assembled guests, the old man laid down his pipe, bowed, took his godchild by the hand, and together they began the ancient and stately round of the *jabadao.*

And this was the way the black-uniformed German *Schutz-Staffel* troops surrounding the house found them when they came streaming in through the door, flooding over the stone garden wall, filling and blocking every exit.

In the first shock, no one moved except the soldiers of death taking up their positions commanding the garden, and in a moment they, too, froze into immovable figures of silent menace. The wedding guests stood like statues, some of them with cups half raised to their lips, or their hands at the plates of refreshments on the tables. None looked at his neighbor. The blind *biniou*-players, sensing the catastrophe through their skins, left off playing, and the last wind from the collapsed bags of their pipes came as a kind of low, dying moan. In the center of the garden stood Yolande and Yves Gourin, petrified, she with an arm about his waist. There came the smart tramp of heavy boots in the corridor of the cottage and the metallic snick and click of the cocking of weapons. A German strode into the garden, an officer with a harsh face crossed by a long, white scar. At the peak of his black cap was a silver death's-head. He paused for an instant to survey the scene from the threshold. Then he marched straight to the old man with the long white hair standing next the bride, and spoke sharply.

"Yves Gourin, you are under arrest!"

The awful moment was broken by the cry of Yolande, who reached up and threw her arms about her godfather's neck. "Oh no, no!"

Still no one moved. No one even dared to look. Only Yolande saw the expression on the face of her godfather, the queer glitter that came into his eyes, which turned into a look of unutterable loathing and contempt. Then, slowly, he reached up and unfastened her arms from about his neck with a kind of shudder as though he were touching something reptilian and put them away from him. Without a word, he turned and followed the officer from the garden. A few moments later the gay, festive little enclosure was as empty of soldiers as it had been before. Outside one heard powerful motors starting up with loud explosions and finally fading away in the distance.

Then only did the people in the garden return to life, stirring, speaking softly, shifting forming into little knots, while Yolande ran to Louis and threw herself sobbing on his breast. The drone of the *binious* resumed again, but it was a Breton lament rather than a dance tune. Afterwards they played merrily again, though not for long, for the spirit was out of the celebration and none was in a mood for dancing. When the food and drink had been consumed, the wedding guests went home.

Later in the day a cart drew up in front of the little shop in the rue Saint-Eloi, and Yolande and her earthly possession, her pots and pans, her bedding and clothes and linens in the carved wedding chest, and her 20,000 francs, were transported to the home of her husband.

Yves Gourin was never seen alive again, and the Germans saw to it that the town heard about what had been done to him before he died. But the town also knew and whispered about the fact that he had passed with his lips sealed and that the Germans had been unable to wring from him the names of his accomplices in the underground.

And there were other things that began to be whispered and gossiped and traded in and about Tregoulac, things spoken softly across the wooden tables at the tavern, after cautious looks about, brief sentences exchanged on corners beneath the leaning, pot bellied houses, dreadful things spoken across the stone and blackberry brier fences of the quiet farmlands.

Who was it had betrayed Yves Gourin to the Germans? Ah well, never repeat it, but one hears. . . . The price that farmer Guizenec paid for his new plot of land was exactly 20,000 francs, was it not? Remember the amount of the reward on the poster, which has now been removed? Whence had one in such modest circumstances as Yolande Plouhet procured such a sum for her dowry? Why did she appear in her wedding dress at the second-story window fronting on the rue Saint-Eloi before joining the guests in the garden? Jean Pelicot, the postman, swears he saw her signal with her handkerchief, and a few moments later the street was full of Germans. Ah, and most damning, did she not single out Yves to be the first to dance with her at the wedding? And was she not hanging on his arm when the Germans surrounded the house and burst in upon them? Such a black deed could hardly be possible. And yet, when one puts two and two together. . . .

Time went on and the talk and the whispers grew, though they did not reach the ears of Louis Guizenec, who was concerned only with the expansion of his farm; but Yolande heard them, or rather felt them. At first she was afraid, but later she rallied. What if they suspected? There was no proof. No one, nothing could disturb her happiness with Louis.

But things were happening beneath the surface of the little town, mysterious boilings and seethings. More and more of the young men of Tregoulac and the district were vanishing into the bush. One heard of the growing strength of the F.F.I., the French Forces of the Interior, the Maquisards and their secret camps, an underground army growing day by day, mysterious parachutings from airplanes that flew over in the night, growing caches of weapons and ammunition, growing boldness on the part of the men of the Maquis. The Gestapo officer of the district himself was said to have been ambushed and captured by the F.F.I., and the Nazi garrison in Tregoulac was doubled.

And now when Yolande came to town alone, there were those who would not speak to her any longer, but stared at her stonily, or turned and walked away when she approached, and into their looks she read an implacable hatred.

Her mood changed to one of defiance. Very well, then, they knew. And what if they did? They dared not do anything to her. The Germans were there to protect her. They would always protect her.

And then in the later winter there was talk in Tregoulac of a coming Allied invasion of France.

To Yolande it was just talk. And if it happened, she had no doubt that it would be defeated. The Germans were so strong. There were so many of them. The coast defenses were impregnable. The Allies would be swept back into the sea, the Maquisards captured and crushed. And in the meantime, the moment of now, through the very ticking of the clock, she had her Louis.

But in the early springtime, when May brought the rose-pink

pear and the snowy apple blossoms to bloom, she felt a vague uneasiness, a tightening of the nerves, the kind of heaviness one feels on a stifling summer's day when all nature stills, the storm clouds gather on the horizon, and one leans one's ear to catch the first faint, distant rumbling. . . .

Not even when the armies of liberation landed in Normandy, though, did she give way to fear. She took courage from the long lines of German tanks and cannon and lorries laden with stout troops in field-gray that rumbled through the town. None could defeat this dreadful might. It was impossible that the swelling combers of war could break over this Army and threaten the happiness of her possession of Louis.

June turned to July. One heard more and more disquieting things —break-through at Saint-Lô, a German army fleeing, another cut off. And then all of one night Yolande lay awake and shivering beside the warm, sleeping body of her husband and listened to the distant thudding of the cannon at Saint-Malo carried to her through the quiet of the starry summer night.

She tried to comfort herself that it was a far-off thunderstorm, but she knew that it was not, for it never ceased, or changed, and every so often she heard a dish rattle or stir in her china closet, and sometimes there would be a heavy thump of air upon a window casement as from a distant explosion. And she lay there all through the night cold as ice and not daring to creep to the warmth of Louis.

It was a few days later that Yolande brought the week's yield of butter, milk, and eggs to market in Tregoulac to find the town alive and boiling with military traffic, staff cars, weapons-carriers, road buses, trucks. The Germans were loading them with every evidence of haste, carrying boxes and crates out of houses and headquarters. It was then that Yolande noticed for the first time that all of the vehicles were pointed, not west, toward the front, but eastward, the line of retreat. Already the first of the trucks and carriers were beginning to roar and rumble out of town.

An icy chill seized her heart as she watched. And now as she reached the market square with her horse and cart, a rattle of small-arms fire broke out from the northwest part of the town, backed by the rhythmic "cha-cha-cha-cha-cha" of machine-gun fire. She heard a German soldier say the word "Maquis!" and then the speed of activity in the square redoubled. Trucks started away with only half a load.

Yolande screamed once, loud and long, but no one paid any attention to her. A Reichswehr soldier carried a duffel bag out of a house and dumped it into a small open military car. Yolande ran to him and shouted, "What is happening? Where are you going?" She tugged at his arm, her hair flying, her face all white and twisted.

The soldier looked at her in surprise, shook her loose, and climbed into the car. He said, "Back to Germany—I hope—before your damned Maquis catch us. . . ."

Yolande clutched blindly at the side of the car as though by holding it she could halt the entire exodus. "But you can't! You can't leave me! You can't go!"

The soldier sniggered unpleasantly and said, "Too bad we discovered each other so late, Fräulein! Well, au revoir!" and he clashed the steel car into gear and jerked it away from Yolande and off through the market square, leaving her sprawling on her hands and knees on the cobblestones. Somebody near by laughed loudly. And from the upper window of a house across the square, the tricolor of France suddenly cascaded in folds of red, white, and blue and hung there mockingly in the brilliant sunshine. . . .

It was two days later, looking out on the farm from the window of her kitchen, that Yolande saw them coming carefully in single file across the fields, toward the house.

There were six of them, men and boys, ragged and whiskered like pirates from their long stay in the bush, clattering with weapons and grenades that hung from their belts, their work clothes nondescript and dusty. But each wore a red, white, and blue arm band around his left sleeve.

The leader, a tall, bearded boy, was clad in the tan battle dress dropped him by the British. The cross of Lorraine was fastened to his beret, and there were three blue stripes sewn to his left shoulder. Over his back was slung a Sten gun, and he carried an automatic pistol.

They moved slowly with a kind of leaden purpose, and Yolande stood motionless at the window, watching them. She did not cry out, or scream, or try to run. She knew that Louis was plowing in the new field beyond the woods, a quarter of a mile away.

The men stopped, deployed before the house, and looked warily for a moment. Then the leader saw Yolande through the kitchen window. He said something to his squad and they relaxed their weapons. They came into the kitchen and stood there looking at her.

There was a curious moment of embarrassment during which some of them shifted their feet and looked away.

The leader cleared his throat. He said, "Yolande Guizenec, we have come for you." That and no more.

She made no reply, beyond a kind of long, tired sigh, a mere exhalation of breath that never seemed to end. Then with fingers that fumbled a little she undid her apron and hung it carefully over the back of the chair. She reached up behind her as though to give her brown hair a sort of pat into arrangement, but paused in mid-air and let her arms fall to her side.

When the leader went to the door, she fell in behind him without a word, the other five following. She did not give so much as a backward glance. And so in single file the seven moved away from the farmhouse and across the green and yellow fields. . . .

I saw the grave of Yolande Guizenec when I visited the secret camp of the Maquis in the Tregoulac district in Brittany last summer shortly after the men of the resistance movement had swept the Boches from their land, and heard her story.

It was not really a grave, but just a bare patch of trampled earth in a grassy field along with eight others, next to the grove that concealed the tents and headquarters of the Maquis camp. But it was set a little aside from the others, this bare patch, so that she slept alone. A cleft stick had been thrust into the ground in the center of the brown earth, and in the cleft there drooped the wilted, browning bud of a wild rose.

The story was told me by the young, bearded captain of the

F.F.I., standing there in his tan battle dress, the double-barred cross of Lorraine pinned to his beret, black Sten gun slung across his shoulder, two German potato-masher grenades hung at his belt. His *nom de guerre*, the only name by which he was identified, was Captain Nemo.

And we stood in the little field with the patches of newly turned brown earth over the remains of those who had died a traitor's death.

Captain Nemo said, "We did not mete out to her the death we reserved for the other traitors, the poniard stab in the breast. It was permitted to her to be shot. . . ."

I asked, "Why? Surely it was a dreadful crime she committed, more wicked than most."

The captain nodded. He looked down and with his toe stirred the edge of the brown earth where it met the fresh green grass. Then he replied, "Yes. She was a traitress. She betrayed her country and her dearest friend. But we had known her all our lives. Many of us had played with her in Tregoulac when we were children together. And then besides—"

He paused, and I said, "Yes?"

Captain Nemo looked at me, and his dark eyes were no longer the eyes of a boy. He said, "It is hard to punish, to mete out justice, and yet it must be done. You see, she did—what she did—because she was in love. And so it was permitted, even though bullets are scarce, that she be shot through the heart. She fell there, against that young oak tree. . . ."

Welcome Home

For this story, the last one I wrote in 1945, I am indebted to the generosity of one of my dearest friends, the late J. P. McEvoy.

One day in the autumn of '45, shortly after Mac had returned on the *Queen Mary* from a tour of Europe, he and his wife, Peggy, came down to our farm for a weekend. After dinner we sat around with a drink in our hands, swapping stories, and Mac told the tale of an incident he had witnessed from the towering deck of the *Queen Mary* when she pulled up outside Sandy Hook to take the pilot aboard. It was wonderful eyewitness story of what had happened to a family that had chartered a boat to ride down the bay to greet its homecoming hero and ran into a pack of sadists. He told it with such felicity and so graphically that long before he had finished I was fairly drooling with desire to possess it.

For even as Mac described what he had seen and heard looking down from the huge liner, I had departed from his viewpoint and had boarded the little launch dancing so gallantly in the trough of the sea. I had peopled it, had named the people, and was already living with them. The entire Soslewski family was coming alive in my head. They were beginning to take shape, to move, and to speak. And their story was making itself up—who they were, what they were like, how they were affected by what transpired, and what happened to them all afterwards. By the time Mac had finished telling about the incident he had witnessed, my story was nearly completed. Sometimes it goes like that and you can make them up in five minutes, or rather they spring to life inside your head with a fabulous speed and energy, whereas other times it may take you five weeks, months, or even years before a story is right and ready. How I loved that piece and longed to write it! I could see it on paper already; I knew its length, its form, and the style in which it would be told. There was only one catch. It wasn't mine. The incident around which it was built had been observed by Mac and belonged to him.

Saturday Evening Post, March 9, 1946.

We all shouted with delight at Mac's narrative, and when Peggy said, "Isn't that cute?" I guess I couldn't keep the desire out of my voice when I half groaned in reply, "Golly, what a short story that would make! . . ."

Mac, grinning like a grizzled imp, said, "Yeah? Do you like it?"

"Do I like it! Why, it's a natural. It's just hollering to be a short story. Why, all you have to do is—" At which point I realized I was hinting with all the delicacy of a drop-forge hammer and shut up. So then Mac said with that generosity which is characteristic of him:

"Why don't you go ahead and write it? I was only going to use it as a paragraph in an article some time when I got around to it."

Well, then I felt like a louse, except that the yearning to be able to write the story was uppermost. There is no desire I know of for anything so great as the longing to write a story that takes possession of one. It arouses a kind of shameless cupidity restrained only by the ethics of the profession, which forbid that one so much as approach the idea of another. Eventually Mac and I effected a kind of exchange, in which an idea of mine was useful to him, which was sufficient to salve my conscience, and the story was mine. I felt as happy with it as a child. One week later it was finished.

If you are interested, either as a potential writer or just as a reader, in the subject: Why is an author's agent? the handling of "Welcome Home" might be a case in point.

Even while the piece was working itself out in my head, I was seeing it as a story for the *New Yorker*. The way it went and the manner in which I thought it ought to be written was, to me, off the beaten track of most magazines, but quite in the style of the impersonal, realistic short stories appearing each week in the *New Yorker*.

I went to see Harold Ober, told him the story, and suggested that he submit it to the *New Yorker*. He was enthusiastic about the idea, but not about my choice of market, and for a very good agent's reason. He looked doubtful and said, "They pay so badly. They're funny people down there."

I said that in this case I didn't really care, I was so in love with the story that I wasn't going to risk spoiling it by angling it for the high-paying magazine market. And I didn't think that any book but the *New Yorker* would touch it the way I planned to do it.

He said at once, "I wouldn't want you to spoil it. We'll offer it to the

New Yorker if you like. But why don't you write it just the way you
want to and then let me see what I can do with it. A lot of my authors
think they have stories that aren't for the regular market and then it
turns out they're sold for a good price in places they never expect."

It was agreed finally that I would write the story without compromise
exactly as I felt it and then turn it over to Harold to try where he
saw fit.

Three days after I had sent it to Ober he called up and notified me
that he had sold it to the *Saturday Evening Post* at five times the sum
the *New Yorker* would have paid. So much for one case of a writer's
editorial judgment.

A FTER they had finished decorating the exterior of the butcher
shop and their apartment above it at the corner of Van
Will and Henry Street in South Brooklyn in preparation
for Johnny's homecoming, they all went upstairs to drink a glass of
beer. Already one of the neighbors had telephoned to congratulate
them on the best display in the block.

Johnny's division was due in three days on the *Queen Mary,* and
the exterior of the butcher shop had been draped in red-white-and-
blue bunting with the big photograph of Johnny above the doorway framed in colored electric lights saved from the Christmas tree,
flanked on either side by the giant replicas of his battle ribbons, the
pre-Pearl Harbor, European Theater, Bronze Star, and Purple
Heart, made by Zella out of cloth and cardboard. The canvas sign—
"OUR JOHNNY"—had been hand-lettered by Myrene, Johnny's
sister, who was twelve and who was supposed to have talent for
drawing. Getting the Christmas-tree lights down from the attic and
using them to frame Johnny's picture had been Mom's idea. Mr.
Soslewski's imagination had not carried him beyond the red-white-
and-blue bunting.

Zella Hyman was engaged to Johnny. She worked as a cashier in
Mr. Soslewski's butcher shop and was already one of the family,
occupying Johnny's room in the apartment over the store until he
returned and they could be married. She was a handsome, capable

girl who liked to use a lot of make-up. In spite of the glasses she
wore for nearsightedness, the bold carmines and pinks she used on
mouth and cheeks coupled with the glossy blackness of her hair
made one think of the Queen of Sheba. Now as she held her glass
of beer, her cheeks flushed with the recent exertion, her dark eyes
moist with anticipation of Johnny's return, she said:

"Gee, does it look all right? I hope he likes it."

Mom moved heavily to the window to give a sidelong glance at
the decorations. She was so stout that she had difficulty breathing
and was always fanning herself with one hand. "It's beaudiful,"
she said. "It's better'n the Gianellis'. That's on accounta what Zella
made with them ribbons. That was your idea, Zella. Wasn't it,
Joseph?"

Mr. Soslewski, thus queried, felt torn between affection for his
daughter-in-law-to-be and the reminder that the touch of distinction
and novelty lent to the display had come from an outsider. He bit
into a salami sandwich and washed it down with beer before con-
ceding, "It's pretty good. Nothing's too good for that boy coming
home a hero. Grover Whalen wouldn't be good enough meeting
him down the bay with a band."

Myrene, who as a concession to her age had only half a glass of
beer, which she was nursing by sucking at the rim of the glass and
letting only a drop or two at a time reach her lips, asked, "Who's
Grover Whalen, Pop?"

Mr. Soslewski mimicked, " 'Who's Grover Whalen, Pop?' You go
to school and you don't know when it's a big shot arrives, Grover
Whalen from the Mayor's Committee goes out in a boat to meet
him?"

"With a gardenia," Zella interpreted loudly to make Myrene
understand.

Myrene, who was so blond her braids were almost albino and who
appeared to have no eyelashes, merely looked baffled and let a little
beer dribble toward her lips. But something odd seemed to be happening to Mr. Soslewski. He was a stocky little man made mathematically in squares and angles as though a carpenter had put him
together. The flat plane of his short-cut, grizzled hair exactly paral-

leled the straight line of his shoulders. His head sat on his torso like
a box. Now the straight lines seemed bent outwards and swelled as
though by some intense inner stress. He glared at his wife and asked
loudly, "What's about Grover Whalen so great he can go any time
with a boat to greet a big shot? Who's a bigger shot than our
Johnny?"

He did not expect a reply nor did Mom prepare to make any. He
set down his glass and began to stomp up and down the room, his
face reddening with the force of the tremendous thought that was
germinating within him. Myrene came out of her glass and asked,
"What does he do with the gardenia?" And her mother said without
emotion, "Shuddup, Myrene, your daddy's busy."

The great inspiration left Mr. Soslewski's innards, traveled upwards through his neck, swelling it out over his collar with the
power of its force and imagination, reached the rectangular confines
of his head, and there exploded in a shout that shook the three
orange-colored globes of the chandelier.

"Listen! Where does it say Grover Whalen is better than anybody else? It's still a free country, ain't it? We could go with a
boat to greet Johnny!"

The result was more than gratifying and restored Mr. Soslewski
as Pasha. Myrene was jumping up and down screaming, "Daddy,
Daddy! On a boat. I kin come too. I'm old enough, Daddy. I kin
come. . . ." Zella's imagination and sense of the dramatic was immediately fired and she cried, "Pops, do you mean it? With a band
maybe?" In her mind she was already choosing what she would
wear. The red dress, the one in which she had become engaged.
Johnny would remember it when he saw it. And carry a big bunch
of red carnations. She saw herself blowing kisses to Johnny from
a boat and Johnny leaning over the rail waving to her while music
played and everyone cheered.

Bewilderment, admiration for her husband, the enormousness of
the project overwhelmed Mrs. Soslewski into a chair, where she
fanned herself with her hand and asked the sixty-four-dollar question for which Mr. Soslewski had been waiting.

"But, Joseph, where you gonna get a boat big enough to go on the ocean? How we gonna afford a boat to go on the ocean? You know what it costs for a boat to go on the ocean?"

"Ha!" replied Mr. Soslewski. "You're asking me! Maybe I'm not Mr. Grover Whalen with a gardenia and pull with politicians, but I got friends." He paused to give them the full effect of what was to follow. "What's the good I go out every Sunday fishing from Sheepshead Bay party boats for five years in the summer if I ain't got friends. I betcha right now I can pick up the telephone and we got a boat."

Zella ran over and threw her arms around Mr. Soslewski's neck and kissed the top of his head fiercely. "Gee, Pops, you're a genius. I'll bet Captain Danahy would lend his boat. You're always talking about him. Gee, call him up. . . ."

"Hmm," said Mr. Soslewski, who would have preferred a little more opposition. And he *had* been thinking of Captain Danahy. He repeated, "I betcha," and when the awe and expectancy had reached gratifying proportions, he moved with recovered majesty to the telephone and picked the instrument from its cradle.

The tidy green and white motor launch, *Daisy D.*, Captain Ed Danahy, Charter Captain Joseph Z. Soslewski, danced unhappily in the choppy swell off Sandy Hook. Behind her lay the winter skeleton of Coney Island, the bones of the parachute drop, and the Ferris wheel sticking up into the sky. It was seven o'clock in the morning, and out to sea the curtain of early mist had not yet lifted. A hundred yards away the pilot boat rose and settled on the incoming tide.

A large wood and canvas hand-painted sign was affixed to the top of the cabin of the *Daisy D.* and ran its length, thrumming in the gusts of salt wind. It read: "WELCOM HOME TO OUR PFC JOHNNY SOSLEWSKI." By the time Myrene's typographical omission had been discovered, it had been too late to do anything about it.

Captain Danahy, whose small exterior of weather-aged leather concealed a heart of gold, had proved a friend indeed, for when he had heard the purpose for which his boat was desired, he had given it for no more than the cost of the gasoline expended.

Mom was snugly ensconced in the bow, a mountain of blankets and shawls surrounded by packages of salami and bologna and bloodwurst sandwiches, hard-boiled eggs, and thermos flasks of hot coffee. In the stern huddled three weedy youths in too thin over-coats with the collars turned up, known in the Soslewski's neigh-borhood as the Three Harmoniacs. They were all sick. The sight of Myrene eating a banana did not help them. Zella kept her hand hooked in the belt of Myrene's warm coat, for twice already she had come close to falling overboard.

Zella looked good. She wore the red dress under her imitation beaver coat, open enough to show it, a hat made of black straw and red flowers; and she carried a bunch of crimson carnations. The sharp air merged the color of her rouge with the tint of her skin. She had decided to wear her eyeglasses and pick Johnny out rather than leave them off and see nothing. Besides, he was used to them.

Mr. Soslewski, his grayish, square head bare, his thick ulster buttoned up to his chin, had never known such sweet power as he wielded now. As originator of The Idea, and charter captain of the *Daisy D.*, he was undisputed master of them all. Everybody had to do what he said. He did not even resent that the presence of the Three Harmoniacs, useless as they appeared to be at the moment, was Zella's doing—for free. Zella was a popular girl. She was president of two neighborhood social clubs and secretary of her high-school sorority. The Three Harmoniacs, an accordion, sax, and violin trio, played at small neighborhood dances and had yielded to patriotic and commercial pressure applied by Zella. They needed her business.

Mr. Soslewski's small gray eyes swept the scene for the hundredth time, checking and rechecking every detail, and what he saw confirmed an added warmth and pride in his heart. But for the jigging pilot boat standing off the Hook, they were alone. There would be maybe some fourteen thousand boys aboard the *Queen Mary* when she came in. And only their Johnny would have a boat with the family and a sign and a band to welcome him home.

From behind the lowering gray curtain to the east a giant voice called distantly at first, "Woooooo . . . woooooo," and then as Mr. Soslewski shouted, "Listen!" more loudly, "Woooooooooooo!" The *Queen Mary*, large as a mountain, her gray sides and cliff tops festooned with faces, came gliding out of the mists.

Mr. Soslewski yelled, "Johnny's coming! He's coming!" and went in many directions at once. Zella, her heart pounding violently, took a firmer grip on Myrene's belt and led her forward, where Mom beamed like a Buddha as the *Queen* increased in size from a mountain to an Alp and from an Alp to the whole Himalaya range. Ed Danahy revved up the motor and swung the *Daisy D.* so that the sign would face the incoming boat, and Mr. Soslewski scuttled to the stern in a crimson fever of excitement and harangued the band to life.

"All right, so you're a little sick. Who cares if you don't play so good? But now you're here anyway, make a noise. Do *something!*"

The suffering Harmoniacs were artists, and nothing if not game. The excitement of the arrival of the big ship and the launch gaining seaway helped them. Greenly they unpacked their instruments and huddled in the stern, giving forth preliminary squawks, grunts, and wheezes.

The *Queen Mary* slid to a halt as the pilot put out in his bouncing rowboat, and because she was so great and so silent now except for the inevitable streams of water gushing from two lower ports and the mewing of her train of gulls, the hush that fell upon the sea and the scene was magnified a thousand times and through it sounded the strains of the Three Harmoniacs in a not-quite-together yet unmistakable rendition of the first thing that came to their minds, which happened to be *One Dozen Roses*.

Triumphant in the last detail, Mr. Soslewski rushed back to join the group in the bow. He waved an American flag. Myrene and Zella also waved American flags. Their cries rose from the surface of the water to mingle with the music and the wailing of the gulls. "Johneeeee . . . Johneeee! Welcome home, Johnny Soslewski! John*neeeeeeeeeee!*"

Mom Soslewski did not wave or cry out, but sat hugely bundled in her rugs like a Mahatma and with her eyes searched hungrily for the face of her son.

There were so many of them, thousands upon thousands of faces. They poked out of portholes and formed pink and khaki patches clinging to the upper decks like shrubbery overgrowing a gray cliff top; they clustered in knots on former gun platforms and emplacements, jamming the rail of the promenade deck, filling the forward and after wells and deck tiers.

The Three Harmoniacs warmed up and switched to *Jumpin' Jive*, which drew whistles from the throng on the ship, as Ed Danahy skillfully took the *Daisy D.* twenty yards distant along the length of the giant liner. They could see the faces clearly now. Their sign boldly stated that all this was for Pfc. Johnny Soslewski, and while they searched, Zella and Myrene shrilly screamed his name. "Johnneeee . . . Johnneeeee!"

High up on the promenade deck a gagster, a funny-man, a lonely family-less soldier who did not know how much he was hurt by the spectacle of the tiny boat bobbing far down below with its tender freight of music and family, the proud old man and the kid sister, the pink-faced girl with the red dress and Sunday hat, the blatant sign, the big fat woman who was so patently Mom and who just stared, cupped his hands to his mouth for a megaphone and shouted down:

"He ain't comin' home. He married a limey!"

His cry penetrated above the gulls and over the thin strains of the music and caused a ripple of laughter all along the rail. Mr. Soslewski, unable to identify the voice or what was said, filled his lungs with pressure and bawled up, "What?"

A dozen GI's nearest the gagster funneled their mouths and joined in the answer. "He ain't comin' home. He married a limey!"

Zella heard it as clearly as though she had been standing on the deck with them. But even as it pierced her heart like a spear, her mind blotted it out, and she cried, "What's that? What are they saying?"

Mom said, "They're trying to say something. Listen what it is, Joseph. Oh my God! I hope something didn' happen. . . ."

Mr. Soslewski bawled toward the stern of the *Daisy D.*, "Shut up the band! You can't hear nothing with such noise." Surprised and hurt, the Three Harmoniacs quit in the middle of a phrase as though their throats had been simultaneously cut. Only Myrene's voice continued to mount shrilly, "Welcome home, Johneeeeee!"

Five hundred throats now hurled back the reply in cadence. "He *ain't* comin' home. He married a *limey!*" A thousand took it up and a thousand more with a kind of compelling hysteria. It spread from mid-deck to topside and the ports below, rolled like a prairie fire fore and aft, the length of the vessel, kindling from mouth to mouth and repeating like a kind of horrible liturgy.

Mom was round-eyed, white, and badly frightened. Her blankets shook with her. She called to her husband, "Joseph! You hear that? They say he's married to someone! Oh my God, Joseph! They say he ain't comin' home. . . ."

The enormity of the phrases and the message they conveyed reached Zella. She opened her mouth but had no voice. Salt spray blurred her glasses and she felt suddenly sick and dizzy and clung to a stanchion for support. In a momentary quiet as the soldiers drew fresh breath, Mr. Soslewski's deep voice barreled upwards as though issuing from Davy Jones's locker.

"We're looking for Private First Class Johnny Soslewski!"

They were ready for him now, the six thousand, plastered over every inch available across the starboard face of the liner, clinging to every hand hold, and the booming chant burst from them like a battleship broadside.

"He ain't comin' home! He married a limey!"

It had such a lovely rhythm to it: "He ain't comin' home." Pause. Then fortissimo: "He married a limey!"

Hot anger, anger against Johnny for spoiling his day, filled Mr. Soslewski, but he did not dare look at Mom, who was crying quietly now with shock and disappointment. Zella was not yet ready to cry. She clung transfixed to the stanchion, her mouth foolishly open, staring unseeing through her salt-encrusted glasses, her ears ringing with the horrible words.

Ed Danahy negotiated the launch at a safe distance past the yacht bow of the *Mary* and drifted her down the port side beneath the towering walls of steel and flesh, and the chant followed them, crossing the ship in a single leap, infecting the soldiers packed on the side facing the sea, overwhelming the people in the little launch with its message of disaster and double-dealing.

Down port and past the stern back to starboard they chugged, pursued by the awful chorus until the *Queen* herself, her pilot now aboard, drowned out the sound with her own great voice as she gave three hoots of warning. White water bubbled from beneath her, and her bow plucked a small feather from the sea. It quieted the soldiers for a moment, and in the hissing silence Myrene asked, "Pop, what's a limey?"

Without meaning to, Mr. Soslewski struck her across the face with his hand and she began to scream, "Johnneeee. . . . I want Johneee!"

"Shuddup!" shouted Mr. Soslewski. "Didn't you hear he ain't comin' back?"

Departing, the GI's drew one more breath and the wind brought it back to the *Daisy D.* in chunks as the liner withdrew into the still misty morning to turn the corner at the Hook. "He—ain't—comin'—back! He—married—a—l—im—e—y!"

The leader of the Three Harmoniacs edged forward miserably as Ed Danahy spun the bow of the *Daisy D.* back toward the dark, desiccated shore. "You want we should play something more?" he asked.

In her room in the apartment over the butcher shop Zella lay on her bed burning with shame and misery, her ears, her body, her nerves still vibrating to the horrible rhythm of the message shouted down from the ship, the unforgettable trumpeting of her humiliation.

Not only had Johnny deserted her, but fourteen thousand of

his buddies had been told and knew the secret of her dishonor. Married a limey . . . married a limey. She knew as long as she lived she would never get the mocking chant of the men out of her head, the derisive dirge that had at last overwhelmed her like the sea itself, battering down her defenses, her refusal to believe, her loyalty to Johnny, until there was no longer any escape from the truth, until her bloodstream and heartbeats were forced to echo the rhythm, "He ain't comin' home. He married a limey."

What did this English girl have to take Johnny away from her like that? It must have happened in the very last moment, because she still remembered Johnny's letter of ten days ago, telling her to prepare for the wedding because he was coming home. He wasn't much at writing love, but he had said, "You better feel the way about me the way I feel about you," and for Johnny that was more even than saying, "Zella, I love you," or sending kisses. He didn't talk much, but he could make you feel what he meant with his arms, or by looking at you.

God, how she hated the English girl, and Johnny too! She made a picture of them standing together on the dock in England, Johnny with his arm around the girl, calling across to the soldiers on the boat as it drew away from the pier, "Tell 'em I ain't comin' home. I'm married."

Why couldn't he have written her about it? Why did he have to tell them all? She would have got the letter and quietly crawled away with it. Now she could never go out on the street any more. Everybody on the block would hear about it. She pressed her face deep down into the bed and pulled the pillows about her ears and tried to drown out the cry of fourteen thousand throats. In the quiet of the bedroom it sounded more loudly and terrifyingly through her head than it had out on the water.

In the living room Mr. Soslewski stomped up and down and reiterated, "He's got to come home some time. And when he does, I'm gonna beat him within an inch of his life. He got no right. Within an inch of his life, man to man."

Mom's eyes were red, but her massive bulk was composed and her face tired but placid, like the features of a soldier many hours after the battle is over and understanding has returned. She was a bulwark against which her husband's spleen was breaking and wearing itself out like combers rolling on shore and diminishing after a storm at sea.

She said, "He's our son, Joseph!"

"Sure he's our son. All right. But what right has he got, when we fix everything to come out on a boat to meet him? What about Zella? She's been like a daughter to us. What do we know about this Miss English-schminglish? You can sit there and? . . ."

This was an old battlefield, and Mom had already counted her dead. "She's Johnny's wife and our daughder, Joseph. We gotta welcome her in our home like our own daughder. It's terrible about Zella, but Johnny's our own flesh and blood. Whoever he brings home, we gotta be good to her."

"Yeah? *You* be good to her." Mr. Soslewski slammed from the room, leaving her to her resignation. She heard the door bang as he went into the butcher shop. She heard the bed in Zella's room creak and felt sorry for her. But above all she was lonely for Johnny.

Mom was tidying upstairs the next morning when the telephone rang. Joseph was in the butcher shop attending to customers. The Gianelli boy had come to help out in the cashier's cage. Zella was packing. She was going up to Fall River to stay with some relatives for a while. She could not face going back to work in the store and meeting everyone. She and Mom had talked it all out the night before, when neither had slept and each with the unconquerable strength of women had made her decision.

Mom laid down her dust cloth carefully and noted where she had left it so that she would not forget and then have to hunt all over for it, and moved her bulk over to the telephone. She picked up the instrument and said, "Yeah, hello."

"Hey, who's this? Mom? Hey, hello, Mom. This is Johnny. I'm home."

"Johnny! Oh my God, Johnny! Oh God, Johnny. You're home? Oh God, I can't believe it. Is—is she with you, Johnny?"

"What's that? Hello, Mom. Is who with me? I'm back."

"Johnny, the— Ain't you married?"

"Ain't who married? Whaddya talking about, Mom. I ain't married to no one. What kinda crazy talk is that? Where's Pop and Zella? Put Zella on."

"But, Johnny— We come down to meet you. We had a boat . . ."

"Yeah, yeah, Mom. I heard about it after we got in. I drew K.P. so I was down below and didn't see nothin'. I'm at Fort Dix, but I'm gettin' a pass tomorrow. Get Pop and Zella. Hello? Hey, Mom! Whatsamatter up there, anyway?"

The matter was that Mom was staring heavily at the telephone receiver and moving as slowly and ponderously in her mind as she moved on foot, trying to replace one image with another, and it was so difficult to do, so hard after what she had gone through to think and know what was right. She had steeled herself with patience and with love to welcome to her heart the strange girl who would be Johnny's wife. The telephone she held almost at arm's length emitted a blasting voice. "Hey, Mom! I can't hear you! Hello, hello, operator. . . ."

Then Mom began to scream at the top of her lungs, "Joseph! Joseph! Zella! Joseph!" and she raised her foot and stamped the downstairs signal on the floor until the chandelier swung and the mirrors on the wall quivered with double images. "Zella! Joseph!"

They came running, Mr. Soslewski alarmed from the shop below with his hands still bloody from cutting lung, and Zella from her room, a buxom wraith without make-up, her glossy hair crumpled atop her head, her glasses awry.

Mom's breath was failing her, but she held out the telephone and gasped out the import of what it contained. "Joseph! Zella! It's Johnny! He's home. He ain't married to no one. He was on the boat all the time. He was downstairs and didn't see us. It's Johnny. Here, Zella, he wants to talk to you. Talk to him, Zella."

She gave the instrument to Zella and plumped into a chair, fanning herself with her large hand, and the tears were quick in her eyes again. "Oh, Joseph, I'm so mixed up. Everything's all right again, and I'm so happy."

Mr. Soslewski stood there wiping his hands and shouting, "I'm going crazy. Why didn't he say something if he was on the boat all the time?"

"He couldn't, Joseph. He was downstairs."

"*Downstairs!*" Mr. Soslewski was yelling now. "I arrange we can go out on a boat like Grover Whalen to meet him and he's gotta be downstairs. . . ."

"Shhh, Joseph. Zella can't hear nothin'."

Zella had the receiver to her ear and was listening, but curiously there was no expression on her face. They could all hear Johnny's voice yelling, "Hello! This is Johnny! I wanna speak to Zella. Hello, is Zella there?"

Zella said in a flat voice not at all like her own, "This is Zella!"

"Hey, Zella! How about it? I'm back. Ya do what I told ya to? About you know! I'm comin' up tomorra. As soon as you're ready we can jump off. Ya gonna be glad to see me, Zella?"

"Yeah," said Zella, "I'll be glad, Johnny."

But she couldn't feel glad yet. She couldn't feel anything but the craving to hide from her hurt and shame. She was still filled with the echoes of bitter thoughts.

She could not yet approach even close to the reality. Johnny was home. Mom had said he wasn't married to anyone. He talked and sounded just like the old Johnny. Perhaps later, when she had time to think and he held her in his arms, she would get over it, but she could not be sure. There was Pop glaring and Mom crying and Johnny's voice in the telephone, but her soul was still shaken and shuddering, her ears and eyes and mind still brimming with the sight and the sound of the massive gray mountain of a ship, the fourteen thousand staring faces, and the hideous, shameful chant from the fourteen thousand throats:

"He ain't comin' home. He married a limey."

The Enchanted Doll

"The Enchanted Doll" was rejected by every American magazine to whom my agent tried to sell it. It was eventually bought and published by a British woman's magazine in London, for whom I changed it into an English story with a London setting.

This is one of those odd stories I can't remember why I wrote or even when or what was the springboard. Reading over it now, I notice a reference to a barrel organ playing "Some Enchanted Evening," which gives us an approximate date, while the theme indicates a momentary interest in psychology and psychiatry which at one time had a great vogue in the United States. Everywhere one went to cocktail or dinner parties one heard snatches of conversations beginning, "My analyst says . . ."

Ah, wait! What would one do without the subconscious, which dredges up the most astonishing things? Somewhere in New York, in some shop I saw a painted doll and fell in love with her. I can't remember where or when, or why I was in the shop and in the doll department, but this was a little creature created by a specialist who had hand-painted the face. The expression, I recall now, was extraordinarily sweet and lifelike, and the little figure touched my heart. If one wanted really to hark back to what the head-shrinkers were saying and doing in those days, one could suggest that this funny little momentary love affair grew out of the fact that I had always wished to have a daughter and instead produced sons.

I remember now the emotion was a strong one. It tugged, and therefore I put it into a short story. Perhaps that is why no American editor liked it or would buy it.

If writers are funny people, so then are editors, and one never knows what will displease them, irritate them, cut across their taboos, personal as well as policy-wise, or just downright fail to impress them as material that will entertain their customers.

But this is a wonderful case in point to confound those who say to you, "Oh, well, of course you've got a name now, you can sell anything," since nothing could be further from the truth. I can think of three stories almost immediately, written in recent years when I was supposed to have a name, that were rejected by American editors and eventually published in Great Britain. They may not have been the greatest stories I ever wrote, but I should say by any standards they were publishable and would have entertained their readers. "The Enchanted Doll" makes us a quartet of rejects from the American market. The truth is, of course, the better your name, the more the editor wants for the high price he is paying. He considers that since he is paying you a top and current price he is entitled to your top work. But any writer knows that if he turns out one or two really first-class short stories in a year, he is lucky.

Looking back over "The Enchanted Doll" and rereading it today, I would say that the writing in it leaves something to be desired, particularly at the end, but the story appears to me to be a good one and sound and possibly moving—at least it did appeal to me and still does. Yet somehow it signalizes the beginning of my divorce from the American short-story market.

At that I might have left it out of this collection, since I have always been willing to admit that my American editors are right and I am wrong, since they are buying for a mass market they are supposed to understand, except for the fact of the post-history of this story.

Mr. Douglas Fairbanks, Jr., was making a series of two-reel half-hour television shorts in England for an American sponsor, and asked my London agent to see my wares. With a wide collection of stories to choose from, he selected and bought "The Enchanted Doll" and filmed it.

I have one final note to add: I have had a number of my short stories, novels, and screen originals made into films and with one exception each one of them was, in my opinion, a catastrophe. Several of them made enormous fortunes in money for their producers, but I hated them when I saw them on the screen. As far as I was concerned, they had failed in every way to realize the manner in which I saw, felt, and created my characters.

The exception was "The Enchanted Doll," which Mr. Fairbanks showed me in the projection room of his studio outside London some four or five years ago. It was the first time that I had ever had the spirit of the story, its emotional content as well as the physical appearances of my characters, faithfully translated to the screen. I can't remember now the name of the actress he employed for the part of the unhappy girl, but I do know that she was tender, wistful, and endearing and brought my character most beautifully to life. The part of the young doctor was most excellently played by Mr. Douglas Fairbanks, Jr., himself.

TODAY is the anniversary of that afternoon in April a year ago that I first saw the strange and alluring doll in the window of Abe Sheftel's stationery, cigar, and toy shop on Third Avenue near Fifteenth Street, just around the corner from my office, where the white plate with the black lettering on my door reads: SAMUEL AMONY, M.D.

And I feel impelled to try to set down on paper some record of the things that resulted from that meeting, though I am afraid it will be a crudely told story, for I am not a writer, but a doctor.

I remember just how it was that day: the first hint of spring wafted across the East River, mingling with the soft-coal smoke from the factories and the street smells of the poor neighborhood. The wagon of an itinerant flower seller at the curb was all gay with tulips, hyacinths, and boxes of pansies, and near by a hurdy-gurdy was playing "Some Enchanted Evening."

As I turned the corner and came abreast of Sheftel's, I was made once more aware of the poor collection of toys in the dusty window, and I remembered the approaching birthday of a small niece of mine in Cleveland, to whom I was in the habit of despatching modest gifts.

Therefore, I stopped and examined the window to see if there might be anything appropriate and browsed through the bewildering array of unappealing objects—a red toy fire engine, crudely made lead soldiers, cheap baseballs, gloves and bats, all a-jumble with boxes of withered cigars, cartons of cigarettes, bottles of ink, pens, pencils, gritty stationery, and garish cardboard cut-out advertisements for soft drinks.

And thus it was my eyes eventually came to rest upon the doll tucked away in one corner. She was overshadowed by the surrounding articles and barely visible through the grime of decades collected on Abe's window, but I could see that she was made all of rag, with a painted face, and represented a little girl with the strangest, tenderest, most alluring and winsome expression on her face.

I could not wholly make her out, due to the shadows and the film through which I was looking, but I was aware that a tremendous impression had been made upon me, that somehow a contact had been established between her and myself, almost as though she had called to me. It was exactly as though I had run into a person as one does sometimes with a stranger in a crowded room with whose personality one is indelibly impressed and which lingers on.

I went inside and replied to Abe's greeting of "Hello, Doc, what can I do for you? You out of tobacco again?" with: "Let me see that rag doll, the one in the corner by the roller skates. I've got to send something to a kid niece of mine. . . ."

Abe's eyebrows went up into his bald head and he came around the counter, the edges of his open vest flapping. "That doll?" he said. "That doll now could cost quite a bit of money, maybe more than you would want to pay. She's special made."

Nevertheless he took her from the window and placed her in my hands and here it was that I received my second shock, for she had the most amazing and wonderful quality. No more than a foot long, she was as supple and live to the touch as though there were flesh and bones beneath the clothes instead of rag stuffing.

It was indeed, as Abe had said, hand-made, and its creator had endowed it with such lifelike features and grace that it gave one the curious feeling of an alter presence. Yet there was even more than that to her. Could a doll be said to have sex appeal in the length and proportions of her legs, the shape of her head, the swirl of her skirt over her hips? Was it possible for an emotion to have been sewn into the seams marking the contours of the tiny figure? For though I am young, I have seen too much, both in peace and war, to be either sentimental or subject to hallucination. Yet to hold this doll was to feel a contact with something warm, mysterious, feminine, and wonderful. I felt that if I did not put her down I would become moved by her in some unbearable fashion.

I laid her on the counter. "What's the price, Abe?"

"Fifteen dollars."

It was my turn to look astonished. Abe said, "I told you, didn't I? I only make a dollar on it. I don't need to make no profit on you, Doc. You can have it for fourteen. Uptown in some a them big stores she gets as much as twenny and twenny-fi dollars for 'em."

"Who is 'she'?"

"Some woman over on Thirteenth Street who makes 'em. She's been there about a couple of years. She buys her cigarettes and papers here. That's how I come to get one once in a while. They sell quick."

"What is she like? What is her name?"

Abe replied, "I dunno, exactly—something like 'Calamity.' She's a big, flashy, red-haired dame, but hard. Wears a lot of furs. Not your type, Doc."

I couldn't understand it, or make the connection between the woman Abe described and the exquisite little creature that lay on the counter. "I'll take her," I said. It was more than I could afford, for my practice is among the poor, where one goes really to learn medicine. Yet I could not leave her lying there on the counter amidst the boxes of chewing gum, matches, punchboards, and magazines, for she was a creation, and something, some part of a human soul, had gone into the making of her. I counted out $14 and felt like a fool.

I felt even more of one when I had got her home and was re-packing her to send her off to Cleveland. Again I felt that powerful impact of the tiny figure and realized that I had the greatest reluctance to part with her. She filled the small bedroom I had behind my consulting room with her presence and brought an indescribable longing to my throat and a sadness to my heart. For the first time since I had come out of the Army and had taken up practice I realized that I was lonely and that sometimes the satisfaction to be derived through helping the sick is not enough.

I said to myself, "Okay, Sam, boy. That's all you need now, is to start playing with dolls. The guys with the butterfly net will be along any moment."

When I came back from posting it to my niece, I thought that would be the end of it, but it wasn't. I couldn't get it out of my head. I thought about it often and tried to reconcile the emotion it had aroused with what Abe had told me of the flashy red-haired woman who had created the object, but I could not. Once I was even tempted to pursue the matter, find out who she was and perhaps see her. But just at that time Virus X hit in our neighborhood and drove everything else out of my head.

It was three months or so later that my telephone rang and a woman's voice said, "Dr. Amony?"

"Yes?"

"I passed by your place once and saw your sign. Are you expensive? Do you cost a lot for a visit?"

I was repelled by the quality of the voice and the calculation in it. Nevertheless I replied, "I charge a dollar. If you are really ill and cannot afford to pay, I charge nothing."

"Okay. I could pay a dollar. But no more. You can come over. Callamit is the name. Rose Callamit, 937 East Thirteenth Street, second floor."

I did not make the connection at the time.

When I pushed the button under the name plate at that address, the buzzer sounded, the latch gave way, and I mounted two narrow, musty flights of stairs, dimly lighted and creaking. A door was opened an inch or so and I felt I was being subjected to scrutiny. Then the unpleasant voice said, "Dr. Amony? You can come in. I'm Rose Callamit."

I was startled by her. She was almost six feet tall, with brick, henna-dyed hair and an overpowering smell of cheap perfume. She had dark eyes, almond-shaped and slanted slightly in an

Oriental fashion, and her mouth was full, thick-lipped, and heavily made up. There was a horrible vitality and flashy beauty about her. I placed her age at somewhere between forty-five and fifty.

The deepest shock, however, I sustained when I entered the room, which was one of those front parlor-bedrooms of the old-fashioned brownstone houses, furnished femininely, but with utter vulgarity by means of cheap prints, cheap satin cushions, and cheap glass perfume bottles. But hanging from the wall, lying about on the bed, or tossed carelessly onto the top of an old trunk were a dozen or so rag dolls, all of them different, yet, even at first glance, filled with the same indescribable appeal and charm as that of the similar little creature that had made such a profound impression upon me. I realized that I was in the presence of the creator of those astonishing puppets.

Rose Callamit said, "Tall, dark, and handsome, eh? Ain't you kind of young to be around doctoring people?"

I answered her sharply, for I was angry, uncomfortable, and irritated. The rediscovery of these beautiful and touching creatures in this cheap, disgusting atmosphere and in connection with this horrible woman had upset me. "I'm older than you think, and my looks are none of your business. If you don't want me to treat you I'd just as soon go."

"Now now, Doctor. Can't you take a compliment?"

"I'm not interested in compliments. Are you the patient?"

"No. It's my cousin. She's sick in the back room. I'll take you to her."

Before we went in, I had to know. I asked, "Do you make these dolls?"

"Yup. Why?"

I was filled with a sense of desolation. I mumbled, "I bought one once, for a niece. . . ."

She laughed. "Bet you paid plenty for it. They're the rage. Okay, come on."

She led me through a connecting bath and washroom into the smaller room at the back and opened the door partly, shouting, "Essie, it's the doctor!" Then, before she pushed it wide to admit me, she cried loudly and brutally, "Don't be surprised, Doctor, she's a cripple!"

The pale girl, clad in a flannel peignoir, in the chair over by the window had a look of utter despair on her countenance. I was disgusted and angry again. The way the woman had said it was in itself crippling. She was not alone telling me that Essie was a cripple; she was reminding Essie.

I tried to observe as much and as quickly as possible, for the doctor who comes into the sickroom must hear and feel and see with this skin as well as his eyes and ears.

She could not have been more than twenty-four or twenty-five. She seemed to be nothing but a pair of huge and misery-stricken eyes and what was shocking was how low the lamp of life appeared to be burning in them. She was very ill. From that first visit I remembered the underlying sweetness of her presence, the lovely brow and shapely head, now too big for her wasted frame, the translucent, blue-veined hands, flaxen hair but limp and lusterless. She had a mouth shaped to incredible pathos, soft, pale coral, and ready to tremble.

But I saw something else that astounded me and gave my heart a great lift. She was surrounded by small tables. On one of them were paints and brushes, on others, rag material, linen, stuffing threads and needles, the paraphernalia needed for the making of dolls.

Her present illness and her deformity were two separate things, yet it was the latter that caught my attention immediately even from the door, something about the way she sat, and made me wonder. The technical name for her condition would be unintelligible to you, but if it was what it looked to me at first glance, it was curable.

I asked, "Can you walk, Essie?"

She nodded listlessly.

"Please walk to me."

"Oh don't," Essie said. "Don't make me."

The pleading in her voice touched me, but I had to be sure. I said, "I'm sorry, Essie. Please do as I ask."

She rose unsteadily from her chair and limped toward me, dragging her left leg. I was certain I was right. "That's good," I said to her, smiled encouragingly, and held out my hands to her. Something strange happened. For a moment we seemed to be caught up in one another's eyes. I felt she was being swept away and drowning in the dark pool of her misery and despair while the air all about me was shaken with the force of her silent cry to me for help. Her hands lifted toward mine for an instant in imitation of my gesture, then fell back to her side. The spell was broken.

I asked, "How long have you been this way, Essie?"

Rose Callamit said, "Oh, Essie's been a cripple for years. I didn't call you for that. She's sick. I want to know what's the matter with her."

Oh yes, she was sick. Sick unto death perhaps. I had felt that as soon as I came into the room. With my glance I invited the big, vulgar woman to leave, but she only laughed. "Not on your life, Doc. I'm staying right here. You find out what's the matter with Essie and then you can tell me."

When I had finished my examination I accompanied Rose into the front room. "Well?" she said.

I asked, "Did you know that her deformity could be cured? That with the proper treatment she could be walking normally in—"

"Shut up, you!" Her cry of rage struck like a blow against my ears. "Don't you ever dare mention that to her. I've had her looked at by people who know. I won't have any young idiot raising false hopes. If you ever do, you're through here. I want to know what's ailing her. She don't eat or sleep or work good any more. What did you find out?"

"Nothing," I replied. "I don't know. There is nothing wrong organically. But there is something terribly wrong somewhere. I want to see her again. In the meantime I'm prescribing a tonic and a stimulant. I'd like to look in again after a few days."

"You'll keep your big mouth shut about curing her cripple, you understand? Otherwise I'll get another doctor."

"All right," I said. I had to be able to return to visit Essie again. Later, we would see. . . .

When I picked up my hat and bag to leave I said, "I thought you told me it was you who made those dolls."

She looked startled for a moment as though she had never expected the subject to come up again. "I do," she snapped. "I design 'em. I let the kid work at 'em sometimes to help take her mind off she's a cripple and won't ever have a man."

But when I walked out into the bright, hot July day with the kids playing hopscotch on the sidewalk and handball against the old brewery wall and traffic grinding by, my heart told me that Rose Callamit had lied and that I had found the sweet spirit behind the enchanted doll. But the cold, clammy messenger of doctor's instinct warned me also that unless I could determine the cause of her decline, that spirit would not be long for this earth.

Her name, I found out later, was Nolan, Essie Nolan, and she was slowly dying from no determinable cause. I was sure that Rose Callamit had something to do with it. Not that Rose was killing her consciously. The red-haired woman was actually frightened. She wanted Essie alive, not dead, for Essie was her source of revenue and meal ticket.

After I had made a number of visits, Rose did not even bother to keep up the pretense that it was she herself who made the dolls, and I was able to piece together something of the picture.

When Essie was fifteen, her parents had been killed in an accident which also resulted in her injury. A court had awarded her in guardianship to her only relative, the cousin, Rose Callamit. When Essie's inheritance proved meager, Rose vented her spite by harping on her deformity. Through the years of their association, the older woman had made her deeply sensitive to and ashamed of her lameness. Her theme was always, "You are a hopeless cripple. No man will ever look at you. You will never be married or have children."

When Essie came of age, her spirit apparently was broken and she was completely subjugated to the will of her cousin, for she continued to remain with her and under her sway, living a lonely and hopeless existence. It was about this time that Essie first began to make the rag dolls, and Rose, for all of her vulgarity, greed, and indolence, had the shrewdness to recognize their unique quality and irresistible appeal. After she had sold the first ones she kept Essie at it from morning until night. Some weeks she was able to clear as much as $300 or $400. None of this, as far as I was able to determine, went to Essie.

Essie was completely under the domination of Rose and was afraid of her, but it was not that which was killing her. It was something else, and I could not find out what. Nor was I ever allowed to see her alone. Rose was always present. Never had I been so conscious of the difference between good and evil as in that room with the girl, whose poor suppressed nature fluttered so feebly in her wasted body, and that gross, thick-lipped woman with the greedy eyes and patchouli smell who exhaled the odor of wickedness.

I did not mention my belief in the possibility of cure for Essie's lameness. It was more important to discover immediately what it was that was killing her. Rose would not let her be moved to a hospital. She would not spare the money.

For ten days I thought I had arrested the process that was destroying Essie before my eyes. I stopped her work on the dolls. I brought her some books to read, some sweets, and a bottle of sherry. When I returned for my next visit, she smiled at me for the first time, and the tremulousness, longing, hunger, the womanliness and despair of the smile would have broken a heart of stone.

"That's better," I said. "Another ten days of no work. Rest, sleep, read. Then we'll see."

But Rose Callamit glowered and there was an unpleasant expression about her mouth. Her huge, overpowering bulk seemed to fill the room with hatred.

The next time I came to call she was waiting for me in her own room. She had seven one dollar bills in her hand. She said, "Okay, Doc. That's all. We don't need you any more."

"But Essie—"

"Essie's okay. Fit as a fiddle. So long, Doc . . ."

My eyes wandered to the old trunk in the corner. There were three new dolls lying on top of it. Was it only my imagination, or was there yet a new quality to these mute, bewitched figurines? Was each in its way a birth and a death in one, a greeting to the beauties, desires, and pleasures of life and at the same time a farewell?

I had the most powerful impulse to push the monstrous woman aside and crash through the doors to see my patient. But the habits of medical ethics are too hard to break. When a physician is dismissed, it is his duty to go unless he has reason to suspect that his patient is meeting with foul play. I had no such reason. I had failed to determine the cause of Essie's illness; Rose was undoubtedly calling in another doctor, for she needed Essie's work for an easy living and would unquestionably try to protect such a meal ticket.

Thus, with great heaviness of heart, I departed. But I thought about Essie night and day.

It was shortly after this that I became ill myself. Imperceptibly at first, then finally noticeably: loss of appetite, loss of weight, lethargy, irritability, at nightfall a half a degree to a degree of temperature, moments of weakness when I felt as though somehow I could not go on with my work. I let Dr. Saul up at the hospital go over me. He thumped and pounded and listened, the obvious routine, and reported, "Nothing wrong with you, Sam. Take it a little easier. You've probably been overworking. Nature's protest."

But I knew it wasn't that.

I began to look shocking; my skin was losing its tone, my cheekbones were beginning to show, and I was hollow-eyed from loss of sleep. I did not like the look in my eyes, or the expression about my mouth. Sometimes my nights and my dreams were filled with fever and in them I saw Essie struggling to reach me while Rose Callamit held her imprisoned in her ugly, shapeless arms. I had never been free from worry over failure to diagnose Essie's case.

My whole faith in myself as a doctor was badly shaken. A desperately stricken human being had called upon me for help and I had failed. I could not even help myself. What right had

I to call myself a doctor? All though one awful night of remorse and reproach the phrase burned through my brain as though written in fire:

"Physician, heal thyself!"

Yes, heal myself before I was fit to heal others. But heal myself from what? If anything, my symptoms resembled those of Essie Nolan. Essie! Essie! Essie! Always Essie!

Was Essie my sickness? Had she always been from the first moment that I had encountered that extension of her enchanted spirit embodied in the rag doll in Abe Sheftel's shop?

And as morning grayed my back-yard window and the elevated trains thundered by in increasing tempo, I knew my disease. I was in love with Essie Nolan. When I could couple the words "love" and "Essie," when I could look up and cry "I love Essie Nolan! I want her! I need her person and her soul, forever at my side!" it was as though I could feel the fire of healing medicine glowing through my veins.

It had always been Essie, the warmth and yearning need, the tenderness that she expressed with her presence, and the odd, off-beat beauty of her, too, a beauty that would only reach its full flower when I had cured and restored her in every way.

For now, as the scales fell from my eyes and my powers were released again through the acknowledging and freeing inside of me of the hunger, love, and compassion I had for her, I knew the sickness of Essie Nolan in full, to its last pitiful detail, and what I must do and why I must see her alone if only for a few minutes if she were not to be lost to me and to the world forever.

That morning I telephoned Abe Sheftel and said, "This is Dr. Amony, Abe. Will you do something for me?"

"Are you kiddin'? After what you done for my boy—you name it."

"Look here! You remember Rose Callamit? The doll woman? Yes. The next time she comes into the store, find some means of telephoning me. Then hold her there, somehow. Talk, or do something, anything to make her stay there a little. I need twenty minutes. Okay? Got it? I'll bless you the rest of my life."

I was in a sweat for fear it would happen while I was on an outside call, and each time I returned to the office that day I stopped by the store, but Abe would merely shake his head. Then, at five o'clock in the afternoon the phone rang. It was Abe. He said merely, "It could be now," and hung up.

It took me no more than a minute or two to run the few blocks to the brownstone house where Essie lived and press the buzzer under another name plate. When the door clicked open I went upstairs, two steps at a time. If the door was locked I would have to get the landlady. But I was in luck. Rose had expected to be gone only a few moments, apparently, and it was open. I hurried through the connecting bath and, entering the back room, found Essie.

There was so little of her left.

She was sitting up in bed, but now the absolute pallor had been replaced with two red fever spots that burned in the middle of her cheeks, a danger sign more deadly than the wastage of her hands and body. She was still surrounded by the paints and bits of colored cloth and threads, as though she did not wish to die before she had put together one more image, one more dream, one last reflection of the sweet self that life had apparently so cruelly doomed to wither.

She looked up when I came in, startled out of her lethargy. She had expected it to be Rose. Her hand went to her breast and she said my name. Not "Dr. Amony," but my given one—"Samuel!"

I cried, "Essie! Thank God I'm in time. I came to help you. I know what it is that has been . . . making you ill. . . ."

She was in that state where nothing escaped her. She felt my hesitation and knew I had avoided saying ". . . that is killing you," for she whispered, "Does it matter now?"

I said, "There's still time, Essie. I know your secret. I know how to make you well. But you must listen to me while I tell you. Your life depends on it."

A change came over her. She closed her eyes for an instant and murmured, "No. Don't, please. Let me go. I don't want to know. It will be over soon."

I had not thought that she might be unwilling or unable to face it. And yet I had to go on now. I sat down and took her hand.

"Essie. Please listen. Give me your mind. When a body is undernourished we give it food; when it is anemic, we supply blood; when it lacks iron or hormones we give it tonic. But you have had a different kind of leakage. You have been drained dry of something else without which the soul and body cannot be held together."

Her eyes opened and I saw that they were filled with horror and a glazing fear. She seemed about to lose consciousness as she begged, "No! Don't say it!"

I thought perhaps she might die then and there. But the only hope for her, for us both, was to go on.

"Essie! My brave, dear girl. It is nothing so terrible. You need not be afraid. It is only that you have been drained of love. Look at me, Essie!"

My eyes caught and held hers. I willed her to remain alive, to stay with me, to hear me out. "See, Essie, a person has just so great a reservoir of love to expend. It is drawn upon through life and must ever be replenished with tenderness, affection, warmth, and hope. Thus the supply is always renewed. But yours has been emptied until there was nothing left."

I could not be sure that she still heard me. "It was Rose Callamit," I continued. "She took away your every hope of life, love, and fulfillment. But what she did later to you was a much blacker crime. For she took away *your children!*"

There, it was out! Had I killed her? Had it been I who loved her beyond words who had administered the death blow? And yet I thought I saw a flicker of life in those poor, stricken eyes, and even perhaps the faintest reflection of relief.

"Oh yes, they were your children, Essie, those enchanted creatures you created. When you were convinced that you had lost your chance to be a woman, you compensated for it by embodying your hopes, your dreams, and, like every creator, whether mother or artist, a piece of your heart went into each of the dolls you made. You created them with love; you loved them like your own children and then each one was taken from you at birth by that money-hungry monster and nothing was given to you to replace them. And so you continued to take them from your heart, your tissue, and your blood until your life was being drained away from you. Persons can die from lack of love."

Essie stirred. Her head beneath the flaxen hair moved ever so slightly. The glaze passed from her eyes. I thought I felt the response of faint pressure from the cold hand in mine.

I cried, "But you won't, Essie, because I am here to tell you that I love you, to refill you to overflowing with all that has been taken from you. Do you hear me, Essie? I am not your doctor. I am a man telling you that I love you and cannot live without you."

I caught her incredulous whisper. "Love me? But I am a cripple."

"If you were a thousand times a cripple, I would only love you a thousand times more. But it isn't true. Rose Callamit lied to you. You can be cured. In a year I will have you walking like any other girl."

For the first time since I had known her I saw tears in her eyes and a tinge of color to her lovely brow. Then she lifted her arms to me with an utter and loving simplicity.

I picked her up out of the bed, with the blanket wrapped around her. She had no weight at all: she was like a bird. And she clung to me with a kind of sweet desperation, so that I wondered where the strength in her arms came from and the glow of her cheek against mine; she who but a moment ago had seemed so close to death.

A door slammed. Another crashed open. Rose Callamit stormed into the room. I felt Essie shudder with the old fear and bury her face in my shoulder.

But Rose was too late. It was all over. There was nothing she could do any more, and she knew it. There was not even a word spoken as I walked past her then and there carrying my burden held closely to me and went out the door and down into the street.

August had come to New York. Heat was shimmering from the melting pavements; no air stirred; water from the hydrants was flushing the streets and kids were bathing in the flow, screaming and shouting, as I carried Essie home.

That was three years ago and I am writing this on an anniversary. Essie is busy with our son and is preparing to welcome our second-to-be-born. She does not make dolls now. There is no need.

We have many kinds of anniversaries, but this is the one I celebrate privately and give humble thanks for—the day when I first saw and fell in love with the message from Essie's soul imprisoned in the enchanted doll that cried out to me from the grimy window of Abe Sheftel's shop on Third Avenue.

The Awful Secret of M. Bonneval

The story of "The Awful Secret of M. Bonneval" is more nearly the awful thing that can happen to a well-meaning and innocent author. In this case it was not myself but a friend and respected colleague who was plunged thereby into the deepest and most horrible embarrassment that can come to a writer. But we will come to this awful *denouement* in due course.

If you have ever toured France you will, of course, have done it with the Guide Michelin in your hot little hand and made yourself thoroughly familiar with the style, contents, and purpose of this wonderful little volume. Then likewise you can see the fascination this would have for a writer and the temptation to weave a story about the winning of an extra star.

If you are not familiar with this guide book, it is sufficient to say that the best restaurants throughout France are designated by one, two, or three stars. But there are only ten three-star restaurants, sixty-six with two stars, and five hundred and seventy with one. You can imagine, then, how the one-star chefs yearn for the second and the two-star cooks strive for that rare third star. Whenever you have something that humans desire and for which they will struggle, you have the basis of a story that your reader can share.

Thus, one day when I was touring the *château* country of the Loire, and after a particularly felicitous meal at the one-star Hôtellerie Château at Chaumont-sur-Loire, M. Bonneval was born. He is, of course, not specifically the host of that particular tavern, but you will find him in France wherever you go to a starred restaurant or hostelry, emerging from the kitchen to look things over in his chef's uniform and tall linen hat. He is usually stout from the joy of his own food and equally usually a genuine artist. Likewise you will find Madame, his wife, presiding over the *caisse*. This combination is almost obligatory for a first-class restaurant, for these are the people with tradition and who really care. Perhaps the most famous, characteristic, and wonderful pair in this category are M. and Mme. Dumaine of the Côte d'Or at Saulieu. M. Dumaine is probably the best chef in France today and his is one of the ten restaurants with the coveted three stars.

The idea, then, was born at Chaumont-sur-Loire in the fall of 1952, and I remember working on it in my mind all the rest of my holiday, driving through Europe, searching for an ending that suited me. The twist that came to me finally was one of those fortunate gifts from on high sometimes bestowed upon writers and for which one can only send aloft a humble "Thank you."

The story was written at the country home of Geoff and Drue Parsons at Moigny, outside Paris. Before Geoff went on to bigger jobs, he was editor of the Paris edition of the New York *Herald Tribune*.

The story was dispatched to agent Ober, who promptly sold it to the *Saturday Evening Post*, which published it under the title "The Secret Ingredient." I should remark here that while this *Post* habit of changing titles is a constant irritant to a writer, the size of the *Post* checks tends to salve the wound.

The tale duly appeared and was a hit, if the quantity and quality of the fan mail it drew was any criterion, and that was that. I filed M. Bonneval away in my mind as a character I would use again if I could come upon an amusing and agreeable plot. You might imagine that in the meantime M. Bonneval would have remained decently buried in the *Post* files; but no. Sometimes by good fortune you endow a character with more life than intended, with the result that he sets off upon adventures of his own; and therein hangs a strange tale of embarrassment.

The victim was one of America's top-flight authors whom I have always admired both as a person and as a writer. Some two years after my story had appeared, this author and his wife set off on a tour of Europe. Like many of us who use our profession to get somebody else to pay for our travels, he signed with a syndicate to send back a story a week in the shape of an essay or an anecdote or a bit of fiction derived from European sources.

When they arrived in Paris, the writer and his wife were invited to a dinner party by some friends, but, unfortunately, the afternoon preceding the dinner the author became suddenly indisposed, not to any alarming degree, but sufficiently to make him wish no part of a large and taxing dinner. He said that he would remain at home in his hotel resting, but there was no reason why his wife should not attend, and she did.

During the course of the dinner conversation apparently the subject of the Guide Michelin, its uses, its integrity, etc., came up and one of the guests said, "Have you heard of the French chef on the Loire who . . . etc., etc.," and thereupon launched into the tale of M. Bonneval and his adventures in gaining the second star for his hostel. Only he told it not as a story he had read in a magazine but as a true story that had been recounted to him by a friend who had heard it from a friend who had received it via another friend of a friend who had been there. My paper puppet had made the transition from ink stamped upon wood pulp to flesh and blood. All the details as well as the plot of my story were there, only recounted as true happenings and vouched for.

Now, any man who takes on the task of producing a short story or even a short essay, incident, or anecdote a week knows what he is up against and everything must needs become grist to his mill. Likewise a good wife will understand her husband's problem and help him by keeping her eyes and ears open. And so did this writer's helpmeet. For she came home to her ailing husband glowing with her prize, which would give him surcease for at least one week, saying, "I heard the most charming true story about a French chef tonight," and then with great accuracy passed on the story. The writer, not a *Post* reader, took it as gospel. He wrote it the following week and posted it off happily to his syndicate, who just as happily shipped it out to their clients and it was duly published, not only in various newspapers in the United States, but also in Europe.

The first I heard of this unfortunate and wholly accidental plagiarism was when I received a desperately unhappy three-page letter with cuttings of the story from the author, with apologies saying that he had received dozens of letters advising him of the identical *Post* story published two years previous, that he had read it with mounting horror and, of course, had notified his syndicate at once to call in the story where it had not yet appeared. There was nothing to be done about those that had already been published. I never felt so sympathetic toward anyone in my life, for it could have happened to me. I got him on the telephone immediately and begged him not to worry. But you can't tell a writer not to worry about such a mishap.

We agreed that the money he had received for the story should be given to charity, which eased his conscience somewhat, and the double existence of M. Bonneval, on paper at least, came to an end. But for all I know he still survives as a real and living person at dinner parties in *la belle France*.

Next time you are touring the château country of France and visit the string of airy castles cresting the hilltops along the placid Loire from Blois to Tours, you surely will drop down from the towered and mullioned keep of the Château Loiret, just below Chaumont, to eat a meal and drink the wine at the famous Auberge Château Loiret at the foot of the castle.

There you will unquestionably partake of that superb and unrivaled specialty of the house, *poularde surprise treize minets,* and find your palate enthralled by the indefinable flavor imparted to the fowl by the mysterious ingredient which is the particular secret of M. Armand Bonneval, host and chef of the *auberge*. And like so many, many others before you, you will attempt without success to identify the famous component X which to this day has defied the most educated taste buds in all France.

You also will encounter M. Bonneval, stocky, red-faced, with short-cut, upstanding, pepper-and-salt hair, youthful-looking because of the energy and kindliness in his face, and Mme. Bonneval, a woman of large heart and girth, who, as always in France, will be seated behind the desk in charge of the cash box and the accounts.

And, either perched on the desk next to Mme. Bonneval or twining at the feet of her husband as he appears at the dining-room door to check on the effect of his cooking, there will be a small black-and-white cat—not a particularly beautiful specimen, owing to the fact that she is somewhat cross-eyed, but nevertheless the beloved pet and pride and joy of Monsieur and Madame, your hosts.

As a matter of fact, the famous and succulent recipe is in a way associated with her, Minette being her name. But "Minet" in France is also the generic nickname for cats, just as we call them "puss," and thus a literal translation of the by-now-world-renowned dish of *Poularde Surprise Treize Minets* might be "Chicken-surprise-in-the-style-of-thirteen-cats."

However, when it comes to inquiring of M. Bonneval how this epicure's delight was named or what it is that makes his *poularde* more tasty, stimulating, and unforgettable than any other in the world, and what unknown ingredient is the key to this miraculous gastronomic blend, you will, I know, run up against a stone wall.

Guarded blueprints for airplanes, battleships, and submarines are traded on an international bourse, diplomatic confidences are whispered over cocktails, the secrets of the atom bomb have been freely bandied about; but up to this moment, not one single person in the whole world outside of M. and Mme. Bonneval has been privy to the secret of the recipe for this famous delicacy.

Permit me, then.

In the days prior to the events I am about to narrate, Armand Bonneval, former assistant chef of the Café de Paris, honorably retired, Cordon Bleu member of the Club de Cent, and now sole owner and proprietor of the Auberge Château Loiret, was consumed with a burning ambition.

In the Guide Michelin for 1951, that tourist's and gourmet's bible, which is the automobile traveler's survey of France, the *auberge* was designated by three crossed spoons and forks, denoting a "very comfortable restaurant." This was not at all bad, particularly for a restaurant in a village as small as Loiret, where the usual indication was one crossed spoon and fork or none at all. But it did not satisfy the artistic and creative soul of M. Bonneval. In his day he had been a great cook. In his old age he longed for the tangible recognition of his genius. A higher rating would likewise make a considerable financial difference to himself and Madame, his partner through forty years of unremitting toil.

The size and location of his *auberge* precluded his receiving the four or five crossed utensils reserved for the big, de luxe restaurants of Paris, Lyon, Vichy, or Cannes. However, the famous Guide Michelin annual has further signs to distinguish the superior cuisines it had tested and listed in villages and towns throughout

France—namely, one, two, or three stars added to the spoons and forks.

Three stars, denoting one of the best tables in the nation, and worthy of a special journey of many miles, were as beyond the reach and hopes of M. Bonneval as the stars that spangled the firmament above the Loire Valley at night. There were but ten of these awarded in all France.

Nor was there any better chance of achieving two stars, indicating an ". . . excellent cuisine: worth a detour," of which there were but sixty-six examples in all the thousands of restaurants, *auberges*, hotels and *bistros* throughout the land.

But M. Bonneval did yearn most mightily with his honest heart and Frenchman's pride to be awarded the addition of the single star which would announce to traveler and native alike that he set *"une bonne table dans le localité"* and that the visitor to his board would be rewarded with something special.

If his winning of the three crossed spoons and forks had already made him an important man in the district, the star would elevate him to the status of distinguished citizen. If now they just managed to make both ends meet, the added star would enable them to amass a competency toward their final days. Alas, there was nothing specific that M. Bonneval could do to achieve this ambition, for the matter was not in his hands.

As he would explain sadly to Mme. Bonneval, when sitting quietly in their apartment above the *auberge* after hours, with his beloved Minette purring in his lap, there were literally hundreds of thousands of eating places throughout France that had to be covered; the inspectors, or official tasters, of the Guide Michelin were only so many; they had but one stomach apiece which would hold only so many cubic centimeters. Worked out mathematically, it might be years before one again appeared to sample the fare at the Auberge Loiret, and perhaps never again in their lifetime.

But if even by some chance one should appear, there was no opportunity for M. Bonneval to prepare the kind of specialty that would be likely to bowl over the taster, for the simple reason that the Guide Michelin conducted its tests and listings with scrupulous integrity and fairness. One never knew when the inspector was in one's midst. He came and went in the guise of an ordinary tourist. The Grand Lottery in Paris was not handled with more honesty and care.

"Ah, if one could but know in advance sometime," he would groan, filled with ambition and desire. "Who knows but with the star I would be able to take you to Italy on that little trip we planned so long ago."

And Mme. Bonneval would comfort him, "Never mind, Armand. I am sure you will receive your star somehow, because you deserve it. And besides, it would not be fair if you should know in advance."

One summer's noon a letter arrived for M. Bonneval that caused him to stare as though he could not believe his eyes, and then call loudly for Madame to come and read it to him again, to make sure he had not been deceived. Madame did so, with her circle of additional chins quivering a little. It was short and to the point.

My dear Bonneval: I doubt whether you would remember me, but many years ago you had the occasion to do me a good turn when I was hungry and on my uppers, and I have never forgotten your kindness.

It so happens that I now find myself in a position to return the favor. Through my connections with the Guide Michelin, upon which I will not elaborate, I am advised that on Friday, the thirteenth of July, an inspector will be passing through Loiret-sur-Loire, and he has been instructed to dine at the *auberge* to check on the quality of your meals. I know that your genius will find the best way to make use of this information. Wishing you the very best of luck, I am an old friend who must sign himself

"XYZ"

There it was—the bolt out of the clearest of skies. Not only was the longed-for visit to take place, but M. Bonneval was actually to have notice in advance and time to prepare one of his more superb specialties, such as duck stuffed with chopped truffles, liver paste, and *champignons* with orange sauce or his own version of *coq au vin*.

"I will be famous! We will grow rich!" declared M. Bonneval, feasting his eyes again on the page of the wonderful letter. But then he cried in alarm, "Great heavens! The letter is dated July eighth, but it has been delayed in transit. Friday the thirteenth, when the inspector is to come, is this very day."

It was true. The calendar on the wall displayed a large red "13." Suddenly the affair assumed an urgency that was not dispelled by the exclamation of Mme. Bonneval, who had glanced out of the window, "And that must be he, arriving this very minute! He has come for lunch."

A large and glittery car had poked its expensive snout alongside the *auberge* and discharged one who could only have spent the major portion of his existence sampling the finest foods and wines, for he was as fat as a prize pig stuffed for exhibition. He carried the Guide Michelin in his hand, and entered the front door with a combined expression of truculence and expectancy.

At once he became identified in Bonneval's mind as "M. Michelin Taster," friend, enemy, instrument upon which he would play his gastronomic symphony, critic and bearer of the laurel wreath, or rather star, that would eventually be bestowed upon him.

However, one thing was patent. There was not a moment to lose. Already flustered by the unexpected imminence of his trial, M. Bonneval rushed off to the kitchen, crying to Madame as he made his exit, "I shall prepare for him *le Homard dans la Lune!*" Which was not at all what he had meant either to say or to cook.

"Lobster in the Moon" was the last thing in the world he would have dreamed of making for such an important test, knowing full well that with lobster it can be this way or that way, whereas your ducks, chickens, and *gigots* are always safe.

For the recipe is a tricky one, calling for one large lobster, *bien vivant*—in other words, a brisk and lively fellow—to be extracted, cut up, seasoned with salt and pepper, and sautéed in oil and butter, after which the oil is withdrawn and a tablespoon of finely chopped shallots or chives and a whisper of garlic is added. To give this mixture a little authority, a glass of cognac and another of white wine are now introduced, after which three tomatoes are broken into small bits with a half-tablespoonful of chopped parsley and a shot of cayenne pepper, and the whole thing is cooked for twenty minutes in a casserole at a steady heat. The lobster is then removed and stuffed into the "Moon," a hollowed-out, crisp *brioche*. Now comes the delicate moment. The sauce is thickened with a little cream laced with a shot of brandy and the whole thing poured over the hot, crispy, lobster-filled pastry.

A man wants to be in complete command of himself to bring off a dish like that, particularly when it meant as much as it did to M. Bonneval. That he was not was evidenced when he almost bumped into Minette, the black-and-white cat, as he charged into the kitchen, bellowing loudly for Celeste, the kitchen maid, and Brazon, the man of all work, her lover.

This served only to unnerve him further, for it so happened that Minette had been so fortunate not long before as to encounter a gentleman friend in the park of the château who had been able to overlook the unhappy tendencies of her eyes to cross, and she was now imminently about to be blessed with the fruits of this genuine affection, and a fair packet of them, too, if one could judge from her size.

Nor was it exactly a happy moment in the life of Celeste, who, a few weeks ago, had been seized with the idea of marrying Brazon, and of course had demanded an increase in pay to support this bizarre notion—a request that M. Bonneval, backed by Madame, had quite sensibly refused, since one did not say yes to such ideas the first time. As a result, Celeste was red-eyed and snuffly a good deal of the time, and not quite herself.

This was a pity, for she was to M. Bonneval what the deft instrument nurse is to the great surgeon. With paring knife and chopping bowl, a veteran of a hundred routines, she had stood at his side ready to supply in an instant what the master needed in the line of utensils, saucepans, casseroles, chopped onions, shaved carrots, bouquets of herbs, and so on.

So there was already a considerable disaster building up in M. Bonneval's kitchen, let alone its being Friday the thirteenth.

The lobster, when produced from the cold room, not only did not answer to the description of a brisk and lively fellow but, on the contrary, was practically in a state of rigor mortis. Cutting him up, hence, was no longer a culinary gesture, but an autopsy. It was Fate giving M. Bonneval one more chance to evade what it had in store for him. Had he been in his right senses he would have dumped the crustacean corpse into the ashcan and started on something else.

But his mind was imprisoned by that inflexibility and rigidity that, in the face of a crisis, sometimes affects the best of cooks and housekeepers. M. Bonneval was bent on making Lobster in the Moon, and so he rushed onward headlong to his doom.

Almost at once there commenced such a catalogue of kitchen catastrophes as can be appreciated only by the housewife or chef who has battled the extraordinary breed of gremlins that sometimes arrive to interfere, obstruct, and frustrate when there is a truly important dinner to be got onto the table.

While Celeste reversed her instruction and scraped a *soupçon* of shallot into a tablespoon of chopped garlic, instead of vice versa, Brazon announced that there appeared to have been a change in the wind, affecting the draft of the huge iron stove, plus a blockade of some sort, and he could seem to put no heat in it, and Odette, the waitress, affected by the mounting tension, upset the soup into the lap of the fat man identified in the mind of Bonneval as M. Michelin Taster. This fetched a bellow of rage from the dining room, matched only by the sound emerging from the kitchen when M. Bonneval discovered that Celeste, ruminating on the inhumanity of man, had taken his sautéeing pan, which for eighteen years had known no other cleansing than with salt and a piece of bread, and washed it with kitchen soap and water.

Disaster followed upon disaster. The stove, stuffed with newspapers, straw, kindling, and coke, emitted clouds of acrid smoke, one whiff of which was sufficient to affect the delicate flavors planned by M. Bonneval. The cream pitcher upset in the icebox, inundating everything therein, and at the critical moment it developed that Brazon had misplaced the key to the wine cellar.

M. Bonneval moved as one in the grip of a hideous nightmare. Matters went from bad to worse as a tin of fat caught fire, the handle of his best frying pan broke, and the lamp upset. Celeste and Brazon went completely haywire, the latter breaking the egg beater and short-circuiting the refrigerator, while the former achieved a new high in destructive confusion by putting salt in the egg whites in place of sugar, and cutting up, on the board reserved for crushing garlic, the almonds destined for the famous *soufflé à la curorange.*

Through all this, red-faced, sweating, the glare as of a wild animal filling his heretofore gentle eyes, struggling to retain his temper and his sanity in the face of trials that would have disjointed a saint, M. Bonneval stolidly attempted to fight his way through the morass of calamities that was engulfing him.

It was a losing battle. Friday the thirteenth was not through with him yet. For just as he was stirring the delicate *sauce vanille* intended to go with the *soufflé* that was browning in the oven, Mme. Bonneval, unnerved by the sounds of panic from backstage, abandoned her post next to the cash box and invaded the kitchen. Her faith in her husband's culinary powers shaken for the first time, she committed the unpardonable crime of opening the oven door to see how the confection was coming along, just as Brazon unlatched the back entrance, permitting a swirl of cool air to tear through the kitchen and smite the *soufflé* where it would hurt the most.

Purple with outrage, M. Bonneval made a lunge to swing shut the oven door. It was at this precise moment that poor Minette chose to make one of her sagging promenades across the kitchen floor just in time to trip and unbalance M. Bonneval and send the *sauce vanille* splashing onto the top of the range, where it made a most dreadful smell.

Something snapped inside M. Bonneval. Flesh and blood could endure no more. Tortured beyond human endurance, he hauled back his right foot and applied it to the rear end of Minette, who happened to be aimed toward the back door at the moment.

With a terrible scream of outraged indignation, the loaded Minette took off like a blimp released from its moorings, and soaring majestically up into the blue, vanished from sight.

Now M. Bonneval turned upon the humans. *"Vache!"* he

shouted at his wife. *"Animal!"* he bawled at Celeste. *"Crétin!"* he nominated Odette, the waitress. *"Cochon!"* he dubbed Brazon.

The reactions were immediate. Brazon resigned; Odette vanished; Celeste threw her apron over her head and had hysterics; while Mme. Bonneval swept from the kitchen, went upstairs, and locked herself in her room. Bonneval himself carried in the *soufflé* and placed it before M. Michelin Taster, where it gave a soft sigh and collapsed flatter than an old-fashioned opera hat.

The fat man took one nibble at the edge of the thing and then let out a roar that shook the dining room.

"Criminal! Assassin! Poisoner!" he shouted. "You call yourself a chef! The lobster tastes of soap, the coffee of kerosene, and your *soufflé* is flavored with garlic! Three spoons and forks they have given you, eh?" and at this point he waved the red-covered volume of the Guide Michelin under M. Bonneval's appalled nose. "Well, when I am finished with you, you will no longer be able to swindle innocent travelers! Faker!"

And with this he tore the napkin from his collar and stalked from the room. When, a few moments later, the car thundered away from the *auberge,* it carried with it, in addition to the indignant fat man, the hopes, ambitions and large pieces of the broken heart of M. Bonneval.

M. Bonneval however was of the breed that wastes no time crying over spilt cream, but faces manfully up to the blows of life and recovers quickly therefrom. But he needed the aid and companionship of his wife. Pocketing his badly damaged pride, he hurried to the door of Madame's locked room, from which emerged sounds of grief, and spoke through the keyhole.

"Come now, my dear, it is all over. Nothing more can happen. I am punished for my sins. The inspector has departed to make his report, and we shall be poor again. But as long as I have you, I shall not lack the courage to make a start again—somewhere in a place where we are not known, perhaps. Come, old friend, we have been through much together. Do not take a little incident so to heart."

From within, Mme. Bonneval cried, "Little incident! You called me a cow!"

Obviously a special effort was required. M. Bonneval now addressed the door as follows: "Dear wife, I was wrong to let petty trifles exasperate me into forgetting myself. But look. Even in my anger against Fate, how careful I was in my choice of animals. For is not the cow the sweetest, the gentlest, the kindest, and the most beautiful in all the kingdom? Does she not, with lavish generosity and warm heart, play mother with her milk to all mankind? Is not her glance melting, her disposition notable, and her character beyond reproach? Does not her soft and expressive face invite caresses?" He ceased when he heard the key turning slowly in the lock.

Thereafter he went downstairs, soothed the waitress, apologized to Brazon, and cured Celeste's hysterics with a promise of a raise in salary should the *auberge* not be forced to close.

Notwithstanding the peace declared within his domain, the heart of M. Bonneval was as heavy as a stone, for by late evening Minette had not returned. His conscience was as black as the night because of the kick he had bestowed upon her, and particularly in the light of her delicate condition. He would rather have cut off his right arm than perpetrate an indignity, much less an injury, upon his little friend. He had called and called, but there had been no sign of her.

She had every right to be angry with him—if she was still alive. How, then, to persuade her of his love for her, and his terrible contrition? The hour was past eleven.

He had been calling her since ten. Suddenly an idea smote him. Minette was mad about chicken. He would tempt her with her favorite food.

Purpose now gripped M. Bonneval, and he said to himself, *Little Minette, I shall cook you a Poularde Surprise Royale all for your very own. For you I will cook this as I have never cooked before, for I am very ashamed of having lost my temper and kicked you from the rear.*

He set to work at once, and everything seemed to work like magic, as though Friday the thirteenth had expanded its malignancy, and Fate was no longer interested in harassing M. Bonneval. The stove functioned like a charm, Brazon was as sharp as a razor, and Celeste was her old, cool, efficient self, anticipating his every wish. Objects not only behaved themselves but positively co-operated, seeming to leap into his hand when he had need of them.

With a series of deft movements he boned the chicken and then stuffed it with goose-liver patty, truffles, and a stew of giblets and kidneys made in meat stock and laced with a jigger of port wine.

Poor Minette, he thought as he added the ruby-red liquid, *after what she has been through she will be in need of a little stimulant.*

Working now with supreme concentration and passion, the recipe burned into his memory the way a conductor knows every note of a great symphony without the score, he set about making a sauce for the bird, using the bones of the pullet, onions, carrots, leeks, celery, and a bouquet, which he fortified with a half-bottle of Bollinger '43. *One gives champagne to expectant mothers,* he said to himself as the yellow wine frothed into the brown gravy.

Exquisite odors began to fill the kitchen. It was art for love's sake, and like all true artists and lovers, he became inspired and began to improvise as he went along, making a daring and radical experiment with here an herb, there a spice, a bit of smoked fat, a glass of very old cognac. *For if she is a little drunk she will become mellow and forgive me the more readily,* he reasoned.

And then it was, as he ransacked his closet of herbs and spices, looking still further to delight the heart and appetite of Minette, that he found and added an ingredient that never before had been a part of *Poularde Surprise Royale* or any other dish.

When the bird was cooked to a turn, he performed some final rites, garnishing it with truffles and *pâté de foie gras,* poured the magnificent sauce over it, partitioned it, and, putting one half onto a plate, went out into the night with this savory harbinger of everything good and perfect that man has learned to do with food.

"Minette! Minette!" he called, placing himself upwind, so that the evening breeze from the Loire would carry the fragrance to every corner of the courtyard where the missing Minette might be lurking. And still there came no answer.

Some time later, painfully and heartbroken and still bearing the dish, he returned to the kitchen, where, at the late hour just before midnight, he found an unaccustomed activity sparked by Mme. Bonneval. Coffee was on the fire, a *soufflé* was in the process of being mixed by Brazon, and the other half of the *Poularde Surprise Royale* was missing.

"Ah, there you are," Madame greeted him. "What a fortunate thing you decided to cook a *poularde*. Only fifteen minutes ago there arrived a traveler, a poor fellow whose car had broken down. He was starving, and begged for a bit of something cold left over. You can imagine how agreeably surprised he was when I was able to set before him your specialty. He is drinking a bottle of the '47 Loiret Suchez with it."

M. Bonneval stared at his wife, aghast. "But, *Maman!* It is impossible. I cooked this for poor little Minette, whom I kicked so bru—"

He did not finish, for the door leading from the dining room opened violently, admitting an excited bespectacled little man with a soup-strainer mustache and wearing a seedy suit, but whose eyes and expression nevertheless appeared to command authority.

He paused for a moment *en tableau*, looking from one to another in the kitchen. Then he rushed to M. Bonneval, threw his arms about him, and kissed him violently on both cheeks.

"It is you!" he cried. "You are the magician who has prepared this delectable, this fabulous, this supreme dish! Chef! Genius! Master! I salute you! Not in thirty-five years have I eaten such a *Poularde Surprise Royale*. And at midnight. A veritable palace of gastronomy, a Sorbonne of cookery. Well, you shall have your reward. A star—no, no, what am I saying?—two stars!" And here he paused, and his look changed slightly to one of cunning. "Three stars if you will tell me the secret ingredient in the *poularde*, the only one I was not able to recognize."

M. Bonneval could only gape at him. Could it have been, then, that the other, that fat one, was not M. Michelin Taster? "I do not —understand," he stammered.

"But it is simple, dear master," the man replied. "Know then that I am Fernand Dumaire, inspector for the Guide Michelin. I was on my way here to test your cookery when that villain of a vehicle I was driving ceased to function. And then, to arrive at midnight and at once to find set before me this masterpiece! Of two stars you are certain, but as a little deal between us, I will risk the third in exchange for your secret ingredient!"

Sweat suddenly beaded the brow of M. Bonneval. "The—secret—ingredient?" he repeated.

"But of course. Naturally, I recognized the chervil and the delicate touch of burnet. It took courage to use the basil, and the idea of applying the marjoram to offset the tarragon was capital, while the amount of thyme and sage was perfectly balanced. I should judge the Oporto in the sauce was a trifle more *sec* than is usual—probably a '39—and the champagne, of course, was Bollinger '43, as anyone with half a palate would notice. But one flavor baffles and escapes me, and I, Fernand Dumaire, must know what it is. For you have changed, improved, and glorified *Poularde Surprise Royale*. It has become a new creation and you shall have the honor of naming it. But first tell me the ingredient that has baffled me, in exchange for the third star. Is it a bargain?"

There was a moment of silence. Then M. Bonneval said slowly, "I cannot tell you, monsieur. I shall be content with the two stars you so generously promised me."

Mme. Bonneval stared at her husband as though he were out of his mind, but the chief taster again fell on his neck and kissed him. "You are right, my friend, and noble and honest. A great chef must never reveal his secrets. I tempted you and you resisted. Well, two stars will distinguish you so that the world will beat a path to your kitchen."

At this moment there was an interruption. There came a sweet little call from the outer darkness, and Minette loped into the room, a thin and shapely Minette, though now more cross-eyed with love than ever. She deposited a newborn kitten in the box that had been made ready at the side of the stove. She retired. She came back with another kitten, and another and another. Thirteen times she departed and returned as they watched and counted, fascinated, and the tears of joy flowed from the eyes of M. Bonneval.

When the last one had been deposited and Minette commenced nursing, M. Bonneval declared with deep feeling, "You said, monsieur, that I might name my *poularde*. Very well, I name it *Poularde Surprise Treize Minets*."

At this moment Brazon produced the *soufflé curorange* prepared from the recipe of M. Bonneval, a dream, a vision, high, potent, sturdy, uncollapsible, a beige cloud, with the interior construction apparently of reinforced steel. They joined around the table, and with a Moët and Chandon '37 they toasted the two stars of M. Bonneval and the *Poularde Surprise Treize Minets*.

So, then, the next time you tour in France and drop in at the Auberge Loiret to partake of M. Bonneval's delectable "chicken à la the thirteen kittens," do not, I beg of you, let on that I have given away his secret ingredient and the reason why he could not reveal it even for the honor and accolade of the third star.

It was simple, but a trifle unusual. As you have already suspected, for love of Minette he had seasoned the *poularde* liberally with that herb beloved of all felines, the strongly scented leaves of *Nepeta cataria*, a plant better known to one and all as catnip.

The Glass Door

"The Glass Door" is a kind of one-minute love affair I had with a girl on Madison Avenue one morning.

I was walking down the Avenue on some errand or other passing a new hotel they had just finished there when through the glass door of the not yet opened building I saw the girl in the bride's costume on the staircase being photographed.

She was a beautiful creature and there was something extraordinarily appealing in the expression of her face. For the instant that I stood there on the pavement (I was not the only passer-by stopped by her beauty, either), she satisfied all of the secret yearnings a man carries about with him, and I was in love with her.

I remained thus for sixty seconds watching her and enjoying that romantic fulfillment never attained in reality. She was, of course, a model being photographed for an agency and her face and figure would later be used to emphasize the necessity for life insurance, silverware, face cream, or under-arm security.

My downtown errand drew me onward, I walked off, the spell was broken. The love affair was over. But out of the sixty-second union with a girl I would never see again grew the story of "The Glass Door."

I can recall several more such instances, or one might even call them "instantaneouses." There was a bareback rider in Ringling Brothers Circus in New York who eventually turned up in one of my Hiram Holiday stories, and another, a redhaired girl with a basket on her arm turning the corner of a street in Amsterdam and of whom I only had a glimpse from my car as I turned off in the other direction, and she evolved into the subject of a fantasy romance published in *Esquire*.

"The Glass Door" became and remains one of my favorite short stories for several reasons, and perhaps one of the chief ones is the economy one is able to practice as a writer in achieving the culmination of a desired romance.

I think one of the hardest lessons learned by the romantic is not to pursue too closely the object of his desires. I remember falling in love in Dallas once for forty-five seconds with a dress model for a famous department store. She was quite unlike the ordinary mannequin, for while her face was young and still lovely, she had gray hair and was a grandmother. This romance differed in that I was offered the opportunity of meeting her, but by that time I was old enough to have learned the lessons I just spoke of. I declined the meeting and retained her thus in my memory, fresh and unspoiled.

All this leads to further development of the premise that there is more to writing than fame and fortune. At the expense of a little paper and ink one can become Don Juan, Casanova, Lothario, and all the rest of those virile frauds rolled into one. No love is unattainable, and having been attained, no woman is disillusioning or ever falls short of the dream, for once she has supplied the initial impetus and stimulus and with her face and figure or no more than the tilt of her head, the softness of her eyes or the pure line of brow or jaw, in the imagination we are able to fashion her as we would have her, and certainly not as she ever is.

If such behavior is "escapism" and in itself childish and fatuous, what is one to say, then, of the original and initiating romantic impulse which sends every man chasing skirts. He knows when he catches what he is after that it won't be what he thought it was. Nevertheless, this has never discouraged pursuit. Another way—the writers way—is to win all along the line. Boy gets girl! Boy gets dream, too. Fiction ancient, classical, and modern is filled with women, characters who have been enjoyed by their creators.

The writing of "The Glass Door" was pure enjoyment and the reading of it now, many years later, brings back pleasurably that sixty seconds of pure romantic fulfillment when I stood outside on the Madison Avenue pavement and gazed with worshipful longing at the incarnation of a long-cherished dream.

Wendy Carrel has not aged, though I have; she is still as she was, young, lovely, bitter, disillusioned, and cynical and withal retaining her innocence and purity of heart as she too cherishes the fragile seedling of romance against the cold, hard winds of reality. She cried out for the one man who would fulfill her, and I still respond to that cry.

I am not so sure about those modern writers of realism who so skillfully portray the less savory human characters and apparently relieve their tensions thereby; nor am I sure who they think *they* are in their stories, or what vicarious experience they enjoy; but the writer of romance or the romantic writer, whichever way you will, not only enjoys his unobtainable goddesses but can even enjoy himself as well after he has completed his metamorphosis. He is a chameleon who undergoes changes to conform with each story he is to tell and each hero in whose guise he appears.

Thus in "The Glass Door" I who am I, and quite unlike Edward Anstey, become a curious combination of brilliant scientist and poet. That I am neither of these makes no matter. During the telling of this tale I am, and likewise it makes my twist at the finish slightly more modest and becoming.

Step with me, then, if you will through that Glass Door that beckons to all of us.

S HE was the most beautiful girl I had ever seen.
        I had never encountered such a tender and exquisite expression on the face of any human being as the one I saw on the countenance of the bride standing on the staircase.

I know there are more lyrical ways of saying this, particularly for a professional poet, which I happen to be. But in trying to tell a story in narrative prose, a medium unfamiliar to me, I have realized that the simpler the statement, the more easily is it understood, the more force and conviction it appears to carry, which is not the case with poetry.

After I had seen her I knew I would never forget her.

Even as I stood there on Madison Avenue, my face close to the glass of the door, with a half-dozen other passers-by in the street, gazing at this lovely apparition within, I knew that I was deeply moved by her beauty, but even more by the emotion, the mystery, and the promise of the look that came into her face and filled her eyes to brimming as she posed at the turn of the stairs holding her bridal bouquet.

I wondered what could be the thoughts passing through her head to make her look so glowingly beautiful, so warmly human, and yet withal so spiritually divine, and I felt an overwhelming longing to be near her.

Never anywhere on earth, I was certain, would I find anything more beautiful than those hidden thoughts that were illuminating her face, turning the corners of her parted lips and bringing to her eyes that shining tenderness, that feeling of being filled almost to overflowing with the substance of the soul.

"Of course," I said to myself, "she is a bride. She is in love." And yet this left me unsatisfied, for the object of her affections appeared to be nowhere about. There was a photographer on the ground level viewing her from beneath his black cloth, while an assistant set and grouped floodlights at his direction. A woman arranged the folds of the bridal gown that fell in a cascade of white satin and cream lace to form a shimmering pool a few steps beneath her feet.

I thought to myself, "Either she has just been married or is going to be married. In any case there can be no hope for me, and what am I to do now that I have seen her and can never again put her out of mind?"

And only a moment before I had been walking down Madison Avenue in the Sixties returning from lunch to my office in the Ajax Building, owned by the Ajax Chemical Laboratories, for I am in the way of being an amateur chemist; that is to say, I earn my living with it on the side, my real profession being the writing of poetry, at which I have had considerable success. Only last week I sold a poem to a magazine for $12, and the month before I received checks for $7.50 and $5 respectively for verse.

Now everything was changed.

The place where I had paused to look was the new Tarleton Hotel, which had opened only a few days ago, and some of the entrance were still locked and not yet in use. It was at one of these where I was standing with the crowd, looking inside. Had it not been locked, I would have pushed inside and asked her what she was thinking of there on the staircase which made her look so beautiful.

Inside the hotel there was a kind of broad foyer with a grand and glittering staircase with double wings curving left and right

upward from the landing some dozen steps up. It was on this landing the bride stood, one hand resting on the golden rail, the other
holding her streamered bridal bouquet.

She was as tall and slender as a calla lily. Her gown and veil
and train were all in white and cream. Her arms were sleeved and
gloved, her hair capped with an orange-blossom wreath; she was
sheathed in lace and satin, all but her face, white and pink with
youth and radiance and of perfection unsurpassed.

So must Helen have looked, for this girl too was without flaw.
It is difficult for me, a poet, to set her attractions down unmetered,
for she had those qualities and perfections that are the aim and end
of every poet's search: the long, dark lashes curled over deep-indigo,
ocean-blue eyes, the lyric curve of her chin, the sweet artistry of
her mouth. She looked as though Phideas had made her of painted
marble and then breathed life into her.

Stragglers departed and thus it was I found myself pressed close
to the long door when the change came over her that turned her
from a statue to a woman, from a waxen figure of perfection to a
human being with all the hopes, yearnings, and sorrows, the hints
of hidden joys and secret laughter, the tragedy of one who, with
every capacity for love and living, is yet unfulfilled.

Who was she? What was she? Whose was she? What thing had
she discovered to light this inner fire that so transformed her? To
the threshold of what Paradise had her mind led her? How could I
touch or share this discovery that, if but for a moment, might bring
man closer to the divinity for which he searched so tirelessly?

There it was. The entire scene, the foyer, the steps, the silken
hangings trembled with it. The people within too seemed stricken
and immobilized through it as though time had stood still for them,
and for that instant the photographer, his light man, and his female
assistant stood fixed under a spell. There came a moment when her
beauty seemed too much to bear, when it seemed one might be
blinded in punishment for having looked upon it, and I turned my
head away.

When I looked back, the expression was gone. It was over. The
light man moved one of his standards closer. The angle of the bou-

quet of white roses and lilies of the valley was changed. It was two
o'clock of a May day on Madison Avenue in New York. I moved
away from the door and walked downtown toward my office. But
nothing, not the green buses or the yellow cabs, the shining shop
windows or the people on the street, looked the same to me, or ever
would again.

I tried to put her out of my mind. I could cloud her face and
form, but I could not shut out the music that she had loosed in my
universe. It was then I first knew what a bad poet I must be, for I
could not distil a single line of the songs, the hungers, the yearnings, the discords, the joys, and the tears that I felt so keenly from
the moment I had seen her. I sat at the deal table of my third-floor
cold-water walk-up flat and listened to the crash of the Third Avenue elevated thundering by, and each passage meant another five
or ten minutes had sped and I could not write a word, or commit a
thought to paper.

If this was what it meant to be in love, if this was what it was
to be a poet, and a poet in love, both were hell.

A week later I saw her again on Fifty-seventh Street, west of
Fifth Avenue. She had hailed a taxi and was just about to get into
it. Even though she was clad in a suit and blouse, and wore a piece
of crimson veiling in her dark hair, I recognized her at once.

And yet I had time to notice that in many ways she was changed.
The perfection of her features was unaltered, but she looked tired
and dispirited. There was no hint of the mystery or the miracle I
had seen through the glass door of the Tarleton Hotel. She was as
beautiful from the crown of her chestnut hair to her tiny patent-
leather feet as any man or poet could ever desire for his own, but
the soul that had animated her when she posed as a bride on the
staircase was missing.

Another moment and she would have been gone. Could I expect
the laws of chance that had crossed our paths twice in this teeming
city of eight million to repeat a third time? Now more than ever it
seemed that I had to know.

I ran up to her and said, "Excuse me! Wait, please. Forgive me, but I must speak to you!" I was badly flustered and must have looked very foolish, for I am not prepossessing, or ordinarily attractive to women. On account of my having such light-colored sandy hair it looks as though I haven't any eyebrows. When I was a child I was considered homely. I was so excited and disturbed now that I forgot even to remove my hat. My face felt red and I was perspiring.

She paused, her gloved hand on the door handle of the cab, and looked at me as though to see whether it was someone she knew. I felt chilled at the strange kind of hardness I saw in her eyes now, and the bitterness that appeared to gather at the corners of her mouth. Made up as carefully as an actress, neat, dainty, efficient, and cold, carrying a small bandbox, she looked like Miss New York, the Fifth Avenue Girl. And my heart was crying out within me, "Where are you? What has become of you? Where did you go?"

For a moment a faintly puzzled expression crossed her face. Then she continued to turn the handle of the cab door. I cried out, "Wait, I beg of you. One moment. I know you. You were the bride on the staircase. Never has any woman looked more beautiful. Could you wait just an instant? I . . . I . . . want to get you an ice-cream soda and ask you something. . . ."

I was very badly upset and not at all the person I had imagined myself to be—cool, collected, and in command of the situation. We happened to be standing just outside of Hicks soda fountain. I could have killed myself for being such a fool. A man of the world would have offered her a drink.

She turned and looked me over slowly and with a strange kind of calculation from head to foot and then said with even a hint of amusement in her voice, "Well, at least that's a new approach!"

I felt myself even more ridiculous, towering over her, since I am so tall that I am inclined to stoop. She was mistaking my desperate attempt to speak with her as an ordinary kind of pick-up. I said, "Look here, I don't mean it as an approach, but it is terribly important that I talk to you for a few minutes. . . ."

She looked up again at me still with a puzzled air. "You did invite me for a soda, didn't you? . . ."

At this moment the cabdriver intervened. He said, "Lady, would it be too much to inquire whether you want this cab or don't want this cab? Either way is okay with me, but if you would make up your mind we might be able to restore the normal flow of traffic on Fifty-seventh Street and earn the undying gratitude of the police department. . . ."

I saw her chin come up and some color mount into her face. She said, "I don't want your cab, and I don't like sarcasm. Good-by." To me she said, "No one has offered to buy me a soda for longer than I can remember. You did say you knew me, didn't you? I want a chocolate, all black with a double scoop of ice cream."

The first thing I noticed as we sat up at the soda fountain and she took off her gloves to eat her soda was that she were no rings of any kind on her fingers. I could have shouted. I introduced myself to her. I said, "My name is Edward Anstey. When I said I knew you, I meant I *felt* I knew you. I saw you that day when you . . . you were posing on the staircase of the Tarleton Hotel."

She reflected for a moment and then remarked, "Oh, the Universal Insurance account. The slogan underneath it will read, 'How Are You Going to Protect HER?' " Then she asked, "Why does your name ring a kind of bell? Where do I know it from? Or do I?"

I replied, "Perhaps you saw the April issue of the *American Review*. I had a poem in it called 'The Sky Dwellers.' "

She looked at me sideways as she sucked at her straw. "You write poetry?"

I could understand her disbelief, for no one ever looked less like a poet than I. I have those Midwestern, washed-out blue eyes and a too-long face. I replied, "I am a poet by profession. I sell my poems. I sold one to *Advance Age* last week."

She gave a short laugh and, oddly, not a very nice one. "This *is* different," she remarked.

Her name was Wendy Carrel, and she was a model. I didn't ask her, but I gathered that she was the most beautiful, famous, and successful model in New York.

I suddenly felt embarrassed that I had intruded upon the time of such a person. I said, "I am sorry. I have kept you from an appointment. I didn't realize."

She said, "Never mind. I was only going home to soak my feet and read a book."

I looked at her in amazement. "Home? I would have thought a girl like you would never be home. I mean that men would be after you all the time for dates."

Wendy Carrel's soda made a little bottom-of-the-glass gurgle. She looked up at me with an entirely different expression on her face and said coolly and succinctly, "Men? I am sick to death of men. I am sick of their dates and their suggestions and their passes, and their clumsy tries, their innuendoes and double talk, and their stupidity and greed, and what I am expected to do in return for a dinner or the theater. I spend most of my evenings home alone. And that is where I am going now. Thank you very much for the soda."

I said, "But I haven't asked you the question yet. That day on the staircase when you were posing as a bride. There was a moment . . . something happened to you—to your face. You were beautiful before that, so beautiful that it took my breath away. But for that instant, you were divine. What were you thinking of? What changed you? Can you remember?"

From the look on her face as she studied me for a moment before she replied I could not tell whether she had forgotten, or, remembering, was not going to tell me. For one brief instant the shadows seemed about to lift from her. Then she looked me straight in the eye and said in a matter-of-fact tone, "I haven't the slightest idea. I never think of anything when I am posing. The ideal of feminine beauty in this city appears to be a perfectly blank expression. I try to achieve it."

This, then, was to be the end of the quest. What I had seen could have been an accident, a reflection of the glass door, a trick of the lighting. I said, "I am sorry. Thank you very much for being so kind."

But it was not quite over. She said, "Don't look so disappointed, as though I had robbed you of something. It was you who came

after me, like all men come after me." But then she added as though
something were still puzzling her, "Is it really true that you are a
poet?"

I said, "Yes. I even live in an attic. That is, on the top floor of a
walk-up."

"And I suppose you would like me to come up so that you can
read poetry to me?" She was bitter again.

"I wouldn't read poetry to you. . . ."

"At any rate you're frank."

"I didn't mean that. I would try to use every moment to find what
I saw that day, to learn whether it was there. . . ."

"No thank you. No sale."

My heart felt like lead. The quest was finished. The adventure
pursued might have been pleasurable, but I didn't want it with her,
beautiful as she was, because of what I thought I had seen.

She rose, took her little model's bandbox and purse, and said
with a kind of hard camaraderie, "It was a good try, Anstey. Sometimes it works and sometimes it doesn't. Write this one off."

I went out with her to get her a cab. It was the rush hour and
we stood on the curb together searching, looking right and left for
an empty. She was my responsibility, but now I wanted to be rid
of her. When you are going to grieve for something lost you want
to be alone.

I turned to look toward Fifth Avenue and thus surprised the
bleakness and misery on her face. Much of the hardness and cyni-
cism had gone out of her, leaving the pain and innocence of a forlorn child. She had become a desperate human being with problems
that were too much for her. Suddenly, what I thought, or felt, or
thought I wanted, all the poet's dreams and beautiful illusions, didn't
seem to matter any more. But she did. Her need for help was immediate.

I said, "Wendy! You're miserable, lonely, and unhappy. Come
home with me."

She turned to me. Her features were dark, her mouth twisted in
an ugly manner, and the bitter note was in her voice.

"Oh, all right. What's the difference?"

I had a double gas burner in an alcove, and I made scrambled eggs with calf's brains and stewed tomatoes, and we had bread, cheese, and coffee and a bottle of Richbourg that I had bought with my last check from the *New Age* for my poem "The Catbird."

At first Wendy was as nervous as a witch and as restless as a cat in a new home. While I cooked she sat on the edge of chairs, chain-smoked, or got up and wandered around the room and studied things, my books and pictures and possessions. She relaxed more during dinner, but afterward she suddenly said to me accusingly, "Where did you pick up the nickname 'Clip'?"

"When I used to play end at Wisconsin, I guess. One of the kids in my outfit overseas remembered it. It's one of those things that sticks."

"Then you *are* the Anstey written up in *Passage* last week under 'Science.' Dr. Edward I. (Clip) Anstey, brilliant chemist who won the Ajax Chemical Laboratories $10,000 prize for synthetisizing Dramitone, the new wonder drug for rheumatic fever. . . ."

I said, "You read a lot, don't you?"

She flared up immediately. "Just because my features match and I don't have pimples, do I have to be a vegetable? So you're 'Wisconsin's gift to synthetic chemistry,' a successful chemist with the 'brightest future in the U.S. field,' and not a poet starving in a garret after all."

It was my turn to be angry. I said, "They're a rotten crowd over at *Passage,* jealous and malicious. They can't stand anybody being a literary success. They sent a girl over to interview me about this —at least that's what she said." I flipped her a copy of the *Asphalt Asphodel,* my book of verse which was published last year at very little expense to me beyond the printing and binding, and which had already sold 347 copies. "She asked me a lot of questions which I answered in good faith. It was supposed to be printed under the heading of 'Poetry.' They double-crossed me. They didn't even mention the book."

She said, "You lied about yourself to me. The article should have said, '. . . brilliant and successful chemist whose hide-out where he brings his girls is an unsuspected Third Avenue walk-up . . .' "

It almost seemed to give her pleasure to say those things as though it was a comfort in a way to have her suspicions verified.

I said, "But, Wendy: chemistry is only an avocation with me. I got into it through a clerical error when I signed up for courses in school. Naturally a man can't exist entirely on writing poetry today, but that's all I care about. And I do live here. I enjoy the noise of the elevated going by. It's like a kind of gigantic metronome. When you're a poet, you don't have to live up to your standards of earnings in outside life. You can live anywhere you please."

She didn't seem to believe me. She threw me an incredulous glance, then got up and went to the window and looked out on the tracks of the elevated and to the washing strung from the windows of the flat across the street. When she turned back to me, there was an expression of desperation on her face.

She said, "Well, when do you start making the passes? Or do you expect me to turn the bed down for you and get in?"

It sounded so hard-boiled and New York, just like so many of the tough kids you meet around. And yet I knew that here was innocence and terror, and something else I didn't understand at all. I waited for the space it took a train to go by. Then I said, "What if there aren't going to be any passes, Wendy?"

She came over, sat down by the table again, and said, "In God's name, Clip, what is it you want of me, then?"

How hard it is to communicate. What a failure are words to try to reproduce heartbeats, longings, and hunger. I tried to explain. "Something I saw in you through the glass door, and that thing was beauty."

I saw her eyes narrow at the word. I said, "It is a different kind of beauty, Wendy, for which every man searches endlessly. It is something that lives in him, perhaps as a memory, perhaps only as a longing. It is his dream of the unattainable woman, the sorceress, the angel, the divine human who will combine heaven and hell for him on earth and into eternity."

I tried to make her understand. "Sometimes he catches no more than a glimpse of it, the contour of a cheek, the sound of a voice in the night, eyes filled with sudden tears, the weight and smoothness of coiled hair, the warm touch of a hand given in kindness, and never in his life does he come any closer to it. And sometimes it stands revealed in all its wonder as it did that day on the staircase when something came into your face that was more beautiful than anything I had ever seen or imagined. It was the end of the search. . . ."

"And now," she said in a hard, flat voice, "it isn't there any more, and I'm just a brat who let herself be picked up on the street like an alley cat, and taken home."

"No, Wendy, you're not."

She sat pulling at her lower lip like a little girl now, for she could change in an instant. Then she said, "I lied when I said I didn't know what I was thinking of on the stairs that day. I was playing bride. I was pretending I was going to go down the steps to be married to the man I loved. He was kind, understanding, unselfish, and honest. I made him up out of my head because I needed him."

She threw me a swift look as though to see if she could tell what I was thinking. Then she continued, with a momentary return of her old bitterness. "Success in New York. The most photographed face in America! And the men who want only one thing from me and who never think of offering me a single bit of their hearts in return. . . .

"I could bear that, but I couldn't bear their minds, their dirty minds, so shallow and empty of everything but themselves, their ambitions and their vanities. Business and sex, and nothing else. And even if I had married one so that he could show me off, it would have been the same. So I made one up. He didn't have much money, and wasn't very successful, but I didn't care about that and neither did he. He cared about me and what I thought about and felt. He thought a lot about things and we talked about them, sometimes through the whole night. He was gentle and considerate and a whole man, strong where others are weak, human and weak where strength is only vanity. To him I was going to give what I have never given to any other because they all held me so cheap, all those who were so cheap themselves. . . .

Now she looked at me gravely, and all the bitterness was gone from her face and eyes. She said, "That's how women dream sometimes. But they can face up to reality too. Take me home, Clip. We have passed one another by, haven't we? Or do you want me to stay? It doesn't seem to matter so terribly to me any more, one way or the other, if it would make you happy. You make the decision for me."

Now the room was full of the feeling of my wanting her; the walls and the floors trembled with it as when the elevated thundered by, but there was no train passing then. There was no hiding this from such a woman as Wendy, my weakness and my desire, and all this coupled with my silly vanity of playing at poet; there I stood before her, a sham and fake, exposed like all the rest.

And yet I did say, "I'll take you home, Wendy. Let's go. . . ."

She laughed, but this time it was a kind of deep, satisfied laugh. "Oh Clip! You've got guts to turn me out. And you *are* a poet."

Wendy lived in a brownstone house in the West Eighties. All the way home in the taxi we did not speak. I did not even try to hold her hand or take her in my arms.

I was thinking, *We will never see one another again because I have been a fool from beginning to end and only hurt her. Why didn't I let her stay with me? How close we almost were. Why would she have stayed with me? What made her give up? What had happened to her, to me? What was it I had missed, and where?*

I took her up the steps of the high, old-fashioned stoop to her door. There I said, "Good-by, Wendy. I can say good-by, I can keep from seeing you again. But I can't keep from telling you that I love you, whoever and whatever you are, and always will. . . ."

She reached up to put her arms about my neck and kissed me. "Clip!" she said. "Don't you know why I would have stayed with you tonight?"

It was my turn to stare at her, not knowing what to say.

She whispered close to my ear. "You fool . . . Don't you know one can look two ways through a glass door? I wove my dreams about you like a silly girl. I said to myself, 'Perhaps he might even be a poet. He could be, with those strange eyes. . . .' You looked like everything I've ever wanted. Later, when I thought you were just like the rest, I was desperate and didn't care. . . ."

And then she said, "Come tomorrow, Clip. Take me out. Let's learn about one another. Let's not rob one another of our courtship. We're just at the beginning. There's so much about one another still to know. . . .

When I went down the steps she remained standing for a moment at the door, looking down and watching me. It was not a trick or illusion of the street lamp's light that gave her face the expression of infinite and exquisite tenderness and beauty. . . .

The Hat

"The Hat" I suppose is an example of how broadening travel can be and of how you never know where the idea for your next story may lurk.

I was returning from research in Israel via one of those delightful white motor ships of the Linea Adriatica which make the four-day boat trip from Haifa to Genoa, one joyous day of sunshine and adventure after another. These ships touch at Cyprus and Piraeus, giving one a day ashore at each after a heavenly sail through the Greek isles and the Corinth Canal, headed for the toe of the Italian boot.

The trip through the Corinth Canal is unspectacular except, as I remember, for the little brown hawks or falcons that make their nests in holes in the steep sides of this big ditch and sometimes fly alongside the ship whistling or circling the masts. A tug hauls the steamer through this passage; one sits or reclines topside in the sunshine and lets it happen. There are no locks; the ditch simply connects with the sea at both ends.

One does, however, pass beneath a bridge, a high, spidery affair devoted to foot and vehicular traffic. I have made this passage four times, and each time as we passed beneath, there was a crowd gathered on the bridge. I can understand their gathering; I would have stopped there myself. There is something quite fascinating about seeing a huge steamer land-locked.

Well, on one of these trips one unknown, unidentified Greek, apparently overcome by the beauty of the spectacle of our passing beneath him like a toy ship in a bathtub, shook his hat at us so enthusiastically that it slipped from his fingers and, swaying and turning like a falling leaf, floated down to land upon our sun deck, where one of the passengers picked it up, waved it at the frantically gesticulating man who had lost it and who appeared to be roaring with laughter, and then set it upon his own head. It was a brown felt hat, much battered, dirty and worn, and that was that.

I fell to thinking about that hat, the journey on which it had embarked and the man who had worn it. I had focused my field glasses on him and saw that he was young, good-looking, and obviously a workman, for he had a pick and a shovel over his shoulder.

Such reflections are bound to lead you into considering the nature of the old, tried, and well-loved garment. A hat in particular becomes part of one, and the longer one has had it and the older and dirtier and smellier it gets, the more does it become an adjunct with which one is loath to part. In fact, man's resistance in giving up an old hat in favor of a new one is a well-known cliché, but, like many clichés, is founded upon fact. A wife can lose the love of her husband by disposing of an old fishing or camping hat behind the back of her spouse.

And so I began to wonder about this man whose hat had left him to go off on a white ship bound for the West and how he would feel about it. Now, this is one of the joys, I maintain, of being a writer: that once fired, the imagination is free to make what it pleases of its contacts with life and people. The man on the bridge probably went home, laughed over the tale of losing his hat, and forgot about it. But not *my* man; he was already beginning to take shape and form in my mind. He was a free and adventurous soul who had only been waiting for that single nudge from fate to break from his cocoon and soar into the blue upon the brightly colored wings of adventure. *My* man was going after his hat.

Thus began this story. As to its developments, who can reflect upon the tale of a poor Greek emigrating to the United States without thinking of the success story of the Skouras brothers? This decided me to lead my hatless man into the world of entertainment and the cinema. It was just at this time too that stereoscopic and stereophonic pictures were making their debut and the lovely complicating feature of a producing company and an exhibitor being indissolubly united by the mechanics of this new art form stood deliciously to hand.

As to the character of Meyer McManus, the Irish Jew who was head of a great motion-picture company, I'll confess I went afield for him by way of Dublin, which at that time was boasting of a Jewish mayor, an anomaly that was attracting considerable attention. I had never met him, but I had read about him. Several years later when I was living in Ireland researching the life of St. Patrick, I had the pleasure of having a drink with this charming gentleman.

Well, there are the ingredients for "The Hat," a thoroughly inconsequential tale which it gave me a great deal of pleasure to write. I have often been damned as a short-story writer with the words "slick" and "craftsman-like," but the point usually neglected is that to stir up ingredients such as I have indicated were tossed into the mixing bowl of this tale and come up with a story in which all the parts fit neatly and to my satisfaction is enormous good fun. There is enjoyment in every moment of doing this, of solving problems, of hitting upon little ideas to enhance the affair and to produce a finished product in which the joints fit as neatly and tightly as they do in a crossword puzzle.

The *Saturday Evening Post* bought "The Hat," and changed the title to "It Happened in Hollywood," which I must admit is a more lively label than mine. The story went forth and I hope fulfilled its function of entertaining its readers.

THIS story begins many years ago on the bridge that spans the Corinth Canal in Greece, that narrow, man-made ditch that makes an island out of the Peloponese Peninsula and saves a day or so sailing time to and from Piraeus.

Viewed from this bridge, a ship moving through the towering brown walls of the cut looks like the vivid toy of a child, and the crew and passengers resemble foreshortened dolls with white, up-turned, indistinguishable faces.

The smooth progress of a ship proceeding overland, as it were, hauled by its black, insect-like outrider of a tug, has an irresistible attraction for spectators above, who wave and shout down unintel-ligible greetings. The passengers reply in like manner from far below and thus there is established a kind of friendly contact be-tween the voyagers and the stay-at-homes.

This was the emotion felt by George Pavlides, a road worker, as he paused on the bridge on his way home from Souidas, where he worked, to Nikodimou, the little village where he lived.

A cheerful, kindly fellow always doing favors for people and known for giving his best on the job, George had not yet amounted to very much in life, but this fact did not weigh upon him, for there was still plenty of time. He was young, no more than twenty-five, strong, and of a generous, happy, and carefree disposition, as sunny as the land of his birth.

He had clothes to cover himself, enough to eat and drink, and the girls had an eye for him, for he was six feet tall with big brown shoulders, a handsome head with dark, curly hair and virile mustaches. In all, he was well content with life.

The craft now passing in the narrow ditch below was snow white with a single buff funnel on either side of which was affixed a relief in metal of a charging winged lion.

This gallant sight delighted Pavlides as it did many other passing likewise on the bridge. They shouted and waved; handkerchiefs fluttered in the hands of the tiny figures beneath as the passengers on the liner returned the greeting. Pavlides removed his hat and swung it violently back and forth in a gesture of salute and bonhomie toward the strangers gliding by.

He waved it, in fact, so violently and enthusiastically that it suddenly escaped the grip of his fingers and wafted first this way, then that, by the strong air currents in the cut, and sank rapidly to land miraculously on the forward deck of the ship at the feet of a passenger, who picked it up, donned it for an instant, and then waved it back at its former owner.

At this, George Pavlides shouted with laughter. He yelled, he chuckled, he roared and bellowed. He pounded his sides; he thumped the back of a policeman standing next to him.

"Look, look!" he cried. "My hat has gone off by itself on a voyage. Where do you suppose it is bound?"

The policeman, who had recognized the Italian flag and the insignia on the funnel as being the Lion of St. Mark, replied, "To Venice, most likely. Was it a good hat?"

"An old friend," said Pavlides. "I have had it for years. Oh-ho-ho-ho-ho! Did you ever see anything so amusing?"

In the meantime the ship was gliding on through the cut growing smaller and smaller, soon to vanish in the distance. Still laughing and shaking his curly, hatless head, Pavlides shouldered his tools and continued on his way home.

But that night he found himself for the first time in his life strangely restless and no longer entirely contented. It was true the hat was an old friend. Now it had left him unceremoniously and gone off to see the world, leaving him behind. Ought he not to follow it? One does not desert old friends thus. It was not the fault of the hat that this had happened. If Venice was where his headgear had gone, then maybe he too ought to journey thither. Soon he felt this overwhelmingly.

The next day Pavlides quit his job and set out to work his way to Venice, where he arrived eventually in good health and full of admiration for this wonderful city.

Unable to speak a word of Italian, he sought out a restaurant where, sure enough, there were some Greeks who explained to the proprietor that this strong, handsome newcomer had come there from Corinth in pursuit of his hat. This so impressed the owner that he gave Pavlides a job as a dishwasher and later, when he had learned something of the language, a post as a waiter.

On day, wandering the Piazza San Marco, Pavlides passed a shipping office in the window of which was a picture of the very vessel onto which his hat had fallen, or at least one like it. He went in to ask about it.

Ordinarily one who offered in broken Italian such a query as, "Eight months ago this beautiful vessel of yours passed beneath our splendid bridge across the Corinth Canal and I dropped my hat. Can you tell me what has become of it?" would have been dismissed as a madman. But Pavlides' smile was so warm and sincere and his brown eyes so trusting that they actually listened to him.

Then, miracle of miracles, a junior clerk sitting at a far desk bethought himself: "I remember something of the sort. There was a passenger who came in here who spoke of such an incident and that he had retrieved the hat."

But he could recall nothing else about him. "I only know that he was on his way to America," he added.

Pavlides thanked him and went back to the restaurant determined to go to America. "For," he explained, "I have found out that my hat has gone there, and if my hat wishes me to go to America, that is where I must go also."

The Italians thought him mad, but the Greeks, being like Pavlides, free souls, understood him perfectly and directed him to the American Consul, where he must apply for permission to emigrate to that country.

This official asked of Pavlides his reason for wishing to go to the New World.

"Because my hat has journeyed there," he explained through an interpreter, "and where my hat is I should be likewise," and he told him the story of the beautiful boat that had passed beneath the bridge and what had transpired.

The Consul—this was before the days of quotas and before the days when U.S. foreign officials had been intimidated—roared with laughter and said to his clerk, "Of all the cockeyed reasons I ever heard . . . Give the chap the permit. I like him."

This was the way it was. Everybody liked George Pavlides. Six months later he left for America, and because he had troubled to learn some English he was able to secure a job as a waiter aboard a Greek-American liner, on which he made a number of crossings to save himself some money before stepping ashore with his wife onto the then more hospitable strand of Ellis Island.

Ah yes, the wife he acquired was a tall, beautiful Greek girl with dark hair—a fine woman—by the name of Sophia Karakeno who came from the island of Kythira and was a stewardess.

George loved her for her warmth and good nature as well as her expressive eyes and her full, uncomplicated femininity. During several voyages he wooed her ardently.

"Marry me," he urged her, "and we will go ashore in America and find my hat together. After all, that is why I have come all this great distance. You will see, it will lead us to fame and fortune."

Sophia looked in despair at this handsome, apparently irresponsible young man who actually did seem to have traveled this far, and for no other reason, in pursuit of an old hat he had carelessly dropped from a bridge in far-off Corinth.

"What is one to do with one such as you?" she protested. "I do not wish to get married, but it is obvious that a fellow like you needs someone to look after him. Very well. I will marry you, but only on condition that afterwards there is no further nonsense about a hat."

And with this, George Pavlides was for the time well content, for he was convinced that in Sophia he had acquired the most wonderful woman in the world.

The rise of those two giants of the entertainment world, George Pavlides, theater magnate, and Meyer ("the Skimmer") McManus, president of Interworld Pictures of Hollywood, was almost simultaneous. Although they had never met, the struggle in which they became involved was the result of an intense personal dislike dating from a contretemps that I shall narrate shortly.

Each refused to give in. Newspapers had printed Pavlides' statement: "If I am ever cotch making business with that skonks I will donate a millions dollars colds cash to Grik orphans tsildrens."

Equally, McManus had been quoted: "Any time I make a deal with that hyena, sure and I'll donate a million dollars to be divided equally between Hebrew and Irish orphans." This split was made necessary by the fact that McManus was one of those oddities of nature, an Irish Jew from Dublin, combining the finest features of each. The various orphans hoped for the best, but in view of the intensity of the feud there did not seem to be much chance of their collecting.

McManus' nickname, "the Skimmer," derived from the fact that since he had flashed like a comet upon the moving-picture horizon a quarter of a century ago, nobody outside his immediate family and a few intimate friends had ever seen what the top of his head looked like. For he never appeared at a production conference, board meeting, financial agenda, story round-table, or big Interworld premier, uncovered.

There were many rumors abroad as to why he never bared his head in public. One was that he was orthodoxly religious; another was that owing to some strange disease suffered in childhood his hair grew only in small green tufts; and a third said that he had not only no hair at all but the top of his skull was missing and you could see his great brain throbbing underneath his scalp.

Whatever the reason he was no fool and held the film world in the hollow of his hand. The only figure that matched him in our era was George Pavlides, the one-time Greek immigrant who rose to the ownership of three-quarters of the great moving-picture cathedrals in the principal cities of the United States.

For the Pavlides who came ashore at Ellis Island with his handsome, strapping wife in the long ago was already a far different individual from the one who had laid down his pick and shovel in the Peloponnesus to follow in the path of his errant hat.

He was now able to speak Italian, a smattering of French, and something that passed for English. He had been around and seen a little of the world and its ways; he had a profession with which he could always earn a living no matter where, as good waiters were scarce. And he was no longer alone.

He retained his cheerful, generous, sunny disposition and his capacity for hard and devoted work. Journeying to San Francisco, he secured a job in a restaurant. He had the gift of being able to deposit a plate of noodle soup or an order of Yankee potroast before a customer with the air of one who has the good fortune to be serving a king. Not only that, but his example infected others of the help working with him.

In no time at all he was head waiter; later he was able to purchase an interest, and when a grateful partner died and left him his share, he became sole owner. His personality, solicitude for his clients, and little generosities such as giving away the after-dinner coffee, mints, bonbons, and cigarettes, plus his wife's excellent business sense, made it a success and shortly after he opened another and another, extending his chain to New York, Boston, Chicago, Detroit, and Philadelphia. Fifteen years from the time he landed in New York, he was a millionaire.

The hat was all but forgotten or at least never mentioned in the Pavlides mansion atop San Francisco's Nob Hill, where he made his home with his stately wife and their three boys and two girls.

In 1939 a fellow Greek who owned a theater in St. Louis found himself in difficulties. With characteristic generosity, Pavlides bought the movie house from him at a price far beyond its worth, bailing his friend out but landing himself with a white elephant.

He promptly went to St. Louis, threw himself into the theater business, and within a year had evolved the famous Pavlides Palace System, in which the patron not only saw the finest feature films and stage shows from deep, plush seats uniform throughout the house, but because of Pavlides' love of people and his desire to share his success with them and make them happy, was the recipient of all kinds of gifts and benefits.

There was a nursery where mothers could leave babies, a television room where fathers could catch the end of the night ball game; free lemonade in paper cups was passed down the aisles during intermission; children were gifted with bonbons and bubble gum, skull caps, six-shooters or ray guns or whatever the fashion was while their mothers received recipe books, aprons, small, useful household articles; there was always a surprise of some sort. In short, everything that could delight the patron, increase his comfort, and enhance enjoyment of the film was freely lavished.

Naturally the result was that the Pavlides Palace in St. Louis became a huge success and soon made money hand over fist. Within ten years there were Pavlides Palaces in all of the key cities of the United States and George stood at the top of the entertainment world. At last he had found a field in which he was truly content. He sold out his restaurant chain in order to concentrate upon his theater empire.

It was at this point he became involved in the battle with Skimmer McManus which shook the nation and eventually threatened both men with ruin.

It came about when Pavlides threw the new McManus picture *Body of Love,* starring Tanya Tanot, a young ex-saleslady better known for outsized glands than histrionic talent, and Ramon Gentile, a Latin scoundrel, out of all the Pavlides Palaces because, as he put it in one of his rare public utterances, "Is steenky pictsoor. Steenky pictsoor is not good for tsildrens to see, bot it is even worses for mothers. We will not play steenky pictsoors in Pavlides Palaces."

Naturally, Skimmer McManus took umbrage, particularly as he was known to have occasional lapses of taste and this was definitely one of them. The phenomenal luck that had characterized his entire career did not desert him and the film cleaned up in other houses, but Pavlides' just criticism stung. McManus permitted himself to be quoted to the effect that that Greek ex-strumberry-pie hustler wouldn't know a picture if he saw one.

This reference to his earlier days as a knight of the black tie and white apron hit Pavlides where it hurt most, through his children, who were now attending fine schools. For the first and only time he lost his temper and referred to McManus as "Abie's Irish Stinkweed," and the battle to the death was joined. No Interworld film could get a Pavlides Palace chain booking. No Pavlides Palace could get any Meyer McManus picture.

Each might have been able to survive this and the feud could have run an uninterrupted course but for the sudden advent of 3D. In the scramble to get aboard the bandwagon, both men committed a fatal error.

Negotiating swiftly and secretly, Pavlides bought the rights to equip his theaters to show Life-o-Scope, the last word in dimensional illusion in which the actors not only came down off the screen and sat in the laps of the patrons, but practically went home with them after the show.

Operating equally rapidly and *sub rosa*, McManus bought the rights to cameras, sound and reproducing equipment of Life-o-Scope.

And there they were. When the news broke, it rocked the film world. For McManus could not show his films in any but Pavlides Theaters, while the Pavlides equipment would now screen only McManus pictures. Yet each would have remained stubborn, preferring to go bankrupt rather than meet one another.

But the pressure was irresistible. For they were not only rugged individualists, but heads of commercial empires upon whom thousands of innocent people depended for a living. The news leaked out that Meyer Skimmer McManus and George Pavlides were at last to come face to face across a conference table to try to iron out the tangle into which they had got themselves.

The meeting was held on neutral ground in Santa Barbara, halfway between San Francisco and Hollywood. Reporters and photographers were foiled by elaborate security precautions. Present be-

sides the two principals, by agreement, were an attorney and a
secretary for each.

An elaborate protocol and time schedule was set up introducing
first the secretaries, who appeared carrying pencil, paper, and sup-
plies to prepare the arena, then the two lawyers, who materialized
with brief cases at the same moment and took up their stations.

At precisely the stroke of 10:00 A.M. the two titans appeared
simultaneously at opposite doorways leading to the conference
table, marched stiffly to the battle ground, and took their seats, for
the purpose of exploring terms and conditions leading to a possible
get-together, each, by further agreement, communicating with the
other only through the medium of their solicitors. Behind the doors
waited a further retinue of lawyers, general managers, vice presi-
dents, and press agents.

At exactly one minute past ten, one of these with a shameless eye
to a keyhole cried out, "Great Jehoshaphat, they're killing one another!" For it looked as though the two principals were locked across
the table in a swaying, clutching, hair-pulling brawl to the death.
But so strict were the orders that none dared enter to separate them.

Yet it was not entirely so. And it is my privilege now, by what
means I am not at liberty to reveal, to relate for the first time what
really happened.

No sooner had the two men seated themselves on opposite sides
of the table when Pavlides was seen staring at McManus like a
man who is viewing a ghost. However, there was nothing ghostlike
about the film producer, who, like the Greek, was a big man and
well built, with a square head, pinkish eyebrows over shrewd blue
eyes. He was dressed in a natty dark suit, with a matching shirt and
bow tie, and the only thing unusual about him was the fact that
he was wearing a . . .

"That hots!" cried Pavlides, pointing to the somewhat disrepu-
table, stained, and crumpled headgear that crowned McManus.
"Where you get that hots?"

McManus, outraged at this incredible demonstration of *lèse-
majesté*, since in his orbit no one even mentioned the hat, much
less asked him where he had got it, started to say, "None of your

gah—" when with an unearthly cry of joy, Pavlides reached across the table and pounced.

"That's my hots what I lose forty years ago."

The battle was thereupon joined. For a few moments it swayed back and forth across the table to cries of "Leggo, you idiot"—"My hots, my hots, my old friend"—"Take your hands off me or I'll punch your nose"—"Give me back my hots"—"Ugh, ye spalpeen, ye'll pay for this—"

Then suddenly Pavlides prevailed. The hat came off and he held it clutched in trembling fingers. The two secretaries and attorneys had eyes only for the top of McManus' head now that his dread secret had been so suddenly and dramatically bared. But there was nothing to be seen there but some quite ordinary strands of pinkish-gray hair to match the eyebrows. Could it be that the secret was that there *was* no secret?

Possessed of the hat, Pavlides turned it swiftly, looked into the sweatband, and then hugged it to his chest with another cry of joy. "My hots, my hots. I knew it." Then he shouted at McManus, "I know where you got this hots. On a ship sailing through the Corinth Canal when it fells from bridge."

All the indignation and fight went out of Meyer McManus and he turned deathly pale. "My God," he said hoarsely, "how did you know?"

"Because," explained Pavlides, waving the hat to and fro in the manner in which he had done so long ago, "I am the fellows on the bridge who dropsing it!"

"Oh, no . . ." McManus moaned, and he suddenly looked twenty years older. And then, "It must be true. There's nobody else in the world would know that." Then he turned his stricken eyes upon his opponent. 'Don't take the hat," he pleaded. "Sell it to me. Sure, and I'll give you anything you ask for it. Just name it." It was a testimony to his basic honesty that he did not try to lie out of it or even question that the hat belonged to Pavlides and that he, McManus, must give it back.

And it was likewise characteristic of the kind of man George

Pavlides was that he did not turn the obvious deep distress of his rival to business uses. On the contrary, his heart was touched. He asked, "Why you want it? What's thees hots to you?"

For a moment, McManus measured his opponent. Then he reached the decision that frankness was the best policy. There was too much at stake.

" 'Tis my lucky hat," he groaned. "Ever since it came floating down from that damned bridge and I put it on, I've had the breaks. I met the girl that I married on that boat and the guy who financed my first picture. I tried it out. When I didn't wear the hat I made mistakes. When I had the hat on, nothing could go wrong."

He sunk his head in his hands for a moment and then continued in a further burst of candor. "It ain't me that's made Interworld Pictures—it's the hat. I've always known it. It's the hat always guessed right. Even that lousy *Body of Love* was a box-office killer even though it was a stinker."

"Hah!" shouted Pavlides triumphantly, "you admit thees was steenky pictsoor!"

McManus looked at him bleakly and then at the hat the Greek had crushed to his bosom. His silence was admission.

"Hokay!" said George Pavlides, "now I tell you what I do. I *give* you the hots! And I give one millions dollars cash to Grik orphans tsildrens."

Meyer Skimmer McManus looked like one reprieved by the governor. Slowly his hands crept across the table; his fingers closed about the hat; reverently he lifted it and restored it to his head. Age fell away from him. Youth and confidence returned. He said:

"I take the hat. And I give one million dollars to the Hebrew and Irish orphans of the world."

"Hokay," Pavlides repeated, his huge face beaming with happiness. "Now I tell you whats we both do. We each give one million dollars to the orphans of United States of Americans because this is such wonderful countries allows bums like us become millionaires."

McManus swallowed and then said, "It's a deal."

"So," concluded Pavlides. "You been wearing my hots for forty years. Anybody wears my hots forty years is my brothers. I do not fights with brothers. McManus pictsoors plays Pavlides Palaces."

McManus averred solemnly, "McManus Interworld Pictures books the Pavlides Palaces."

"Only," Pavlides suddenly admonished, "when I say a pictsoor is steenky—IS steenky!"

Choler came to the McManus countenance, but only for an instant. Then his fingers once more caressed the brim of the battered old hat.

"IS steenky . . ." he assented.

The two men reached across the table and gripped hands with respect and the beginning of a deep affection.

That night when Pavlides arrived home he said to his wife, "Ho, Sophia! You know whats? Today I find my hots what I dropsings off the bridge at Corinth. You know who is under it? Meyer McManus. He is my brother now. We don't fights any more. This is lucky days for me. What a good thing back there in Nikodimou I make up my mind to go where my hots goes."

Sophia Pavlides, stately and beautiful with age, who had grown with her position into the sweetest and best-loved matron in San Francisco, went over to her huge, friendly-eyed husband, who was a man from the top of his grizzled curly head to the tips of his shoes, and kissed him.

"What a good thing, foolish man," she said, "that I make up my mind to follow where my heart goes."

Saint Bambino

This story is pure nostalgia. I wished to bring the late Babe Ruth back from wherever he had gone, Heaven, Hell, Purgatory, or Limbo, and so I did, and once more exercising one of the more joyous privileges of the writer, I made him a saint, the patron saint of baseball and of the small boys who try so hard to play it well.

Theoretically and theologically I feel within my rights. I know of some far less attractive characters assigned to the Pantheon to act as assistants to God. And if one wishes to be technical, one can ascribe a number of genuine miracles to the living Ruth, for he snatched not one but several boys back from death's portal by the mere majesty and awe of his presence.

These were sick children given up for dead. He visited them, sat at their bedsides, autographed baseballs for them, and promised them a private and individual home run. I am sure with his bulk and bustle he edged aside the skeleton with the scythe. At the very least he restored them their will to live. And incidentally he always came through with the promised home run.

If you considered the background of Babe Ruth, his lusts, his appetites, his mode of living, you might have written him off as a rough, vulgar, gargantuan, and not entirely attractive man. Yet he had a number of saintly qualities. One of these was devotion to his God, which in this case was the game of baseball, and the other was an equal devotion to the boys of the country who loved the game as well. He cared about them and about the problems that their worship of him as an idol set him as an individual in his personal behavior and daily life. Because of the public opinion of a host of small boys he made a change in his manner of conducting himself.

The urge to write this story began, as I remember, one evening in the chalet in Liechtenstein, thinking about Babe Ruth. Perhaps it was during World Series time. I used to get the live broadcast from the

World Series over the armed-forces network from Munich. These broadcasts made me sentimental. The broadcasting booth must have been near the Press box, because I could hear the telegraph instruments, the bugs of the operators clicking off the play by play dictated by the baseball writers, most of whom had one time been my colleagues. And the silence as the crowd awaited a crucial pitch would be broken by the sound of bat meeting ball wafted to my ears across three thousand miles of sea, and I suppose I fell to thinking of the days when I was a sports writer and covered baseball, and from there one would naturally reflect upon the man who was truly baseball's giant, physically, ethically, psychologically, spiritually, box-office, any way you cared to look at it.

To say that I loved him might sound curious, but it is true. I loved him for his humanness and his greatness. We were never intimate, though there was a time one winter when we used to play handball together two or three times a week in Bill O'Brien's gymnasium on Broadway. But I must have covered many pounds of paper writing about him.

When he died he had long since retired from baseball. He was not considered the type who could fill the job of baseball manager and so his connection with the game was severed, but there was still a generation of small boys who remembered and venerated him.

I recall one time when I was staging a water show at Jones Beach and I asked the Babe whether he would consent to be the star of the show. He would have to do no more than appear, be introduced, and fungo-bat a dozen or so baseballs out into the bay. He consented readily and made his appearance.

We had many performers and competitors in the show, which was half a swimming meet and water show and half a circus, and they were gathered around the semicircle of Zach's Bay where the show was staged. No sooner had Ruth started batting the baseballs for vast distances out into the water when the bay was made black with several hundred heads of youngsters threshing out to sea. It was one of the most astonishing sights and experiences of all my years as a sports writer. They were all competitive swimmers and the speed of their passage churned the blue surface of the bay into a froth. What was it all about? What were they after? The baseballs that had become endowed with magic properties from their contact with the bat of

Babe Ruth. Baseballs touched, hit, or autographed by the great man became talismans to youth.

And thinking back upon those things and those days with Ruth interred in his coffin and vanished from the scene, I found myself wondering what had become of the essence of the Babe, the driving force, the towering, overpowering, ebullient personality. As a sinner he would perhaps be doing time over a slow fire in Hell, but as the idol of the American small boy he certainly belonged in Heaven.

And if one cared to consider the Christian Heaven, peopled with saints engaged in mortal business, such as Anthony in charge of the Lost and Found Bureau, Christopher looking after travelers, Peter at the door, and a whole host of others acting as messengers and advocates, it seemed to me that if ever there was a perfect candidate for a patron saint of sports and someone on high to intercede for and look after the interests of small fry in the U.S.A. who were troubled with such maladies as batting with one leg in the water bucket, misjudging a curve, or unable to get anything but the handle on to a pitch low and inside, Babe Ruth was the one. During his span upon earth he had done nothing but good for the game of baseball and everything and everyone connected with it, including myself. If anyone was to understand the distress, the emotions, and the yearnings of a small boy, it was Ruth, for he himself never grew up.

This story, then, is a kind of compendium of thoughts and memories and emotions and not only my missing a man for whom I had profound respect and affection, but also my nostalgia for a profession and an era that I had left behind me and that as a writer I could re-create for myself and thus once more enjoy the presence of the great Bambino.

And in the process I cannonized him. I hope you don't mind.

I DON'T say you should believe this story.

Maybe the whole thing is just the imaginings of an old man who ain't got much more time left to sit in the sun in the grandstand behind third base and listen to that sweet sound when the ash is applied to the middle of the old horsehide and you know the apple is heading for Railroad Avenue the other side of the fence.

Could be I just dreamed it all, or maybe it was Jimmy Jr.'s dream that I got into somehow. But I know I seen and talked with a real saint.

I seen him just as plain as you're looking at this page, that night a year ago when I went into Jimmy Jr.'s room feeling licked and lower than a snake's piazza because I wasn't getting anywhere with what Jimmy's mother asked me to come to New York for and live with them, which was to try to make a man out of him. You see, the kid didn't care about baseball. That was a terrible thing. Twelve years old and he don't know Mickey Mantle's or Ralph Kiner's batting average, and can't tell you who's leading the league in R.B.I.s.

How bad it is, he don't even know or care who's topping the League, American or National. His teacher in school said he was a natural pull hitter and could make the team if he cared. But all the kid wanted to do was read about space rockets and trips to Mars, and look at Captain Universe on television.

What made it worse is who his father was. And his grandfather. That's me, Harry Murphy.

So this night I am going to tell you about. I'd come back from a night game at Yankee Stadium, which was just across the way from where Janet, Jimmy Jr.'s mother, had her flat on Edgecomb Avenue, and I couldn't sleep. Vic Raschi beats the Detroits 6 to 5 and Mantle hits one in the clutch; I sat alone back of third base. Used to be a time when I'd dreamed of sitting there with my grandson. But the kid wasn't having any. He stayed behind to look at a television show. And it wasn't baseball.

That Yankee Stadium was like home to me. I let out a couple of blasts at the Yanks, but it wasn't the same like the old days when the Babe and Lou Gehrig was there and everybody knew me.

I lay there thinking about what the kid was missing, and what I could do about it. Maybe I did ask for help. You wouldn't want to see any boy of yours grow up without caring how the home team made out, would you? Why, sometimes that's all that holds the country together when things gets tough.

The next thing I know, it's two o'clock in the morning and I thought I heard a noise in Jimmy Jr.'s room next door. So I got up to look, thinking maybe he wasn't well or wanted something.

But when I came in, I could see he was sleeping peacefully, for there was a moon over Coogan's bluff lighting up the Polo Grounds on the other side of the river, and it came in the window. Then I saw the stranger sitting by his bedside.

He was a great big guy built like a beer barrel. I shoulda jumped a mile high from scare, but right away I saw there was something familiar about him. He was wearing a big camel's-hair polo coat with a belt, and a tan camel's-hair cap. His head was turned and he was looking down at Jimmy Jr., but when I came into the room he switched around so that the moon lit up his face and I saw who it was. I'd of known that big ugly mug with the little piggy eyes and the nose spread all over his face anywhere in the world.

And at that moment I didn't even stop to think that he'd been dead five years. I said, "Hello, Babe!"

He said, "Hello, keed. How's things?" but didn't get up or offer to shake hands. He just sat there, his jaws moving on a big plug of tobacco he had in his mouth.

I couldn't think of anything to say but, "The Yanks won tonight, 6 to 5. Mantle got hold of one in the eighth."

He nodded. "Yeah, I know. I was there. That's a good kid that Mantle, but he ought to stick to one side or the other. Them switch hitters ain't never consistent."

"Boy," I said: "Babe Ruth. Am I glad to see you!" All of a sudden it come home to me who I was talking to. "Hey," I whispered so as not to wake Jimmy Jr., "what's going on? You're dead, aren't you?"

The Babe grunted. "Uhuh! Deader than Kelcey."

"Then what are you doing here?"

The Babe chewed on his plug for a while before replying, "You sent for me, didn't you?"

"Me?" I was so mixed up by this time I couldn't remember who I was talking to.

"I dunno," the Babe said, "you oughta know what's cooking. We got a call about a half-hour ago. The manager told me to get my pants off the bench and take a look in here."

It came back then, what I'd been doing a half-hour ago. I ain't much of a religious man, but when it comes down to it and a member of my family is in trouble like Jimmy Jr. was, I ain't ashamed to pray.

I said, "I remember now. I asked the saints to help me."

"Okay," the Babe said. "What's on your mind, keed?"

Much as I loved the big monkey, I couldn't help letting out a snort. "Hey! What are you giving me? You a saint?"

The Babe for a second actually managed to look modest, which was never one of his long points, though maybe sheepish was a better way to describe it, and he said hastily, "I know, I know. I done all kinds of fat-headed things when I was around here, didn't I? Women, liquor, horsing around . . . But *they* got a way of over-looking those, if you say you're sorry when you get *there*, or if you were too dumb to know what you were doing. So after I'd been there a couple of years and kept my nose clean, *they* made me a saint."

I couldn't figure it out. In my book, the Babe was the greatest man that ever lived, but they got rules for that sort of thing. I said, "I thought you had to be made a saint from down here."

The Babe's ugly puss busted into a big grin. He replied, "Up there they don't always wait. Particularly when they got use for a guy."

I asked, "How did it happen, Babe?"

He chawed a while and then replied, "I dunno. One day one of them came along and says, 'Hey, Babe. What about that time you got up at that dinner to Jimmy Walker and promised to turn over a new leaf for the sake of the dirty-faced kids in the street?' I says, 'What about it?' He says, 'Were you on the level? Did you really mean it?' I says, 'What do *you* think? Ain't you never seen a kid with his heart broke because something or somebody he believed in went sour?' He says, 'Okay, Babe. That's all I wanted

to know. You come along with me. We got work for you to do.'
So they put me on the roster."

I said, "Well, what do you know? What are you saint of? What
do I call you?"

He shifted his chew and said affably, "Call me Babe. Up there
I'm known as Saint Bambino, but I don't go much for that
stuff. Baseball, of course. It's the biggest thing in the world, ain't
it?"

I started to say "You're tellin' me . . ." when he continued.

"There's millions of kids in this country to whom baseball's
mighty important. They worry, and snivel themselves to sleep
because they can't hit a curve ball, stop pulling back from a fast
one inside, or hold a hot liner with the meat hand. Or maybe they're
weak on grounders hit to the left of them, or don't like to block
the bag at second when a bigger guy is trying to steal or stretch a
single. Sometimes it's a matter of timing. Others, it's moxie. I'm
in charge of that."

"Yeah, is that right? What do you do?"

Babe turned to the window and let go some tobacco juice.

He said, "Oh, I dunno. Take a look around and maybe ask
Number One, the manager, to give 'em a hand. Unless they ask
for me personally, like some do. . . ." He grinned again. "There
was that kid last week in Biloxi, Mississippi. He threw wild to home
plate from left field, let two runs in, and lost the game. All the
others kids picked on him. That night he asked me if I'd ever
pulled one like that? He kept bellerin', 'Babe, I bet you never did
that. Babe, I'm no good. I wanna die. Help me.' "

"So what did you do?"

"So I reminded the kid about that time in Cleveland in 1925
when we were two games out of first place for the pennant the last
week in August."

I said, "What happened? I don't remember that one."

The Babe laughed that big old deep rumbling laugh of his.
"We're leading 6–5 in the last of the ninth. The Indians got two
on and two out. What's-his-name, their shortstop, comes up and I

figure him for a short single between first and second if he hits, and come in to take it on the first hop."

"And does he?"

"Sure. And I got the runner for home out by a mile, only I'm still full of beer from the night before and throw the ball right over the top of the Press box. Boy, Hug was sore. He slapped a hundred-dollar plaster on me. I told him to keep his shirt on, I'd get the games back for him."

"And did you?"

"Sure . . . I got hold of two the next day. Day after I clobbered 'em. I got a single, a double, and two triples, and threw Whosis, their second baseman, out at the plate with the tying run from the right-field fence. Hug took the plaster off."

"What about the kid from Biloxi?"

"He quit blubberin'. He'll go out and try to win the next three games and make 'em forget his error. Remember how they used to razz me when I struck out? They'd forget all about the strike-outs when I got the wood onto one."

I moved so that the light from the moon through the window fell onto my face. The Babe suddenly took a good gander at me.

"Say," he said, "I seen you before some place. Hey, wait a minute! Ain't you that red-faced turkey used to sit back of the boxes behind third base in the stadium and ride me all the time in the old days? I can't remember the name. . . ."

Babe never could remember anybody's name, not even the guys on his own team. But I could of busted with pride and almost cried to think he knew me.

"Murphy," I said, "Leather Lung Murphy!"

The Babe slapped his knee. "That's the son-of-a-sailor," he said. "Boy, that brass voice of yours used to get under my skin."

How it all came back to me then, those years when I used to give it to him back in the old days. The Babe would come up to bat, and I'd holler, "Strike out, ya bum! Oh, what a bum!" And if he'd hit one I'd bawl, "Oh, you lucky stiff!"

They said my voice would carry all the way down to the 138th

Street Harlem River bridge. The crowd would whoop and holler
and laugh and turn around and point me out, saying, "That's
Leather Lung Murphy from Detroit. He always rides the Babe."
The papers wrote pieces about me and the kids would come up
and ask for my autograph. I was as famous as any of 'em.

It was like I could close my eyes and be back there more than
twenty-five years ago and see Yankee Stadium on a summer's afternoon with the Babe up to bat. The outfield seemed greener then,
the ball whiter, the uniforms brighter, the crowds bigger and better.

There would be the Babe at the plate. He had a body shaped
like a pear and he'd stand up on those thin, pipe-stem ankles of
his with the number "3" on his back, leaned over a little, waving
his big bat a little. I remember how the elevated trains would slow
down as they passed the stadium so the motorman could see
whether the Babe got hold of one. Nobody could make any mistake,
no matter from how far, who it was up.

He'd have his big paws wrapped around that bat handle so it
looked like a matchstick in his fingers. The pitch would come; he'd
miss it with an almighty swipe and wrap himself around so his
legs was twisted like a pretzel. A roar would go up and on top of
it would be me like a brass trumpet yelling, "Strike out, ya bum!"

There'd be another throw and he'd be taking a backswing before
the ball got out of the pitcher's grip. Then you'd hear a click—it
wasn't a crack, or a bang, or a thud, but a click like no other sound
you ever heard; it was never different, and it always meant the ball
was out of the park over the right-field fence.

Boy, that roar! And that big ape trotting around the bases on
them too-small dogs of his, tipping his cap. And maybe giving me
a grin when I handed him the bird as he rounded third base.

Pretty soon the game'd be over, the fans would be streaming
across the diamond. I'd go home to a big thick steak my good wife,
Ellen, would have cooked for me and tell my Jimmy, who was
eight, what his big hero the Babe had done that day. That was
the life. It was never so good, before or after.

The Babe shifted in his chair next to Jimmy Jr.'s bed and said,

"What was it you had it in for me in them days, Murph?"

"Nothing personal, Babe," I replied, "I come from Detroit, so there was only one ball player in the world for me, Ty Cobb."

It was true. I was born and raised in Detroit. After you'd watched the Georgia Peach play you couldn't see no other diamond jockey for dust. When I come out of the Army in 1919, I stayed in New York and got a job as a mechanic. Afterwards I got into the garage business and made my pile. But I'm always a Tiger rooter because that's how I was born.

Babe was scratching his head like he was trying to think back on something. Finally it come to him.

"What made you quit riding me, Murph? Seemed like one day all of a sudden you wasn't there any more. I missed you, keed. You used to get my goat so I'd want to bust that apple clear out to Hunts Point."

I said, "On the level, don't you remember, Babe?"

He looked at me with surprise. "Naw," he replied. "What happened, keed?"

"Don't you remember little Jimmy Murphy in St. Agatha's Hospital, the kid who was so sick the doctors give him up?"

The Babe still looked blank. Me, I could hardly choke down the lump in my throat. Ever since I come into the room and see him sitting there by Jimmy Jr.'s bedside, I got another scene in my mind just like it, when my boy Jimmy was dying back in 1926. Some sports writer got wind of it and fixed up a visit from the Babe because my kid was as crazy a fan for Babe Ruth as I was for Ty.

I can still see it like yesterday, the big monkey sitting next to my Jimmy's bed in the hospital. It was God come down from Heaven in a tan polo coat and go-to-hell cap, holding an auto-graphed baseball. He said, "You lissen to the game on the raddio tomorrow, keed. I'm gonna bust one for you." He did, too. I was with Jimmy and seen the glaze go out of his eyes and the color come back to his cheeks. After that, am I going to razz the Babe any more? To me, he's just the greatest man in the world.

"Yeah?" said Saint Bambino. "So what happened?"

I said, "You come to the hospital, autographed a baseball for him, and promised to hit a home run for him."

"Yeah?" said Saint Bambino, "did I? How'd he make out?"

He didn't remember. I suppose he visited a lot of kids in hospitals in his career. There was that Johnny Whosis for whom he hit a home run in the World Series, and a boy in New Jersey, one in Chicago, and another in Boston.

"I said, "He got well. But he wouldn't of if it hadn't been for you."

"That's good," Saint Bambino said. "He must be a big guy now. Whatever become of him?"

I swallowed so I would steady my voice. "He was leading a company in the Hurtgen Forest in the last war," I said. "A Heinie threw a potato masher. He covered it with his body to keep his men from being clobbered."

Saint Bambino chewed his wad for a considerable time before he nodded and said, "That's bad."

I nodded toward Jimmy Jr. asleep next to him. "That's his kid there."

The saint looked down at him. I never would have thought such tenderness could spread over that ugly mush. For the first time I noticed a faint glow that seemed to surround or come from the wide-brimmed camel's-hair cap on the big head. "Is it, now?" he said. "What would be his trouble? What made you send for me?"

I had to swallow again hard before I spoke. "Saint," I said, finally, "he don't care about baseball."

The Babe chewed and let another stream out the window. When he spoke again it was to say, "That's real bad. How did that happen?"

"After his father was killed, his mother never remarried," I explained. "Women don't understand about baseball like men. The kid's father was the greatest Yankee fan in the world, but Jimmy Jr. grew up without a man around the house. All he wants to do is look at television shows and read space comics."

"That's terrible," Saint Bambino said. "Comics is okay if a game is rained out and you got nuthin' else to do. . . ."

"A year or so ago, his mother smarted up to what was going on," I continued. "The boy was pale and didn't eat good. He shoulda been out with the other kids running the bases beltin' that apple and have his head full of something worth while instead of them bum television jokes. I was back in Detroit where I had a string of garages. When the good wife, Ellen, died six months ago I sold out and retired. Janet—that's Jimmy Jr.'s mother—telephoned me to come here and live with them and work on the boy. But it's too late. He just don't care."

So we sat there a minute, looking down at Jimmy Jr. He was a good-put-together kid with his mother's mouth and his father's fighting chin, but he was thin and his color wasn't right.

Saint Bambino leaned forward a little in his chair and began to talk in a low, deep voice. Only he wasn't talking to me any longer, but to the kid.

"Jimmy Jr., lissen to me," he said. "Don't you make no mistake. Baseball's the greatest game in the world, and any man can be proud to have a connection with it no matter what, even if it's only sitting in the grandstand and keeping a box score and yelling for the hometeam to git out and get them runs."

I thought Jimmy Jr. would wake up, but he don't. He just moved a little in his sleep.

"Do you know what baseball can do, Jimmy Jr.?" the saint continued. "It can take a nobody out of the gutter, maybe somebody that's seen the inside of a jail or a reform school, and make him a bigger man than the President of the United States. Now, you tell me any other game that can do that and I'll kiss your fist."

The moon was starting to slide past the open window now, and it seemed like the glow coming from the camel's-hair cap on the big dark head was brighter.

"Don't kid yourself, Jimmy Jr.," the saint went on. "You gotta be a man to play baseball. It's the toughest game in the world, because you gotta have everything. You gotta have condition, co-ordination, speed, science, know-how, hustle, and moxie. Plenty of moxie, son, because if you ever show a yellow streak, the pitchers'll dust you, the base runners'll cut you to ribbons, and the bench jockeys will ride you right out of the league.

"You can't let up for a minute, keed. You got to give it everything you got and use the old bean besides. You let one get by you in April, and maybe you find out it's the error that's cost you the pennant in September. You can't slack off, or ease up. When you're in there at bat, or running the bases, you got nine guys working against you, and a big brain sitting on the bench as well figuring out how to make a monkey out of you."

I never heard such earnestness in any man's voice as in the saint's. He leaned a little further forward and went on.

"Keed, there never was a game figured out prettier to test a man for speed and guts and the old whip; whether the runner gets to the bag first or the ball beats him. Ninety feet between bases, and guys like Ty Cobb was fast enough to steal home, while the pitcher is winding up and letting it go. Sixty feet from the pitcher's mound to home plate and you got maybe a half a second while the ball is in the air to pick out whether you're going to be a hero or a bum. It takes real men to put together a double play and make it look easy and graceful-like.

"Why do you suppose so many millions of people, grown-up men and women as well as kids, Jimmy Jr., love baseball? Why, for so many reasons I could sit here all night long and tell ya. Some of the finest men that ever breathed the air of our country has been in baseball, men everybody can look up to and be proud of because they never give anything but the best they had.

"It's a game, and yet it's like life, keed, and it gets you ready for it. Maybe the score is 10 to 0 against you in the ninth with two out. Half the crowd is heading for the exits because they figure you ain't got a chance. But you know you ain't dead until there's three out, so you go up there to the plate and take your cut and next thing you know the pitcher is walking to the showers, the new one ain't warmed up good, and you clobber him; the fans stop walking out and five minutes later you got the game in the bag. Nobody ever played baseball, keed, or followed them that did that wasn't the better for it."

His voice dropped even lower, until it was just like a deep, soft, friendly growl. "It's a team game, Jimmy, and it's ours. It come out of the guts of this country. That's why we're so hard to lick when the chips are down, because when we get into a jam, we play it like a team instead of every man for his self. A soldier or a sailor or an airman will back up his buddy because maybe he's learned somewhere on some sandlot, or inside a stadium, that a pitcher can throw his heart out, but you gotta spear those liners and pick those drives off the fences and then go out and get him some runs, or it don't do no good. It's like you're a family, or a lot of brothers working together. It's the only game you don't have to play to feel the good in it and learn the lessons that are gonna help you some time when you're in need."

The saint paused for a moment, then gently patted Jimmy Jr. on the thin shoulder that was sticking out from under the sheet.

"That's all for now, keed," he said. "Think it over. Good luck. I may be seeing you again some time. . . ." I thought that Jimmy Jr. seemed to smile in his sleep. The saint turned to me. "Okay, Murph. I guess I won't be needed around here any longer so I'll be beating it. The kid'll be okay. If you ever need me again, holler. I'll be keeping an eye on him."

I was all choked up, but I managed to say, "Is there anything I can do for you, Babe—I mean Saint Bambino? . . ."

He thought for a moment, and then got up from the chair. The moon was gone, but from the glow on his cap I could see a kind of sheepish grin on his big mug.

"Yeah," he said, "maybe there is. Things are kind of quiet-like where I am. Just for old time's sake, gimme the old razz. I'd like to hear the old leather lung just once more."

"Which one?" I asked. "I hate to do it to you, Babe."

He grinned again. "The strike-out one. It used to keep me on my toes."

I saw he was on the level, so I let him have it just like I used to with all the brass and steam I had left. . . .

"Strike out, ya bum!"

For a moment I thought I could hear the roar of the crowd again, and the sharp "CLICK" that meant the management was out another baseball.

Jimmy Jr. woke up with a start, but when he saw me he quieted right down. "Oh, Granddad," he said . . . "Was that you? I was having a dream about Babe Ruth and baseball. . . ."

I started to say that the Babe, or rather Saint Bambino, was right there, but when I looked to where he had been he was gone. Instead, Jimmy Jr.'s mother came hustling into the room in her dressing gown, saying:

"Land's sakes! What's happened, Dad, you yelling fit to wake the dead?"

I said, "I was only showing Jimmy Jr. how I used to holler at the Babe in the old days."

"At this time of morning when the child ought to be getting some rest. I declare, you men . . ."

But Jimmy Jr. just lay there looking up at the ceiling. After a little he said, "That was a funny dream, but I liked it. Granddad, can I go to the ball game with you tomorrow?"

Yeah, there's one more part to the story, and you don't got to believe that, either.

Last week Jimmy's school nine is playing in the crucial game with Jimmy Jr. catching and batting in the clean-up position. It's two out in the ninth, Jimmy is up. The bases are loaded and we need those runs. In a couple of seconds the pitcher, a big, tough kid with a nasty eye, has breezed two strikes past my Jimmy Jr., and one of 'em is a duster that almost took the P.S.A.L. lettering off his chest. Two and none, and I can see the boy is shaken by the duster. We're in a bad hole.

All of a sudden I hear a familiar voice say, "Move over, keed." I look up, and it's the big guy in the tan polo coat and go-to-hell cap. He sits down next to me.

"Babe," I said, "you got here just in time. The kid's in a spot. . . ."

The saint laughs his deep rumbling laugh. "Take it easy, keed," he says, "just you watch him."

I look. And there's Jimmy Jr., standing at the plate, his bat over one shoulder, and with his free hand he's pointing out to the center-field fence just like the Babe did that day in the World Series in Chicago. It rattles the tough kid just enough. He lets the pitch go. SMACK!

No, it wasn't a homer, but for what was needed, just as good, a triple to deep center that clears the bases.

The saint laughs again, deeper and more satisfied. "The old trade mark," he says, and grins out to where Jimmy Jr. is roosting on third base. "That's the keed. Didn't get enough of the old back porch into that one. A little more meat on your piazza and it's over the fence. Gotta work on them wrists of yours, too. Ain't quite cocking them enough on the backswing. Well, so long, keed. . . ."

I heard that big laugh again as he vanished, and then it was lost in the noise of the crowd cheering for Jimmy Jr.

The Silver Swans

There is, of course, no end to the diversity of material from which a story can originate—memory, personal experience, frustration, ambitions unadmitted, incidents and happenings in daily life—for that matter, there is hardly a waking moment when one is not surrounded by or in contact with story material. "The Silver Swans," however, came out of work connected with another story.

To satisfy your curiosity in case you have skipped this preamble and read the story, Alice Adams, the heroine, is Miss Dorothy Tutin, the brilliant young actress; Richard Ormond Hadley is based upon the professional activities of my friend and one-time fellow Liechtensteinian, Dr. Hans Haas, the underwater photographer from which I also took the liberty of borrowing his beard; and the third character in the story, Dr. Fundoby, is rather what I hope and expect I shall be like when I am seventy-five.

In 1955 I was working with the late Henry Cornelius, the motion-picture director who made those two enchanting films *Whisky Galore* and *Genevieve,* in an attempt to get a film script out of a short wartime novel of mine called *The Lonely.* That we didn't succeed may be attributed to a number of causes, one of them being you can't photograph what goes on inside a person's head; but at the time the project was a serious one and the picture was scheduled as one of the J. Arthur Rank productions.

At the same time that we struggled with the adaptation we were casting and looking for an actress who could play the heroine, a girl by the name of Patches. She was an A.T.S. officer who became involved in a romance with an American flyer. The American boy was nothing in particular in the story, but the girl somehow had turned out to be something special and we wanted, therefore, someone special to play her, for the success of the book had been based upon her character and personality. When the book was closed and laid down, Patches was the one who one remembered and would have wished to have known. Corny and I talked to two of the younger British actresses. One was Virginia MacKenna and the other Dorothy Tutin.

Miss MacKenna had commitments, as I remembered. Miss Tutin would have been ideal: she had a flat, round little face with a tiny nose, and a gravelly voice which she attributed to the presence of nodules on her vocal chords. She had a warmth and personality of compelling charm; also, she was then already, having hardly reached her majority, a first-class actress and was nightly filling the theater in a Graham Greene play in the role of a tender young girl in a Catholic household who, having been seduced and abandoned, destroys herself.

Although Miss Tutin was eighteen at the time, she managed to look fifteen and play with the assurance and art of a woman of forty. I remember inviting Miss Tutin out to dinner one Sunday night to discuss the role, the story, the screen play in the making as well as to learn more about this person into whose mouth I should be putting speeches, words that must not clash with her personality and projection.

We went to a place in London called the Club Casanova, one of the few spots in London where one can get a decent meal on a Sunday night, in spite of the fact that the proprietor insists upon serving his hors d'oeuvres and his sweets from the same trolley.

Miss Tutin, who I think liked the Patches role and the story of *The Lonely,* chose to turn up that night in a little-girl dinner dress, reminiscent of graduation day from grammar school. This, with her gamin face, made her look exactly twelve.

We occupied one of the red plush banquettes, part of the Casanova's decor, amidst glowering looks from the other patrons, which at first I took for jealously, but later interpreted properly as hostility toward what seemed to be the most blatant cradle-snatching of the season.

The Casanova employs a dance band, to divert or annoy the customers, and when I asked Miss Tutin whether she would care to dance, she did, and we did, and it was during this *pas de deux* that I seemed to feel the crystallization of the sentiments of the other patrons into "Just look at that dirty, lecherous old man out there with that pure, innocent child—how revolting!" I got Miss Tutin off the floor and back to our banquette, where for the rest of the evening I tried to hide behind the huge silver-branched candelabra on the table. Nobody had recognized the most accomplished actress of the London season.

But that isn't where "The Silver Swans" came from, or why. The story derived from the fact that Miss Tutin *did* live aboard a houseboat named *Undine*, moored at the foot of Cheyne Walk, and everything aboard, including the occupant, was as described in the story. The first time I met Miss Tutin I visited her in her strange and interesting abode and at once thought of this as a background for a short story and someone very much like Miss Tutin as the heroine. In fact I am afraid that during this visit the new story quite overtook the old and drove it out of my mind, so much so that I became completely fascinated with Miss Tutin's houseboat, her manner of living, and her personality, and asked whether she would mind if I put her lock, stock, and barrel into a short story. She said she didn't.

Thereafter the story is, of course, pure fiction, but it springs from the kind of character I thought Miss Tutin to be and from what she would have done, or might have done, had the circumstances I invented ever presented themselves to her. And this to a great extent is what fiction writing is like, or turns into. You invent a character or you come up against one and learn to know or recognize it as a character, and then to make it stand out and illuminate the page, you reveal it against the background and a set of circumstances.

If when you read the story you will accompany me aboard the *Undine*, now renamed the *Nerine*, you will see that as I was shown this unusual home or sat out on the stern with Miss Tutin looking across the muddy Thames and watching the unlaundered and cantankerous-looking swans glide by, all the elements of this little tale were there and only needed to be swished around in *that* kind of mind a bit to come into being. I think that the octopus as well as the heroine's proficiency on the theorbo were my inventions. I have always been a fascinated admirer of the concerts of the Dolmetsch group. The quasi-Elizabethan poet, author of the lyrics of "The Silver Swans," which the heroine sings in the story, is, I am afraid, myself. I can't think now, five years later, why one should learn to recognize one's true love when the "Silver Swans come gliding," but it sounded nice to me and seemed like a good idea at the time.

When the story was finished I showed it to Miss Tutin, who approved of it. My agents showed it to the *Saturday Evening Post*, who bought it. It caused no stir whatsoever when it was published, but I like it and that is why I have included it in this volume.

To round off this narrative, the attempt to film *The Lonely* was abandoned because I wrote a very bad script and never did solve the problem of showing what my characters were thinking and feeling. Miss Tutin had the nodules removed from her vocal chords and went on to honor the roles of Portia and Cressida with the Old Vic. I have one more dampening item to add to the history of this story. I gave it the title "The Silver Swans," one that seemed to me gentle and gently intriguing and in keeping with the tone and nature of the tale. The *Saturday Evening Post* editors, closer to the public and to what they felt would stimulate, excite, and compel them to read this item for which they had already shelled out the price of the magazine, retitled it "Waterfront Girl."

I, DR. Horatio Fundoby, one of the assistant curators at the British Museum, always take my Sunday afternoon constitutional along Cheyne Walk on the Chelsea Embankment of the Thames, where I am frequently mistaken for an artist because of my white goatee, blackthorn stick, and battered hat, to which I have clung for more than forty years.

I am pleased with the sights and sounds of the river, the cries of the gulls and their exquisite flight, the marine traffic passing beneath Battersea Bridge, the colorful collection of ancient houseboats colonized at the moorings of the Chelsea Boat Company, and the faint smell of the sea borne by the tidal waters.

On this Sunday of which I am about to tell there was much of interest to contemplate as I stood on the Embankment near the entrance to the boat company. There was stationed in midstream a graceful white steam yacht, the *Poseidon*, with a curiously constructed stern, which I recognized as belonging to Lord Struve, the sub-sea explorer. A lovely motor ship from Panama was anchored near by, and a rusty Spanish freighter from Almería.

My eye was caught likewise by the heterogeneous selection of colors that had been splashed over the houseboat *Nerine*, apparently since the week before. The boat itself was a weathered gray, but the companionway and door had been painted blue, the hatch a bright vermilion, and the chimney yellow.

Indeed, at that moment the red hatch was pushed halfway

back from within and the head and shoulders of a young girl appeared in the space, striving to thrust it fully open. She did not succeed and, on the contrary, it soon became apparent that she had managed to wedge herself in so that she was able to move neither forward nor backward.

Her eyes caught mine at this juncture and even from that distance I was astounded by their extraordinarily luminous quality. She did not cry out, but her lips silently formed the words "I'm stuck!"

Without further thought, I hurried down the steps and across the gangway as rapidly as my aging legs—I shall be seventy-five in November—permitted, past a rusty water pump, a group of malodorous dustbins, and a clowder of contemplative cats. Reaching the *Nerine*, which was resting on the likewise malodorous mudflats, the tide being out, I struggled with the recalcitrant hatch.

It had stuck through the drying of the paint, but by means of judicious leverage with the blackthorn I was soon able to move it and free her. She was very young, I judged, hardly more than twenty, clad in paint-spattered dungarees and a gray T shirt, not at all beautiful in the accepted sense, but with a haunting quality that made itself felt immediately.

She did not break into an effusion of thanks but contemplated me with serious self-possession out of enormous gray eyes flecked with green, the loveliest and most startling feature of her face.

"Do you know who you are besides being a love?" she asked, and then continued, "You're the Kindly Old Gentleman—"

"Out of *Punch*, whom one encounters in the British Museum," I concluded.

Her contrition was charming. Her mouth, which was wide, could be extraordinarily wry and mobile. "Oh, I wasn't meaning it to be rude."

"But I am an old gentleman," I said, "I do feel kindly toward you, my years leaving me no other choice, and it just so happens that I *am* from the British Museum—Dr. Horatio Fundoby, Assistant Keeper in the Department of Medieval Antiquities."

"Oh," she said, "the British Museum." She fell silent for a

moment, pulling at her lower lip as she contemplated me solemnly. Then she asked, "Would you like to see my octopus?"

When I declared myself delighted, she led me down the companionway through a small galley into the main room of the houseboat, where it was cool and green. I was aware of a bunk, bookshelves, paintings on the wall, light filtering through green curtains, and two tanks, one small, the other large. The former contained a pair of sea horses floating smugly, the latter an octopus, an ugly specimen of *Eledone Cirrosa* at least a foot in diameter.

She was staring at it fascinated. "Isn't it beautiful?" she asked. "Sometimes I sit and look at it for hours."

"What do you call it?" I asked.

"Call it?"

"Hasn't it a Christian name?"

She looked at me, startled. "But it isn't a Christian. It would be an impertinence to it to give it a name. I call it Octopus, or sometimes O, Octopus."

"And yourself?"

She hestitated a moment before replying. "My name is Thetis."

I nodded. "Thetis was one of the Nereids, the daughters of Nereus and Doris who lived at the bottom of the sea. She was wooed by Neptune but married Peleus and became the mother of Achilles."

She pulled her lip contemplatively again. "Actually," she said, "my name is Alice. But I took Thetis. I would like terribly to live at the bottom of the ocean."

To tell the truth, in the little cabin one had the impression of being under water, the drawn curtains, the illumination of the tanks contributing to the illusion. The paintings on the wall were sub-sea scenes in blues and greens, but the creatures that one saw through the veils of water were weirdly unfishlike and full of fantasy. I suspected she had painted them herself. And she, with her tiny nose, huge eyes, and aureole of short-cut brown hair, might well have been a nymph.

She asked, "Would you care to have me sing for you?" and when I begged her to do so, pulled from behind a curtain a long-necked, oddly shaped stringed instrument constructed on the principles of the lute, which made me start. It was a fifteenth-century theorbo.

"My dear, where on earth did you get that?"

She looked surprised, as though I ought to have known. "I saved up and bought it—from Arnold Dolmetsch of course. I always wanted one. Please sit down. I am going to sing."

She closed her eyes and tilted her head back, revealing the exquisite line of her chin and throat. Her fingers touched the strings and the theorbo gave forth a deep bass twang. She announced the title of her song, "The Silver Swans," and then sang in a husky voice that was infinitely moving in its simplicity.

> "How shall I know my true love?
> When will my true heart speak to me?
> O, when the silver swans come gliding
> Then will I know my true love,
> Then will I with my true love be,
> Forever with my love abiding."

There was something inexpressibly touching about her, and some mystery, too, for behind the dewy youth was something ageless and wise, yet wholly innocent. But there was yet another enigma. The verse might have been the work of any of the minor Elizabethans, but the genuine line of the plaintive sixteenth-century melody eluded me—who should have known.

A sigh escaped me. "Ah, you have sung it beautifully. But who, who?" I racked my brains and enumerated, "Dowland? Weelkes? Thomas Morely? Willbye or Gibbons?"

Thetis opened her eyes. "Oh no, it is mine. Don't you see? That was why I needed the theorbo."

"Do you often compose authentic Elizabethan verse and music?" I asked.

"Only when it comes into my head." She leaned forward suddenly and spoke with an odd vehemence. "How *will* I know my true love? How shall I tell when I love?"

"How old are you, Thetis? Have you never been in love?"

"Twenty-one. I don't think so. How will I know? What will tell me when I am? You are so old and wise. Cannot you help me?"

It was a cry from a young and anxious heart and deserved reflection. I thought deeply and replied, "When he is desperately and unbeautifully ill and you are able to love him. Then you may be sure."

She mused to herself, "When he is ill and unbeautiful . . ." and was lost in thought for a moment. She returned swiftly. "How rude and forgetful I am. Won't you have a drink, Dr. Fundoby?"

When I replied that I never refused, she produced a bottle of black Jamaica rum, two drinking tumblers, and filled them each two-thirds full. She lifted hers and repeated, "When he is ill and unbeautiful. Oh, thank you, Dr. Fundoby!" smiled bewitchingly, and drank it down at one gulp, this astonishing creature, and never turned a hair, or at any time later showed that she had had so much as a single drop. It took me a good half-hour to consume mine while we talked.

She had parents who lived somewhere in Bayswater, but she preferred to dwell by herself on the rotting old houseboat because it was by the water, which she loved. She had a job that kept her busy nights but did not say what it was. She had been poor.

Was it the drink, or was it the craft that had stirred, causing something inside me to react uneasily? Before I could determine what it was, Thetis proposed that I might like to go out on deck.

Deck at the stern of the craft proved a narrow space perhaps several feet in depth and four feet wide, just room for us both to stand. To my surprise, we were afloat. The tide had come in and we were rocking gently, a motion that threatened to become more formidable as the curling wash from an ascending petrol-motor barge approached.

Past us drifted four of quite the filthiest swans I had ever seen, their yellow beaks and unfriendly eyes gleaming out of a dark-gray background compounded of oil, grime, coal dust, and soot from the river commerce, which twice a year makes it necessary for them to be collected and taken to a station on the upper Thames to be laundered.

Thetis regarded them musingly, but I teased her. "The Silver Swans," I said.

"Tarnished silver," she replied, slightly defiantly. We heard the thumping of oars in rowlocks, and around the corner of a half-sunken barge there came a sailor in a rowboat. He was a big fellow, in a blue jersey. He had curly black hair and a spade beard and eyes of a strangely light color.

"Oh, hello there!" he hailed, white teeth gleaming magnificently against the dark beard. "I say, do you suppose I might borrow a needle and thread for a moment? I've split meself rowing against this perishing tide."

"Certainly. If you want to come aboard I'll do it for you," Thetis invited.

The sailor grinned. "Can't. Embarrassing spot."

"Oh!" Thetis went inside and fetched a small sewing basket and, selecting a spool of thread, stuck a needle into it and tossed it into his boat. "Blue," she said.

The sailor caught it. "Bright child," he remarked. "Much obliged. I shan't be long." He let the tide carry his boat into the barge, where he made it fast, and, turning his back, bent to his repairs.

The wash from the petrol barge arrived and the *Nerine* began to rock alarmingly and a few moments later fatally. I believe there is no illness with which mankind is afflicted that can compare with the horrors of *mal de mer*. Certainly it is the only one in the entire category which causes man to long for and cry out to death to come and take him. The motion of the *Nerine* was one such as I had never endured before.

Just in time, Thetis turned from her interested contemplation of the blue-clad back of the brawny sailor and noted the color I had turned. "Oh, you poor dear!" she cried. "I'd forgotten it sometimes affects people. Come along quickly."

She took me by the arm and guided me to the bunk inside and gently helped me to recline. Then she opened a small cabinet, secured a tablet from a bottle, and popped it into my mouth. "Trigemine," she said. "They discovered it during the war. You'll be right as a trivet in five minutes. Just lie quietly." She went out on deck again.

I heard her hail the sailor. "Ahoy the sewing circle! What's your name?"

"Hadley. Richard Ormond Hadley." The name rang a bell, but owing to the struggle between the Trigemine and the violently rocking craft, I could not tell which.

I heard his return hail. "Ahoy the nursery! What's yours?"

"Thetis."

A moment of silence. Then the sailor: "Oh. You're the girl Neptune jilted because it was prophesied your son would be more famous than his father."

Thetis said, "I think that was silly. I should think that a father would be proud if his son turned out greater than he."

"Yes? Wait until you've been a father. And by the way, speaking of fathers, what's become of yours?"

"He isn't my father. He's a kind old gentleman who was visiting. He got seasick and is lying down inside. I gave him a Trigemine."

The sailor's snort traveled across the water. "What? Seasick on that scow? Why, it's practically dry land." Another ship must have gone by, for the *Nerine* rolled even more violently. But the Trigemine was getting in its work. I thought Thetis' reply was surprisingly mild.

"It isn't a scow," she said, "it's my home. And she does roll at certain states of the tide. You have to have a frightfully strong stomach."

"Hoh! I'll wager."

Thetis said, "Really, this is quite different. You might get sick yourself." I realized she was speaking to comfort me.

The sailor roared with laughter. "Who, me? Listen, brat, I've sailed every sea and ocean there is in all kinds of weather and haven't been sick yet."

I heard Thetis say, "There's always a first time. You wouldn't care to try, would you?"

"Let me know some time when it gets really rough." His boat bumped against the stern. "I say, you're not really as much of a child as I thought you were. I do apologize. Maybe I'll try out your craft some time. Well, thanks for the repairs."

The Trigemine had triumphed. I felt I might survive. When I went out, Thetis was standing on the deck shading her eyes from the descending afternoon sun and looking after the diminishing figure of the sailor rowing in the direction of the fine white yacht.

"Oh," she said, "you're better. I knew it. It always works. Wasn't he beastly?"

I commenced to reply, "We-e-ell," when she continued: "But wasn't he *beautiful?*"

I did not see my new friend for several weeks. Then on a rainy Sunday as I walked along the Embankment past the boatyard I heard my name called. "Dr. Fundoby, Dr. Fundoby!" Thetis ran across the gangway and up the steps to the road. There was anxiety in her bearing. "Dr. Fundoby! What shall I do? My octopus has eaten off one of his own arms."

I said, "They often do when kept in captivity, no matter how well you feed them."

"Oh!" She fell to reflecting, pulling at her lower lip. "Then I suppose I'd better call him Septopus. Thank you very much." She turned and went back to her boat.

Just before she vanished down the companionway I called after her, "Did your sailor ever come back?" She nodded her head vigorously in assent and then disappeared.

It was shortly afterward that a friend invited me to see a play, *The Unwanted*, at the Wyndham Theater, featuring Alice Adams, a rising young English actress, and due to close soon, after a long run.

Imagine with what astonishment and emotions I sat spellbound when Alice Adams made her first entrance and proved to be *that* Alice, the Nereid Thetis of the Chelsea Embankment.

In the role of a sensitive girl who is seduced by an older man and abandoned, and who in the end destroys herself, she brought a maturity of interpretation and understanding I would not have thought possible in one so young and essentially innocent. Her performance was as moving and haunting as she herself and I wept unashamedly at the close.

I took the liberty of calling on her the following Sunday. The already tiny cabin was further cramped by the addition of a new tank. In it were two pike with saucer eyes and a huge eel. She had been sitting in front of it watching them. She gave me a Trigemine at once, which I took gratefully even though the *Nerine* was fairly quiet.

"My dear," I said, "why didn't you tell me who you were? I was at the Wyndham Theater last week."

"I did," she replied. "This is who I am here. It's who I really want to be."

"You moved me very much in the play. How can you who are so young and say you have never loved reproduce all the pain and yearning of love, night after night?"

"Oh," she replied, thinking a moment. "That's the other side of me. I just do it."

She saw me looking at the newest additions to her undersea home, the unblinking pike and the somnolent eel. "He gave them to me," she said.

"The sailor? Where did he get them?"

"From the bottom of the river."

"Indeed. How?"

"He said he went down and looked for them until he found them."

Now I knew who Richard Ormond Hadley was and wondered whether she did? And whether her heart was to be broken, and her role in the play perhaps even repeated in real life? I took the liberty granted my by my years and asked, "Is he in love with you?"

Thetis shrugged. "He's frightfully rude to me. Is that a sign?"

"And you? Are you in love with him?"

She replied, "I don't know," and then repeated twice more, each time more intensely, "I don't know. I don't know! Oh, Dr. Fundoby, how terrible it is to be young!" and with that she leaned her head against my shoulder and began to cry, while I comforted her as best I could.

Accustomed to walk, rain or shine, I came along Cheyne Walk the following week in a violent windstorm. The wash of river traffic added to the already choppy Thames had set the *Nerine* to rocking alarmingly at her moorings, and, looking down, I suddenly feared for the safety of the child, remembering the narrow cabin and the heavy glass tanks even though she took the precaution of keeping them but half filled so that they would not slop over.

Noting that the hatchway was open, I hurried across the gangway to the deck and down the companionway. I had not yet reached the bottom when a deep groan of mortal anguish emerging from the interior caused me to hasten my steps even more.

An astonishing sight met my eyes. Reclining in the bunk of the cabin, apparently *in extremis*, was the sailor, Richard Ormond Hadley. Thetis was sitting on the edge, cradling his head in her arms. He was green, was my Lord Struve, the color of one of Thetis' sub-sea paintings; his brow was clammy, his hair matted, his eyes agonized. For one moment I thought the poor wretch was dying and then as the cabin lurched and a sudden qualm struck me I realized his trouble was that he was not.

"Thetis!" I gasped, "the Trigemine! Quick! Where is it?"

"Oh-h-h!" groaned the unhappy man on the bunk, "won't you all go away and let me die peacefully?"

"I love him!" Thetis cried joyously, cradling the ghastly head closer to her breast. "Oh, now I know I love him. He is awfully ill, isn't he, Dr. Fundoby? And I love him even more than when he is well."

I staggered to the cabinet where I knew the Trigemine was kept. It was locked. A look of guilt combined with stubbornness came over Thetis' features. "He won't say that he'll marry me," she said. "I don't mind in the least being poor and sleeping in a hammock."

The miserable fellow, who was evidently too weak to arise and escape to land, groaned again. "All right, all right. Anything, anything if you'll just go away and let me die!"

I gathered my own failing strength. "Thetis! For shame! This is medieval torture. Give me the key at once."

Meekly she produced it from a chain around her neck, and handed it to me. "He's sailed every sea and ocean in all kinds of weather," she murmured.

I secured the Trigemine bottle, popped two tablets into my mouth and three into the unhappy orifice of the great sub-sea hunter, diver, and marine biologist, Richard Hadley, Lord Struve, and then lay down on the floor to wait for them to take effect.

Thetis looked down at me. "Will you come to our wedding, Dr. Fundoby?" she asked.

The drug within me had not yet made contact. For the first time I was put out with Thetis. "If he consents to marry a blackmailer, torturer, and assassin, I shall be convinced that he is out of his head," I replied.

The dose had apparently begun its work on Struve, for he suddenly sat up and said, "I'm glad to hear you say that, Dr. Fundoby. Promises made under duress—"

"But it was your idea to come aboard at this state of tide and weather after I warned you," Thetis said plaintively.

"Dammit all!" growled the peer, the color beginning to return to his face. "I came to tell you I loved you."

"Well, then," Thetis asked simply, "why didn't you?"

His lordship had the grace as well as the ability now to blush. "Because I was unexpectedly taken severely ill. Look here, Thetis. You'd better know what you're in for if you're going to marry me. Do you know who I am?"

"I don't care who you are, or what you've done," Thetis replied, "I love you." Then half to herself she murmured, "In sickness and in health."

I was feeling better and sat up. "What about your stage career?" I asked severely.

Struve looked blank. "Whose stage career?" he asked.

"Good Lord," I cried, "are you both blind? This is Alice Adams, featured in *The Unwanted* at the Wyndham Theater for the last two years."

Struve stared. "This child? She is a child, isn't she?"

Thetis nodded absent-mindedly. But I said, "England's most promising young actress. She's all of twenty-one."

He stood up. "Great heavens! I remember reading something ages ago. I've just come back from the Galápagos and haven't seen a paper for eighteen months."

Thetis sprang to her feet and went to him. "Oh please," she pleaded, "all my life I've wanted to go to the Galápagos. Are sailors allowed to take their wives with them when they go?"

Struve burst out, "Hang it all, Thetis. I'm not a sailor. I'm a—" He hesitated, since it is somewhat embarrassing to announce yourself as a lord, and then concluded, "—a sort of marine biologist. I do things under water. Your career—"

Thetis interrupted. "Bother my career. I never wanted to be an actress. When I went for a job they said I had talent. I only did it to get money to rent a houseboat and buy myself things like theorbos and octopuses. Do you know what a good octopus costs?"

Struve took her by both arms. "Thetis, can you be serious for a moment? Do you really mean you'd give up all that for me and come away?"

"Of course. What I really want more than anything in the world is to walk at the bottom of the ocean at the Galápagos, with you, now that—" She hesitated, reflecting a moment. "Now that, thanks to Dr. Fundoby, I'm sure I love you."

For still another moment Lord Struve held her two arms and, looking up to heaven with an expression of sheer gratitude on his dark countenance, mumbled something which I took to be thanks. Then he sheltered her in his own arms with a tender and protective gesture so that her face was buried in his blue jersey, and looking at me over her head he said softly, "You know, Dr. Fundoby, God is sometimes just too awesome, the way He will pause in His works to answer the need of one single, puny man."

And thus the prophecy of the silver swans was fulfilled. So too, in this incarnation, with myself at the wedding, Neptune married his nymph Thetis, and if the son turns out to be indeed greater than the father, he has only himself to blame.

I still promenade Chelsea Reach, but Cheyne Walk by the boat company is no longer the same. Lady Struve, her husband, her theorbo, and her quintopus (it having devoured two more of its arms) have gone off to some tropic isle where they dive and work together in the wondrous marine gardens.

A family from Chipping Barnet have taken the *Nerine,* painted her a hideous brown, and renamed her *The Nelson.* I see her rocking in the wash, dressed from bow to stern in the international white squares that signal the presence of small, damp fry. And I wonder as I pass whether they too have frightfully strong stomachs, or have likewise discovered the miraculous powers of Trigemine?

The Lost Hour

"The Lost Hour" is a fairytale based upon what must be considered, I suppose, a bygone era of travel, the five-day transatlantic voyage, and one that surely in this jet age will strike the reader as dated and anachronistic as the tales of the windjammers and clipper ships read to me as a boy.

Five days to cross the Atlantic? Six hours is the established time, at least as this book runs through the high-speed presses. Still, new keels are being laid, new superliners projected, and perhaps there will always be a passenger list for a leisurely sea voyage. It is certainly the way I travel by preference.

"The Lost Hour" is also an example of a story, in this case a long short story that has been termed a novelette, based upon a fantasy idea in which one plays with the imaginative elements behind the truth or fact.

The truth in this instance is that there is a five-hour difference in time between New York and London, and when one travels west, the clock is stopped for one hour at midnight to make up the difference in time. The fantasy behind this truth is: what becomes of that lost hour at midnight when time stands still, when the vast liner with its thousand passengers, a thousand different souls, steams through the sea between time, as it were?

And then one picks up from there and begins to weave a story.

The R.M.S. *Gigantic* is, of course, the R.M.S. *Queen Elizabeth*, the ship that in a way is like another home to me. If it is at all possible for me to arrange the time of a transatlantic crossing, I will do so to fit in with the schedule of the *Elizabeth*—both ways. I have lost count of the number of times I have crossed with her and her chief purser, Lionel Carrine, O.B.E., whom I count as one of my oldest friends.

Publications do not like real names of ships or products or things, and so in the *Saturday Evening Post*, where this story first appeared,

349

the *Elizabeth* became the *Gigantic*. But in the film later made from this story, about which I will tell you, she was the proud and beautiful *Elizabeth* and much of the story was photographed aboard her and the premier of the film also took place in her cinema.

But to return to the idea of "The Lost Hour" and the characters that then had to be fashioned to fit the notion, almost before I knew it the character of Edwin Reith-Jones was born and prepared to play his part. For what kind of man would it be who would make use of the magic inherent in the timeless hour but one who lacked the courage or presence to make use of seconds, minutes, hours, and days that were timeful?

Essentially the basis of this story is as old as the hills—the mouse who turns into a lion, the timid man who finds courage. It has been reiterated all too often that there is no such thing as a new plot, and indeed this is so; there is only an occasional new twist to an old one. The novelty of this story is contained in the idea of that magic sixty minutes each day of a five-day journey when time stands still. I can still see myself sitting in the smoking room or the lounge of the *Elizabeth* looking at that clock stopped at midnight with the chatter of conversation going on all around me or dancing, music, and laughter, and no one noticing or caring that the hand of the clock had been stilled. I suppose in a way the timidities of Edwin Reith-Jones reflected my own, except that I only dreamed of what one might do during the time the clock was stopped and my character did something about it.

The character of Lisa Lisbon I visualized in the glamorous persons of either Miss Joan Crawford or Miss Rosalind Russell. The part was eventually played by Miss Betsy Drake.

The rest of the cast of the story soon fell into place or were invented to do their work. Some stories begin with characters and then take over and often go their own headlong and headstrong way. But for a story of this kind you create or engage symbols to carry out your designs almost as you would engage actors, where the director phones central casting and asks for such-and-such types. You may then say, "But then these are not real-life characters." But then this is not a real-life story, either. I warned you at the beginning that this was a fairytale in which the author himself escapes from that sometimes too grim and unhappy thing known as real life.

In reading a story and condemning it as "escape" fiction, one is too prone to forget that it is more than a pastiche designed to dope the reader and enable him or her to escape momentarily from the complications of life. It is the writer himself who is frequently the fugitive. Writing stories is often more relaxing and revealing and certainly cheaper than the psychiatrist's couch. For the weeks that I worked upon "The Lost Hour" I was able to flee wholly from a difficult period and trying problems and became Edwin Reith-Jones all-powerful between the hours of midnight and nothing.

The story was written in my mountain-top chalet in Liechtenstein and published by the *Saturday Evening Post*. A year later it was bought by the late Henry Cornelius, the director-producer. The sale excited me more than any I had made in a long time, for at last it looked as though I was due to have a good and successful picture made out of one of my stories, a picture that I could enjoy. Alas, it didn't work out that way, for Cornie, though he himself was not aware of it, was a very sick man all during the time that he prepared and directed this picture. The story passed through many hands; the characters were altered, and in the end only the *Queen Elizabeth* and the gimmick remained as I had conceived them, and with the new turns and twists the story had taken and the casting, not even the gimmick was valid any longer. The picture, called *Next to No Time,* was not a success. Cornie died before it was released.

E DWIN REITH-JONES, painfully shy and, as always, suffering from lack of self-confidence, sat by himself at the far end of the deserted Veranda Bar of the R.M.S. *Gigantic,* westbound, and contemplated the ship's electric clock over the doorway, the hands of which had stopped at midnight. It had been some ten minutes since they had been in that position.

Clad in a dinner jacket with red carnation, the uniform aboard the *Gigantic* after six P.M., he regarded the stalled timepiece and the sign above it, which read, WESTBOUND ALL CLOCKS WILL BE STOPPED ONE HOUR AT MIDNIGHT, through a haze in part compounded from Scotch whiskies he had consumed in his loneliness and in part from the fears and worrisome thoughts that dogged him.

They never should have sent him on this trip. He simply wasn't the man for it. Indeed, he remembered painfully the conversation overheard outside the chairman's door in the office before he was admitted.

"Reith-Jones? Good heavens, you can't! The man's an absolute rabbit when it comes to dealing with people! He'll never put it over!"

And the reply, "At least he's honest. It's wretched luck, but I don't see that there is any choice."

Nor had there been. A concatenation of circumstances, including an illness and an accident, made Edwin Reith-Jones, chief accountant for the Manchester cotton firm of Selwyn & Havas, the only responsible member available for the important mission of journeying westward aboard the *Gigantic* and contacting Sir Malcolm Gordien, the London financier.

Sir Malcolm was on his way to the United States to seek American aid for the cotton industry and to offer in return a kind of cartelization which, in the event of war, would mobilize British production with American. The small but growing firm of Selwyn & Havas wished to be a part of the scheme and share the aid. It was a job requiring the ability to meet and impress people as well as knowledge of the business.

Edwin's unobtrusiveness was so marked as to be almost obtrusive, for his hair was so fair as to be nearly white, as were his eyebrows. He was forty-five, but with his pale-blue eyes, pink skin, and plain, innocent features, he looked half that. Only a slight truculence about the chin seemed oddly out of harmony with his other, negative qualities. Sitting alone at the bar—most of the passengers having congregated for the dancing in the lounge—he gave the impression that he wasn't there.

His thoughts turned to Lisa Lisbon, the Hollywood film star. He had seen her descending from the Veranda Grill, trailing perfume, the rustle of expensive clothes and men behind her.

She would be in the lounge now, dancing with any one of the group of powerful and notable men rumored to be in love with her —Victor Vaughn Craig, the explorer and writer; Senator Austin Gregg, of the Foreign Relations Committee; or the Earl of Morveigh.

And then in his mind's eye he himself held her in his arms and she was dancing with him. She was a wondrously beautiful woman with roan-colored hair, exquisite brown eyes, and most delicately chiseled features. She was so beautiful it made the heart ache to regard her. He remembered that she was dressed in a gown of copper sequins that exactly matched her hair. She was a more famous actress than even Greta Garbo had been.

He dismissed his dreams. As much chance of realizing them as bearding Sir Malcolm Gordien and persuading him to include Selwyn & Havas in his combine. He did not even know Sir Malcolm by sight. And furthermore, he could not dance—at least not any known intelligible step. He could only sit, a nervous, socially timid, useless fellow, alone at a bar, absorbing Scotch whisky.

He said to the bartender, "May I have another or is it time?" referring to the British closing laws.

"Ain't no time at sea, sir," the bartender replied, setting up a new glass and pouring. Then, with a nod toward the halted clock, he added, "Ain't no time at all now. We're between time."

Was it the whisky or the words that had the most curious effect upon Edwin Reith-Jones? Surely not the former, for he held his liquor like a gentleman. No! The phrases ran through his mind and blood like fire. He felt suddenly different—strong, brave, gregarious, powerful. The barkeep had said it. Time was standing still.

Between Time! There was a difference of five hours between Great Britain and the United States. For an hour each night then, at midnight, they were adrift not only upon a trackless ocean but in a boundless universe where no time was kept.

Suddenly it came to him that with Time standing still, everything during that hour was unreal and taking place in a vacuum. Nothing really counted—not the Scotch he was downing, the glasses the bartender was polishing, the miles the ship's vibrating screws put behind her, nor words spoken, actions done, contracts signed, beliefs expressed.

Slipping thus in-between Time, a man could escape at last from the straitjacket of his nature. During that nonexistent hour he could be anything, do anything, including—the idea came to him almost as an inspiration and a command—invite the most beautiful film star in the world to dance and proudly whirl her in his arms before the envious and admiring eyes of all. Forty-five minutes of the precious lost hour remained.

Inside Time, Edwin Reith-Jones discovered when he reached the lounge, was a peculiar clarity, a sharp awareness of people, of tensions, but particularly of himself and his own powers, which he had never experienced before.

Lisa Lisbon was not dancing. She sat, looking neither bored nor entertained, with Craig, a handsome giant; Senator Gregg, a gray-haired man with a beautifully sensitive face; and the lean, red-headed Earl of Morveigh. Near by were two other suitors—Saul Wiener, president of American Pictures, and a pink-faced, boyish-looking man, playing canasta at a small side table.

There was yet another member of the group, a gaunt fellow with snapping dark eyes, high cheekbones, and a long, humorous nose. He had big hands, which were at the ends of arms too long for his sleeves. A man of forty-odd, with grizzled dark hair, brush-cut, he was smoking a black cigar and watching everything with amusement. This was Cy Hammer, Lisa Lisbon's agent.

There was another party adjacent that impressed itself upon Reith-Jones. It consisted of a typically well-to-do American family —a father and mother with two girls in the awkward thirteen-to-fifteen age bracket. But the girls were not sisters. On the contrary, they could not have been more different. The one was a wide-eyed, innocent-looking child, blond and breathless, who resembled her sweet-faced, well-mannered mother. The other, taller, pale, self-possessed, with Italian-cut black hair in the latest style, looked sophisticated and hard. Yet there was about her, Edwin felt, a curious yearning quality of desperation that did not seem to match her artificially brittle voice and laugh and the shocking fact that, though she was obviously still a leggy, undeveloped child, she wore lipstick, mascara, and eye shadow and her fingernails were painted bright red. Although she was chattering animatedly, she never took her eyes off Lisa Lisbon.

Secure within the confines of the hour that did not exist, Edwin Reith-Jones marched up to the movie star, bowed, and asked, "May I have the pleasure of this dance, Miss Lisbon?"

The group looked up in surprise at the intrusion, Saul Wiener pausing in the discard of a queen to remark, "So who is this guy?"

Victor Vaughn Craig's cold eyes appraised the newcomer. He said stiffly, "You must excuse Miss Lisbon. She does not care to dance."

In Time, Edwin would have blushed to death on the spot. Outside the clock's iron jurisdiction, he said evenly, "Why don't you let Miss Lisbon answer for herself?"

Lisa's rich, warm laughter rang out. "Why, it's the Boiled Turnip!" she cried, but with such immediate and engaging friendliness that Edwin could only take it as the dearest of compliments. "Oh, that's dreadful of me, but I always name everyone. Of course I'll dance with you."

Craig said sharply, "Lisa!" and the Earl of Morveigh raised an eyebrow. But the star was looking across to Cy Hammer, who removed his cigar, winked at her, and merely said, "Have fun, kid."

Lisa Lisbon arose and cast her magnificent glance over her assembled swains. "Why shouldn't I dance with him?" she inquired. "You boys have been boring the garter belt off me for the past hour."

Edwin was suddenly caught up in two near-by dark eyes staring into his for a moment, and felt that a message of deepest despair was being sent forth to him. But what it was, or why, he could not fathom. The eyes belonged to the strange, tall child with the make-up. Then Lisa Lisbon gave herself into his arms. The band was playing a fox trot.

At that moment the ship lurched, as it had been doing for some time, due to the fact that the *Gigantic* had passed Land's End and an angry following sea snapped at her from the Channel. She rolled all of the dancers, adept and tyro, including Edwin and Lisa Lisbon, the width of the dance floor, shrieking and laughing.

With a surprisingly deft movement, Edwin swung Lisa around at the end of the slide, so that it was he and not she who crashed into a pillar.

"Nice going, Turnip," Miss Lisbon chuckled in her sweet, deep contralto. "Hang on, kid. Here we go again," as the reverse roll started them sailing back. They made two more trips before the band leader ended the set and Edwin brought a breathless Lisa Lisbon back to her party.

"Oo-oo-of!" she said. "Haven't had so much fun since I used to slide on the ice as a kid back in Milwaukee."

The men all arose stiffly to receive her, their faces trying to register disapproval of this odd albino Englishman who had crashed their midst.

"Thank you very much," Edwin said. Then he added, "I say, would you perhaps care for a turn up on the top deck with me, Miss Lisbon? It's jolly nice up there."

Victor Vaughn Craig loomed a menacing six feet four. He said, "Miss Lisbon would not care for a turn on deck. You've had your dance. Now how about making yourself scarce?" Implied was: "while you've got your health."

The Timeless Edwin Reith-Jones said succinctly, "Why don't you go soak your head, old boy?"

Cy Hammer was grinning like a gargoyle. Lisa's laugh temporarily postponed the crisis. "That's telling him, Turnip. . . . Victor, when I have my dialogue written for me, it will be by a script writer. . . . O.K., Turnip. We'll go topside and look at the moon. I think I like you."

She took Edwin's arm and marched out of the lounge with him, followed by the stares of some two hundred or so passengers and the adoring gaze of the queer, made-up child.

When she reappeared alone, the orchestra had packed up for the night and the entourage and most of the other passengers had gone from the lounge. Cy Hammer still remained there, waiting.

He stared in astonishment as the star came in. The immaculate axis of Lisa's gown no longer bisected her exactly. One false eyelash was gone, her lipstick displaced, and an appreciable amount of the magnificent roan-colored hair was disordered. Her cheeks were pink and there was a shining in her eyes.

Hammer regarded her quizzically and said, "A limey did this?"

Lisa fell into one of the overstuffed lounge chairs next to him. "Wow, what a man!" she said. "That was close. Two more minutes and it would have been all up with little Lisa." She felt the air with her fingers where the missing eyelash should have been, and then hastily stripped off the remaining one.

Hammer smoked tactfully for a moment, and then, since he was devoted to Lisa and her business and there were no secrets between them, he inquired, "What broke it up?"

Lisa replied, "I don't know," and then, "Yes I do. We were up forward. The ship's bell struck. He looked at his watch, said, like a bad actor, 'Great heavens, what have I done? Can you forgive me, Miss Lisbon?' and bolted before I could say a word."

She sat there a moment with a reminiscent and girlish smile about her mouth. Then she said, "The sweetness of him, the tenderness, the sweetness of the things he said to me. Nobody is ever sweet to me, Cy. He made me feel like a woman again, instead of like a doll or a prize animal."

The agent regarded her with astonishment. Then, without speaking, he reached over and patted her hand. Lisa turned her warm smile upon him. "Take me down to my cabin, Cy," she said. "I want to dream."

The tall, dark-haired child with the sophisticated make-up and manner was Melanie Holcombe, the unhappy shuttlecock of the notorious Chicago Holcombe divorce case of a decade ago. She was returning alone to her father in Chicago from Paris, where she had been living with her mother in the European whirl that meant Cannes in the winter, London in the season, autumn for the racing, St. Moritz for New Year's.

She had been befriended on the boat by the Chamberses and their daughter, Florrie. They had taken the unhappy child under their wing, sat with her at the table, taken her to the movies and provided a kind of base for her.

All this, Edwin Reith-Jones had found out by accident, when he had gone to the purser's desk to make inquiries about Sir Malcolm Gordien, and, finding the chief purser in conversation with the ship's doctor, had been too shy to intrude.

"It's a rotten shame," the purser concluded. "The old girl's just taken a new lover—one of the De Neuilly boys. Melanie was in the way, so she's sent her packing back to her father."

The doctor asked, "Won't that be better for her? Girls usually love their fathers."

"True, but old Holcombe won't have any use for her. He's just married again—some young television actress. I saw pictures of them, taken at Sun Valley. She looks a real featherbrain. I feel sorry for the kid."

Reith-Jones felt sad and depressed. He knew now the reason for the unhappy expression in the girl's eyes. It was the same look of seeking and longing found in the eyes of a stray dog searching every passer-by for the one who will eventually take him home and give him love and shelter. He forgot about Sir Malcolm Gordien and went away. He wished somehow he might talk to the child.

That evening Edwin emerged from the moving-picture theater through the smoking room, which was crowded in anticipation of the big auction pool on the ship's run.

Lisa Lisbon, in blue-and-silver lamé, surrounded by her entourage, saw him pass and called to him, "Hi, Turnip! Come over here and sit with us!"

Crimson with embarrassment, he could do no more than go over as he had been bidden, and face the hostile or indifferent glances of the important people with her. It was Cy Hammer who made place for him and ordered him a double Scotch, which he downed quickly to give him courage, and another on top of that.

The ship was sorting itself out and Edwin was learning names and faces through listening. The pink-faced man engaged in the eternal canasta game with Saul Wiener was Hamlin Mason, another suitor, head of National Motors, of Detroit. And the man a few tables away with the too-large head and perpetually sneering expression on his face was Frank Patch, the left-of-left British Socialist M.P., labor leader and good friend of the Communists.

Edwin wanted to ask which one was Sir Malcolm Gordien, but did not wish to parade his ignorance before the others. He searched the room for one who might possibly be he, and felt the tension of expectation as the time for the bidding neared. The gambling lust already lay thick over the room, like the layers of blue smoke from the rich cigars. Syndicates and combines were forming to bid for the favored high numbers.

He watched the smoking-room steward searching for a volunteer auctioneer among the passengers. A famous comedian turned it down with "No, thanks. I'm on vacation." A well-known journalist took one look about him at the assembled money power and, with a quiet shudder, asked to be excused.

The steward finally went to his desk, rang a bell, and pleaded, "Ladies and gentlemen, we know everyone is anxious for the auction to begin, but we have not yet been able to secure an auctioneer. Won't some gentleman kindly come forward?"

A buzzing hum followed as people at various tables urged others to go up and sacrifice themselves.

Edwin Reith-Jones's pale eyes found their way to the smoking-room clock the hands of which were fixed at midnight. Time was suspended again. He rose to his feet.

Lisa Lisbon laid a quick, detaining hand upon his arm. "Turnip, sit down," she said. "They'll eat you alive."

But Edwin Reith-Jones, the famous wit, entertainer, and auctioneer, walking confidently to the desk across a planet that had ceased to revolve through space, seized the gavel and said, "Ladies and gentlemen, and fellow cutthroats—"

In the gasp that followed, Victor Vaughn Craig, "What an egregious little bounder."

But Lisa's anxious expression cleared as she breathed, "I think he's going to get away with it."

"There's one rule to this auction," Edwin was saying. "When the hammer falls, it's final. Any opening bid of less than fifty pounds from this aggregation of captains of industry, financiers, millionaires, and plain, unassuming second-story men will be treated with the contempt it deserves."

There was a titter. Saul Wiener said, "What did he call us?" and then added, "What's with his face? I never saw a feller without any eyebrows like that before."

Lisa said, "He has them, only they don't show."

Cy grinned at her. "You find out everything, don't you, Snooks?"

The steward drew the first number from the bowl. Edwin went to work. He was fast, funny, accurate, and hypnotic as he drew bids from all quarters of the room. The pool grew to record proportions.

Low Field came up. The sea was smooth, the big ship racing through the night. Nobody bid for it. Edwin cupped the number in his hands and then cradled it. "Poor little orphan," he said, "nobody wants him."

"Oh," cried Lisa, touched, "Cy, you buy it!" But Hammer's call of £50 was immediately jumped and spirited bidding resulted, with Edwin finally knocking it down to him for £250.

"What happened?" Hammer said. "He put the whammy on me. I need this number like a hole in the mind."

"That's my li'l' ol' Turnip," Lisa purred; and then soothed, "Never mind, Cy. Something may bust during the night and slow us down."

"And now, ladies and gentlemen," Edwin cried, "the number you have all been waiting for, number five hundred and seventy, the captain's choice." One number in the pool was always supposed to be the captain's estimate of what the run might be.

A prebattle hush fell over the throng in the smoking room as Edwin's washed-out eyes wandered over them, weighing them. By now he knew all the big combines and syndicates, as well as the wealthy individuals and for all he had mental names. The Wolves were on the starboard side, the Tigers to port, and the Hyenas dead center. Then there was Mme. Vulture, Mr. Snake Eyes, and Old Veins-in-the-Nose.

The Tigers opened the bidding at £100, the Wolves raised it to 200, and the Hyenas said 300.

"Right," Edwin called cheerfully. "Now let's separate the men from the boys. Who'll say five hundred?"

Veins-in-the-Nose did. He was a florid, portly man with a great shock of white hair and possessive eyes. Mme. Vulture raised it to

£550; Snake Eyes said 600; and to the surprise of everyone, Victor Vaughn Craig bid 650. It was a fantastic sum, but the record amount in the pool made it a good gamble.

Too rich for their blood, the syndicates dropped out. Veins-in-the-Nose growled 675. Pale as a zombie, Mme. Vulture, a Parisian *couturière*, whispered 700. Craig took her off the hook with a call of 795, drawing an admiring look from Lisa. Her big guy might not have a sense of humor, but he knew how to fight.

Edwin now had them in his net, and swept them along by 25's, until to a hushed room he said, "Nine hundred and twenty-five pounds am I bid by Mr. Craig." He pointed his hammer at the florid gentleman. "It's against you, sir. Would you care to continue? I'll take ten pounds."

Veins-in-the-Nose stared heavily before him, but remained silent.

"Going, then, at nine hundred and twenty-five pounds . . . going—" Edwin brought the hammer down with a smart crack on the desk top.

"Nine thirty-five," said Veins-in-the-Nose.

"Sold to Mr. Victor Vaughn Craig at nine hundred and twenty-five pounds, and congratulations, sir!" Edwin called.

The florid gentleman was on his feet. "I said nine thirty-five, Mr. Auctioneer."

Edwin said, "I beg your pardon, sir, but you were too late. The hammer had fallen."

"Sir, I say the hammer had not fallen! My bid was in time! I demand that you accept it!"

At once the room was divided into two camps shouting, "Yes, yes!" or "No! Stick to your guns, auctioneer!"

Edwin declared firmly, "I repeat that your bid was too late. I stated the rules clearly at the beginning. The number goes to Mr. Craig, and that is final."

Lisa Lisbon breathed, "Oh, Turnip, Turnip, I love you," and Craig muttered, "The little guy's got guts," causing Lisa to remark, "Oh, hadn't you noticed that?"

But the old gentleman with the veins in his nose was shouting in uncontrolled temper now. "Sir, you are impertinent! I tell you my bid was in time and insist that the bidding be reopened! I guess you do not know who I am!"

A harassed-looking assistant purser arose. "Just a moment, Sir Malcolm. I'm sure this can be straightened out. . . . Mr. Auctioneer, in view of the strong protest made by Sir Malcolm Gordien, do you think it might be advisable to reopen the—"

The name "Sir Malcolm Gordien" rattled about in Timeless space and bounced off the incorruptible hide of Edwin Reith-Jones, who interrupted with, "I think nothing of the kind."

There was laughter, which angered the purser, who said, "I am afraid, sir, I am going to have to ask you to alter your decision and reopen the—"

"You mean you are ordering me?" Edwin stared at him incredulously.

The assistant was in a bad spot. Sir Malcolm was a V.I.P. Traveler. "As an officer of this ship, I am. Sir Malcolm is entitled to—"

Edwin laid down the gavel quietly. "Very well. You may damn well go to hell and run your auction under any rules you jolly well please. I'm through with it. My decision stands. You can do as you like. You, Sir Malcolm, are, in my opinion, a cheat and a bully. And now permit me to—"

He paused midway in this dramatic farewell. His eye had caught the smoking-room clock. The hands stood at eight minutes past twelve, and, as he watched, twitched to nine after. Time was on the move again.

He turned as white as his hair. His countenance seemed to be a void pierced only by two pale, terrified eyes.

"Oh, dear," he murmured, "what have I done? What have I done?" He looked up at the clock again and once more repeated, "Oh, dear," and Lisa Lisbon, her heart riven for him, expected at any moment he would add, "Oh, my fur and whiskers! I shall be late! What will the duchess say?" exactly like the White Rabbit in *Alice in Wonderland*.

Instead he put down the gavel and incontinently fled from the room up to the sun-deck railing, where he was sick. Then, limp and weak, he went to his cabin, thus missing the final act of the little drama in the smoking room.

The assistant purser, having taken over the gavel, said, "Mr. Craig, do you consent to the reopening of the bidding at nine hundred and twenty-five pounds?"

The big man said, "Your question comes a trifle late. However, I do." There was a murmur of applause and approval.

Sir Malcolm cleared his throat. "Nine thirty-five."

"Victor," Lisa Lisbon said, "shut up. I have a hunch."

Craig reflected a moment, studying the beautiful girl and liking the sincerity of the expression about her eyes. "Have you now, kitten?" he said softly. "That's good enough for me." To the purser he said, "Thank you. That will be all."

The number was knocked down to Sir Malcolm Gordien for £935, something over $2,600.

A little later a fourth engineer appeared at the door, whispered to the smoking-room steward, and went away.

The steward pounded the gavel once and said, "Ladies and gentlemen, the engines will be stopped for a half-hour or so at one o'clock for a minor adjustment. We are advising you so that you need feel no alarm when we lose way."

A rebel yell issued from Cy Hammer. Then he cried, "Lisa, you witch! You called it! I love you!" and he reached over and kissed her. The delay would drop the twenty-four-hour run covered by the pool well into the figures of the Low Field.

Lisa Lisbon had arrived at her eminence in her profession as well as her emergence as a woman through hard work, brains, and the devotion and prescience of Cy Hammer. He had picked her a little over eleven years ago, when she had been an almost unknown M-G-M starlet, one of a dozen on the roster, used mostly for cheesecake and publicity stills. At that time, too, she had been crushed by the loss of her husband, Mark Lisbon, a script writer whom she had married when she was twenty. He had enlisted in the marines and was killed at Iwo Jima.

Hammer had penetrated the exterior of what seemed to be a

brittle and unhappy girl to the talent beneath and had offered her work, self-sacrifice, and stardom. Once she had accepted, she had never wavered, and they had formed an extraordinarily successful business partnership. Hammer had never made a mistake in choice of vehicles and directors in her slow, steady climb to the pinnacle. She had never let him down.

Theirs was an unusual relationship in that he was likewise the repository of all her thoughts and secrets. She kept nothing back from him and consulted him about everything, including her dressmaker, hairdresser and love affairs. When one broke up badly or she was hurt, she came to him and he was there to pick up the pieces. And because they were united in a business partnership, there was nothing that could not be discussed between them—no shock, no outrage, and, above all, no censure. Each deeply respected the other as a grownup, with no personal ax to grind.

The next day, on her way to the lounge, Lisa encountered Sir Malcolm Gordien in the main-deck passageway, and he acknowledged her presence with a slight bow, though they had not been formally introduced.

Walking alongside him, Lisa said, "You know, you were a rotten sport last night. You ought to be ashamed of yourself."

Sir Malcolm replied with icy indignation, "I did not ask you for your opinion, Miss Lisbon. You realize that you are being extraordinarily impertinent."

Lisa stopped and, perforce, Sir Malcolm had to do likewise. She turned the full shock of her beauty and smile upon the financier and looked him levelly in the eye. "When your face makes up the way mine does, Sir Malcolm, you can get away with it."

For a moment they dueled wordlessly and she triumphed, for she had reminded him that his success in making millions of pounds was no more than hers in enslaving as many people who flocked to see her pictures.

Sir Malcolm suddenly melted and laid aside the dignity which he had acquired overnight with his title. "I suppose you can," he said, smiling, "particularly with an old man."

"You know you didn't make your bid before the hammer fell."

"Of course I didn't. But the silly twerp irritated me."

"Don't you think you ought to apologize to the Turnip?"

"The who? Oh, the Reith-Jones fellow." Sir Malcolm looked at her with the sheepish air of the delinquent, and asked in the tone of voice used by a small boy ordered to do something unpleasant, "Must I?"

"Yes, you must."

"Very well, then, I will."

Lisa reached up, kissed one corner of his mustache, and for an instant leaned her velvet cheek against his. "Oh," she cried, "I like men!"

Sir Malcolm said, "I'll look him up. Come, let us drink a glass of champagne. I haven't felt so good in years." They continued on, arm in arm.

There were two further incidents that third evening, and both occurred during that hour when midnight stood still. In one of them, a mild and unobtrusive Englishman with pale eyes and albino hair, seemingly reading a book near by, turned upon Frank Patch, smug, bitter Left Wing Member of Parliament, who had been sounding off to a group within earshot of Senator Gregg, to the effect that Britain would no longer support American imperialistic war-mongering policies.

Edwin Reith-Jones, secure once again, unhampered by Time or consequences, laid his book down sharply and said, "You are a liar, sir. You sit with the Socialists, but you speak for the Communists. Englishmen will never abandon their friends or knuckle under to yours."

In the startled silence that followed this outburst, Sir Malcolm Gordien said, "Hear, hear! Well said, sir," and Senator Gregg looked up sharply and asked, "For whom do you speak?" This had been a voice he had not heard in recent days in Great Britain.

Edwin answered almost irritably, "For every Englishman who has a roof over his head and isn't a Nazi slave and doesn't wish to be a Communist one. We are myriad." He turned upon Patch again and cried, "You are base and traitorous, sir! You belong to Russia and have the vicious ingratitude of the runny-nosed little boy who flings mud at his benefactor! You have no sense of brotherhood or honest blood in your veins! Brother answered brother and blood stood with blood in 1917 and 1941! You are no Englishman, sir, but a Communist, and we will never support you!"

The incident ended when Patch, flushed and angry, arose and stalked out. History might have received an infinitesimal nudge. Sir Malcolm's plan might now fall upon slightly more receptive ears. But the second incident was perhaps the more important one, for a human soul was saved.

It began innocently enough with a good-night kiss. Near by where Melanie Holcombe sat with her friends, Florrie Chambers got up and said, "Good night, Daddy. Good night, Mother." She put her arms about her father's neck and kissed him, and then did the same with her mother.

Mrs. Chambers held her tightly as she said, "Good night, darling. Sleep well." For yet another moment the two lingered in embrace, gazing at each other with love and intimacy.

But Edwin Reith-Jones had been watching the expression in the eyes and on the painted face of the other girl. Only that day he had talked with her for an hour on deck, and gauged something of her loneliness. Now he experienced a thrill of horror.

Florrie said, "Coming, Melanie?"

"No." Florrie went. A minute later Melanie arose stiffly and said, "Good night, Mr. and Mrs. Chambers. Thank you very much for all your kindness," and walked away, but with ever-increasing pace, so that by the time she had reached the far door of the lounge, she was running, and Edwin Reith-Jones after her.

For, from those who have succeeded in escaping the confines of Time, there are no secrets, and to him, the expression on the face of Melanie during the simple, tender good-night scene had been that of one already dead.

Lisa Lisbon arose impulsively. Cy Hammer lazily stretched and put a hand on her arm. "What's up, Snooks?"

She said, "Let me go, Cy. I feel that something dreadful is about to happen. Didn't you see? He felt it too. . . . No. No. Let me go alone." The glances of all the men who were in love with her followed her to the door.

At the boat-deck starboard rail, Edwin reached Melanie in time. But she had one thin leg over and was poised to plunge into the roiling, black, phosphorescence-coated eternity below.

"No, no, Melanie!"

He pulled her back from the rail and sheltered her in his arms, where she collapsed, sobbing. He let her cry herself out; then commenced to talk to her in the darkness, quietly, soothingly, about herself and the life that animated her.

He said, "Listen to me, old girl. Look at yourself. Feel your body. Hear the beating of your heart. This is a wonderful thing. You must not destroy it. You are alive to see, hear, think, and know. Some people are born to be loved, others to give it. To give is good, too, Melanie. There are so many in this world who need it."

And he said further, "Melanie, you are old beyond your years and will understand. Do you wish to kill the body in which sleep the unborn children to whom you will be able to give the love that has been denied to you? Someday they will be awakened and will cry out and reach for you. And between you and them will pass just such a look as you saw tonight betwixt mother and daughter, because it will be yours to give."

And he said finally, "Have courage, youngster. Take care of this you which is so perfectly made, against the day when you will surely know the happiness of receiving as well as giving love."

Lisa moved out of the darkness. A ship's light fixed the tears on her cheek and made them shine like the jewels at her ears and throat. She said softly, "Melanie," and then, "Edwin. My dear, good Edwin."

At the masthead a bell chimed. Simultaneously all over the racing vessel electric impulse surged through the clocks again.

"Take her," Edwin said hoarsely, and gently shifted the child from his arms to those of Lisa. "Take her and keep her. Her father will make no objections. She worships you. You can make her into as fine a woman as you are. But first you must help her to be a child again. Let her stay with you."

He was gone. Lisa remained with her arms about the girl, her cheek resting on the small head with the too glossy hair.

"You may come with me if you like, Melanie," Lisa said to the child, who was crying softly again. Then, gently, with her handkerchief, she wiped the ravages of the mascara from the cheeks of the too-soon woman who was to have her girlhood restored to her.

It was the following night that Lisa, troubled, searched the ship for Edwin. Half of that hour during which the moving finger wrote not was gone by the time she found him standing at the stern rail below the Veranda Grill, looking out across the white wake and into the stars, dreaming she could not guess what dreams, except that they were bounded neither by Space nor Time.

She stood beside him, taking his arm and leaning against his shoulder in silence. She said, "It's the enchanted hour, isn't it, Turnip?"

He looked at her. "You know?"

"I guessed. It wasn't difficult. This is that hour between Time when one may be wise and brave and all-knowing. I came to you because I need help, Edwin."

"Yes, Lisa."

"Whom shall I marry?" He did not reply at once and she continued. "I want to marry again. I am living a lonely, selfish life." She counted her suitors off on her fingers. "Shall I be Mrs. Victor Vaughn Craig, keeper of a literary lion; or Mrs. Saul Wiener, queen of Hollywood; or Mrs. Hamlin Mason, ruler of motor society; the Countess of Morveigh, with a castle; or Mrs. Austin Gregg? Gregg is being talked of for the presidency."

"Which one do you love?"

"In each one there is something that I can love and respect."

"Who will make you happy?"

Lisa reflected. "I despair of that. Besides, that wasn't what I asked."

Edwin, staring out after the broad white track their ship painted on the dark surface of the ocean, replied: "Take the one who is kind. Kindness outlasts everything else."

Lisa nodded gravely and remained lost in thought.

Edwin turned to her and for a moment seemed to look her through and through.

"Lisa."

"Edwin."

And thus they remained, recognizing, knowing, and loving each other. They loved beyond words, beyond even the taking of each other, for in the sharing of this magic hour they were for one shattering moment too deeply moved by what they experienced.

Here was that perfection of which each had dreamed and sought at some time through life; that understanding tenderness, and unawakened passion, that blending of heaven and earth that men and women look for in each other and so rarely find.

At that instant they were one. They could have lived together into all eternity; they could have died together with equal happiness. They did not even kiss, but remained lost in each other, enveloped in such sweetness as neither had ever dared to hope for in mortal life.

And yet both knew in that moment that they were also lost to each other, for it was the enchanted hour, and as unreal and illusory as a dream. But, unlike a dream, neither of them would ever forget what they had seen in each other and what they had felt, the heights of human affection they had scaled in that moment of halted Time they had shared, the exquisite surge of love that filled their eyes with tears and their hearts with pain.

With the striking of the ship's bell reality would return.

Lisa said gently, "You're married, aren't you, Edwin?"

"Yes. For twenty years."

"Happily? Is she kind to you?"

"No."

"Why not, Edwin?"

"It is my fault. I never had confidence in myself. When I married her she was sweet and lovely. I didn't turn out the way she hoped. I'm nothing more than a clerk. It made her bitter."

"And is there no escape?"

"No. She needs me. I am that cherished daily reminder to her of her wasted life. I am all she has."

Lisa said, "Not to believe in oneself is a sin. We are punished for our sins."

Edwin replied, "Yes, I know," and looked at her again, but differently, for this was their final parting, his acknowledgment of the weakness that would forever send them different ways—two who had so nearly gained paradise.

He glanced at his watch. "Lisa," he said, "there is one minute left!" He put his hands on her arms, holding her away from him, looking into her eyes. "Close your mind and open your heart."

For the first time she appeared confused and unable to meet his glance. She asked, "What do you mean, Edwin?"

He held her for an instant longer to emphasize his words. "Look close to home, Lisa!" Then he let her go.

From for'ard, borne on the wind of the ship's thrust, came the sound of the striking of the bell. Lisa shuddered quietly, turned and walked away into the darkness.

For the fifth and last time on that strange voyage, the motionless hands of the clock marked the enchanted hour. Lisa Lisbon and Cy Hammer stood at the rail beneath the Veranda Grill, from which came the gleam of pink table lamps and the sound of music.

They were in the shadows, almost where she and Edwin had stood the night before. The deck beneath their feet was shuddering with the turning of the twin screws as the giant vessel raced through the night to keep her rendezvous with the tide in the early morning in New York.

Lisa was silent, for she was thinking that there were many kinds of enchantment, if one believed in them, but only one from which there was no escape in the end, no matter what the hour. And yet, in a sense, this queer, magic Timelessness that the shy little Englishman had evoked helped now to give her the courage to face what must be faced with this man at her side, and which might spell an end to all enchantment forevermore.

Hammer, who had been looking out at the wake as Edwin had the previous night, turned to her with his friendly, quizzical glance and asked, "What's the matter, Snooks? That little Britisher get under your skin?"

For the first time, Lisa wished to deny it, but she could not. One spoke only the truth when all clocks stood still. She replied, "Yes, in a way he did—unforgettably."

Hammer nodded. "It's funny where you find it, isn't it? I think perhaps he was the best of them all. But it won't work, will it?"

"No," Lisa replied.

"Badly hurt this time, kid?"

"No," Lisa replied again.

Hammer said, "That's good," without surprise, and Lisa was aware that he was not curious as to why, or when, or what had happened, but was only expressing deep relief that she was not in trouble.

Beneath their feet the deck quivered. All about her, non-Time quivered too. This had been Edwin's gift to her.

"Cy," she said, in a voice so filled with timidity that she hardly recognized it as her own, "will you answer me a question truthfully?"

"Sure, Snooks. What's on your mind?"

"How long have you been in love with me?"

Hammer glanced at his watch, and Lisa's heart seemed to stand still. What if he replied, "And what makes you think I am?"

The gesture with the watch reminded her of that of the Englishman twenty-four hours ago. And she thought how much like him Hammer was in kindness, gentleness, goodness, and steadfastness. How quickly he had understood and approved of her decision to take the miserable, difficult, abandoned girl, Melanie, to live with her. And yet she now knew there was something further that Hammer had. He was strong. When the ship's bell chimed, he would still be there. He would always be there.

Hammer had finished his calculations. He replied quietly, "Eleven years, seven months, two weeks, three days, fifty-eight minutes, and eighteen—no, sorry, nineteen—seconds, twenty now."

"Why didn't I ever know? How could I have been so blind?"

Hammer's warm, slow smile spread over his face, crinkling his eyes, which were full of tenderness. "Agents aren't supposed to have hearts."

"Or actresses either, if it comes to that," Lisa said almost bitterly in self-reproach. Then, "Cy, will you marry me?"

"If you ask me prettily," he replied lightly, but she saw that he was deeply moved, as indeed she was at having found her love at last, and with a sense of homecoming.

She leaned her forehead against his shoulder to press and feel the dear, comforting boniness of it. The ship's bell struck the end of the enchanted hour.

"Please marry me, Cy," Lisa Lisbon asked humbly. "I have been in love with you for a long time, I know now. Everything else is and was an illusion."

He took her hand in his and held it firmly and tightly clasped, and they remained standing there for a long time, shoulder to shoulder, looking out over the star-illuminated waters and thinking of the joy and comfort they would bring to each other in the days to come.

Lisa Lisbon and Edwin Reith-Jones encountered each other for the last time on the crowded, noisy pier the following morning. Lisa and Hammer had been eased through customs quickly, and they had collected Melanie. There had been no one at the pier to meet the child, though there was a telegram instructing her to proceed to Chicago. They were on their way out when Lisa saw the Englishman. He was standing, with his sparse luggage, by a window, gazing out forlornly over the midtown skyscrapers.

She pressed Hammer's arm, and then went over to Edwin, and it was characteristic of Hammer that he only nodded understandingly and then went on with Melanie to await her at the exit.

Lisa said, "Good-by, Turnip."

Edwin blushed crimson, reached for his hat, found he was not wearing it, and finally managed to take the hand she extended. "Good-by, Miss Lisbon—Lisa."

She said, "You're unhappy. You shouldn't be. You've got Sir Malcolm Gordien eating out of your hand."

He replied bleakly, "It was expected of me. It's what I was sent for."

Lisa continued, "You saved a life and a soul; you've spoken up for your country before important people and done it a service; you have helped me to find a happiness that might have passed me by. Cy Hammer and I are going to be married."

"Oh, splendid!" Edwin said, and then repeated, "Splendid." Yet the bleakness did not leave his countenance, and beneath Lisa's questioning gaze he said finally, "What will happen to me? I've stolen five hours and done things in them I've never done before."

"What did you do with the final hour?" Lisa asked.

"I prayed," Edwin Reith-Jones replied, and the girl nodded almost as though this was what she had expected him to say.

She said, "It is true. You live between Time on five borrowed hours. You will have to give them back."

"Yes, but how?"

Lisa smiled. "On the return journey. They'll be taken from you again, willy-nilly. There's never anything for free. You pay or give back."

"But what will I be like afterwards?"

"The same good, sweet, gallant, greathearted gentleman you have always been. But you will probably never make love to another girl or beard another lion."

"And is that all that will remain?"

"No," Lisa said gently. "There will be dear and tender memories. This is all we ever really steal from Time. God bless you, Edwin."

She reached over and kissed him, then turned and walked away to where Cy Hammer, Melanie, and reality were waiting for her.

Edwin Reith-Jones remained standing there and watched her go, but the expression in his pale eyes and on his unobtrusive countenance was no longer either bleak or forlorn.

The Silent Hostages

In the spring of 1955 the United States exploded an atomic bomb at the Nevada proving grounds, designed to test its effect upon a human habitation, and called it Operation Teapot.

"The Silent Hostages" was a story born out of a night of controlled horror that I spent in Las Vegas, ninety miles from the explosion. I was visiting Las Vegas in the course of a ten-thousand-mile trip around the United States, a kind of "rediscovering America" assignment for *Reader's Digest*.

Adela Rogers St. Johns had come from Los Angeles to join me there and we were spending the evening with friends of ours, Ray and Gwen Bolger. Ray was dancing in the show of one of the big hotels and gambling casinos there and after he had finished his last performance we went to the bar while he had some food and then retired to his room to sit up and talk and wait out the half-hour to dawn when the explosion, some ninety miles away, was scheduled to take place. For at the zero hour we had been promised the flash that would light up the heavens followed by the mushroom cloud climbing into the sky, the twentieth-century symbol of the ultimate idiocy of mankind.

That night remains with me today as vividly as then. Las Vegas is a curious place. Depending upon your sophistication or your point of view, it is either appallingly naïve or equally appallingly wicked. That night, for instance, Adela and I saw two or three shows that were irreproachable for entertainment and good taste. And later on in the aforementioned bar where Bolger was taking on some much needed nourishment, the last hour was horrid and depressing.

The entertainment was supplied by a band and a band leader, the latter being a most unsavory and unappetizing specimen. The songs he sang were suggestive and the movements of his body as he sang them were revolting. Nothing can be quite as tiresome and disgusting as inept and reiterated pornographic performance. The place appeared to be

374

filled with amorous drunks. The whole smoky, noisy room seemed to be centered around one great, dirty leer.

And one knew that less than a hundred miles away men were preparing to tamper once more with one of the secrets of the Universe. Small wonder that one had thoughts of Sodom and Gomorrah and what had happened there. I remember a remark made by Gwen Bolger as we talked after escaping from the bar. "Dear God, I hope they know what they are doing."

It was odd, or perhaps not so odd, that all of us for that half-hour experienced a sense of guilt and a sense of doom.

What we felt we all wanted after that hour spent in that cesspool of a bar was a bath with plenty of hot water and soap, but this was not practical at the moment and, besides, we were waiting for them to detonate that atomic bomb.

Gwen Bolger had voiced the fears in every heart each time we or the Russians set off one of those things in experiment. "Dear God, I hope they know what they are doing." If one of those things went wrong and set up a chain reaction, it might mean wiping humans off the face of the earth. And when they got those things going *right*, we were faced with the same prospect. And at that moment we were not sure but that perhaps all of us might not have wanted a bit of wiping. We had taken no part in that dirty performance in the bar, nor had we liked it, yet we were the brothers and sisters of those who had.

Over the radio we listened to the sands of time running out and the moment of the explosion drawing nearer. The sense of impending catastrophe was increased. The ninety miles intervening between us and what was about to happen seemed suddenly infinitesimal. It appeared that that *thing* was aimed at us. We reflected, each silently and to himself, I am sure, upon our past lives and I suppose made a quick catalogue of major sins. One had tried to live life according to some rules or concepts of ethics and morality and one realized that one had not always succeeded. One realized that one was not in a position to peg any rocks at the poor clowns still besotted in the bar; if the time was really at hand when the Creator was to tire of His puppets, nobody would be excused.

These were morbid thoughts, but it was also a morbid moment, and we were writers and professional people.

When the final countdown started we went outside, where dawn had begun to overtake the night, and looked toward the north. A great glare lit up the horizon. We heard no thunder, for the wind must have blown the noise in another direction, but shortly after, the horrid cloud appeared.

We looked at one another with a kind of sheepish relief; we were still there. We kissed one another good night with more than usual tenderness and went off to our respective hotels. I remember feeling a little sick as I drove back. When I looked over my shoulder, the mushroom cloud seemed to be coming nearer.

The next day Adela and I drove to Los Angeles, and while we were crossing the desert, flat and endless with only an occasional building of adobe or a distant water tower to break the monotony, I thought of the idea for "The Silent Hostages" and told it to Adela. Two professional writers in a car and on the spot, so to speak, and the story didn't take long to build and complete itself, though the final twist I only thought of after I returned to Liechtenstein and sat down to write it.

I should add that this story doesn't stem from the morbidity of our thoughts the night before, but rather from the nature of the experiment the Atomic Energy authorities had conducted. Of course had I not been so close, it might not have occurred to me.

You may or may not remember what the nature of that experiment was. If not, I shan't remind you, as I don't want to spoil the story for you.

T HE car carrying the two escaped killers, Wylie Rickman and Art Hoser, nosed carefully into the unidentified desert town, its headlights burning blindingly. It was that darkest hour before dawn of a moonless, starlit night.

Rickman driving, small, dapper, with cold, saurian eyes and bloodless mouth, judged it to be Parumph in lower Nevada. Somehow they had missed the Fairbank Ranch in the dark.

Ever since they had murdered their three hostages, the woman and her twins, and shot their way out of Beatty, northwest of Yucca Flat, they had been attempting to find their way southwest toward the Mexican border, twisting and turning, driving without lights on back roads and wagon trails, avoiding the glow of towns, fighting the panic of the hunted.

A few hours back they had listened to a news broadcast that caused them to change their plans and begin searching for a settlement where the alarm might not yet have reached. They desperately needed fresh hostages.

Now they approached carefully a brief main street between the small cluster of buildings that mushroomed abruptly out of the desert. They were jumpy, nervous, half drugged by fatigue, and deadly dangerous.

Fat Art Hoser, who had needlessly killed the policeman the day after they had escaped from the penitentiary at Carson City, had turned to a vengeful jelly of cowardice, for he knew what the police did to cop killers. Rickman was even more vicious, for he murdered in cold blood and was prepared to sacrifice a human life for every extended hour of his own if necessary. He was aware that if daylight found them without a shield of living flesh, they were finished.

The town was apparently an early riser, for many of the buildings were blazing with lights. But this was not surprising. Life in desert communities frequently began before sunup.

Caught in their headlights, the tall saguaros cacti, which with the stunted greasewood shrubs and sagebrush grew right to the edge of the town, pointed aloft like warning fingers. But as yet there seemed to be no one abroad in the streets.

They passed the usual filling station on the outskirts. Rickman drove cautiously, his Magnum .38 on the seat at his left side. Two rifles and a sub-machine gun were between his partner and himself. Hoser had a double-barreled shotgun resting on his lap crossing his fat legs and beer belly.

A sedan with its engine running was standing by the pumps. Inside they spotted the white-overalled attendant with another man, apparently making change. It reminded Hoser of the gas-station jockey, no more than a kid, they had killed and robbed near Tonopah. Rickman thought only of the hostage he wanted. A woman, preferably with another kid or kids.

As they moved by, Rickman sought to assess the buildings of the town. There seemed to be a two-story brick hotel, a general store, some shops, a livery stable, several frame dwellings, a café, the usual adobe buildings, and, at the end of town, a small power station with what appeared to be a tall radio mast next to it.

A lounger was apparently asleep on the porch of the hotel, chair leaned back, shovel-shaped Stetson tilted over his eyes. A ranch wagon was parked in front of it and a rancher sat at the wheel. Hoser nervously moved the shotgun. Rickman picked up his gun and said savagely, "You shoot again before I tell you to and you'll get this across the bridge of your nose."

They drove quickly by. The rancher did not even bother to turn his head. It was Hoser's nervous and wanton shooting of a policeman after they had escaped from the prison that had started the hue and cry at their heels prematurely.

Glimpsed through a grimy window, the café appeared to be filled, with the counterman at his griddle and the waitress serving coffee across the bar. A jukebox bawled from the restaurant. An asphalt-carrying tank truck and a big freighter with trailer were drawn up in front, their drivers apparently breakfasting inside.

As they drove on, voices emerged from several of the houses where radios had been turned on by early risers. In a near-by house a telephone was ringing and there was a thumping noise of some kind of pump or gasoline engine. A window a few houses down showed a family seated at early breakfast. It seemed as though only the first rays of the sun were wanted to send the inhabitants of the town spilling out onto the streets and about their business.

They passed a frame house with a big sedan parked in front and the blinds up, revealing the occupants. A man in trousers and shirt with suspenders hanging down was shaving himself in front of a cabinet mirror. In the kitchen, a woman in an apron was bending over a mixing bowl. There was no one in the living room, from which the radio was playing loudly, but in an adjoining bedroom they snatched a view of a cot with a girl of five or six asleep on it and a crib in which there was a baby.

Rickman's thin mouth curled with satisfaction. This was a prize he had not expected. With the baby they might even reach the border. And there were keys, he noted, in the ignition switch of the sedan. The two-tone maroon and cream car they had taken from the salesman they had kidnaped and shot between Tonopah and Goldfield was marked.

Hours before, they had sat in the vehicle, lights and motor shut off, and, concealed by a fold in the foothills miles from anywhere, listened to a news round-up from Las Vegas, which was largely devoted to the harrowing story of the murder trail of the two escaped convicts.

Without emotion, coldly and clinically, Rickman had listened to the list of their killings: the guard at the penitentiary, the policeman at Wilson's Gulch, the boy in the gas station at Tonopah, the salesman at Goldfield, and finally the woman and two children at Beatty, where they had snatched them.

And a mile away, a man sitting in a shack by a gate of barbed wire, sick and clammy, listened to the same broadcast over a portable radio, the beads of sweat running from his cheeks and temples as the announcer detailed:

"As the chase spread out down the highway from Beatty, with the bandits firing from their car, police did not dare to shoot for fear of hitting Mrs. Nellie Bassett and her twins, Tina and Joey, aged seven, kidnaped as hostages an hour earlier by the fleeing pair.

"Apparently when police braving the fire attempted to force the fleeing car off the road, Rickman, Hoser, or both shot the mother and two children, threw the bodies from the car, and escaped as the horrified pursuit ground to a halt. The children were dead, but Nellie Bassett was still alive and was rushed to the hospital in critical condition. . . ."

The man in the shack fought and lost his battle between duty and instinct, switched off his portable, entered his car, and drove off to the north. The sound of his motor and the glow of his headlights caused the two killers to finger their weapons apprehensively, until the noise and the beams of the headlight faded in the distance. Then they had listened to the details of the tri-state police dragnet set for them.

"We gotta get us another hostage. The Fairbanks Ranch ought to be where that car came from. There'd be women there."

Driving blacked out, they crept to the spot from whence the vanished car appeared to have come. The rutty road continued on the other side of the wire fence, which to Rickman denoted the ranch he sought. The gate was open and they drove through past the shack and large property-posting sign. By star glow he was able to read the big letters "KEEP OUT!" He did not want to show the light necessary to read the rest.

Hoser said, "You sure you know what you're doin'?" and then added, "I'm getting sick of all this killing."

Rickman reached over and hit him on the cheekbone with the barrel of his .38. The fat man stared down at the blood dripping onto his hand and said nothing further. He was afraid of Rickman. They had floundered in the darkness for several hours, but found no ranch. Then, shortly before five the lights on the horizon had announced the presence of the town in which they now found themselves.

Rickman drew up behind the parked sedan. "Shift the stuff into the car ahead and start her up," he ordered Hoser. "When she's running, come in and grab the kids. I'll take care of the other two. . . ." He slid out from under the wheel with a movement that was almost obscenely sinuous, shifted the heavy .38 to his right hand, and ran into the frame house.

From the entrance inside the unlocked door he could see both the man shaving and at the back the woman at her kitchen table. He threw his gun down on the former saying, "Don't anybody move. This is a snatch. Stay where you are. Do as I say and nobody's going to get hurt." Then he called to the woman, "You in the kitchen; if you open your yap, I let your husband have it."

The man in the bathroom froze obediently, motionless, his razor at the side of his cheek. The gunman could see his own face reflected over his victim's shoulder in the mirror. The woman, apparently terrorized, did not stir or utter a sound.

In the next room the radio blatted loudly. Rickman did not listen to it but was satisfied it provided cover. Seconds ticked by. Hoser should have had the rifles, guns, ammunition, and their small stock of food transferred to the other car by now. The gunman heard the starter whir, then the sound of the engine catching and turning over with a steady beat. He waited until he heard Hoser's footstep on the threshold and then pulled the trigger, shooting the man through the back on the left side.

Hoser rushed in howling, "For God's sake, you crazy fool! Are you killing again? You'll have the whole town on us. . . ."

For once Rickman did not turn on his partner, but stood with the already recocked pistol staring blankly at the round hole that had appeared in the back of the man's shirt in the region of his heart. The fabric of the garment was smoking slightly, but the man, oblivious to the shock of the bullet or the fact that he should be dead, remained standing.

Rickman bawled at Hoser, "Grab the two kids in the bedroom!" Then he raised the heavy gun, aimed it at the back of the man's head, fired twice, and endured the shock of seeing his own pale and deadly image vanish as the cabinet shaving mirror shattered under the impact of the slugs.

With two holes through his head, the man, the razor still grotesquely held at the side of his cheek, yet refused to fall and die like the others had.

With a cry of rage Rickman leaped forward and brought the gun barrel down on the fellow's skull, which split like a melon into a hundred pieces just as Hoser came in from the bedroom calling, "Hey! These ain't no kids. These are dolls. What's going on here?" In one hand he held the baby made of bisque, its blue china eyes open and staring innocently. With the other he dragged the mannequin of a five-year-old girl with dark chestnut curls.

Rickman's nerve broke. He yelled, "What the hell is this, a trap?" Berserk, he pulled over the body of the headless dummy by the broken mirror, kicked it, then knocked down the lifelike wax figure of the woman in the kitchen, swearing incoherently. Then, ignoring the shaking Hoser, he dashed through the door pulling a heavy automatic from a shoulder holster as he did so.

But there was no police-patrol car or posse of armed citizens converging upon the house. The streets were still empty. It was beginning to grow light. From the house across the street the telephone kept ringing.

Down the block at the filling station the customer and the attendant were still immobile at the cash register. The lounger slept on undisturbed tipped back in his chair on the hotel porch. None of the figures in the Café and Eatery had stirred. In the near-by station wagon the rancher remained unmoved at the wheel.

Rickman, his guns held before him, ran over, yanked the door open, and pulled at the rancher's arm. The wax figure obediently slipped out from under the wheel and fell to the ground.

The gunman suddenly became appallingly aware that for all the noise that filled the village street there was not the sound of any human voice that did not come from a radio, or a single living thing to be seen or heard. Somehow they had blundered into a settlement populated solely by department-store dummies. And still the whole truth did not dawn.

He went back to the charnel house of the murdered waxworks, where he came upon Art Hoser kneeling in the living room before the radio, his whole person quivering abjectly from his buttocks to his belly, chin and lips, the sweat pouring off him in rivulets.

He did not even look up as Rickman came in but stared transfixed at the instrument that he seemed to be praying to as a kind of animate responsible being, mumbling, "No, no! Please! You got to wait!"

Rickman, clutching the two guns that had decided so much for him but that would never conclude anything again, focused his attention on the radio as the announcer was saying tensely:

"Everything is in readiness now. The tanks are in position three miles from ground zero: the Civil Defense workers are in their places on Media Hill. And in just exactly one minute from now, Survival City, or Doomtown, as the newspapermen have called it, the guinea-pig village peopled solely with dummies distributed throughout in human attitudes of daily life, will be subjected to the disintegrative force of an Atom blast twice that which leveled Hiroshima. . . . Now I will pick up the time signals to zero hour. Twenty seconds . . . nineteen . . . eighteen . . . seventeen . . ."

Rickman ran screaming into the empty street, where he could still hear the telephone ringing in the house across the way. "No, no!" he bawled. "Hey! Wait a minute! Do you hear me? You can't! We're here. For God's sake, wait!"

The last thing he saw was the steel skeleton of what he had thought was a radio mast. But now, outlined against the dawn a dark, torpedo-shaped package hung from the five-hundred-foot tower top. And the last thing he heard was the unison chant from all the live radios in all the dead, dummy-filled houses: "Five seconds . . . four . . . three . . . two . . . one . . ."

A little while later, the guard who that same morning had deserted his post at the No. 3 Desert Gate of the Restricted Area between Beatty and Mercury, returned alone, a half-hour before his relief was due.

His name was Joseph Bassett and he was the husband of Nellie Bassett and father of the twins Tina and Joey. He had managed to reach the bedside of his wife and hold her in his arms a scant twenty minutes before she died. Dazed by the completion of the tragedy, he had returned to his duty from force of habit.

Still in a state of shock, he could not cope with the ominous mystery of the tire tracks, west to east, that crossed his post and, entering through the open gate, went straight as an arrow eastward toward where the brown mushroom cloud of the recent explosion had begun to lose its shape and drift with the wind.

Someone had entered during his absence. He stood staring down uneasily at the tracks, wondering who it had been, what had happened to him and what it might portend for him—if ever it came that someone had entered there during his absence.

Shut Up, Little Dog

Of all the title changes through which I have suffered with my dearly beloved *Saturday Evening Post*, the one I found most painful was the switch on this next story from "Shut Up Little Dog!" to "The American Ingredient." Perhaps it was a bid on the part of the editors to revive memories of the previous story about the same character which they called "The Secret Ingredient," but to me it sounded flat and uninteresting. "Shut Up Little Dog" was my idea of the way a literal-minded Frenchman might translate that wonderful native American dish known as the hush puppy.

That character, of course, is our friend whom I hope you have learned to like, M. Armand Bonneval, of the Auberge château Loiret on the Loire.

M. Bonneval, in his first experiment with cats and catnip, had won many friends, and so I thought I would try him again. I therefore wrote a second story entitled "The Murderer of M. Bonneval," which had to do with the plight in which the little chef found himself when a visitor to his *auberge* who appeared to be a dangerous and wanted criminal also turned out to be a first-class gourmet and worshiper of the culinary art. This story was rejected out of hand by the *Saturday Evening Post*, which had published the first one.

I cite this incident neither in hurt nor in anger at this decision of the editors. "The Murderer of M. Bonneval" was just not as good a story as "The Secret Ingredient," and therefore they were quite justified in turning it down. For the prices they were paying me, they had a right to ask for nothing less than the best.

The story, I might add, wasn't all that bad, for it was published with considerable success in Great Britain. To illustrate another of the hazards of free-lance writing, as the original character, M. Bonneval, had appeared in the *Post* first, my agent could not offer the story to any other magazine, nor would any other magazine have touched it. Bonneval was considered a *Post* character. Therefore that story for the United States was a dead loss, a fact not taken into account or recognized by the Bureau of Internal Revenue. A merchant or manufacturer with unsold stock on his shelves may deduct value of same at the end of the year. A writer may not.

Nevertheless, in the writing profession it doesn't do to let oneself become discouraged; and, besides, the rejection made me determined to sell the *Post* another Bonneval story.

In my introduction to "The Silent Hostage" I made mention of my ten-thousand-mile trip around the United States in 1955 on a "rediscovering America" tour for *Reader's Digest*. The idea for this story stems from that trip.

My itinerary took me through the capital of the noble and elongated state of Florida, where signs almost every block informed me that I was now in the home of the famous Tallahassee Hush Puppy—Try One! I did. In fact I became practically an addict during the deep South portion of my tour. And this set me to wondering what M. Armand Bonneval would both say and feel when confronted with this strange *gâteau frite*.

From there my thoughts went awandering on to the general subject of food and the fact that while there was a good deal of hoo-ha on the subject of French cooking, there are a number of American dishes and foods and places where one can get them superbly prepared which are unsurpassed. In fact, much of my trip around the United States was a constant gastronomic surprise, and the further I went and the more native and indigenous dishes I sampled, the more I felt that M. Bonneval, as an honest man and a culinary artist, would likewise appreciate these goodies and give them full marks in any kitchen.

From there it is not difficult to follow a line of fictional reasoning: what would happen if M. Bonneval were called upon to prepare a dinner for a famous French club of gourmets and elected to produce a dinner of American dishes? Having both lived and traveled in France for a time, I thought I knew.

To paraphrase the *Post* title editors, what was missing in this mélange of thoughts and ideas was "the final ingredient"—that is to say, that ingredient which brings about the climax and sews up the story neatly and satisfactorily to an unexpected conclusion.

This final ingredient was finally supplied unconsciously by one of the very *Post* editors who had been instrumental in bouncing my second Bonneval story—Stuart Rose. For one day, I fell to thinking about Stu who was a friend of long standing as well as my editor, and about his hobby or recreation, which was fox hunting. He was one of the few Americans—in fact the only one—I ever knew who followed the hounds and made it a part of his life. He had a farm in Pennsylvania outside Philadelphia, kept his own horses, and was a member of a Pennsylvania hunt.

Rose, hunt, hounds, hush puppies—and there was the final ingredient and I could devote myself to setting down on paper the manner in which my M. Armand Bonneval, of whom by this time I was more than a little fond, was able to win the coveted rosette of the *Légion d'honneur*.

I F THERE is one thing longed for by the average honest middle-class Frenchman even more than a competence for his old age, it is to wear the rosette of the *Légion d'honneur*.

By virtue of his diligence and superb mastery of his art plus the caution and thrift of Madame, his faithful partner through life, M. Armand Bonneval, Chef of the Cordon Bleu and Honorary Member of the Académie Culinaire of France, retired, and now owner of the Auberge Château Loiret, was reasonably well secured for his declining years.

The supreme decoration of France, however, had eluded him. Nor was his position in such a modest village as Loiret on the placid Loire, even though it was on the trail of the tourists visiting the *châteaux* in the summer, likely to bring him the prominence that might result in such a coveted reward.

But one could always hope, and each time the stout and graying little chef read of the cross and rosette having been bestowed upon some scientist or man of letters, he would sigh, not with envy, but with longing.

And Mme. Bonneval, as rotund as he, clad in honest cashier's black, seated at her accounts in her tiny office off the foyer of the *auberge*, would comfort him with, "It is you who deserve it if any-one does."

"It is for your sake even more than mine," Bonneval once said, glancing down at his immaculate white chef's jacket almost as though the rosette were already looming in his buttonhole. "When we went for a promenade and the decoration was admired, everyone would look to see this paragon of a wife who had assisted her husband to such eminence."

"Ah, Armand. I do not need any ribbon to convince me of your worth!"

Yet the yearning remained, even after the extraordinary piece of good fortune of their holiday trip to the United States. This was the gift of an impetuous Texas oil millionaire steered to the *auberge* by the famous Guide Michelin's rating of three crossed spoons and forks and two stars. After a delicious dinner he fell into conversation with the little chef.

"Boy, that was a mighty tasty meal, I don't mind telling you. But we got some mighty fine cookin' back home, too. You ever eat barbecued spareribs?"

Bonneval indicated politely that he had not.

"What? Don't tell me you never had a real southern fish fry with hush puppies, or hot jowl with collard greens and potlikker?"

Baffled, Bonneval shook his head.

"Why, Monsoor," cried the Texan, "you jes' ain't never lived. You and Madame gotta come over and be my guests. We got the finest cookin' in the world in the U.S.A."

Have you ever encountered a Texas oil millionaire suffering from an aggravated fit of hospitality? They have not only the necessary persuasiveness but also the cash. The result was that when M. and Mme. Bonneval closed the *auberge* as they always did from January to April, they embarked at the expense of the millionaire upon a coast-to-coast gastronomic tour of the United States.

And the interesting part was that M. Bonneval discovered that the Texan was quite right. For the chef was too great an artist himself with the skillet and saucepan to be a chauvinist. He greeted and acknowledged perfection where he encountered it. And he was enthralled by some of the recipes and dishes he discovered in America.

However, upon their return, life resumed its normal tenor and his ambition to achieve the final honor to crown his career remained strong.

Now, there is this about an *auberge* honestly conducted and starred by Michelin: namely, that you serve many hundreds of people in a month; they arrive; they order; they consume; they call for the bill and depart, and you do not know whom you have entertained, satisfied, or even charmed.

One day a letter arrived at the *auberge* out of the blue that sent Bonneval and Madame into an absolute hysteria of excitement and happiness.

It was on the stationery of the Circle Intimes des Grandes Gourmets de France—in other words, that sacrosanct inner circle of all the gastronomic organizations of the country, those supreme knights of the aesophagus and the gizzard, formed of the most sensitive and exclusive over-eaters of a nation devoted to defying indigestion on many fronts.

The missive read in part:

As you may know, this club tenders an annual banquet to His Excellency the President of France and for which each year a French chef of outstanding accomplishment is selected to compose the menu and cook the dinner.

Not long ago, the Duc de C. happened to dine at your *auberge* while en route. A member of this club, he has professed himself an admirer of your art, and has forwarded such an unstinted and glowing report of your accomplishments, and such is his influence in our club, that you have been unanimously nominated for the post of Chef du Cercle for this year's dinner.

Write us that you accept, *cher* Maître Bonneval, and send us at once your menu and choice of dishes so that it may be printed and given to the press in advance of the banquet, which is next month. You are of course aware that the entire responsibility for the dinner will be yours, and once you have made your choice, there is none can interfere in or alter your decisions.

M. and Mme. Bonneval read and reread this eloquent letter with tears streaming down their faces and then embraced one another, for the selection as Chef du Cercle for the annual banquet ten-

dered to the President and a few members of the Corps Diploma-
tique almost automatically carried with it the coveted award of the
cross of the *Légion d'honneur.*

"My dear husband, I am so happy for you," Mme. Bonneval
wept. "Now at last your true genius has been recognized."

"Oh, would that I were indeed worthy," cried Bonneval in a
seizure of becoming modesty, "and could somehow give something
extra in return for this great honor that has come to me."

And then, like a bolt of lightning from the sky, compounded in
part from his deep sense of gratitude and the memory of his recent
visit to the vast and fruitful land across the sea, an idea struck M.
Bonneval. The idea embraced how he might be the instrument to
perform a good work, earn his decoration, and at the same time
indicate his gratitude to the generous host from Dallas who had
made it possible for him to learn the culinary secrets of the Texans
with their chilies and enchiladas, the Alabamans with their *fritures,*
the New Englanders with their soups and dumplings, the Idahoans
who produced a fabulous *pomme de terre,* the Californians who
roasted meat in a charcoal pit.

"*Maman!*" he shouted to his spouse, who was already seeing the
receipts in the black japanned cash box doubled once her husband
wore the red rosette. "Do you know what I shall do? I shall combine
all that I have learned on our recent trip and cook a United States
dinner for the President of France, thus proving my skill and
originality as well as cementing Franco-American relations. Will
this not constitute a sensation?"

"Perhaps it might be wiser . . ." began Mme. Bonneval, but then
concluded, "Prepared by you, I am sure that it will be a most wonderful repast." Had the chef not been so gripped by excitement and
pleased with his marvelous notion, he would have seen that her
reply was slightly less than enthusiastic. Often women have a fatal
intuition. . . .

Shortly after, M. Bonneval, having accepted the invitation, forwarded to the Cercle his menu, consisting of ten courses and demi-
courses spreading from New England to the Mexican border,
bounded on the east by the Atlantic and on the west by the Pacific.

A secretary acknowledged receipt of this novel and interesting bill of fare and confirmed June 15 as the date at the Ritz in Paris. He noted also that although this was likewise the occasion of the annual dinner at the same hotel of the Chantilly Hunt Club, an organization devoted to the chase and supported by wealthy British and American sportsmen currently residing in the charming area of Chantilly, there would be no interference. The Ritz would provide M. Bonneval with his own kitchen and all the assistance he needed.

And in due course, also, there appeared at the Auberge Château Loiret a scruffy-looking reporter from a Paris paper with dirty cuffs and even dirtier fingernails. In France it is not unusual for representatives of the press to appear in less than immaculate condition. Hence, M. Bonneval was neither on his guard nor, in his innocence of the world, aware that this specimen was filled with the gall, wormwood, and general overflow of malevolence characteristic of his affiliations.

The fellow named his paper, which meant nothing to M. Bonneval, whose reading was confined chiefly to a sheet giving intimate details of the love and home life of bicycle-race riders. The reporter then said, "I have seen the menu you have presented for the annual capitalistic orgy of . . . that is to say, the *Fêtes des Gourmets* of the Cercle, and wish an interview."

"But of course, *mon vieux*," replied the unsuspecting Bonneval. "Ask me what you wish to know and all shall be made clear."

"This idea of presenting North American dishes . . ."

"Ah yes. An American millionaire from the famous state of Fort Dallas, in the country of Texas, invited me there. In gratitude to him and this great nation that is aiding us so nobly in combatting the evils of communism, I shall cook United States."

The reporter coughed, produced a crumpled cigarette from a soiled packet, extracted a frayed vesta, and lit it. Then, consulting Bonneval's menu from a mimeographed sheet, he asked, "This strange item here in the middle of the repast called the 'hush puppy' —what is that?"

"Oh, oh! The hush puppy! This is a most famous and extraordinary food of the inhabitants of the city of Florida in Tallahassee where I have visited."

"Indeed. How, for instance, would you translate this dish?"

M. Bonneval reflected. "To be exact," he replied, "it would be called *'tais toi, petit chien.'* Is not that adorable?"

"Quite," agreed the reporter. "But what is it and how did it come by this astonishing name?"

"Ah, ah!" said the delighted Bonneval, "well may you ask. It is the most touching of stories. It is a dough comprised of white maize flour, baking powder, salt, milk, water, and a large chopped onion and fried in the fat devoted to a *friture* of native fishes. . . ."

"Yes, yes, but the origin of the name," pressed the reporter.

"I was arriving at this," said M. Bonneval. "It is the custom in the southland after the hunt or the fishing to gather about the camp-fire for a fish fry. There the hunters relate exaggerated tales to themselves and their faithful Negro retainers with their dogs of the hound variety who sit around the outer edge of the firelit circle of the camp where the evening meal is cooking.

"The odor of the food frequently excites the younger animals in charge of the darkies, causing them to make the disturbance with barks and whines. Then one of the hunters detaches a piece of this marvelous maize-and-onion cake fried in the fish fat and hurls it at the animal, saying softly, 'Hush, puppy. Be quiet, little one!' The satisfaction of this food, it is said, is miraculous, and once a beast has engulfed a portion of it, no further sound emerges from him and thus the evening's entertainment may proceed without further disturbance. Is this not a beautiful custom?"

"Quite," said the reporter and, having pumped M. Bonneval a little more, permitted the friendly little chef to treat him to a meal and a bottle of wine and then departed for Paris.

The storm broke three days later.

It began of course in the Communist paper with a story head-lined: "U.S. INSULT TO FRANCE! GESTURE OF CONTEMPT! NATIVE CHEF BRIBED TO GIVE FRENCH PRESIDENT MIXTURE FED TO DOGS OF NEGRO SLAVES IN FLORIDA CONCENTRATION CAMP!

The Radical Socialists, fearful that the Communists had latched on to something this time, took it up, as did the parties of the Center and the Right.

The menu that had been composed by M. Bonneval for the Cercle and that had previously been ignored by the press was now published in every newspaper with stinging comments and editorials reflecting all political and cultural shades and opinions.

FRENCH CHIEF OF STATE TO DINE ON DOG BISCUITS,

trumpeted one. DISHES OF THE SAVAGE INDIANS OF THE MOUNTAINS OF TEXAS FOR FRANCE'S PRESIDENT, headlined another. HAS BONNEVAL BEEN BOUGHT? asked a third. "Can it then indeed be true," inquired a fourth, "that it is seriously proposed at the annual banquet of the sacrosanct Cercle to compel the elected head of the French Nation to consume a drugged cake used to calm hysterical hounds belonging to the uncivilized inhabitants of a still barbarous portion of the United States?"

The De Gaullists took the nationalistic line and demanded to know since when had the classic French cuisine not been good enough for Frenchmen. The Socialists wrote of further evidence of expanding American imperialism and interference with the internal affairs of France.

Bonneval was denounced as a traitor in the Assembly, the first time the members of that body apparently agreed on anything; there were repercussions at the Quai D'Orsay and the ripples eventually reached the State Department in Washington, causing a query to be cabled to the American Ambassador in Paris.

Poor Bonneval found himself plunged into a sheer hell of notoriety. He was badgered by the press. Hordes of reporters descended upon peaceful Loiret. He was the recipient of petitions and blackguarding mail and was subjected to abuse and pressure of every kind.

The Cercle itself, consisting for the most part of aristocrats and professional people disinterested in politics, took a strong line and issued a statement to the effect that the banquet was traditional and once the chef was selected, the entire responsibility for the menu remained with him. The club would under no circumstances interfere.

But this left Bonneval alone to weather the tempest, buffeted hither and thither. He was no reed, however, but a man of courage and considerable stubbornness. He knew himself and his intentions to have been honorable, the dishes superb; he was a Frenchman and independent and he refused to budge.

And of course as the pressure and fury redoubled, all hope of his *Légion d'honneur* faded, as the President would not dare award it under the circumstances. Indeed, the police claimed to have discovered a plot to bomb the hotel.

The harassed chef had one silent rooter in the person of the American Ambassador, a cultured and patient man who was already fed to the teeth with the dangerous antics of French politicians in international affairs and who diplomatically refrained from taking any part in this controversy. But privately he remarked to his wife, "By George, the little fellow has courage. If he serves that dinner I'll see that he gets a decoration from the U.S.A. if it's the last thing I do."

But the unhappy affair was taking its toll. With all the concentrated venom of the America-haters turned against him, the unfortunate chef began to lose some of his comfortable rotundity. Lack of sleep and worry drained the cheerful stove-side red from his face.

But the dignity of M. Bonneval under these attacks was something splendid to see as he stood firm on his decision to present the best dishes of France's old friend and ally from across the sea. His physical as well as moral courage was an example, so much so that a few more daring souls even began to speak up in defense of his rights.

And then, suddenly and inexplicably M. Bonneval yielded.

At first the news was received with astonishment and skepticism until it proved to be true, confirmed by the Cercle. The pressures had apparently been too much for Bonneval to bear, and, giving in, he had presented a substitute menu in honest French for the President's banquet.

Most saddened by this news was the American Ambassador,

so much so that he almost canceled his acceptance to the invitation to the dinner, but on second thought and the persuasion of his wife, he reconsidered.

The Communists crowed; the De Gaullists exulted; the Socialists pointed with pride. And only two people really knew what final straw had proven too much for the back of this stout little culinary camel. It had been none other than Mme. Bonneval.

Unable any longer to bear the spectacle of her gallant husband withering away before her eyes, she had said to him a week before the date of the affair, "Armand, I beg of you. Do what they wish. You cannot hold out against all of France."

"Never! No one may dictate what I, Armand Bonneval, shall cook!"

"Armand, my husband, do this for me. I cannot bear these attacks any longer. I shall have a breakdown."

Bonneval regarded his wife long and fondly. "There is no power on earth could make me give in but you," he said finally.

"Oh, Armand! Do you promise?" Madame was deeply touched, for she knew that never had a greater compliment been paid her.

"Very well, then. I promise."

"Ah! I am so happy. See, I did it only for you. Now you will receive your *Légion d'honneur*. In the end you would have regretted having lost it, besides making yourself ill."

"Wretched woman, what have you done?" cried Bonneval. "I should never have yielded for myself. Give me back my promise."

But this Madame refused to do, insisting it was true that the strain was too much for her, and in the end Bonneval went into the little office and mused upon the devious ways of women. Then, suddenly, with a curiously intense expression on his countenance, and removing his chef's toque and napkin for greater freedom of thought, he penned the substitute menu and sent it off to Paris. I have a copy of it before me and reproduce it as it appeared in all the French newspapers:

Bouillabaisse des Palourdes de Normandie à la Crème
Saumon de Loire Diable sous Cendre, Sauce d'Enfer

Entrailles de Jeune Porc à la Bama
Feuilles de Navets au Lard,
Quenelles de Maize Blanc au Pays Fleuri
Poulet de Bresse, Terre Marie
Pommes de Terres de Sénégal douce sucié.

Soufflé Indienne
Salade Rouge de Avocado

Gâteau de Courge

You have no doubt read in your news magazines of the tremendous success of the banquet of the Cercle and the cheers that echoed for the great chef who cooked it. But you will not know about the strange affair of the disturbance next door, plus the astonishing behavior of the American Ambassador.

The matter of the interference from the adjoining banquet hall will remain your secret and mine when I have revealed it, but there were several in the vicinity of the American Ambassador when he seemed to be in the grip of an unfortunate seizure of near apoplexy who declared that his difficulty appeared to be, as the dinner progressed, to keep from laughing himself to death.

But first we should glance backstage to the special kitchen of the Ritz where guest chef Armand Bonneval, like Toscanini, conducting without a score, created his fabulous banquet wholly from memory and without referring to any text.

Refusing all assistance provided in the form of fryers, sauce makers, and junior cooks, he buzzed about the kitchen, a veritable dynamo of energy, whipping salt pork, minced clams, potatoes, onions, and cream into the wonderful *bouillabaisse,* with his own hands preparing the hot sauce containing onion, catchup, vinegar, Worcestershire, various peppers, paprika, and chili powder for the charcoal-grilled salmon, and crisping the long, sausage-shaped *quenelles* in the fat wherein frizzled the fascinating dish of swine's intestines flavored with cloves and chopped red peppers.

With deft touch and loving care he golden-browned the tender Bresse chicken sections creating the thick cream gravy to pour over them. To the tubers imported from French Africa he added honey, orange juice, and brown sugar; he took particular care with the vegetable pudding and the avocado salad and lavished attention upon the dessert browning in the oven.

Marvelous odors, rich and spicy, filled the kitchen and were wafted out to the two banqueting rooms beyond, the one where the Cercle waited hungrily and next door where the Chantilly Hunt Club was likewise dining in great state, formal red coats and all.

Reports tell how the members of the Cercle were enthralled by the very first dish, the wonderful soup concocted by their guest chef; they began to applaud with the appearance of the fish course with its new and marvelous sauce and their enthusiasm knew no bounds with the arrival of the pork dish accompanied by the *quenelles,* the like of which, for flavor, they had never tasted before.

Tears were shed over the chicken course with its accessories of fabulous potatoes and extraordinary soufflé. Excitement mounted to a fever pitch with the unusual salad, and when the fragrant, mahogany-brown, spicy *gâteau de Courge* appeared, the dignified members of the Cercle, stuffed to the eyebrows, were prepared to carry M. Bonneval in triumph upon their shoulders.

However, this had to wait upon the address of the President of the nation and the summoning of the guest chef to the banquet room to receive the plaudits of the members and France's highest decoration.

It was at this moment, just as the toastmaster announced, *"Messieurs, le Président de la République,"* that the disturbance next door broke out, precipitating a crisis such as not even the oldest member of the Cercle could recall.

For as the Chief of State rose to his feet, several dozen hounds collected in the hall without, gave tongue simultaneously in shrill whines, barkings, yappings, yelps, and shrieks. It was the famous Chantilly pack being brought to the banquet for the annual ceremony of being blessed by the Bishop of Chantilly.

Held in leash outside the banquet hall in the foyer, they yelled vociferously in both French and English, while the President of France stood on his feet, unable to hear himself think, much less speak, and the chairman and members of the Cercle turned crimson with embarrassment. No one knew what to do. Indeed, there seemed to be nothing to be done to save the situation.

But attend! Likewise outside the door up to his knees in baying beagles there waited one who was also in possession of a tremendous secret. It was none other than M. Armand Bonneval ready to be called inside to take his bow. He saw the impasse. He realized the solution. For him to see and to know were to act.

"*Vites! Vites!*" he called to an assistant near by. "Bring the *quenelles!* Run! Fetch the remaining *quenelles* at once!"

The assistant ran. He returned with a huge dish heaped high with crispy, fragrant, brown, sausage-shaped cakes. Bonneval seized them and flung them by handfuls to the screaming Chantilly pack. "*Tais tois, méchants chiens!*" he cried.

The animals flung themselves upon the succulent offerings. They gobbled. And a moment later nothing but silence, golden silence, broken only by almost inaudible canine snufflings of joy, filled the foyers and banqueting rooms. The President commenced to speak; ten minutes later M. Bonneval made his entrance, to be greeted with a standing ovation and ringing cheers as the distinguished new member of France's *Légion d'honneur.*

And outside in the hall, a baffled Negro kennel boy in the employ of an American film man, owner of the Chantilly pack, fingered one of the golden-brown, sausage-length cakes and, shaking his head, said, "He called 'em '*quenelles*,' but dey looks like, dey smells like, dey tastes like, and dey sure enough *acts* like good old-fashioned Tallahassee hush puppies. . . ."

Ah yes. By now you will have guessed what that wicked M. Bonneval had done to revenge himself upon his tormentors, evade the promise extracted by his wife, and maintain the dignity of a chef of the Grand Cordon Bleu, retired, to whom nobody tells anything about what he shall or shall not cook, or how.

But if not, you will only have to imagine yourself a mouse at a quiet and almost secret investiture in the American Embassy, where M. Armand Bonneval was decorated with the U.S. medal of the Legion of Merit, the citation reading in part: "For courage in the face of great adversity and an unexampled demonstration of supreme friendship for the United States of America."

For, being the only American present at this exclusive feast of the Cercle, none but the Ambassador, who had been born in Alabama, educated in the Midwest, attended Harvard Law School, and practiced law on the Pacific Coast, was aware of the true nature of the French-sounding repast prepared by M. Bonneval.

Picture the diplomat's joy, for instance, when the *bouillabaisse* arrived and he found himself eating the finest Boston clam chowder to be had outside of Gallagher's Fish House on South Market Street. Imagine his delight at next being presented with barbecued salmon with round-up barbecue sauce as it is prepared in the Columbia River section of the Northwest, where the big Sockeyes run, followed by Alabama hog chitlins with turnip greens, potlikker, and genuine Florida-style hush puppies.

His enchantment, amusement, and affection for the little chef grew with the appearance of Maryland fried chicken with cream sauce, candied yams, and old-fashioned southern-style corn pudding, was augmented by the good red *guacamole* the way they used to make it in Monterey, and climaxed by the appearance of the famous *gâteau de Courge*, which any French dictionary and a little imagination and skill translates into good old New England pumpkin pie.

None of the above, of course, appeared in the citation; the Ambassador never mentioned it to anyone, nor did Bonneval ever breathe a word, not even after his red rosette was securely implanted in his buttonhole.

Nevertheless, the facts have somehow managed to leak out and appear in this space, unfortunately or fortunately, as you may care to look at it, considering that that great delicacy, the Tallahassee hush puppy, has probably made its last appearance in *la belle France*.

Love Is a Gimmick

Sometimes the work researching one story will suggest another as one is taken far afield into strange and interesting realms. The idea for "Love Is a Gimmick" was born while researching *Too Many Ghosts*.

Too Many Ghosts is a mystery novel, a thriller that appeared in serial form in the *Saturday Evening Post* in the United States and in *John Bull* in Great Britain before its publication in book form. It introduced what I hoped was a new kind of detective, a ghost breaker and de-haunter of haunted houses.

To gain the necessary information and knowledge to write this book required a library of more than a hundred diverse volumes dealing with every form of spiritism, charlatanism, psychical research, and the subject of ghosts, poltergeists, and things that go bump in the night. The research took eighteen months and led me through psychical research, legerdemain, photography, chemistry, psychiatry, spiritualism, stage illusions, poltergeist phenomena, etc.

A part of this reading was a study of the life and work of the late Harry Houdini, the illusionist and escape artist and certainly one of the greatest showmen and magicians of all time.

There was still a third facet to this fascinating man, namely his implacable enmity to the fake spiritualists, ghost-message writers, clairvoyants, trumpet mediums, and all the rest of that kind of trash which flourished during his heyday. Houdini called them all cheats and liars and challenged them to produce a manifestation that he could not duplicate. None ever did so successfully. The man himself was a wonderful character because he actually wanted to believe in another world. He was sentimental about his mother and after her death would have welcomed a genuine communication from her. He was shocked and dismayed by the drivel poured forth by the mediums and the infantile mechanical methods employed to gain their effects.

It was inevitable after Houdini's death that a book should be written revealing how he accomplished his almost incredible escapes, and through these accounts coupled with general study of the subject, one learned that super-normal phenomena were far from confirmed and that when tricks were performed upon the stage in the form of illusions or escapes which appeared to be impossible, they actually were that—plain and simply impossible. They were done either with the aid of an accomplice or a gimmick, "gimmick" being a carnival word to cover a multitude of tampering.

But what glowed through it all, the stories and revelations, was the strength and the courage of Houdini, and while he was extraordinarily powerful in his wrists and fingers, it was his courage that attracted me. Even if your escape is planned, rehearsed, and the gimmick familiar and fool-proof to you, it takes more than ordinary human nerve to permit oneself to be handcuffed or straitjacketed, padlocked into a mail sack, nailed into a wooden coffin, and dumped into an icy river in the middle of January.

Courage, particularly the kind of courage that I myself lack, has always fired me, and therefrom sprang the basic idea for this story.

Houdini faced many kinds of challenges during his career and in one way or another beat them all. Some of the means he used to beat them are revealed in this story. But even when he was dead and gone (and incidentally no so-called medium ever established contact with him, though Houdini had promised to try to communicate if he found there was a life after death), the challenge remained. Could Houdini have been defeated? This problem I carried about in the back of my head for a year.

And then one day I was walking along the famous Bahnhofstrasse in Zurich, the street in the Swiss capital which corresponds to Bond Street in London and Fifth Avenue in New York, and looking into the window of a toy shop that had a display of magic equipment and boxes of tricks for young people. Among them I noticed a gadget I hadn't seen since I was a child at the turn of the century with my own magic box. This was a straw-plaited finger grip.

You slipped one on to your forefinger, or preferably that of an uninitiated companion, and the harder he tugged, the more impossible it was to get it off, for the interwoven plaits of straw simply gripped more tightly under pressure of pulling. This principle has been used even commercially for lifting certain articles by crane. The way to get it off, of course, is to push against the finger instead of pulling. The plaited straw then enlarges and the finger is easily freed. But as long as the strands of straw used in the plait are intact, it is impossible to pull them off the finger. The skin will come off first.

I went inside, bought five of them, took them home, and experimented for an evening and knew that I had my gimmick. Now the short story based upon Harry Houdini could be written.

Houdini's method of escape from the normal straight or restraining jacket was based on muscle control, agility, and strength. No one was ever able to put one on him without Houdini's gaining sufficient slack for him to begin to maneuver his arms over his head and in a position to manipulate the buckles of the jacket. Then, using his extraordinarily muscular fingers, he would open the buckles *through* the canvas.

But supposing someone could devise a way to deny Houdini, or my Houdini character in the story, the use of these powerful fingers? And this is where the straw-plaited, child's-magic finger stalls came in as used by my unsavory villain in "Love Is a Gimmick." That villain, incidentally, is a composite of several unappetizing officers of the law I encountered during my days as a reporter.

This was the means used to deny my escape artist the use of his fingers, for when they were inserted into those straw traps, he was as good as dead. The harder he pulled to free himself, the more tightly they would cling. It was a horrible gaff, and thinking of it at night sometimes gave me the cold sweats until I had the story written and out of my system.

There is one more amusing footnote to be connected with the adventures of this particular tale and has to do with my late agent and loved and life-long friend Harold Ober. Harold was a very careful man with his authors and spent a good deal of his time walking the tightrope with them as far as he, his office, and the writer as well were concerned. There was really only one criterion for whether a story submitted to him was good or bad—namely, would it sell?

This made Harold cagey. Indeed, when a story came into his hands, if he overpraised it and the story was rejected, his author would feel injured and ill-treated by the magazine. If he condemned it and ordered changes, he was taking an editorial responsibility upon himself.

Harold usually walked right down the middle when I sent him a story, saying it *seemed* to be a good story and he *thought* the *Post* would like it. We had had several instances when he had gone overboard over certain stories, praised them, and said he felt sure the *Post* would buy them. The *Post* didn't.

"Love Is a Gimmick" is one of the few stories I ever sent Harold which he thoroughly disliked, discredited, and condemned. He simply hated it and wrote that he didn't even wish to show it to a magazine.

As you can imagine, this came as a considerable shock. Over the years I have schooled myself to accept criticism. I prefer praise, but I don't go to pieces when I am intelligently criticized by an editor or even a friend.

But this one threw me. Like many writers, I am always close to that dark borderline of self-deprecation where I am able to convince myself that I have lost what is known as "the touch" and will no longer be able to produce that combination of words and ideas which can be turned into rent and groceries.

However, in this instance my common sense came to the rescue. I had been writing and selling stories professionally for a quarter of a century. I had, I knew or felt, put this story together soundly, my facts were authenticated, my main character a reasonable facsimile, and my final twist at the finish both legitimate and accounted for. It was not the greatest story I had ever written, but it didn't seem to me to be all that bad either. So I wrote to Harold asking whether as a favor he would get me another editorial opinion on this story. I asked him to show it privately and off the record to Stuart Rose, associate editor of the *Post*. If Stu concurred with Harold's opinion, I would agree to jettison the story and not ask for it to be submitted for sale.

For ten days I heard nothing from Harold. On the eleventh day I received a cable from him: "POST BUYING LOVE IS A GIMMICK AM PLANNING DINING ON FRESH CROW TONIGHT HAVE YOU ANY SPECIAL RECIPE. LOVE HAROLD.

I WENT back today and looked at a diary I wrote thirty years ago and put away in the bottom of an old theatrical trunk. It was the account of the end of the Great Armando.

And I got out something else, too, and looked at it again for the first time since it had come into my hands so long ago. It was a canvas straitjacket with leather straps, the metal buckles rusted from contact with the waters of the Detroit River.

Still sewn into the sleeves was the gimmick, that simple and devilish device of a mean and murderous man which, I wrote in my diary back in 1925, killed the Great Armando as surely as a bullet in the brain or a knife stuck in his heart. Only we never found his body afterwards.

The Great Armando was a farm boy from Perrysville, Ohio, whose real name was Joe Ferris. I was his partner for five years and loved him like a brother. He was a queer, gutty, moody fellow whose father was American and mother Polish. He was the strongest man I ever knew, particularly in his fingers, hands, and wrists.

He wasn't even a big guy, being no more than five foot ten and stocky, with shoulders and chest like a barrel. And I guess the most important thing in the world to him was the legend we'd built up about his escapes. He boasted that there wasn't a prison cell, manacle, lock, or restraint that could hold him.

And it was true, in a way. He was the greatest showman I ever knew, with piercing black eyes and a big shock of black hair which he wore long for effect. When in public he talked with some kind of Spic accent he'd picked up from a Mexican knife-thrower during his carny days. But in private with me, he was as American as chewing gum, cornflakes, and batting averages.

When he was a kid, a carnival came through Perrysville and he ran away with it from his old man's farm. He picked up everything good and bad a kid can learn around a carnival, but when he met an Australian who taught him to escape from rope ties, he found his life's work. Thereafter he concentrated on escapes and worked up a fair living with an act devoted to getting out of rope ties, straitjackets, handcuffs, and so on.

But he didn't become the Great Armando and hit the big money until I joined up with him in 1920 after the war.

If that's blowing my own horn, Joe Ferris would have been the first to acknowledge it. It just happened I had what he needed to take him out of the class of the mediocre performers barnstorming the country with cheap carnivals and put him in the ranks of the world's great illusionists whose names will never be forgotten, like Robert-Houdin, Maskelyn, Hermann the Great, Thurston, Harry Kellar, and Harry Houdini.

My name is Carl Hegemeyer, master mechanic and locksmith. My father came over from Germany in 1888. He taught me the accumulated knowledge of eight generations of locksmiths which could also be summed up in the sentence "Anything that can be locked can likewise be opened provided you have the right key or instrument."

But I had another accomplishment that made me indispensable to the myth of the Great Armando. I could look at a key and several hours later duplicate it from memory. When we traveled around I had the finest little portable power-driven metal lathe and key cutter with me. I could plug it into any hotel room, or in emergencies run it off the battery in our car.

An hour or so after a preliminary conference on any escape challenge at which I saw the key used to lock the device, Armando would have a duplicate. Slipping it to him or concealing it was no problem for a man with his training in sleight of hand.

There's no such thing as magic. You know that. You've seen a lot of magic shows from out front where the magician performs the apparently impossible. Well, it not only seems impossible; it is. There's a gaff to everything.

"Gaff" is the carnival word for the gimmick, the trick, the concealed device, the common-sense explanation of how it is done. And usually the gaff is something so simple you don't want to believe it. You'd see the Great Armando buried handcuffed in a stone sarcophagus, and three minutes later he'd be out of it, taking his bow. Common sense would tell you he couldn't do it unless he had superhuman powers or assistance. But the kind of showmanship he'd give you would make you want to believe in the superhuman powers. That's what you paid your money for.

Yet in nine cases out of ten he had assistance. I provided it. With my help he escaped from a sealed subway caisson, a time vault in the subtreasury, a four-thousand-year-old Greek stone coffin, the punishment cell at Alcatraz, and countless types of manacles and restraining jackets.

But don't forget, he had moxie along with it. Even if you know the gimmicks, it takes guts to let them lace you into a straitjacket, stuff you into a government mailbag, padlock it, nail you into a packing case bound with rope, and drop you into an icy river in midwinter.

The only one to come near the Great Armando was Houdini, and everything Houdini did, Armando did better. Houdini did the riverescape trick, only he used handcuffs that he could get out of in ten seconds. Nobody but Armando dared to do it with the straitjacket and letting an expert truss him up.

Yet, as I wrote in my diary, the straitjacket finished him—leastways, the gimmick in it. And a woman put it there. The only woman he ever loved.

He was a queer duck, was Joe Ferris. Nobody ever knew him or got close to him, not even me, and I was his trusted partner. I suppose that was the Polish in him. Often he was moody and suspicious. He kept his money stashed away in cash in safe-deposit boxes under different names that I never even knew. He thought only of his reputation and the myth of the Great Armando. He said to me, "Remember this. Whatever happens, the Great Armando never fails."

Yet he was no fool, either, and knew the risks he was running. He once told me, "The first time I get a real bad scare, I'll quit and nobody'll ever hear of the Great Armando again. But up to now I haven't seen anything we can't beat."

But that was before we met up with Sheriff Jules Massin of Ossowo County in the tough River Rouge section of Detroit, where we were doing the water escape as preliminary publicity to Armando's being booked into the Michigan Palace Theater in Detroit. The sheriff had taken up our challenge to lace Armando into a straitjacket from which he could not escape.

On the face of it, it was routine. There was no straitjacket made that Armando couldn't get out of in less than a minute. But we never took chances. It was a condition that Armando guaranteed to get out of any restraining device provided he could inspect it first. The padlock on the mail sack had to be closed and opened in our presence. This gave me the necessary gander at the key. And the packing case had to go on exhibition in the lobby of the theater before and after the stunt. That's when we gaffed it.

We thought we had every angle covered. Only we never figured to come up against a man with murder in his heart.

There was a crowd in the sheriff's office the day we went there to inspect the restraints and set up the stunt: deputies, detectives, police, reporters, and photographers. The sheriff's wife was there, too. His office was on the ground floor of his home. At first I didn't notice her. She had a scarf bound around her head, European style. She had pale cheeks and prominent gray-green eyes that seemed absolutely devoid of expression. They did not even flicker when the sheriff, noticing her in the forefront of those crowding around his desk, snarled, "What the hell you doin' here, Tina? Can't you see I'm busy?"

She was submissive to his abuse; every line of her body proclaimed her to be cowed and hopeless. Yet she did not go, and soon other matters claimed the sheriff's attention.

The sheriff was a mean man. Mean, dirty, and dangerous. He wasn't a copper for nothing. He liked it. We meet all kinds in our racket from plain smart alecks who think it is fun to make a monkey out of a performer, to cops and jailers who don't like to see you make a monkey out of them. But we'd never run up against a guy nursing murder in his heart, because it was for free. Armando always signed a release.

That was the sheriff. I knew him for a killer, a killer inside the law from the moment I walked into his office. He was over six feet tall, fat, burly, and dirty. His clothes were dirty, as were his skin, his fingernails, and his teeth. His breath was bad. He wore a fancy gun in a belt holster, silver- and ivory-handled. You could see he loved the power it gave him.

Massin threw a straitjacket onto his desk and sneered, "Anything wrong with that?"

It was an ordinary violence-restraint jacket with straps and buckles, the easiest type for Armando, for the canvas was not unusually thick. No matter how strong the manipulator, Armando, by swelling his muscles, could always reserve enough slack to get his arms over his head. Then he opened the buckles *through* the canvas. I told you he had the most powerful fingers in the world. In that department he was superhuman. That's why he was called great.

I picked up the jacket to show Armando. But he wasn't looking. Something strange had happened. He was staring instead at Tina Massin, and on his face was an expression such as I had never seen there before.

I had to catch my breath. Her head cloth had fallen back upon her neck, revealing hair so ash blond it was almost white, and the perfect oval of her face. She looked like the pale, imprisoned princess in the book of Grimm's fairytales I had when I was a kid. The impression she made upon me at that moment was one I would never forget.

Have you ever known it to happen that you see someone for the first time and in that moment you know his life story almost as though you had read it in a book? She was of foreign extraction, maybe Polish or Finnish. I guessed she had been taken from an institution or orphanage into the sheriff's establishment, as household drudge. She had no doubt first been abused and later married because it was more convenient to own a wife than a servant. There are some women who become the hopeless, submissive captives to the most appalling men. Such a one was Tina Massin.

They were caught up in one another's eyes, these two utterly different and contrasting strangers, the showman with the long black hair and piercing glance, the pale girl with the silken-thick hair and eyes that were for the first time alive and filled with a kind of pleading. Any moment it would become obvious that two people had found one another, had fallen in love, and were attempting to communicate.

I created a diversion by tossing the jacket back onto the desk. "That's okay," I said.

The sheriff sniggered unpleasantly. "It's the way I strap 'em into it," he said. I was satisfied to let Armando deal with that. The post-office inspector produced the mailbag. I bent over to examine the thickness, fittings, and padlock. I had a dozen keys that would open it. Armando would have two of them concealed on his person attached to a fine wire. Once out of the straitjacket, a matter of sixty seconds, he would push out the key and manipulate it, again through the material of the sack.

It was okay. Nevertheless, I made them open and shut the lock several times to make sure it hadn't been gaffed with shot or sand. Mrs. Massin dropped her handkerchief. Armando stooped to pick it up as did she. Their fingers touched for an instant. I was still bent over, examining the mailbag. I heard her whisper to him, "For God's sake, don't do it. . . ."

The time set was ten the next morning at the Western and Lakes railroad pier, where there was a big traveling crane. The document releasing the sheriff's office and Detroit police from all responsibility was produced and the photographers jostled for position. Somebody handed Armando a pen. Mrs. Massin made a slight gesture with her hand. Their eyes met once more. She licked dry lips and, almost imperceptibly, shook her head. The sheriff missed the byplay, but sniggered again. "Going to welch?" he asked and then, addressing everyone in general, said, "I say all greasers are yellow."

Joe Ferris flourished the pen dramatically. "Armando he nevaire welch," he said, and signed. The light in Tina Massin's eyes was extinguished. All the life went from her. She was hopeless, despairing, submissive. She turned and went out of the room.

I went to see Harry Hopp, an old-time reporter friend on the *Free Press*. I told you we never left anything to chance. I didn't like the set-up for two cents. I asked, "What's the background on your fragrant sheriff of Ossowo County?"

Hopp said, "Can't tell you anything good about him. And as long as you're asking, he hates carnivals and the carny crowd. They can't get the time of day in his county. You better watch out for that baby."

"Yeah," I said, "I got that. But why?"

"Shakedown," he replied. "There was a carnival through here five or six years ago really loaded with grift. They shelled out plenty to the sheriff to operate, but when he came back again for a second hand-out they beat him up and threw him out. Maybe your boy-friend even was with the carny and saw it happen. He's death on anything connected with traveling shows or midways."

That night I said to Armando, "Lissen, Joe. Were you ever with a grift show that beat up a sheriff around here before you started in with me?"

He reflected and then said slowly, "So that's where I know him from. When he tried to shake me down I poked him and that started it."

I said, "I don't like it. He's got it in for you. Let's call it off. We can do it in Cleveland next week."

He looked at me as if I were out of my mind, and asked, "Have we got all the angles covered?"

I went back over things in my mind. There was nothing that could happen that we hadn't thought of. "Yes," I said.

"Okay," he said, "we go. We can't afford to back out."

But I was wrong. There was something I hadn't thought of, something so simple and elementary as a means of destroying Armando that it never dawned on me until it was too late.

The day of the test was damp, cold, and sunless. There were chunks of ice floating in the river. In spite of the raw, blustery weather, the pier and several adjoining docks were black with people. We'd had a big press in advance of the attempt. . . .

The stunt was routine and we'd done it a dozen times before. The gaff was this: as soon as they started to nail the cover onto the box, Armando would start working his way out of the straitjacket and the mailbag, while I'd stall, suggesting putting in more nails or tying the rope tighter until I got a signal from Armando that he was out of the restraints. The crate had been gimmicked by us the night before with a concealed sliding panel in one side. Fifteen seconds after the box disappeared beneath the surface, he'd be out of it.

It was that simple—like all stage or escape illusions, except it was the way Armando did it that made it look so good. It is a part of the showmanship in that kind of an act that when you really think a guy is in danger he's as safe as he'd be at home in bed. The real deadly stuff doesn't show. Like staying under holding your breath for more than three minutes in freezing water and then coming up amidst ice floes or risking being carried away under the ice by the current. He had a right to call himself the Great Armando and to be proud of his rep.

When Armando and I arrived, there was a big bunch of reporters including Harry Hopp, several sob sisters, a horde of photographers, and newsreel movie men. Captain Harry Stevens of the river police was giving directions to a police launch that was to pick Armando up if and when he appeared. He was not too pleased at being used for a publicity stunt and greeted us sourly. He said, "Okay, okay, let's get going and get out of here. You fellows signed a release, didn't you?"

Sheriff Massin, wearing a big sheepskin-lined coat, said, "Yup. Got it right here."

Armando slipped out of his cloak. Underneath he was wearing trousers and sweatshirt of light, warm wool, and sneakers. The sheriff stepped over with the straitjacket, a nasty, self-satisfied smile on his face. Tina Massin was there in the front row. She wasn't pretty any more. Her face was tear-stained and filled with fear. Her eyes were fixed upon the jacket.

I spotted something about the sleeves that had not been there the day before. My stomach started to sink. I said, "Here, wait a minute. Let me see that jacket. It's been gimmicked."

The sheriff said, "They're stalling," but handed it over.

I turned out the sleeves. Inside, ten finger grips of plaited strips of colored straw had been sewn to the canvas lining. You've seen them in any magic or trick store, or child's magic set. Once they are slipped over a finger, the harder you pull, the more tightly they grip. A device also use commercially for hoisting, there is no possible way of tearing loose from it. The secret of escape is to push against the grips. The plaits then contract and enlarge so that the finger can be removed. But fastened inside the long, narrow sleeve of the jacket, there was no leverage to push. And deprived of the use of his fingers, the Great Armando was as good as dead.

I saw Armando's eyes narrow when he saw the deadly trap and the sweat bands form on his upper lip and under his eyes. It was the first time I ever saw Joe Ferris afraid. I said, "What the hell is this? Those things weren't in there yesterday when we inspected the jacket."

Massin sniggered. "Well, they're in there now." Tina Massin seemed about to faint. I had a picture of her sitting up all night with the sheriff standing over her, sewing in those terrible devices designed to kill a man for free.

Captain Stevens came over, took the straitjacket and looked at it and the innocent-looking toy finger grips plaited in reds, yellows, greens, and purples. "What's the idea, Sheriff?" he asked.

Massin bustled truculently and replied loudly so that all the press could hear. "This feller says he can get out of anything, don't he? I had a nigger once I hadda take to the loony house. Killed three guys. He got out of the jacket. He had hands like a gorilla. I fixed him up like this. He didn't get out. Okay, so let this greaseball put up or shut up. They seen them kinds of grips a dozen times before in their racket."

Captain Stevens looked doubtful, but I could sense that he was secretly pleased, in a way, that a performer who had put them to a lot of needless trouble was going to be shown up. He said to us, "What about it, boys? You don't have to go through with it if you don't want to, but make up your minds and let's get out of here."

Harry Hopp, the *Free Press* reporter, said, "Don't let him do it, Carl. It's sheer murder. I'll see that he doesn't get the worst of it in the papers."

Massin laughed his loud, dirty laugh. "I knew the fourflusher would welch."

"Welch nothing!" I shouted. "Our contract clearly stated—"

"Quiet, everyone!" It was Armando. And even in that crisis he didn't forget the phony Mexican accent. "Shut up, Carl." But he wasn't looking at me. He was looking straight at Tina Massin and she at him. There was no mistake. They were in love, all right.

They had found and lost each other in the same moment. They were saying good-by, for there was no hope for them. She was the wife of a brute who would never let her go. And he was faced with an insoluble dilemma. Because if he went through with the stunt he was a dead man. And if he backed out he might as well be dead because he would never again be the Great Armando.

He said, "All right, Sheriff, I am ready."

The sheriff stepped forward, laughing. "So long, sucker. You asked for it." Things moved fast then as he went about his for-free murder, forcing each finger of Armando's hands deep into the plaits of the straw finger grips, then pushing his knee into Armando's back in order to haul the straps tighter.

And all the time Joe Ferris continued to look only on the white face of this girl he had come to love in such a strange manner and who had been forced to become his executioner. Her eyes were lost in his. Her lips moved though no sound come, but I would have sworn they were communicating for the last time.

When four men lifted the mailbag with Armando inside it into the packing case and the electric crane traveled over and lowered the lid into the top, Tina Massin gave a soft cry and crumpled to the pier in a dead faint. The sheriff laughed, saying, "Now, what the hell's the matter with her?" A newsreel cameraman shouted, "Hey, Sheriff, willya look out! You're in the way of the shot." I felt like it was me who was going to die.

I jumped up onto the box to stall as long as I could and give him a chance even though I knew it was hopeless. There was no signal from him as usual to let me know he was out of the jacket and sack waiting for the plunge with his finger on the gaffed panel that would slide open and free him as soon as he sank beneath the surface.

Then he hadn't got out. The child's toy had defeated him. The legend of the Great Armando was a thing of the past. But I was determined to save the life of Joe Ferris.

The sheriff cried "Lower away!" and there was a cheer from the crowd as the steel cable paid out. The weighted crate went in with a splash and began to settle as the water poured in through the interstices.

I had a sickening vision of Armando trussed up like a mummy in the horrid canvas jacket, his fingers helplessly trapped in the straw grips, the icy water pouring into the case, the mail sack filling up, his last gasp for oxygen, then the hopeless last-minute struggle, tugging against the inexorable grips, and the final bubble bursting from the tortured lungs. And after that silence.

Air was rushing up in a dirty surface swirl as the case sank with its burden. When my stop watch showed two minutes and there was no sign of an arm or dark head breaking the gray river surface, I bawled in panic, "Haul away! Get him up out of there. Something's gone wrong! Get him up, do you hear!"

There was some confused shouting and I could see the police captain shouting futilely at the man in the hanging operator's booth of the crane. But there was no rattle of machinery or running of steel cable over the wheel. Something had happened to the crane or the power, for I could see the operator wrestling with his levers.

I went over the side of the pier into the water. Men and women were screaming. I had a crazy idea I could swim down, work the panel, and get him out of there, sack and all, and up to the surface. I fought the cable and my bursting lungs. Then the police launch came and fished me out. After ten minutes the power came on again and the crate was raised. But there was not a chance in the world that the Great Armando was still alive. The sheriff had won.

Workmen attacked the case with axes and crowbars. Internes from an ambulance, their white trousers showing beneath their dark overcoats, stood by with a Pulmotor. With a splintering and wrenching the side of the case broke away revealing the locked mail sack.

And I was the first one to see that it wasn't full enough!

With a yell I broke away from Harry Hopp, seized the key from the postal inspector, and opened the padlock.

It was empty! No, not quite empty. Inside, buckled as though it had never been unfastened, the terrible finger grips still in place, was the straitjacket neatly folded. But of the Great Armando there was no sign. He had accomplished his greatest escape!

It was his last, too, for he was never seen again. The police dredged, grappled, and dived for three days, but his body was never recovered. He had defeated the vicious finger grips, the jacket, the mail sack, and the case and got out, and then perhaps at the last moment, exhausted from the struggle, his strength exhausted, he had drowned and been swept down river or under a pier.

I went to a hospital myself with pneumonia. They said I swore in my delirium I'd kill Sheriff Massin for murdering my friend and partner. It turned out it wasn't necessary. Six months after the disappearance of the Great Armando I read in a newspaper that Jules Massin was shot to death in a saloon by the saloonkeeper he had attempted to shake down. I never heard what became of Mrs. Massin after that.

A couple of months after I got out of the hospital, Captain Stevens of the river police sent me the straightjacket complete with the sheriff's deadly gaff as a souvenir. I couldn't bear to look at it and put it away with my diary of how it all happened, in the bottom of my trunk. Then I went back into the locksmith business.

All that was thirty years ago. Now I am holding the jacket in my fingers again. For two days ago I saw Joe Ferris, the Great Armando! And with him was Tina Massin! I'll swear it! I couldn't have been mistaken, even though his hair was white and his features changed. She looked almost the same, except happy. It was coming out of a movie house in Athens, Georgia.

I said, "Joe! Joe Ferris! And Tina Massin!"

They denied it. They stopped politely, but their expressions remained blank. The man said, "You must be mistaking us for someone else. My name is Vernon Howard, and this is Mrs. Howard here. I'm in the grain and feed business. Anyone in Athens knows me. And now if you'll excuse Mrs. Howard and myself . . ."

Vernon Howard's Grain and Feed Store was at the corner of Boulevard and Pecan streets. When I instituted inquiries as to how long it had been there, the invariable answer was, "Oh, 'bout as long as I kin remember. . . ." But when I got down to cases, no one seemed to remember them back for *thirty years, or longer.*

When I returned to New York I dug out the straitjacket of Sheriff Massin. I hadn't touched it since the day I thought it had killed the Great Armando. The color on the finger grips of plaited straw had run, but otherwise they were exactly as they had been on that fatal day. I examined them. Then I took a magnifying glass. I tried them out by putting my fingers in and yanking. They pulled loose. And after that I knew the secret of how the Great Armando had escaped from the inescapable trap laid for him by vindictive Sheriff Massin. The finger stalls had been subtly and efficiently gaffed, by his wife.

The straw plaits had been cut with scissors in such a way as to defy casual inspection, but in every case destroying the tension of the plaits so that they no longer pulled against one another.

I remembered the look between them, the money he had stashed away in safe-deposit boxes, and his remark: "If I ever get a real scare, I'll quit and nobody'll ever hear of the Great Armando again." And how easily he could have swam ashore under cover of the panic and excitement, and vanished, to return when he read that Sheriff Massin was dead.

Yeah, we'd thought of everything, except one thing. And in the end it was Joe Ferris, the Great Armando, who had the guts to put his faith in love as a gimmick.

Orchestration for Twelfth Night

This story has probably the most curious history of inception of any that I have conceived. It was not written to make money or to sell: it was not written on speculation. Instead it was conceived partially as a kind of Christmas gift to a magazine of which I was very fond and to its late publisher, who while he was alive was for many years my friend and highly amusing companion, the late David Smart, founder and publisher of *Esquire*.

David was a curious man, tough, cynical, experienced in life and disillusioned by same, and all this was levened by an inner softness and sentimentality and exquisite sense of humor. He was one of the few millionaire publishing tycoons who could laugh at himself. I had enormous affection for Dave Smart. There are certain editors and publishers one enjoys being associated with and David was one of them.

I worked for him as a columnist, writing a monthly piece called "This Man's World" for *Esquire* for many years. We had times of violent and raucous disagreement when I would resign or he would fire me, but before too long "This Man's World" would be back in the magazine again.

I thoroughly enjoyed writing this column, for in it I could give vent to the most outrageous ideas or notions and write them as I pleased. I was happy to be able to get gripes off my chest monthly, and the preparation of copy for *Esquire* was always a joy.

David was an odd man with a curiously blind spot for writers and writing, and in particular writers of fiction. He simply had no concept of how we or our minds worked. He also found it difficult to pay writers. David had been brought up in the clothing business, where you get materials for your money. He never quite mastered the idea of such an abstraction as writing being likewise a commercial commodity. I had encountered this frame of mind before in the days when I worked on the *Daily News*, and as editor of the sports department found myself involved with the business department. You could get them to shell out for presses, drinking fountains, lavatory fixtures, paper clips, but what did you have when you spent money for writing?

Dave also could not understand why if one had the ability to write a successful story or book, one could not repeat it immediately. If a cutter could cut a suit of clothes which sold, he could do it again and again. I remember there was one story of mine which was a favorite of David's and which later appeared as a book called *The Small Miracle*, and as a film, *Never Take No for an Answer*. It all seemed so simple and easy on the face of it, and he would be at me to ask why I didn't keep on doing this. I had the formula, hadn't I? Why not turn out a whole series of such tales and grow rich?

I remember arguing with him about this one Thanksgiving when I was a guest at his home outside Chicago. He wanted a Christmas story and why couldn't I put one together the way I had put together "The Small Miracle"? So I said all right, we would take a rainy afternoon and try to synthesize a Christmas story that would be popular. We would do it together.

At the end of a four-hour session we were exhausted; we had no story, but David had learned something. I had let him flounder with me through the morass of story-making—the plot twist that won't stay bent, the characters who insist upon going their own way, the forbidden use of the long arm of coincidence, the problems of cause and effect, and the difficulties of producing the effect of a piece of life in a small compass of space. In working up the proper, valid, and watertight plot, one thinks up a hundred ideas that are self-defeating. The professional writer doesn't get discouraged by this because he knows that the hundred and first or the hundred and fifty-first idea may lead to a solution. He can, if need be, turn his story inside-out or upside-down, or look at it both ways from the middle and each time get a new slant and possibly new ways of solving the problems. The layman merely sees insuperable obstacles and unsolvable dilemmas. What is that reiterated cry I hear from frustrated or would-be writers? It is, "I know I could write but I can't think up any plots."

I think if I did nothing else for my fellow craftsmen, I did in David Smart's lifetime somewhat increase his respect for them and certainly elevated the prices he paid them. His sudden death left me forlorn. I missed him greatly; I still do. Some years later I went back to writing my column for *Esquire* again for Arnold Gingrich, David's one-time editor and after his death the new publisher of *Esquire*.

This is a long way of getting around to the "Orchestration for Twelfth Night," but in my own heart it was a Christmas present to the memory of David Smart; it was that Christmas story which he and I failed to work out that rainy afternoon on his estate in a suburb of Chicago and which didn't work because we were trying too hard and, anyway, that isn't the way good stories are written.

For technical reasons my *Esquire* copy had to be in between four and five months in advance and even further in advance for the huge Christmas issue of the magazine, and I used to write of snow and ice and the jingle of sleigh bells and the glitter of Christmas-tree ornaments in the heat and greenery of July.

Over the years that I wrote this column I had rung almost all of the changes on Christmas I could think of—sentimental, nostalgic—and the particular July that still another column for Christmas was due I somehow couldn't face going through all this again, or finding some new variation to the old Santa Claus themes, and so I fell to thinking about what I would really like to do and about the magazine that had been good to me for a long time, and in particular about David, who thought that one could simply sit down and knock together a Christmas story, and I decided that that is what I would do for that Christmas issue instead of writing my usual column. I would write a Christmas story and it would be a kind of present to David.

There was no trouble about this one, for all of the ingredients must have been simmering in my subconscious for a long time (and that is really where stories come from).

The ingredients are familiar—the three kings from the East bearing gifts to the child in the manger; but the setting has been altered, and the kings are three odd people, all of whom I have encountered and all of whom I like for their own integrity.

It was a treat for me to write this story. Since it was going to replace my regular column, it didn't have to compete for the editor's eye or for space or for a big fiction check. I could just write it as my Christmas contribution, send it along, and it would appear.

I don't know whether David would have liked it had he read it; I don't know whether anybody did like it when it appeared—possibly not, because nobody said. And in this instance I didn't particularly care. I liked it; I thoroughly enjoyed writing it and that is why it appears in this book.

THE three men struggling each from another direction against the gale-lashed rain that drenched the dark Eastchapel street hard by the bend in the River Thames bore upon the light that gleamed out of the pitch darkness of the miserable, stormy Twelfth Night that engulfed London. Each hoped to find temporary shelter from the cold and the soaking storm.

The light shining from the covered loading shed of the deserted brewery and refracted by the downpour beckoned like a star. It was past midnight. The morning of January 6, twelve days past Christmas, had been born. Shivering and huddled to themselves, the three men hurried their footsteps and arrived almost simultaneously beneath the shelter of the roof of the loading platform where it was at least dry, and where their welcome was pronounced by the pair who had arrived there before them.

The woman who lay on a pile of sacking only moaned and whimpered and then cursed softly, but the man kneeling beside her in the shadows said bitterly, "Gor! It's got to be a nigger, a Jew, and a bloody drunk wot turns up 'ere."

The three, startled by the voice, brushing and shaking the rain from their clothing, looked at one another for the first time and saw that the man had spoken truly.

The Negro was young and dapper in a tan raincoat. His head was as round as a leaden musket bullet. He was hatless, and the drops of rain glistened beneath the light as though his kinky hair was shot through with diamonds. He wore gold-rimmed spectacles and his skin was ebon-dark. The whites of his eyes were creamy and the eyes themselves were of extraordinary luminosity.

The Jew wore the long, square-cut beard of orthodoxy and it was mottled with gray. He was clad in what once had been a Chesterfield overcoat and a bowler hat and his back was bent beneath his peddler's pack, from the straps of which he now eased himself. In his eyes was the melancholy of his race and lot, but the lines of his face were set to reflect good nature and cheerfulness.

The drunk was an apple-cheeked Cockney with a red nose, gnarled chin, a mouth gaping with stained and missing teeth, and naughty, piggy little eyes. He wore no coat and his checked jacket and trousers were rain-sodden, as were his traditional neckcloth and peaked cap. But he was so half-seas over from beer that he did not mind, and he stood in the circle of the light grinning boozily and occasionally shaking himself like a terrier.

The kneeling man, a big bruiser in rough clothes whose heavy, lumpy features were stormy with anger and self-pity, repeated, "A Jew, a bloody drunk, and a nigger."

None of the three men thus characterized appeared to take offense. The Jew, with his pack divested, poured the water from the rim of his bowler hat, ignoring the appellation as one who had grown used to it and no longer even heard it.

The drunk uttered a strange gibberish—"Be-deet da bedeedle um bum"—while at the same time stamping and shuffling his feet and waving his arms in apparently some new way of getting warm, his grin expanding to show his bad teeth, his wicked little eyes twinkling.

The Negro said to the man and the woman in the shadows of the raised loading platform, from which in the daytime the beer kegs were rolled onto the drays and hauled away by big gray Percherons, "Are you in any difficulty? I hear the woman moaning. I should like to be of assistance. I am *Mister* William Matumbwe of Nigeria." His voice was as musical and mellifluous as an organ note. The curious manner in which he emphasized the "*Mister*" caused the Jew to cease drying his hat, put it back on, and glance at him interestedly, but led the rough-looking man to spit and rasp, "No nigger is *Mister* to me. . . ."

The Negro smiled, and the smile brought a curious and comforting kind of beauty to his round face. "Oh yes," he said, "there is one who must be, and that is myself. For I have worked long and very hard to earn the title and it is the greatest title I have ever had and the one of which I am justly proud."

The man spat again, but Mister Matumbwe continued cheerfully. "Oh, you are lucky perhaps that I am a highly educated nigger. Bachelor of Science, Christ Church College at Oxford—'The House,' you know—and degree of Master of Surgery from the University of London, where I have just completed my studies. That is why I am entitled to be called 'Mister.' If the woman is ill, you could not have a better nigger happen by here, I am sure."

The Jew, who had not been paying much attention to what Mister Matumbwe was saying, brushed a small puddle of rain from the top of his pack and loosened the cover. "Could I sell something, perhaps, to any of you gentlemen, or the lady? I have many interesting articles. It is still not too late to acquire a small gift for someone. Everything is reasonably priced."

The drunk had subsided against the far side of the loading shed balanced on his heels, bent in the middle with his rear braced against the wall in the attitude of one who is about to sit down. There was an expression of great concentration upon his face, and his lips and fingers moved rhythmically.

The man with the ailing woman cried, "Gor, you mean you're a doctor? Why the hell didn't you say so before? My old woman's time's come. Bloody National 'Ealth Service. Try and get 'elp when you need it. I was wanting to get her to the 'orspital when she got took on the way. Reckon the kid'll be here any minute. . . ."

"Ah . . . I thought so perhaps," Mister Matumbwe said, and moved to climb up onto the loading platform, but the woman screamed and then shouted, "No, no! Get away! I don't want any dirty nigger touching me. . . ."

But the Negro completed his climb and talked to her soothingly as he would to a child. He said, "Shhhhhh. Do not be afraid. I fear, madam, that you have no longer any choice in the matter. But you will see, I am very gentle."

He moved over to her and placed a hand upon her stomach. His touch was indeed gentle and curiously it quieted her at once, so that she left off cursing and only whimpered a little and stared at him out of frightened and pain-racked eyes. She was still handsome in a strong, blowsy way, though no longer young.

Mister Matumbwe nodded his head and said, "Not just yet. But soon. Quite soon. I take it this is not a *Prime Ibs?*"

"Not a wot? Blast yer, talk English."

"Her first child."

The man laughed unpleasantly. "Not bloody likely. She's 'ad four wot we can't feed decently now. Wot's she want to go and 'ave another for, that's what I'm asking?"

Mister Matumbwe replied, "Sometimes these matters are determined elsewhere." He arose and faced the two men below him as though he were addressing them from the lecture platform. "Gentlemen, we are about to experience an emergency. Fortunately, I feel myself well qualified to cope with it even though it will be my first delivery outside the hospital. However, I shall require some assistance—that is to say, we must make do with what we have."

He leaped down from the platform and crossed to the drunk, who was still in his almost sitting position against the wall, and addressed him respectfully. "You, sir, who are you, and what is it you do?"

The little fellow's mischievous eyes looked up at Mister Matumbwe out of deep crinkles as he asked without rancor, "Wot's it to you?"

Mister Matumbwe had the most endearing quality of never being, or appearing to be, offended. He replied, "Oh, it is only to ascertain whether you might have any particular skill that could be put to some use at the moment of crisis. . . ."

The Cockney stood up, threw his head back, and roared with sudden laughter. "Skill, is it? 'Arry Napes is the name. 'Arry Napes from Eastchapel. King o' the buskers, they call me. I'm a whole bloomin' performance by meself." Then he sang, "Be-dee, be-da, bedeet-do-da!" and did a shuffle and kick.

Mister Matumbwe gazed at him in bewilderment for an instant and then his magnificent white teeth appeared framed by his smile. "Oh, but of course. A busker is one who performs in the streets for pennies to the queues waiting to get into the theaters. And you are their king. . . ."

"Ask anyone in Eastchapel about 'Arry Napes. I'm me own bloomin' orchestra as well. Took in more'n a couple o' quid tonight by the Palladium where the panto is playing. Coo, I'm not 'arf a panto all by meself. Here's a example." He sang, "Hi tiddlyum-ti, bedeep ba boop ah beedley um bum," and danced a creditable buck and wing.

Mister Matumbwe pressed his hands to his forehead in deep thought and concentration and then dramatically pointed a pink and ebon finger at Napes. "Oh, excellent. You will be the anesthetician when I call upon you."

He turned to the Jew. "And you, sir, are a peddler."

"Moshe Konig, at your service. But I do not understand what is to happen. You spoke just now of an emergency."

"The woman is about to have a baby. I shall deliver it."

"Ach, the poor! On such a night and in such a place. What is there I can do to help her?"

"Have you by any chance some alcohol in your pack?"

Konig shook his head. "Alcohol I do not carry—but wait. I have some most excellent eau de Cologne and bottles of scent, almost as good as French, and very cheap. I always try to procure the best for my clients at low prices. I will give you what I have. There is alcohol and spirits in it."

Mister Matumbwe's happy smile illuminated his countenance. "Yes, it will do as disinfectant in the emergency. How kind of you to offer it. Any kitchen utensils?"

"A few. But the knives, I am afraid, are not very sharp. With prices what they are, goods are not what they used to be."

"Oh, not, not knives, but if you have something curved as well as flat in the manner of a . . . well, a cake lifter, for instance . . ." The peddler was already delving into his pack and spreading out his wares. "Oh, excellent, Mr. Konig, most excellent. Those will do splendidly. I am sure it will not be a difficult delivery. . . ."

"Hoi," called the man on the platform, "Hoi, Mister . . ." He could not bring himself to speak the name tacked on to the

"Mister" and so he finished, "Mister Doctor, what about getting on with it?"

Mister Matumbwe turned to him. "Your wife will let us know when she is ready. In the meantime, what is your name and occupation, and your wife's name and age?"

The man looked down in surly fashion upon the young surgeon and finally muttered, "Sam Boles. Dock worker. The old woman's thirty-two. Name's Anna."

"Ah. A dock worker. You must be glad the strike's over, what with another baby coming." He climbed back onto the loading platform.

The word "strike" acted upon Sam Boles as though he had been touched with a live wire.

"Gor!" he yelled. "Strike! I've lost three months' wages on their blinking strike, me with a fambly, for a six-penny rise. It'll take me two years to make back what I've lost by them making me stay out. 'Oo are *they?* That's what I'd like to know. Strike, says they; go back, says they; lost yer seniority, says they; arbitrate, says they; *they've* raised prices again, they say. All right, you and your bleedin' education. YOU tell me who *they* are."

Mister Matumbwe reflected deeply for a few seconds, his round chin in one cupped hand. Then he replied somewhat inconsequently, "Better perhaps to ask who He is?"

"He? Wat he? Wotcher talkin' about?"

"Him," said Mister Matumbwe. "He who is more than all of them and us too, put together. God whose dream it all seems to be. . . ."

"Coo," commented Harry Napes, who had moved over closer to the loading platform. "You sound like a ruddy preacher."

Mister Matumbwe looked pleased. "Yes, do I? There was once a question in my mind whether I would study for the ministry or medicine. But I am glad I decided—"

A cry from Anna Boles interrupted him, but it was one of despair and anger rather than pain. "I don't want another. I tell you I don't want it. God knows I never wanted another."

Mister Matumbwe was at her side in an instant, his eyes searching her tortured face and figure with anxiety and tenderness, as his fingers gently examined.

"Yes," he said, "now is the time," and then, "Madam, if God knows, then He has decided otherwise for His reasons, and you had best take it in good part, for the child is coming now."

But the woman would not be hushed. She complained. "What's anyone get out of anything? Drudge and slave for what? Not so much as a half-crown to go to the flicks once a week." Her voice rose querulously. "What's in it, one kid after another, always one asuckling and pulling the life out o' you?"

Mister Matumbwe looked reflective before he replied earnestly, "There is a very good formula, National Dried Milk, three level tablespoons, one and one-half teaspoons of sugar, mixed with four ounces of boiled water, in a sterilized bottle, five to six feedings a day. And the Infants' Welfare Center will give you cod-liver-oil compound and concentrated orange juice. But of course breast feeding is the best for the child if you are able to do it."

But now another cry burst from the woman, no longer one of self-pity or complaint, but vibrant with animal anguish. Mister Matumbwe turned to Harry Napes. "Dance, Mr. Napes," he commanded. "Divert her. You are the anesthetician, the only one we have. We have nothing to give her to take her away from pain but you. Give your best performance."

Just beyond the loading shed the rain was still seething down out of the black, gusty night. Mister Matumbwe ordered the peddler, "Collect rain water in your bowler hat, Mr. Konig: we shall need it to wash the child."

The busker had pushed his cap onto the back of his head and taken up position within sight of the woman in labor, where he began slow and comic gyrations to his self-made music. "Da da da-DEET-da-da, beedle-de-o, beedle-do-o, boompa tum boom."

"Watch him, Madam," Mister Matumbwe said to the woman, "and you will see a better show than the Christmas panto at the Palladium, for he is the king of the buskers."

Then he removed his sack coat, rolled up his sleeves, doused his hands well with eau de Cologne, and turned to the business of ushering a new life into the world.

He did so with humility but also with great love in his heart toward this woman, for she was his first patient. To maintain his own courage even in the face of what appeared to be a simple cephalic presentation, he muttered Latin medical phrases such as *"Occipito dextra posterior,"* which for all of any of the others might have been incantations.

And yet, through it all, he was also living a dream, and in the dream the little head that was presenting itself was coal black, for he was back in his native Africa, and this was but one of a steady stream of coal-black heads he would deliver with equal skill and tenderness in the hospital he planned to build, and the mothers would recover free from infection and the babies would survive, properly fed, cared for, and looked after, and ignorance and disease would be banished. . . .

"Rum-tum-tummy tum hi-de-vo-do . . ." The busker was dancing and grimacing with his rubbery face and froward eyes, now like a hula girl, now executing buck and wing and soft-shoe. The rhythms came through to Mister Matumbwe like the beat of the jungle bongo drums that he remembered as a child before he was sent down to the lowlands to the mission school.

At his elbow was Moshe Konig with his bowler hat full of soft rain water. Sam Boles stood looking down, his hands working nervously, an expression of anxiety on his lumpy features.

Racked with pain as she was, the woman Anna could not keep her eyes from the jigging, bouncing figure on the floor of the loading shed and the gargantuan shadow cast by the single yellow light that accompanied him.

Mister Matumbwe, Mister Surgeon Matumbwe, applied skill and imagination to help her, but there came a time of desperation when the birth slowed. He dared not trust further the primitive instruments at his command and he did not know what to do.

"Beedeet da CHA!" croaked the busker, leaping into the air to his left and clicking his heels together. "Bee doh dee CHA!" He leaped to the right, again cracking his heels. "HOI!" and he rose straight up into the air in the manner of a ballet dancer attempting an *entrechat*. Coming down, however, he landed in a puddle in the middle of the stone floor, made when the rain had run off their clothes, his feet shot out from under him, and he fell on his behind, throwing out spray to all sides from beneath him.

"Blow me!" he cried, "it's like a bleedin' skating rink!"

The woman Anna gave vent to a great and convulsive blast of laughter, for she had never seen anything quite so comic in her whole life, and the child was expelled, giving notice with a thin cry that pierced the laughter.

Mister Matumbwe did what was requisite and then, almost like an offering, held the infant aloft for a moment and his beautiful voice filled the cavern of the loading shed.

"Behold," he cried, "the miracle!"

The others, looking, saw only a newborn babe, red, wrinkled, and incredibly ugly, not knowing that the black man referred only to the miracle of the handing on of the flame of life in man's interminable relay race down through the ages and at which he had been privileged to attend.

"The boy better be wrapped in something warm," Moshe Konig remarked, and delving into his bottomless pack, he produced a woman's white flannel nightgown in which he carefully and gently wrapped the child while Mister Matumbwe attended the mother and made her comfortable. Then the peddler, freeing the child's head from the swaddling clothes, laid it squalling in the mother's arms. Searching in his pack further, he found a golden butterfly on a stick, which he laid beside it. Or rather it was a butterfly cut out of paper-thin copper with jeweled eyes and springlike coiled wire feelers that quivered as the mother's breast rose and fell; but beneath the rays of the single yellow light the toy gleamed like red gold.

Sam Boles said, "Look 'ere now, we carnt pay nothing. . . ."

Moshe Konig bent over the two on the sacking, looking down

upon them with a grave, sweet smile, moving the toy so that it shivered and made a dry rattling sound with its wings. "Sha, sha," he said. "Who is asking?"

But Boles was filled with suspicion. He looked angrily from one to the other and asked, "Wotcher expect of me?"

Mister Matumbwe looked up at the question and his grave glance behind the gold-rimmed spectacles took in the busker, who had come over to the loading platform to inspect the baby and was grinning his impudent, broken-toothed smile, and the bent figure of the old peddler curved over the pair huddled on the sacking as he rattled the golden toy, and he found himself filled suddenly with an unearthly joy and exaltation.

"Nothing!" he cried, "nothing at all. Take all that has been given as a gift of the Magi. For, gentlemen, do you not know what night this is?"

They stared at him. The baby had stopped crying and outside the shed the storm had suddenly abated. The wind had dropped and the rain fell now only gently.

"It is the night of Epiphany, the Twelfth Night. And do you remember the Gospel according to St. Matthew, Chapter Two?" His face filled with wonder and his voice vibrating with the sincerity that filled him, Mister Matumbwe began to quote:

" 'Now when Jesus was born in Bethlehem of Judea in the days of Herod there came wise men from the east to Jerusalem. . . .

" 'And Herod sent them to Bethlehem and said, Go and search diligently for the young child. . . .

" 'When they had heard the king they departed; and lo the star which they saw in the east went before them, till it came and stood over where the young child was. When they saw the star they rejoiced with exceeding great joy.

" 'And when they were come into the house they saw the young child with Mary, his mother, and fell down and worshiped him; and when they had opened their treasures, they presented him with gifts; gold, and frankincense, and myrrh. . . .' "

Moshe Konig turned his sad, wise eyes upon the black man and asked, "What is it you are trying to say, Mister Surgeon?"

Mister Matumbwe replied ringingly, "Only that this morning something very great and wonderful has happened: a babe was born. For there is not an infant delivered into this world, white, yellow, brown, or black, who does not have the breath of Jesus in him, who does not at the moment of birth in his innocence and the immediacy of his arrival from the breast of the Creator share in the spirit of Jesus." But he finished on a lower, shyer note. "So you see, perhaps it was suitable that we should bring him gifts. For who shall say that we are not Three Kings come out of the East, following the star that led us hither?"

The silence was broken by the long, deep sigh of Moshe Konig, in whose head and heart old legends and prophecies were stirring.

"Oh, yes, it might well be, gentlemen," Mister Matumbwe continued, "for you, Mr. Napes, are a king, the king of the buskers, a king out of Eastchapel, are you not? And the very meaning of your name, Mr. Konig, is 'king.'" His warm, earnest, friendly smile embraced them both.

The face of the busker parted in his jagged grin. "And 'oo's the ruddy third king?" he asked, and then, nodding his head in the direction of the confused and dour Boles: "Not this bloomin' Happiness boy 'ere?"

"Oh no," said Mister Matumbwe, simply. "I am." And it was as though there had been a ruffle and fanfare.

Moshe Konig sighed again. "Ahhhhhhh. This must be so. Only kings and Jews possess the dignity never to feel offended."

"Yes," Mister Matumbwe repeated. "I think indeed we are Three Kings from the East bearing gifts of gold, frankincense, and myrrh."

And here Mister Matumbwe seemed to increase in stature and beauty as though the majesty was swelling within him as he explained, "You see, at home in my own country in the Northern Province of Nigeria, I am King Matumbwe the First, for my loved and honored father, King Nkukawa, but recently died there while I was completing my studies here. But when I return I have decided I shall not be King, but *Mister* Matumbwe, graduate of the College of Surgeons of London, for of this title I am most proud of all."

A strange voice broke in. " 'Ello, 'ello, what's all this going on in 'ere?" They all turned and saw the constable, his shiny black rubber mackintosh and helmet glistening in the yellow overhead light of the loading shed.

The spell was broken. The sound of the drums and bugles of royalty faded. Mister Matumbwe replied for them in the precise, careful English of the African student. "There has been an emergency birth here, constable. I am a qualified surgeon and have seen it through successfully with the aid of these kind people. Mother and child are doing excellently, but I recommend they be taken to a hospital now. If you will arrange to telephone for an ambulance . . ."

The police constable had finished the voluminous entry in his notebook; the ambulance was on the way. Moshe Konig's pack was closed again; Harry Napes had pulled down the peak of his cap and turned up his coat collar around his neckcloth. Mister Matumbwe once more had lapsed into the guise of an insignificant, dapper young African in tan raincoat and gold-rimmed spectacles. Sam Boles stared down at them all from the height of the loading platform, still dully suspicious, for he could not believe that he was to get off scot-free without payment for what he had received.

Napes gave the "thumbs-up" gesture, nodded cheerily at Mister Matumbwe, and said, "Well, good night, guv'nor. You're a bit of all right. . . ."

Moshe Konig shouldered himself into the straps of his pack. He said, "God bless you, Mister Surgeon. You are greater than any king."

Mister Matumbwe laughed nervously. "Oh, do you think? How kind of you to say so." He looked up at the woman with the child and the golden butterfly once more, and counseled, "You will remember the formula for bottle feeding I told you. It is most efficient. But of course, if you could see your way clear, madam, breast feeding is the *very* best. Well, good night, and good luck. . . ."

The three passed out of the loading shed into the gentle rain and their separate ways.

Some Conclusions for Young and Old

Well! It's been a long book. . . .

It's over, with the exception of this vermiform appendix I feel inclined to write about editors, publishers, agents, their relationship to the writer, the writer's relationship to the public and vice versa; and if you'd be interested, I'd be glad to have you stay on while I conclude chapter and verse on some thirty years of writing for the popular magazines.

Outside of the self-inflicted occupational neuroses that bedevil him, a writer of stories lives a wonderful life, and I would have no other. He comes and goes as he pleases, wears no man's collar, and has a ready means of expressing himself if he can. He is looked upon as a harum-scarum artist and semi-magician rather than as a businessman or a man with a profession. In fact, the magazine publisher who is a businessman is always a little upset when he contemplates the way a writer earns a living, one that frequently enables him to exist on the same scale as the publisher; and while the latter recognizes the link between writer-pull, circulation, advertising rates, and profit, he is always a little resentful of the methods used by the writer, which do not seem to him quite ethical. To pay out so much money for an abstraction looks and feels like bad business, and yet it is good business. Somewhere there appears to him a fallacy, and it is probable that he does not believe and never can that the writer works hard enough for his pay or that an equity has been arrived at when a writer delivers a little bundle of manuscript in exchange for a large check.

I remember back on the *Daily News* on the seventh floor, where the editorial offices were located, I always felt myself a kind of sandwich between two layers of contempt. On the eighth floor was the business department, forever crabbing about the sums of money lavished on the intangibles and imponderables of the editorial department, the reporters, feature writers, columnists, dramatic critics. If you bought a machine you knew what you had. If you bought a writer—well, anybody who had the time could be a writer.

And below us on the sixth floor was the composing room, under the captaincy of Gus Smith, and a regiment of artisans, linotypists, copy-cutters, typesetters, make-up men, stereotypers, and others, to whom we were so many lines of type daily, and that usually late. Gus's reaction to my outpouring of deathless sports prose was contained in his usual greeting: "Is that crap of yours going to be on time tonight?"

No one but a writer considers writing work—not the publisher, not the editor, and surely not the reader, who through ignorance rather than malice has the greatest contempt for the craft as a profession, even though he admires and conceives an affection for authors who have entertained or touched him.

Every writer has run up against the fellow or female who says, "I've always thought I could write. Some time when I can get around to it I've been thinking of knocking off a story myself." Not all people say that, but most of them think it. And the upsetting truth is that every so often someone turns up who not only thinks and says it but actually does it. These are great exceptions, but they occur frequently enough to keep us humble and not too cocksure that we are craftsmen or magicians. It always comes as a nasty shock to me when I read that some matron who never touched a pen before has taken time off from counting the laundry and getting the children to school to turn out a thumping good novel or short story. I find writing hard and elusive work. I never know enough about it. I never catch up. I never do a story but what in retrospect I realize I might and should have done it better.

I like editors. I do not subscribe to the popular theory that an editor is a frustrated writer. I do not believe there is any such thing as a frustrated writer, because of all the arts, expression in it is most easily achieved. It just takes pencil and paper. Failure to sell or gain recognition is a different kind of frustration and might lead to acquiring a job in the editorial rooms, in search of sublimated vengeance, but I don't believe it. Editors edit because they like it and have a talent for it. There are all kinds of them, including editors who can write. An editor only becomes a frustrated writer when he turns down *your* story.

I like editors even though their idiom frequently cheapens me. In discussing what they are about to buy or what they have on hand in the shop, they frequently talk about our work as a commodity, like so much hamburger or so many yards of cloth. Then I find that I, who have so often considered a piece of my own work as just that, a commodity to be exchanged for the wherewithal to live, am having my feelings hurt. I want them to consider me as an artist and poet and not as a pants-maker or sausage-manufacturer. So I want to have my cake and eat it too. There are some editors who, while they never would be so impolite as to say it, manage to convey the thought to you: "Why, you're nothing but an author," and at those times I have shriveled with the utmost guilt feelings, just as I did the fatal night when I heard the spectator holler at a fight-writer pal, "Siddown, you're nothing but a sports writer." I suppose actually a fellow couldn't edit unless he felt himself superior to an author, just as an author couldn't write unless he felt himself superior to everyone else. It is reasonable to suppose that there are occupational maladies connected with working as an editor just as there are with being a writer. Editors don't like authors, and probably maintain their sanity in that fashion.

The reason why I like editors is simple. They have helped me beyond measure—not all of them, but in sufficient numbers to prejudice me incurably in their favor. Always along the road there was someone to hold out a helping hand.

Of these I owe the greatest debt to Frances Whiting, first associate editor under Harry Burton and then editor in chief of *Cosmopolitan* until she resigned in 1946 to marry Paul Schubert. Miss Whiting was an editor who loved her work. She encouraged me to write stories that were well off the beaten magazine path. She did more than encourage. She would sit up with me until five o'clock in the morning helping me sweat out a knotty problem in a yarn. She sent me off on assignments, twice to Europe and once to South America. In 1939, when I was sick and unable to work for four months, I went broke. Frances Whiting made trip after trip out to Connecticut, where I was living, to help me work on a serial that would put me back on my feet. I wrote two chapters of it in bed. A sick man cannot write. The serial was unusable. But *Cosmopolitan* through Harry Burton and Miss Whiting paid me half the price of the serial just as though they had accepted the chapters I wrote. I don't know of any other magazine that would have done that. They gambled that when I got well I would write them a serial they could use. It worked out that way, with Frances struggling with the new story through my convalescence and its completion.

Vanity Fair was a veritable incubator for young writers. From 1927 on, with the help and encouragement of Frank Crowninshield, the late Don Freeman, and Clare Brokaw, later Congresswoman Luce, I made the transition from sports articles to fiction. They let me try anything and, after I had tried, published it. Even a rejection from the Chesterfieldian Mr. Crowninshield was like an acceptance from any other magazine. I brought in a piece once that he didn't like. After reading it he took me affectionately by the arm and murmured, "Dear boy, what a masterpiece! How beautifully thought out! What color, what fire! It's truly magnificent writing. It's so poetic. Do take it over to *Harper's Bazaar*, where they will really know how to appreciate it. . . ."

Those were editors who made me believe I could do anything, and backed their belief by opening to me the columns of the smartest and wittiest magazine of the day. To a young fellow trying out his wings, unsure, but passionately excited over the medium of story-telling, they brought faith, stimulus, and enormous incentive.

I had only one meeting with the great George Horace Lorimer, before he died, the man who made the *Saturday Evening Post,* but that was enough to fire me, to make me want to write for him. He had praised my early work and imparted to me his formula "Write me a good story and I don't care what your background is," and while he was alive I wrote not for the magazine, or the readers, but to try to give Lorimer what he had asked for—a good story.

The late Dave Smart of *Esquire* was another who could make writers write. He was strange and difficult and hard to get along with, but he had that something which, when you wrote a piece for him, compelled you to want to make it an extra-good one. Goodness knows he didn't do it with money, so there must be more to him and to us than mere financial consideration. He had one priceless asset as both editor and publisher of his magazine. He'd dare anything, try anything, and printed pieces many another magazine would lack the courage to publish, if they happened to tickle him. If you had the urge to try a wicked or completely *outré* literary handspring, you knew that Dave would print it if it came off. It made you feel good to have a guy like that around.

Herb Mayes is an author's editor with a passionate devotion to good stories. If Mayes buys it you know you've done more than just made a sale to round out a magazine's literary vaudeville show. You've written a good story.

I used to find the *Saturday Evening Post* staff somewhat difficult to work for, as they were aloof, distant, and detached. They simply don't believe in coddling writers and in particular writers of short stories, for the competition to land a short story in the *Post* is so keen and so many writers and agents are bombarding this magazine with stories that the editors are able to maintain that acceptance, the check that is forwarded within three days, and publication in the magazine are the highest accolade they have to bestow. To add personal praise after having bought a story would be painting the proverbial. What they have to sell to the aspiring writer is the point of great pride in "making the *Post.*"

The editors of this magazine rarely ask that a short story be rewritten. They either buy it or they don't. The rejected story goes back to the agent with the simple comment, "Didn't quite make it," or, "We didn't like this one," leaving you to try to figure out why.

In the beginning my relationship with Stuart Rose, who was the editor with whom I had personal contact at the *Post,* used to worry me, for the only comment I could ever get out of him was that a certain story they had bought was "in the groove." This phrase always gave me the shudders and the feeling that what I really needed and wanted was to get out of that particular groove, whatever it was, at once. Later, however, I came to realize that in an attitude that seemed cold and impersonal, Stu was paying me the compliment of regarding me as a "pro." Pros were supposed to know their business and to have enough spine to stand up without having it patted constantly.

Whenever I visit the United States I go to Philadelphia to spend a weekend with Stuart at his farm, and there we drink bourbon and talk shop far into the night. But the editorial staff lunches I sometimes attend in Philadelphia I find diffident and not particularly inspiring—inspiring in the sense to make me wish to rush forth and write them all a fine story that will give them pleasure and call forth praise as well as payment. I don't feel them looking over my shoulder approvingly as I work, as I used to with the late Bill Williams, one-time editor of *True,* whose chuckles I could hear mentally when I had turned a phrase well. I wanted to please him as well as sell. Still, I realize that my presence in Philadelphia is a guarantee that I am taken seriously by them and am an old and established *Post* writer; nevertheless, beneath my rude exterior there beats a timorous heart. I often need and want to be coddled.

So you see, it's more than just money with us, no matter what we say about the necessity for it. Harry Burton used to keep me rolling on my back and wiggling like a puppy by the simple procedure of calling me on the long-distance telephone wherever I happened to be—England, Havana, San Francisco—to tell me that a piece of mine was doing well in the magazine. A telephone call from Miss Whiting, in the voice she reserved for such occasions, to tell me that a story I had just submitted had hit meant more to me than all the money *Cosmo* could stuff into my bank account. Crowninshield used to send telegrams of congratulations. Dave Smart wrote little personal notes from Chicago. It doesn't even matter if we are aware that it is astute editorial policy and accurate judgment of their man that leads to these mash notes. Once when I had been squawking to Smart for more money, Arnold Gingrich, who was then editing *Esquire*, called me up from Chicago and said, "Look, kid. We know you've got to give an author one of two things, either money or lovin'. Well, we've been so busy here of late we've been a little remiss on our lovin'." After I got through laughing, I listened, purring, to five minutes of long-distance lovin'.

Do cats eat bats, do bats eat cats, do authors need agents? And what is an author's agent and what does he do? It is a queer profession, this middleman who bridges the gap between writer and editor and concerns himself with the peddling of fantasies for rent and groceries money. And who created this gap between writer and editor, does it exist, and is it necessary? And why doesn't the editor pay the agent a percentage for services rendered as well as the author?

The value of a literary agent to the sale of a good story to the right market for the right price varies from nil to seventy per cent. No literary agent I know of has ever sold a bad story to a magazine because of his ability to sell or blarney. If the story is not right and salable the agent is helpless. An agent rarely, if ever, has been able to persuade an editor to change his mind and buy a story after he has turned it down. The layman is often baffled over the functions of an agent and why he exists at all. This section may help to clear the mystery.

To the editor, the purchaser of magazine fiction, the agent represents a certain standard of quality. Since an agent lives off the ten per cent he charges his clients, he is interested in handling only writers who either are successful or have shown definite promise of developing. Under those circumstances he would automatically screen out clucks, the same hopeful but inept crew of amateurs and dilettantes who bombard the magazines with bad manuscripts.

The good agent is in effect a kind of pre-editor. For a young writer to acquire a competent and recognized agent is half the battle in the psychology of getting the editor to consider his work in the light of purchasable material. We know that a great story will sell itself, but to get that great story through to the attention of the responsible editor is not always so simple, since members of the editorial staff of a magazine are human beings as fallible in their profession as are writers in theirs. But this we know: when an author's story appears on an editor's desk bound in the distinctive cover used by the agent—mine uses black paper with a red and white title label, which immediately identifies it as "Ober Associates story"—it is a guarantee of three things: that the agent has sold the writer's work before and believes him a good business risk, otherwise he would not be handling him; that he has read this particular story; and that he believes the story is right for the style, type, and needs of the particular magazine to which it has been sent. The editor, if he trusts the agent, knows that his time will not be wasted in reading the piece and he is ready to render an accurate and impartial judgment of the piece strictly on its merits. Sometimes a telephone call from the agent to the editor calling his attenion to what he believes is a particularly good piece of work will further prepare the ground for a quick and interested reading. Thereafter the piece is strictly on its own. If it clicks, the editor spares a moment of warmth for the agent who enabled him to acquire this fine piece of property instead of sending it to another. If it flops, a black mark goes against the agent as well as the writer.

I shall never know whether I would eventually have made the big magazines without an agent, merely by submitting stories by mail with a return envelope, because when after an eight-year hiatus writing sports I turned once more to fiction writing, my first story and every one thereafter were sold through the office of Harold Ober. I had acquired him as an agent as far back as 1930, when I began to sell sports articles to *Red Book*, the *American Magazine*, and the *Saturday Evening Post*.

A pal of mine on the *Daily News,* Dick Carroll, who subsequently went to Hollywood, had had some stories placed by Ober. Dick introduced me to Harold. I showed him one of my pieces and he agreed to add my name to his stable. That was all. We have been together ever since without a contract or so much as a single scrap of paper between us, and although he is dead, I still remain with his Associates and his office.

Could I get along without an agent now? I don't know, because I don't intend to try. No professional writer will. To one another we curse and damn and decry and complain about our agents and what they don't do for us in return for the ten per cent and expenses they clip us, but no established writer would dream of dispensing with this middleman.

Among other things, the agent is deemed necessary because it is quite true that the average writer is a poor businessman and does not know how to place a proper value on his work or services. Also the agent remains as a hangover from a period when there was something faintly discreditable about writing for money, and the days when the publishers took shameful advantage of the scribblers. The writer was a poet who was supposed to dwell at least on the side of Olympus if not at the top, and haggling for dollars and cents was considered far beneath his dignity.

Today the agent does our haggling for us and protects our tender sensibilities from contact with the vulgar commercial aspects of the business that might have a tendency to stifle the beauty in our souls. He sets the prices, wangles us raises, cushions the shock of rejections, sends out clean copies when the old ones get frazzled from too much editorial thumbing, listens to our complaints and gripes, sympathizes when editors fail to agree with us on the epic qualities of a story, lends us money when we are broke, gives matrimonial advice, makes appointments with editors, listens to offers that come in and screens out the clucks, crackpots, and cheapjacks, supervises contracts, gets the income tax made out, takes the blame and acts as the fall guy when we pull a boner, and generally makes himself useful as a business manager as well as a steady and loyal friend in time of need.

He has his dark side and frequently cannot be counted on to battle a big magazine (or movie studio). This is an understandable outgrowth of a queer business. Possibly fifty per cent of the agent's income on his percentage of sales made from all the authors in his stable may very well come from one magazine or one company. He does not dare to alienate this magazine over the difficulties of one individual author, thus jeopardizing not only himself, but other writers in his stable. He walks a tightrope warily, and his life is not an easy one. An agent can show bad judgment in offering a story to the wrong magazine, or even, if the writer is so unsure or stupid as to let him, offer the writer bad editorial advice on a story, but that's not my agent; it's always the other guy's who does that.

When I had an idea for a story or an article, a book, a play, a movie, or whatever, I would call on Harold at his office and discuss it with him. If it needed to be discussed with an editor, he organized and arranged the appointment, either in his office or at lunch. When the script was finished I sent it to him and was through with it except for the worrying. When it was sold he called me up and told me. He charged me for the typing and any other patent expenses incurred, but I know there are many expenses for which he never billed me.

And so they clip us our ten per cent, and sometimes, because we are human, greedy, and bad-tempered, we wonder what the hell for and complain to our wives about it, but we cling to them throughout life and even beyond, because after we are gone we expect them to collect and market our immortal works and provide an income for our families. Sometimes a top writer will change agents. But be without one? Never!

When I was a student writer the chief criticism leveled at the big slicks, the high-paying magazine market, and that chiefly by unsuccessful writers, was that they insisted upon the "happy ending," and that you could not sell them a story that did not make this concession, or which did not conform to popular standards or tested formulas. The magazines have changed over a period of twenty years; they have become broader and more courageous and are encumbered with fewer taboos; but the criticism still persists among the uninitiate, would-be fiction writers, who because they are unable to find a market for their bad scripts excuse themselves by saying that realism and the unhappy ending cannot be sold and that the entire magazine market is in a conspiracy to flatten out life and present it in terms of sugar-coated falsehood.

It's the bunk, at least as far as I am concerned. Never at any time in my career have I had a story rejected because of a so-called "unhappy ending," or has any editor ever suggested that a story might be acceptable if I would change the ending and make everything come out all right.

No, it just won't do as an excuse for not making the grade—if the slicks are the grade you want to make—and when you hear complaints that the popular magazines will print nothing but phony stories, you are listening either to someone parroting a cliché or to a writer who is suspect.

It is true that the majority of the high-priced popular magazines feature the formula story with the sarsaparilla ending, and many of these stories are so much junk, but there is no rule against the realistic or honest story provided it is readable and entertaining, and if there is a good deal of cheap and shoddy writing in slick magazines, who is to blame, the writer or the editor? I would be inclined to blame the writer and the law of supply and demand. Every big editor I ever knew lets out a shout of joy when he gets his hands on a really good story. Many of them are story fanatics, genuine worshipers of the art form, and they will make the fortunes of men and women who can write them. They would like to see every story in every issue a gem of its kind. There simply are not enough good writers to go around, and issues must be filled.

Also there is no law that just because a story is bitterly or misanthropically realistic and has a sour-puss ending, it automatically becomes a great piece of literature. My recollection of the story-tellers who have withstood the test of time to become classics is that they maintained about the same ratio of happy to unhappy endings as do the modern magazines. The one thing they never neglected was to be entertaining. The villain who gets hisn, the poor boy who overcomes obstacles to become wealthy and famous, or who marries the daughter of the boss, the two lovers happily united after many vicissitudes, were not invented by the *Saturday Evening Post, Cosmopolitan.* The story in which the inequalities, terrors, and injustices of life yield to things as they ought to be, in the very best of all possible worlds, is a very ancient dream and was first expressed in folklore and fairytale. Maybe such stories are bad for us, but if so many millions of people love them and are diverted by them, then they are a part of the people and their lives and there must be something to them. You tell me what's wrong with romance, and since when.

The popular magazines on their various levels, and with consideration of the audiences they are aimed at, demand that primarily their writers shall be entertaining. You may quarrel with an editor over differences with regard to what he and you consider entertaining, but not with his motive, which is honest in every respect, including that cardinal sin which is known as pandering to public taste. I see nothing particularly wrong with public taste or in pandering to it from the point of view of the editor who is charged with putting together and selling a volume every week or every month. If he fails to meet public taste, circulation falls off and he loses his job.

Magazines of all classifications are no better or no worse than their readers want them to be, and the material contained in them is always the best they are able to purchase in the open market. The time test of a story does not depend upon whether it was published in the *New Yorker,* the *Saturday Evening Post, Harper's, Western Stories,* or *True Confessions.* Nobody today remembers the names of the periodicals that published Charles Dickens, Rudyard Kipling, G. K. Chesterton, Conan Doyle, O. Henry, Mark Twain, Edgar Allan Poe, Bret Harte, and others, but their stories live on because people liked them.

I have no objection to anyone who wishes to look down his nose at American magazines so long as his criticism is based upon personal reaction to the contents and distaste for it rather than the snobbery that comes from swallowing false clichés or approaching a tale from the standpoint that if it appeared in a popular magazine it can't be good. If this sounds like an apology for my own stories, forget it. In magazine form they were once turned loose to entertain and divert many millions of people. If the majority of them in this volume have entertained you, that will satisfy me.

If I were to offer gratuitous advice to would-be writers of short stories, or, for that matter, would-be writers of anything, I would suggest that they keep in mind change of pace and change of subject matter. They will live longer as writers.

This takes some doing in the face of the fact that the magazine editors will often offer you self-destroying advice, particularly if you hit upon a good character. They will ask for more and more of the stories using that character, if it is a successful one, but the result is that you become a "Johnny One Note." Eventually the public tires of your character, and even if there is still lively interest in him, if you try to write on another subject you find yourself handicapped in the editorial offices. They will want you to do for them "another So and So," naming your successful character.

Nothing is more easy in the competitive magazine world than to become typed, and once typed, you have had it! You will see from the diversity of the stories in this book how I have struggled all of my writing life against this typing. Just as soon as an editor or a magazine thought they had me typed I would switch to another background and another style, or an entirely different character, and in later years I have tried to do the same, alternating long novels with very short ones, animals with people, gentle stories with tough adventure and mystery thrillers. Perhaps I will never write a great novel in this manner, but at least I hope I will continue to be interesting.

At the time that I sold my first story to the *Post* I followed it up with a sports story or two which likewise found acceptance by that magazine and earned me an invitation to Philadelphia from the late George Horace Lorimer, the editor generally credited at the first part of the century with making the *Post* the great, successful magazine it was.

This was really a summons from on high, and my knees started shaking already as the train drew into the outskirts of Philadelphia.

At last alone in the sanctuary with the great man, I waited for what he had to say to me. It was that he was pleased to see me and in particular was happy about the sports stories I had submitted; he felt that this was my field and that the *Post* had great need of stories with sports backgrounds. He looked to me to supply them with these in the future.

I remember that instead of being delighted I was aware of a sense of desolation at these words, and young as I was, I knew that I was already in danger of being typed and must protest at once, and that unless I protested immediately it would be too late.

I thanked Mr. Lorimer for the kindness of his praise but added, rather plaintively, that I was afraid I wanted to play Hamlet.

He looked across his desk at me somewhat gloomily and asked, "And what form does your Hamlet take?"

I then confessed that I didn't want to be restricted to sports stories and that I wanted to write stories with newspaper backgrounds as well as other.

Mr. Lorimer looked me over for a moment and then said, "Young man, let me tell you something; I don't care what your background is, or your characters, or where it is set if you will only tell me a story."

I went back to New York with that sentence ringing in my head, "Tell me a story," and I have never forgotten it. I even once used it in a title, "Tell Me a Love Story." It has never been far from the forefront of my mind as I sat down to write. I hope you will conclude that down through the years I have kept faith with Editor Lorimer and myself.